A Fallen Lady

ELIZABETH KINGSTON

This is a work of fiction. Similarities to real people, places, or events are entirely coincidental

A FALLEN LADY

Copyright © 2015 Elizabeth Kingston

All rights reserved.

ISBN: 978-1543014815
ISBN-10:154301481x

For all the Helens I have known, and all the Stephens who have loved them.

Other books by Elizabeth Kingston
THE KING'S MAN
FAIR, BRIGHT, AND TERRIBLE

In collaboration with Susanna Malcolm:
THE MISADVENTURES OF A TITIAN-HAIRED
GODDESS AND AN OUTRAGEOUS HELLION

PROLOGUE

It was a simple story, really. But somehow it was never easy to tell. Whenever she tried to recite it to anyone (not that there were above a very few who ever heard it), her tongue would become paralyzed. Her eyes would seek out the corners of the room, looking anywhere but at the listener, searching for any sign that she was not the girl speaking. Her ears would shrink from hearing the sounds forced out of her. It was as though a massive hand pressed on her chest as on a bellows, and the words came out full of breath and scant of timbre.

And so the story of her ruin was little more than a rarely heard cluster of breathy syllables that made no sense, not even to herself. There was a dark wood and an innocent-looking shaving kit. There was blood and blue eyes and shouting – and ribbons, a token for an orphan child. She knew it was an incoherent tale, the way she told it. Years later, it remained a disjointed blur of images and sounds.

She should have run. She should not have been there at all. Silly girl. Mostly, she remembered the warmth of his neck on her forearm, his pounding pulse against her wrist, the words that she had spoken, and the running, running, running.

A simple story with a simple outcome. It perfectly

explained why she came home from Ireland three weeks early with no husband, an Irish maid, a thoroughly ruined reputation, and a tangle of cheap ribbons. It was her own difficulty in telling it that complicated things and rendered it – and her – powerless.

CHAPTER ONE

September, 1820
The Earl of Whitemarsh
Baird House
London

Dear Whitemarsh,

I am now installed at my home in Herefordshire, not more than an hour's ride from the village of Bartle-on-the-Glen. Having arrived only a week hence, I have not made great progress in that Task which I have undertaken at your request and to the benefit of our mutual interests. It is true that the dower house is indeed without a boarder, much as Lady Helen's solicitor warned. Failing any sudden breakthrough with the clannish villagers, I fear my Investigation may proceed rather slowly.

However, it has come to my attention that a certain Mme de Vauteuil resides in the village and is described with some respect by frequenters of the local public house as "real Society" — which phrase I can only assume to mean that she is not averse to receiving callers and, one hopes, is as enamoured of gossip as any member of Society. I have said that the villagers are not forthcoming. In particular, their responses to inquiries concerning your sister are uniform. They invariably become hostile and suspicious of any motive in seeking her out, while simultaneously refusing to admit they know or have even heard of her. The information of Mme de Vauteuil I obtained myself, my servants having now gained a reputation in the village as intrusive outsiders who ask far too many questions.

I hope you will send word immediately if you have any knowledge of Mme de Vauteuil for her name seems familiar to me, though I cannot place it. She may be the only route by which Lady Helen may be found.

As I have no other pressing matters to attend to in the coming months and my affairs can easily be managed from this location, I am prepared to stay for the whole of Autumn. The manor here wants improvements which I am now at leisure to oversee.

I shall keep you informed regularly of my progress in pursuit of your sister.

Your Servant,
Summerdale

༄༅

The knock came just moments before afternoon tea. Marie-Anne was in high humor, laughing at Helen's attempts with the bobbins.

"No, no, mademoiselle, you must always keep them in order!" It was a laughing scold.

Marie-Anne leaned over her as they both giggled. Her practiced hands moved the bobbins to their proper positions on the pillow and tried to untangle the mess of threads laced around the pins.

Helen wailed, "I shall never learn! I am more like to make a proper nesting place for mice." She dissolved into woeful laughter at the sight of her handiwork. Really, it was awful. "And a rodent's nest need not waste so much of my time and effort. Nor your thread!"

Marie-Anne plucked the whole contraption of pillow, frame, and dangling bobbins out of Helen's lap. Her fingers began to work among the threads. It looked rather a hopeless task to Helen.

"You only need more practice, and when you have learned, you can make the finest lace nest for that family of mice in your cellar, if you like."

They spoke in French. Marie-Anne often missed her native language, and found it easier to communicate the details of lacemaking when she could be certain of her vocabulary. Helen was glad to have a chance to use the language at all. There were few enough calls for French in Bartle-on-the-Glen, and it was pleasant to hear the lovely, exotic tones of it while knowing she brought some comfort to her friend.

Poor Marie-Anne seemed baffled at the profusion of loops and knots in front of her. "Perhaps Maggie knows a simpler design, though Irish lace is just as lovely."

And no doubt just as complicated, thought Helen wearily as she reached for the letter in her pocket. Her solicitor had given it to her at their last meeting, only a week ago.

"The Huntingdons will not be coming this autumn. Joyce says the baron is unwell." She scanned the page as she had a hundred times in the last week, searching for any sign of Joyce's displeasure. Her friend was normally quite straightforward, and Helen had no reason to doubt the baron's illness. Still, one could hardly expect a friend to write that it was impossible to visit because one was an embarrassment.

Marie-Anne looked up from her lap in dismay. "But that is too bad! I hope it is not serious?"

"I suspect it is his gout, though she does not specify. She writes of it as if he is most tiresome. Her tone would be more serious if the illness were grave." Helen attempted a smile. "We shall have to make do with each other's company, it seems."

The visit would be sorely missed. Joyce Huntingdon always brought with her an air of gaiety, sharing the gossip from Town and insisting to them that they were most fortunate to be well out of marriage. The baron was not an ideal mate, and being a wife was not nearly as pleasant as one might think, she would tell them. Helen knew her friend always took a risk to socialize with her, and her efforts to keep The Fallen (as they referred to themselves with laughter) entertained were most appreciated. Thinking of the chance she took even in writing to them, Helen was ashamed at her obsessive reading of the letter. Joyce was a good friend.

Marie-Anne looked worried. "Will this not reduce your income this quarter?"

"Indeed," answered Helen, re-folding the letter and carefully slipping it into the pocket of her brown homespun dress. "But it is by no means disaster. All our plans are well laid. I have discussed it with Thompkins and I shall manage, so long as there are no unforeseen expenses."

In truth, it was worrisome. When were there *not* unforeseen expenses? A lady, whether fallen or not, was entirely confined to her quarterly income unless she had an easily influenced husband with deep pockets.

In the absence of such, Helen depended on the rent from the dower house to add a bit to her income against any small expenses. The Huntingdons had rented it at least three months out of the year for the last six years. It was a small sum, but welcome nonetheless. In any case, she saved money simply by closing up the dower house. The very thought of heating it throughout the winter made her blanch. No, she did very well in her small lodgings on the edge of the village. If her situation became unbearable, it was her right to sell the dower house, as it had come to her directly through her mother and was independent of her brother's estate. She would not sell it unless forced to do so.

Trying to turn her thoughts away from such a grim alternative, she lightened her expression and adopted a bright tone. "Which means I shall have to stop wasting thread on this pitiful excuse for Bruges lace."

Marie-Anne looked at her for a bare instant before returning her eyes to the mess of thread in her lap and matching Helen's tone. "Another noble pursuit abandoned, with a single visit to the solicitor. I wonder if they know how well they can depress us, these solicitors."

"Well, as long as they don't confiscate the tea from our cupboards, I shall not stoop to cursing them." Helen stood up. "After all, Mr. Thompkins is an excellent man. And I should hardly call *that* noble," she said with a nod toward the lace pillow. "Perhaps a valiant attempt, at best. Now, shall I include the berries Maggie found on our tray?"

"I had Mrs. Gibbons turn them into the most delightful-looking tartlets. You'll find them in the larder." Marie-Anne spoke as her friend headed into the kitchen. "You are quite sure all will be well, *ma chère?*"

Helen paused at the doorway. Marie-Anne's income was more than her own, though still just enough to keep her comfortably situated.

"Quite well, my friend," she answered quietly. She clenched her lower lip between her teeth and conjured a mischievous smile. "And if not, then perhaps I can interest Thompkins in a lovely new style of trim for his cuffs." She nodded again at the mess of thread in Marie-Anne's lap. She began to giggle at the image that formed in her mind of dear, sweet Thompkins tangling his fingers in a profusion of confused threads. "I could tell him it's all the rage"

She'd managed to set Marie-Anne to giggling by now.

"Without doubt, we could start a new fashion. We shall spread it about that a man is judged in a moment by his skill in keeping the trim out of his soup," said Marie-Anne with a wide smile.

Helen laughed her way into the kitchen. They really should not make fun of dear old Thompkins, but he was most ignorant of fashion. The thought of his spindly fingers catching in the knotted loops of thread set her to laughing again as she warmed the pot and measured out tea leaves. Well, the notion of selling a travesty of lace to a gullible old solicitor was certainly more appealing than asking money of Marie-

A FALLEN LADY

Anne. Both of those options were infinitely more palatable than going to her brother.

And then she heard the knock at Marie-Anne's front door.

                    §

Not for the first time in his life, the present Earl of Summerdale asked himself what he could possibly have done to avoid the strange situation in which he found himself.

He stood at the door of a small home at the edge of a quaint village and listened to the charming laughter of unseen women inside, and knocked. He was probably disturbing them in gossiping over their needlework. He would much rather have caught Madame de Vauteuil at tea as he had designed, preferably alone. Having never made her acquaintance – and by everything he knew of the village, he was not likely to happen upon an obliging neighbor – the best ruse he could think of to approach her involved acting the dimwit.

His horse stood at the gatepost, looking perfectly fit and docile. Anyone who cast a discerning eye would doubt the beast was impaired in any way. It must be Stephen alone who would employ his scarce acting abilities and more abundant powers of persuasion to gain entrance into the Frenchwoman's home. Deceiving ladies, he knew, was not his forte. But in his experience, they did often seem to thrive on assumptions and rejoiced in leaping to conclusions. The thought gave him some hope that, with just the right approach, he might succeed here.

Before he had time to dream up a sound reason

for actually entering the perfectly nondescript little house in the perfectly nondescript little village, the door opened. A lovely, petite woman with honey-colored hair stood at the threshold. It was impossible that she was the maid.

Looking into her expectant face, he felt a complete fool. He decided to be every inch the nobleman, in hopes of inspiring some feeling of obligation from the woman.

"Madame, I beg your pardon for disturbing your afternoon. It seems my horse has been so unobliging as to lose a shoe in a place unfamiliar to me." Thus did he launch into his inadequately prepared plea for aid. He made sure to mention the dustiness of the road and to interrupt himself with a dry cough, in hopes of being invited in to a cup of tea.

"I seem to have ridden quite a bit farther from my home than I intended." He began to falter under her pointed gaze. He had the most distinct impression that she knew exactly who he was, and he sensed a slight hostility whose origins he could not fathom. At the same time, she seemed to be laughing at him. It was a most uncomfortable feeling. "I thought perhaps..." What the devil had he meant to say? "Pardon me, madame, but have we been introduced?"

She seemed highly amused at that, but only smiled pleasantly. "I do not believe so, sir."

He should have expected her to have an accent. There seemed to be a thousand things he should have expected at this meeting, but he never expected the strong impression that she had sized him up and summarily dismissed him at a glance. She stood there, looking at him out of those dazzling blue eyes as if she knew precisely who he was and why he was there, and yet she took him to be a colossal joke. He found it maddening.

He chose to play the haughty aristocrat, curious to see what effect it might have on her demeanor. It was easy enough to raise his brows and look down his nose at her. "Permit me to introduce myself, in that case. I am Stephen Hampton."

She did not miss a beat. Beaming at him and offering her hand, she said, "A pleasure! And I am Marie-Anne de Vauteuil, scandal of high society, four seasons past."

How she expected him to respond to that, he couldn't dream. Numbly, he took her hand and made a bow over it. He instinctively felt that gaining her respect would be much easier if he stopped pretending and simply told her immediately that he'd come looking for her. Besides, he found himself amused at her brazen ownership of her scandalous reputation. Her humor was infectious.

The answering smile that spread across his face was genuine. "How very fortunate, madame. It was in the hopes of making your acquaintance that I came this way."

He had gained some ground with that, he saw, and something else. She looked somewhat suspicious of him.

"And who told you to come looking for me, *monsieur*?" she inquired politely, though nervously.

Suddenly realizing how it must sound to a fallen woman to hear that a man was seeking her out, he hastened to explain. "I came of my own accord, I assure you. I had hoped to see how you were. I counted the late Mr. Shipley as a friend, you see." That appeared to reassure her somewhat. "I was aware of his very great affection for you. His loss was a tragedy."

A sweet, wistful sadness came over her face. Shipley, he had recently been reminded, had been her lover. The story of their *affaire* had been the talk of London four years ago and was still told, he was sure, to young girls at their coming out. A more effective cautionary tale against giving in to fleshly temptations was hard to come by. Shipley had died of a terrible fever quite suddenly, before they could marry. And this lovely woman – who couldn't be above 28 years old – had been left pregnant, disgraced and alone, with no legal claim for herself or her child.

She had miscarried, he understood, shortly after Shipley's death. His family of unrepentant snobs had never approved of her, but it seemed she had some means of income. Undoubtedly, she'd come to England because of the war in France. Why she would choose to live out her days in Bartle-on-the-Glen was a mystery to him, until he noticed how her smile had become almost forced, an effort. Perhaps she had had enough of living in society.

"Well," she said warmly, "it is a pleasure to meet a friend of Richard. You said your name is Hampton?" She looked into his eyes and suddenly opened her own wide in recognition. "Oh, then you must be the Earl of Summerdale?"

He smiled, enjoying the hint of the throaty r's, the full vowels, the slight nasal tone. "My title is most lovely when graced with the proper French accent, I find."

"*Mais vous devez parler français, non? Chez moi, on parle français quand possible.*"

Good God, not French.

Grimacing, he made sure his horrible French was instantly established, despite his embarrassment. "*Oui, madame, mais je ne parle pas...le parle*, that is." True enough that he didn't speak it. He said nothing about understanding it. "My lamentable tongue is purely English, madame. My tutors often despaired of me, I assure you."

She looked slightly taken aback by his shameful accent. His inability to properly pronounce even the simplest words was far from an act. He could not pretend to speak it as badly as it naturally fell from his mouth.

"*Bien*," she managed to recover from her horror, "then by all means we shall speak English."

"Please," he gave his most charming grin by way of apology.

She seemed transfixed for a moment. "Ah! Yes! Your horse." Snapping to attentiveness, she turned away from the door and called down the hall behind her. "Hélène! Is Jack in the forge today, if you know?"

A voice – the other source of the earlier laughter, he assumed – called back, "No. He's helping the newlyweds with their roof thatch today. Why do you ask?"

Mme de Vauteuil looked back at him for a moment, calculating. "It seems you may be stranded for a time." As though deciding something, she nodded briefly and called back to the house's other occupant. "We shall be three for tea, mon amie. A guest!"

He supposed one could not expect a woman who flaunted her ruined social status to care that such exuberant shouting was unmannerly. He consciously lightened his features against their natural tendency to show his shocked displeasure at this display. Any lack of polished manners could easily be overlooked in light of the fact that he had just, he assumed, been invited to tea.

Mme de Vauteuil ushered him in hastily and showed him into a sitting room. He watched as she picked up what looked like a ragged pillow in the midst of being repaired out of a chair and invited him to sit in its place. Casting the pillow (at which she seemed to be laughing) next to her, she sat on the settee across from him.

She was most charming, with her French accent and her deep blue eyes, he thought. Perhaps this would not be so difficult. She seemed to trust him well enough so far.

And then the girl entered the room, carrying a full tray. She wore a plain dress, horribly cut and of rough fabric; her dark hair was pulled back into a tight chignon, low over the ears. Such an unflattering style.

Her eyes, a dark brown rimmed in heavy black lashes, caught his own. She was... there was not a single word that came to his mind to describe her. Plain. She had a pleasant enough face, pleasant brown eyes. She was pleasant-looking. But at his second glance, he realized his mistake. She was beautiful. Breathtaking.

It was as if her beauty were hiding in plain sight. She obviously did little enough to showcase her looks, and her beauty was unassuming. But there was no way to hide the fineness of her bones, the depths of her eyes, skin like porcelain. She was like a magnet. He found he could not look away. And every moment that he looked at her, he discovered she was more beautiful than the last.

A housemaid, he told himself. Or no, perhaps a village miss who visited to practice her French. All he could think was that she was too lovely to be hidden in such a place as this, and that she would look so much more beautiful in a pretty yellow dress and her hair worn high to show her neck.

Gradually, he realized that Mme de Vauteuil was speaking, and the girl was looking down at the tea tray now with a closed expression on her face. An instant before she looked away, he thought he'd seen something like fear in her expression. He forced himself to listen to his hostess.

"You must meet Lord Summerdale, a friend of my dear Richard."

He stepped closer as she made the introductions, assuming that this was, in fact, *not* the maid. He was ridiculously close to nervousness as he prepared to take the girl's hand. She looked away from him. Shy, he thought. Shy and enchanting.

"And this is Hélène Dehaven, my lord," said the Frenchwoman placidly.

The shock came belatedly, after his brain had time to sift through the heavy accent on her name. He had a hard time hiding the surprise that flashed across his face, not the least because Helen Dehaven looked full at him with a contempt he had never seen directed at himself from a stranger. For reasons he could not hope to know, her look was full of distaste and, he fancied, resentment.

He was sure they had never met before. Even if she knew him to be acquainted with her brother, it would not account for such a force of feeling. She would surely have snatched her fingers back as he briefly bowed over her hand, if she could have managed to do it with any grace. Instead, she was coldly formal.

"A pleasure to make your acquaintance, my lord." She said *my lord* almost as though it were a scathing epithet. Even through the lack of warmth in her tone, the first thing he acknowledged was that her voice was, like everything else about her, exceptionally pleasant.

"Enchanted," he said. A moment ago, he would have meant it. Now, if he were to be honest, he found her baffling. It seemed she despised him, and to find that confusing attitude alongside her agreeable appearance was jarring.

They all sat as Helen Dehaven silently served tea. He noticed as Mme de Vauteuil chattered on about Jack, the village smith, and his newly married nephew's roof, that the chilliness in the room was not entirely Lady Helen's doing. Marie-Anne de Vauteuil seemed to have retrenched from her earlier friendliness. He began to feel like an intruder, which was a familiar enough feeling. There was an invisible line in the sand, and he was clearly on the opposite side from his lovely hostesses.

Lady Helen did not speak at all. She seemed content to let Mme de Vauteuil and him carry on the meaningless conversation. After explaining that Jack was two villages away and would most likely be unavailable well into the evening, Marie-Anne turned to Helen Dehaven.

"Will Daniel Black perhaps be able to help a stranded gentleman, Hélène?"

Lady Helen scrupulously avoided his eyes and spoke directly to her friend. "He could not help except to offer his cart for hire." There was not a trace of any emotion in her voice.

Stephen cleared his throat and tried not to stare at her. He knew he was searching for signs of her personality, and he knew just as well that she would show none. It was telling enough that they were both obviously on friendly terms with the common inhabitants of the village. But then, she could hardly afford to be choosy about the company she kept.

"I beg you both not to tax yourselves with solving my predicament. I can only thank you for your kindness."

He realized how he had stupidly created the perfect opening for his own departure. He hadn't meant it to sound as if he intended to leave at that moment. A stupid mistake, one from which he must immediately recover if he was to establish any kind of rapport with Helen Dehaven. He felt clumsy in the face of their vague animosity.

He addressed Lady Helen directly. "If you could direct me to Mr. Black?"

Fortunately, both women seemed at a bit of a loss. From Mme de Vauteuil's confused explanation, it seemed Daniel Black was difficult to find. Down the road and past the pub, on the opposite side of the village, down a dirt track, but not the track that led straight, it curved to the right and was half-hidden by a tree older than anyone currently living. His head reeled with the thought of finding the man. It was perfect. He proceeded to misunderstand every turn of the path until it was abundantly clear he would never get out of the village without their direct and immediate help.

Taking a deep breath, Helen Dehaven spoke. "He lives not far from where I am going after visiting with

Madame de Vauteuil." Her tone was reluctant, as if he had tortured her for the information. "I shall be happy to show you the way, my lord." She sounded anything but happy about it.

He found himself taking his leave of Marie-Anne de Vauteuil at her front door, with Helen Dehaven standing next to him and tying her bonnet. After the difficulties he'd had in finding the woman, it seemed incredible that she should be preparing to accompany him on a ramble through the village. He wanted above all else to understand her apparent hostility toward him. But that was not why he had sought her out.

"I am so sorry to see you go, Lord Summerdale. We did not have much opportunity to speak of Richard, and I do enjoy to meet his friends," Mme de Vauteuil murmured. She was not exactly insincere, but she left no doubt that she in no way wished to suggest he was welcome to stay longer.

The villagers had described her as "real Society," and so he must attempt an appeal to her social graces. Fortunately, she seemed not to have lost them along with her virtue.

"I would be most pleased to visit with you again sometime, madame. Under less inconvenient circumstances, one hopes. I hope I may call on you again?"

He watched her face turn into a stone wall as she seemed to grope for an appropriate response. Almost imperceptibly, she glanced toward Lady Helen before answering.

"Of course, *monsieur*, it will be a pleasure to have you call again, but surely you will not be here in Bartle often?" She made it sound as if he proposed to visit her in the Sahara.

"My manor is not far, and I plan to stay for some months in the area. I'm sure I will not be able to resist your company again, madame. As I said, I wish to assure myself of your welfare, for the sake of Mr. Shipley's memory." There was no need to inform her that he and Richard Shipley had met exactly once, and that he was much better acquainted with the man's horrible family. "I shall be passing this way again next week," he stated with finality.

Before she could find an excuse to be unavailable to visitors next week, he turned toward Lady Helen expectantly. In the late summer light, her hair shone.

"*Au revoir, Marie-Anne. Ne te préoccupe pas.*"

Do not worry. For Mme de Vauteuil did look slightly worried for her. The two of them were protective of each other, anyone could see. She took leave of her friend with a kiss to the cheek. He offered his arm to her as she turned to the path. She failed to notice it, purposely. There was no mistaking her coldness.

As he led the horse into the road, he watched her walk ahead of him. She carried herself stiffly, as though marching toward an important task. There was no suggestion of leisure in her step. The dress she wore emphasized nothing in her figure. Of average height and medium build, she was really physically unremarkable; even her face was unassuming at first glance. Walking ahead of him, she was just a drab sketch of a country woman. He had a growing suspicion that she took great pains to appear so, with her dress and her hairstyle that would horrify the London ladies.

Any other man would not have looked at her twice.

"You live here in the village, Lady Helen?"

Her pace slowed and she turned her head in his direction to answer. "Not far from here." That was all.

He remembered the laughter he had heard before he had entered the house earlier. "You have been friends with Madame de Vauteuil for long?"

"Since she moved here." She was obviously disinclined to converse. He could feel her impatience, and was glad to let the horse walk slowly. It was difficult enough to find topics to discuss with someone whose dishonor followed her everywhere, a fact which he could not let himself forget. But she made it worse with her reticence. He never thought he'd long for the chatter of a typical woman.

"And were you acquainted at all with Mr. Shipley?" he asked casually.

She paused before answering. "No." She suddenly gave him a sharp look. "Were you?" she demanded.

If it was as long a walk to Daniel Black's cart as he'd been hoping, they seemed destined to come to the point of it eventually. He felt a certain respect for the girl for taking the offensive with her rude question.

"You believe I lied?" She did not look away from him, and a part of him almost felt like cheering her on. The other part of him was appalled at her brass. "I suppose I should be insulted. I did know Shipley, slightly. But it is his father the baronet who is better known to me."

It was as if he'd given her a focus for the anger she'd been holding back since his appearance. Her jaw tightened. "And so you've come here to spy on her? Does the family demand a report of her behavior, to be assured that she does not sully their beloved son's name?"

She was vehement and cold at the same time, with a voice that could wither the trees. When he did not answer immediately, her look changed. No less outraged, her expression shifted to one of contempt.

"Or perhaps you wish to try your hand at blackening *her* name further?"

Her words enraged him in a distant way. It was quite a novel thing, to be so thoroughly insulted without provocation. He let her see exactly what he thought of her eagerness to challenge his propriety, returning her look of disgust in full. It galled him that she would presume to judge him, as if he had given her any reason to think he would act as dishonorably as she once had.

"I have no such intentions." His voice was terse. "In fact, it has been my intention to make *your* acquaintance, madame, though I am sure I now regret it."

The hardness of her face dissolved a little, a sudden look of fear coming over her features. Her eyes seemed to take him in all at once, as though the reason for his presence would be written on his shirtfront or tucked under the fold of his cravat. He was botching it badly, he knew. Her brother had been accurate in his assessment of her perceptiveness. She had known on first sight of him that he hid his intentions, and in his anger he had confirmed her worst suspicions.

"I have not sought you out to insult you, or to offer you offense of any kind, Lady Helen. On the contrary," he said with a conscious softening of his tone, "I have come on behalf of your brother."

She looked a bit lost at his change in tone and when he mentioned her brother, it was as if everything within her stilled. She stopped in the road, frozen in place and staring at nothing.

"My brother?" she asked. Her voice was harsh. "What does my brother—"

She stopped herself abruptly, and gave a convulsive swallow. For someone on the verge of tears, she controlled herself very well. When she finally looked at up at him, her face was composed and definite, her tone certain.

"My brother does not wish to know of me." And she began walking along again, her chin level, neither proud nor ashamed, as she fixed her eyes on the road ahead.

It was plain to see that she would not be easy to convince. They walked in silence together. He did not often find it so difficult to hide his thoughts about another person. It was because of her past, of course, and because she had angered him. He surreptitiously looked at her profile and tried to reconcile what he knew of her with what he saw next to him.

If he had not known of her past dishonor, he would be inclined to think she looked an admirable young woman. But he did know of it, and knew there was little to admire in it. She had been betrothed to Lord Henley and, though Stephen himself had been abroad during the season of that infamous courtship, even he had heard how shamelessly she had comported herself. Tongues had begun to wag even before her return from a visit to Henley's estate in Ireland, where she had been seen by more than one guest in an unmistakably compromising position.

It would have been a trifling thing, that she had

given her virtue to her betrothed before they were wed, but her true sin was that she had then refused to marry Henley. Even knowing it would drag her family, her friends, and Henley down with her, she had simply refused. Six years later her brother, who had been in India as it all happened, remained angry and baffled. According to him, she had simply written that she would not marry Henley, and would remove to the country house she had inherited from her grandmother. And when her brother at last came home to England and demanded a satisfactory explanation, he had not got one.

Wild stories, her brother said vaguely, *meant to excuse her crying off. They evidently fell out, and she no longer wished to marry him.*

It was hard to imagine why she would act so foolishly. In one misguided act, she had utterly ruined herself. In the aftermath, she had alienated her brother, her only remaining family. As far as Stephen could tell, Lord Whitemarsh truly was unsure what to believe, insisting that Lady Helen had told him wild, incomprehensible tales of her visit to Ireland. Now her brother felt he must learn the truth of it, discreetly. Which was how Stephen found himself here.

Uncertain how best to proceed, he allowed the silence to stretch between them until he judged himself able to continue in a more tolerant vein. He needed to learn her own account of why she had refused Henley before passing his judgment on to her brother, and to do that he must avoid scenes like this.

They were approaching a turn in the path, where she led him around an admittedly ancient tree. The way was narrow and she walked ahead quickly into the shade as though anxious to get to the open light on the opposite side.

"I am sorry if it pains you to hear of your brother, Lady Helen. He hoped that there may, one day, be a reconciliation between the two of you." He remembered the look on Whitemarsh's face as he spoke of his errant sister. There was love there, and a kind of loyalty. She should be reminded of it.

He had spoken softly, but she startled at the first sign of his voice and hurried ahead. Too late, he realized they were alone, in a secluded spot. Without a chaperone, she did as any well-bred lady would do by seeking a more public place to converse with a man. She waited for him in the sunlight.

Keeping her eyes on the horse he led behind him, she steadily asked, "Since the day I left London, he has never implied that he wished even to know me. Yet now he seeks a reconciliation?"

He chose his words carefully. "I believe he wishes to know if it is possible you might welcome his affections. And also," here he gambled that she still cared for her only remaining family, "whether such a reconciliation is warranted."

They went a long time down the path before she answered.

"So he sends you to try to discover my worthiness?"

When he did not answer this rather uncomfortably insightful comment, she continued. There was no mistaking the chill in her voice.

"I suppose you are meant to be the objective observer. Will you tell me what accounts for this sudden desire to conditionally forgive me?"

"For my part, I am here because I wish to be

here." That much was true. "Your brother has been urged by his new bride to make a peace with you. I must tell you she is an excellent woman, whose only wish is your brother's happiness. But he hesitates. He is not yet convinced of the wisdom of it. I came of my own desire to be of service to him."

"So he did not precisely send you to me?"

He did not wish to lie, so he did not answer.

They had reached a small cottage surrounded by fields. She turned to him, waiting for his reply. A boy running toward them from the house saved him.

"Miss Helen! Have you brought the lace? Mum will be so happy and I've saved my penny for the thread and all, and if you can—" He stopped the breathless chatter to register the stranger and the horse. His eyes opened wide and then narrowed at Stephen. "Who's this, then?"

How had Helen Dehaven ever become so friendly with villagers who obviously treated all outsiders to such suspicion and mistrust? The boy looked back and forth between them as if waiting for a kidnapping to take place before his very eyes. Lady Helen laid a hand on his shoulder.

"I am very sorry, Danny, but my attempt at lace was dreadful," she said in a softer tone than Stephen had yet heard from her. She actually smiled. "We shall have to ask Maggie if she has something that will do. And this," she said with a gesture toward Stephen, "is Lord Summerdale. He has come to see your father."

The boy was still looking at him uncertainly. Stephen felt as if he'd suddenly sprouted cloven hooves.

"I'll run and get him, then?" the boy asked Lady Helen. She nodded and gave him a gentle push toward the house, watching him leave.

Stephen felt awkward, standing beside her. He should say something. Instead, he held the reins in his hands, looking at the cracked and worn leather as if it were the most absorbing thing he'd ever encountered.

She turned back toward him, her expression unreadable. "I shall leave you now. Your concern for my brother is laudable, but this is a misguided gesture, sir. Mr. Black will be happy to help you on your way."

He would not be dismissed so easily.

"Have you nothing to say to your brother, then?" He searched her face, but it was no use. She gave nothing away. Whether this cost her at all, he would never know. "Anything that might make him more... inclined to... attempt a resumption of his affections?" He could think of no less clumsy way to ask if she wished to alter her account of her fall from grace.

She was looking down at her hands, presenting him with a picture of demure simplicity. She thought a moment, and then replied. "If he wishes to know anything further of my actions or my choices, you may tell him that he is already in possession of the relevant facts." She looked him in the face again. "If I am to be given his regard once more, it must be on the strength of what he knows of me."

She turned to leave. Before he could think of a way to stop her, she had already paused. Turning her head over her shoulder, she spoke again.

"And if he is concerned for my welfare here, you may tell him that I do quite well without him. He need not bestir himself, or anyone else, on my account."

And then she was gone, walking across a field in the opposite direction from which they'd come.

Before she disappeared into a small copse of trees, the sun reflected once more off her tightly bound hair, sending the light back to him.

CHAPTER TWO

He would be back. Helen half-ran to the door of her cottage, thinking of nothing else but his return. He would come again with his eyes that saw too much and his all-too-friendly demeanor; he had said so. In a week. She knew, no matter how dismissive and final her words to him had been, that he was not going to give up so easily.

Her hands shook as she reached for the door. It was good that Maggie was not yet returned from her work at the Brandens' house. The jobs Maggie took as help in others' homes often kept them from growing exasperated with each other's company. Now, as she pulled off her tattered gloves in the entryway, she was glad for a moment alone to compose herself. She could not explain her agitation to Maggie any more than she could explain it to herself, so she was relieved to go upstairs to her comfortable little room and sit on the edge of the bed. There she put her mind to sorting it all out.

It wasn't as if she'd forgotten her brother, or that he was never spoken of. His presence was everywhere in her life, like a ghost in the house. It was because of him that she was here. It was because of him that she lived the way she did, hiding from the larger world and searching for some meaning in a meaningless existence. But she'd never thought he would reach out to her again in her lifetime.

Was that what this was — an attempt at apology? He'd chosen a safe enough way to do it, sending someone else in order to preserve his precious pride. Someone else to decide if she was worth the effort of forgiveness.

She could still feel Lord Summerdale's eyes on her, green like the soft moss that grew in shaded places. They looked quite harmless, even warm and kind, but they never ceased assessing her every movement and word. It almost felt as if he could look all the way through her and compel her to speak when she did not wish to. She admonished herself to take care in not speaking too freely around him. Her brother had chosen well, if he had truly wanted the man to come. Summerdale was friendly, and it was a constant task to remain cold toward him. His mouth smiled easily, his voice was rich and kind when he wanted it to be, his face open and handsome.

She clenched her jaw, slightly, almost angry at this last point. He was far too handsome, with his dark hair and green eyes, his fine broad shoulders. He looked like the kind of man that women fairly swooned over on a regular basis. That he seemed utterly unaware of it only made one more likely to swoon. She must not allow herself to let down her guard, but the truth was that he made her feel as if she'd like very much to dance again. In a dress of ice blue silk, with chandeliers of a thousand candles overhead.

Perhaps Alex thought she might respond to the combination of good looks and breeding in the man. But as an ambassador from the land of the civilized, Lord Summerdale was unable to entirely conceal his distaste for her. She rather doubted there was a speck of mud on his name, the way he wore his propriety like a perfectly tailored waistcoat. She smiled to herself, recalling his scandalized expression when she'd implied that he had come here to seduce Marie-Anne. It was a natural enough assumption on her part, even if it was indecorous to give voice to it. Marie-Anne's virtue was as questionable as her own, after all, and an easy and obvious target for a man's lust. But Summerdale seemed the kind of aristocrat who would rather starve than use the wrong fork at the dinner table, so she doubted he would be here at all if he had not been compelled by her brother.

Then again, perhaps Alex had not compelled him. He had not said he'd been sent. He might have come of his own accord because he wished to effect a reconciliation for the sake of her brother, or her new sister-in-law. How stupid of her, really, to think Alex would go to the trouble. It gave him too much credit. This ridiculous softening in her heart toward her brother must end, for he was probably still quite glad to be rid of her. She was in ruin, after all. And her brother had no place for ruined relations.

Her hand pressed against her mouth. She would *not* cry over him again. In six years, she had made a life for herself here, asking nothing of her brother in all that time. The letters he had sent in the beginning were at first scathing, then terse. They had always been brief, and she had scorned to answer them. She instructed Thompkins to answer, should Alex ever ask after her, that she was well and would trouble him no more. After a couple of years, the letters had stopped. She had cried then, a little, when she realized that no more would come. Then she had vowed not to shed another tear at her brother's disaffection. He obviously had shed none for her.

But now he was married. Six months ago, Thompkins had handed her a note. She still had it in her desk drawer downstairs, tucked far back and away from the pens and paper so that she would not be tempted to answer it. She knew every word by heart, short as it was.

My Dear Lady Helen, it read. The script was cramped but still graceful, unmistakably a woman's hand. *I wish to offer my warmest greetings to you as your new sister, or soon to be. I understand that it has been some years since you have had contact with Alex, but I would like to extend my most heartfelt invitation to you and hope that you will attend our wedding. I shall pray that you come, as I believe Alex will be very moved by your presence.*

Foolish woman, Helen thought, our dear Alex would be appalled if he even knew you'd been bird-witted enough to invite me. He'd be moved to boot me out of the church. The new Lady Whitemarsh seemed either very bold or else simpleminded.

An image came to her of her brother when he was fifteen and full of himself. (But then, she snorted to herself, he'd never stopped being full of himself.) He was lecturing her seven-year-old self on how to be a Perfect Lady in order to catch a Suitable Husband.

"You must never be too bold or outspoken,

gentlemen don't like that," he said. When she asked him if a woman must always remain quiet to please a man, he'd pulled back his shoulders and said, "I would only marry a woman who did as I told her. She'll have to listen to me and do as I wish."

She gave a sad smile at the memory, wishing she could tell his new wife about that conversation. And she would also tell how, afterward, she'd refused to put on her boots for her riding lesson, and Alex had reasoned with their parents to let her go barefoot. He'd told them she was young, and would not always be able to do as she wished, so why not indulge her this once? He was forever doing that sort of thing - lecturing her on propriety and then allowing for her unladylike, childish whims. He had trusted her to outgrow them, and she had.

It looked as if his new wife was not the woman he'd predicted for himself all those years ago. Helen had not even considered going to the wedding for an instant, certain that the invitation was unknown to her brother. If he knew that his bride – *Elizabeth Cabot*, read the signature – had even written of the nuptials, he would probably have ridden any number of horses to collapse in order to intercept the note. She decided the new Lady Whitemarsh showed admirable spirit in defying her brother. Yes, it would make sense that Alex would marry someone strong-willed, and not lacking in wit.

Helen longed to know her. An excellent woman, Lord Summerdale had said of her.

Lord Summerdale. He had come here, but perhaps not at her brother's request, just as Lady Whitemarsh had written her without her brother's knowledge. She must know more about the man: whether she could trust him, why he had come, if he was truly her brother's confidante. When standing under his penetrating gaze, she felt defenseless. He knew everything of importance about her. She knew nothing about him at all. She had thought the heir to Summerdale was named Edward, and that she had danced with him once at a ball, a hundred years ago. She could only vaguely recall what the man looked like, but it was not this same Lord Summerdale.

He would be back. She had thought so often of writing her new sister-in-law that for a moment this seemed the perfect excuse for it. Surely Lady Whitemarsh would know her husband's friends, and she seemed eager enough to hear from Helen.

Hardly thinking further than that, she flew down the stairs and to her desk. It was opening the drawer where she kept the writing paper that reminded her what a daft notion it was. Behind the neat, white sheets was a tangle of carefully preserved ribbons that had belonged to a dead woman, a woman she had watched die. It hit her like cold water, this reminder of everything her brother had refused to hear. There was too much that lay between them, the estrangement too complete.

What could she possibly write to her sister-in-law? Though we have never met, and I have no reason to offer for my curiosity in the local Lord Bountiful, please tell me everything you know of the man? It would sound like the pathetic plea of a moon-struck backwater miss. Or worse, like a hopeful courtesan looking for tidbits to help land a new benefactor.

She accepted the bitter truth of that. After all, she was a fallen woman, and her new sister was firmly in place atop Society's pedestal. As was Lord

Summerdale. They had every reason, to their own thinking, to believe the worst of her. She stared at the blank page, tasting bile at the back of her throat.

But she still had one friend in London who would tell her whatever she knew. She picked up her pen and began to write to the Baroness, Joyce Huntingdon. A friend. One who would not think ill of her, she hoped.

*

It was hardly, he thought with a sinking heart, a rousing success.

As he jolted down the road in Daniel Black's sturdy cart, he wondered if any good had come of meeting her. A good bit of time alone with the girl, and what had he learned? Precisely nothing, except that he was not likely to learn anything at all.

He was not in the habit of failing in this arena. In his life, he had been used to learning people's secrets. It was all he had been good for before Edward's death. As a younger son he'd been obliged to acquire some kind of usefulness, so he had made himself an invaluable friend to several important people. Gossip ran like wildfire through every level of society, and was so often wielded as a weapon by those who professed themselves in the know. But Stephen had observed early on that the truth behind the gossip could prove even more valuable.

For years he had kept his ears open and his mouth shut, and found himself in a position of relative power, advising dukes and counseling the king. When a gentleman had sensitive matters to discuss, and no one he trusted with whom to discuss them, he quite often found himself turning to Stephen Hampton. For years, he had been known as the one to consult when in need of a map of the terrain, so to speak. In a few words, he could tell someone – if he wished – that a split in the High Tory vote was probable, or that the youngest son of the Duke of Heatherleigh was not to be trusted with a prime naval appointment. How he knew these things, no one asked. And no one cared, so long as he was right.

He only paid attention, dodged and danced on the peripheries of others' deepest feelings and thoughts, their fears and ambitions. Then he slipped away with the truth and used the knowledge he gained. Discreetly, of course. Always discreetly, or else he would no longer be trusted.

Two years ago, Edward had died of the influenza. The shock of losing his elder brother and realizing that he was to inherit the title, much to the everlasting chagrin of his family, had barely worn off before his father passed on earlier this year. Now Stephen, who had grown to hate tawdry secrets and intrigue and subtle fluctuations of influence, had become an earl. It was laughable: he was in a better position than ever to use his knowledge for his own benefit, but he had no wish to do so. He only wanted out of London and away from the whispers that kept it all going.

Instead, he found himself here. He had known it would be impossible to avoid such games altogether if he was to manage his business affairs. Secrets and inside information were unavoidable, but he was used to the secrets of men. Women, he knew with bitter certainty, were quite another matter.

Helen Dehaven and her friend were different from the women he had known, though. Hardly accustomed to the company of ruined ladies, he had not known what he would find. But he had never expected the hostility he had found from either of them. Suddenly he realized that he had thought they would want to please him, because they were less than respectable and he was... well, what he was: nobility, society, the world that had rejected them. Instead, it seemed as if they had rejected his world, and him.

It was more galling than he liked to admit to himself. He thought of Lady Helen's tightly bound hair and simple dress, her cold speech. How well and thoroughly she shut him out. The moment when he had mentioned her brother came back to him vividly. She'd wanted to believe, for a moment, that her brother cared for her still.

He was acutely aware that she stirred a sympathy in him, despite his rational understanding that she was everything he considered selfish, ill-bred, and unthinking. But her brother seemed willing to consider a rapprochement, which indicated there was doubt about what had happened with Henley so long ago. Instinctively, he knew that to find the truth he must continue to act as if he were there only to bring brother and sister to an understanding. Perhaps she was suspicious, but she missed her only family. If he could play to that emotion, he might have a chance of gaining her trust.

If he could not soon manage to meet again with her, he would learn whatever possible from her friends. Marie-Anne de Vauteuil might be charmed, and Daniel Black had thus far treated him with less suspicion than either woman. As the cart bumped along, he turned to the spindly man at his side.

"I had hoped to return for my horse tomorrow

and thank Miss Dehaven for her help. She is a neighbor of yours?"

"Aye, that she is, and a better neighbor I'd not have looked for in a young miss." For the first time since their meeting, the man gave him a doubtful look. "You din't know her afore today, then, your lordship?"

"I am a friend to her family. I did not know until today that she lived in the village."

"When my Barbara was down sick with the childbed fever, that was Miss Helen's first year here in Bartle. She come over and looked after the boy, brought us dinner each night and herbs for the wife," he smiled. "Didn't hardly know what to make of such a fine lady treating us like that, but it's only that she has a good heart."

They rumbled along in silence as Stephen digested this. The other man shot him a critical look.

"Miss Helen's never mentioned her family much. Been right happy just where she is, away from all the fine lords and ladies." He kept his eyes on the horse's backside. Obviously he didn't shy from implying that Lord Summerdale was entirely unnecessary in this town.

Stephen took his chance to establish his motive. "I think her family has missed her," he said pointedly. "I believe they'd like to know that she is well."

Daniel Black's expression turned sour. "They'll not be coming out here, I'm sure, and she won't be leavin' for no London, neither, if that's what you mean. If she wants nothing to do with a family then there's no cause for you to pester her with it. Beggin' your pardon, lordship." His face closed like a trap.

"You think it's your place to tell me I should not

call on her again?" He was careful to use a neutral tone, though he was torn between outrage and humor at the man's impudence.

"It's not my place to tell you nothin', your lordship," he grumbled. "But I know her and you don't. Never asked her why she come nor why she stayed, but I know enough that she's only gotten grief from your kind. Like I said," he finished, "best leave her be."

So much for the opinion of the common man. This morning, he might have taken the advice. But now, seeing the loyalty she inspired in those around her and knowing of her lurid past, he did not wish to leave her be. Outside of his original purpose here, Helen Dehaven intrigued him. She could not hide forever, no matter the walls she had built around herself. And no matter what her neighbor advised, he would be back to see her again.

CHAPTER THREE

The fine weather could not continue much longer. Already, there had been a number of unseasonably mild days filled with sunlight and soft breezes. The late-blooming flowers would replace the ruinous lace as a gift for Danny's mother, if only she could manage to cut them free without gashing herself.

The dress she wore was a plain homespun, one of three she kept on hand. All of her old dresses had been sold or packed away or, more often, cut up and salvaged for the expensive material and trim. It had caused her no anxiety to be rid of them. In the purge after her banishment from high society, it had been a welcome task to re-define her wardrobe and, as a consequence, her entire persona. She almost enjoyed looking ghastly in the threadbare gown, the dirty apron. She laid the cut blossoms on the grass next to her and was looking for any more that might be presentable when she heard the beat of approaching hooves.

He rode up on a fine piece of horseflesh, leading the other horse beside him at a trot. He looked like a heroic figure from a painting, she thought with no little humor: Gallant Officer Leads the Charge. She had rather forgotten how very attractive a good-looking man on a blooded horse could be, and almost forgot that she was frightened of this meeting. So absorbed was she in the sight of him that she didn't notice Danny riding alongside. As the two reined in close to where she rose from the grass, she suddenly felt horribly provincial. Her hair, her dress...what must he think of her? Her stomach fluttered even as she told herself such concerns were trifling and unworthy.

When she looked up at him, she knew precisely what he thought of her. He was obviously appalled. The corners of his mouth turned down in distaste as he fairly glared, horrified, at her dress. She would not allow herself to be nervous, nor care one whit what he thought of her, no matter how disappointing it was to watch his mouth turn severe. She had half-decided something since last she'd seen him and it would be harder to know what to do with any certainty, if she let her mind be clouded with cares of what he might think. So instead of looking at him, she turned to an extraordinarily pleased Danny, who was calling her name.

"He let me ride the horse, Miss Helen, and I did well, I did! It's a fine horse — as fine as any gentleman would ride, Jack says!"

The boy lost a little enthusiasm when he looked at her. It was terrible that she could not bring herself to laugh for him, or even give him a smile. She seemed unable to move a single muscle in her face when she felt Lord Summerdale's scrutiny of her.

"That's wonderful. You ride well, Danny," she said faintly into the silence. She nodded. "Lord Summerdale."

"Lady Helen," he returned, dismounting fluidly as Danny scrambled off the horse. Probably he had practiced since their last meeting to keep the contempt from his voice. He had succeeded admirably. If she had not felt it so acutely yesterday, she would have thought he thoroughly respected her today.

"I've cut some roses for you to give to your mother, Danny. They'll do much better than the lace, and you can keep your penny for sweets." It was an effort to keep a light tone.

Poor Danny tried quite hard not to show disappointment at this announcement. "Then Miss Maggie don't have none?"

She found a grin somewhere within herself for the boy. "No, and Miss Marie-Anne has only a half-finished bit of it. The flowers are all we can offer just now." She watched Danny shift his feet and fought against doing the same.

"It's a well-known fact that women in every corner of the globe love flowers, Danny." Lord Summerdale's rich voice reached out to them. Danny turned to him with the look of an adoring puppy. "There is nothing better to get a man out of trouble, isn't that right, Lady Helen?"

"Indeed," she replied. "Not that you're in any trouble, at least lately, Danny. And we should get these in water right away. No, I will not take the penny, you'll have need of it one day and they cost me nothing. They provided me a perfect excuse to enjoy the fine weather. Now handle them with care, they're easier than you think to crush." She could not seem to stop herself rambling on as she picked up the roses and fussed over them. "They'll keep for a few days with fresh water, you know. Your mother will know how to care for them. We may even be able to add a few blooms if the weather continues fine, as I think it is likely to do."

She stopped herself from launching into a treatise on the weather. Probably she *had* become provincial. There was no other reason for her senseless chatter. Living for so many years in Bartle, with only Marie-Anne and a few others who were schooled in the art of conversation, had left her with rust on her words. Perhaps she would be lucky enough to bore the fashionable Lord Summerdale into leaving her alone. If that was indeed what she wished, for she was not sure any more that she wanted him to give up on his mission.

Danny thanked her profusely and turned to go. He did not leave until he had thanked Lord Summerdale for the ride and admired the horse at length. When he finally scampered away, she stood silently in her dirty apron, staring at the soil beneath her cracked fingernails.

"I'd hoped to see you and thank you for your kindness in aiding me yesterday."

She heard him clear his throat when she did not respond. Her heart began to beat faster, thinking that she must find the right words to keep him here. She had determined she must learn more of her brother, of this chance to reconcile through such an unlikely intermediary as Lord Summerdale. The letter to Joyce had been sent off this morning, and she knew she would have no reply for at least ten days or more. Without some notion of who Summerdale was, she was at a loss for safe conversation. It was unthinkable to blurt out that she wished to hear everything he knew about her brother's current attitude toward his ruined sister, or his new wife, or even the state of Alex's beloved Thoroughbreds.

The thought of her brother's horses gave her a mundane topic to cling to. That much she remembered from her season in London – mundane chatter.

"Your horses are most impressive, my lord. It was kind of you to let Danny ride. He'll talk about it for ages."

His grin was like the sun bursting out of the clouds. "I couldn't very well have passed up the opportunity to thrill him. He looked at the horse like a starving man. He has a good seat."

"Yes, he's always loved to ride. He'll find any number of reasons to take the carthorse off the traces and ride over to Hillside." She found herself warming to him, because there was no sign of his earlier disapproval. He was so friendly and easy. With a little laugh, she told him, "One would think there was a social event of monumental proportions every week in that town, to hear Danny tell of it, but really he only rides the nag there for a few minute's talk with the tanner's boy. Then he rides back and turns it into the most fascinating discussion in all the parish."

His smile made her forget to mistrust him. "And what do they speak of?"

Such a silly and simple miss she was, to stand here with a man like him and talk of a farm boy's exploits. To wish she had her straw bonnet, so that she could peek from behind the brim to take in more of his delicious grin. It transformed his face, mischief breaking out of a marble sculpture, as if a stone Apollo had decided to become a puckish boy.

"It usually has to do with some vital technique of farming, but the dear boy can never quite explain how a tanner's boy should know so much about spreading manure."

He let out a laugh, the sound of it curling around her toes. "It sounds like they are both quite practiced in the art of manure-spreading. Never doubt that young boys are all expert at it, of necessity."

She could not resist smiling back at him, until he raised his brows and asked, "Would you care to ride with me?"

She had a thrilling vision of the countryside speeding by as the wind whipped through her hair. But she had no sidesaddle. Nor any riding habit. Her hands, twisted in the grubby apron, itched with dirt and leaves and tiny scratches.

"I do not ride," she said, and felt her heart close up like a crocus faced with a sudden nightfall.

She stared resolutely at his boot in the stirrup, feeling the distance of the worlds that stood between them. That quickly, she no longer wanted him there, in front of her little home. It was plain he did not belong here.

"In that case, I shall tether the horses," he said. Before she could think of a reason to protest, he said, "It's a pleasant day for a walk, and I should enjoy seeing the village."

She could feel him staring at her, the top of her head fairly afire under his gaze. The returning memory of a favorite straw bonnet with the wide blue ribbon, abandoned so many years ago, tied her tongue into a knot. She could not think past the way the smooth silk of it had pressed under her chin on warm days like this.

She reprimanded herself. He was waiting for an indication of where he should tie the horses, and she could only obsess over a silly bonnet. She could not imagine it, a walk with him.

"I've put a spot of tea on to boil, milady."

Maggie's voice behind snapped her fully back into the moment. She glanced back at her apparently shy and docile maid (an excellent act, indeed) and then looked back at the earl, unable to speak just yet. It was visually arresting to look so quickly from Maggie's blazing red hair and round freckled face to Lord Summerdale's quietly handsome features, arranged into a polite and patient inquiry.

He raised his eyebrows and spoke as if he were inviting her to refreshment in his own home. "Or perhaps something to drink, Lady Helen?" It was the slowness with which he spoke, as if she were a dimwitted child, that prompted her to nod quickly and indicate the post where he should tether the horses, when she was not even sure that she still wanted to speak with him.

Maggie bobbed a curtsy at him and led the way into the house. It was because of Maggie that she had decided to at least try to speak to the earl. The small but fierce Irishwoman had not sympathized with Helen's recalcitrance when she'd heard of this chance to have some sort of contact with Alex. "He's your only family, and if he's come to see he's been a cruel idiot, what more could you be wanting?" she had asked last night. "It's a sorrow to you, not having his love. I see it every day, there's no use pretending."

From the servile manner Maggie affected in front of Lord Summerdale, one would never guess at her complete lack of feudal obedience. Helen had never felt any desire to treat her as other than a dear friend, not from the moment Maggie had taken her out of Ireland and stayed with her throughout her unceremonious banishment. A fist of fear closed briefly around her heart when she thought of Maggie's impending departure. Back to her family, back to Ireland, where Helen would never go again.

She shook off the thought as they stepped into the house. Looking at the walls around her, she acknowledged once again how lucky she had been to find Maggie on that most horrible of days. Sunlight poured in through the windows and bounced off each gleaming surface. The furniture was simple, taken from the servant's quarters at the dower house, but it was solid and in good condition for the most part. Helen had not known what to do with this house when she rented it; Maggie called it "grand" and had set to work tidying and beautifying everything that fell under her hands. Now, it was a cheery little home.

Out of long habit, she looked down at her feet to see that she did not trail dirt across the polished pine floors, and noticed that she still wore the rag of an apron. Hastily, she untied the strings behind her waist and pulled it off. Maggie's hand was there immediately to take it, which she did with another quick bob. She had not seen such humility since Maggie had come into her employ years ago. The illusion of the humble servant was shattered when Helen glimpsed the stern look in the girl's eye. If she did not go through with the effort to speak civilly to

Lord Summerdale, she had no doubt that Maggie would make her feel like a wretch before the day was done.

"Are you enjoying the ruminations of Marcus Aurelius, Lady Helen?" At his question, she turned around to see him looking at the slim volumes on the table.

Books. She could talk about books, yes. "Indeed, my lord. I find his writings to be fascinating, and not a little bit humbling."

"'Look at the yawning void of the future, and at that other limitless space, the past,'" he quoted. Of course he would know the most suitable quote for her situation.

"'Look beneath the surface; let not the several quality of a thing nor its worth escape thee.'" But she said it mildly. It would gain her little, to engage in such a battle with him. "His writings are intriguing," she finished lamely.

"Not nearly so intriguing as the writing of Mr. Franklin," he answered, holding up the other book. "Wherever did you manage to procure his account of the American negotiations with England?"

"A friend on the continent delights in presenting me with scandalous literature, and I have a certain affection for the subject. It is outdated, and surely written with a sympathy for the colonies, but I confess to the same sympathy."

"Do you really?" He looked at her with an expression that was amused, impressed, and somewhat surprised. The grin did not reappear, for which she was enormously thankful, but laugh lines formed faintly around his eyes. He had such a friendly, open face, as though he were eager to smile.

She realized with a shock that he was seeking to find some point of interest between them, a common ground, and she thought with trepidation that she might come to enjoy the sight of those fine lines radiating out from his eyes. "So do I, in fact. My late father met Mr. Franklin many years ago, but was not impressed by the man. Do you follow their politics, then?"

A discussion of politics was odd, but infinitely preferable to so many other topics. She answered honestly. "I do, yes. As a child, I was fascinated with their President Washington. Such an admirable man, I've always thought."

She waved the earl to a seat and sat on a chair across from him as Maggie glided soundlessly from the room to fetch tea. Once they were seated, he looked about the room and said, "I confess myself curious as to why you have chosen to settle in Bartle. Your grandmother's home was not far from here, I gather?"

"Just a few miles east of the village."

"You must prefer your lodgings here?"

She refrained from voicing the reply that came immediately to her lips. "It is more agreeable to me to remain in the village. I have made many friends here. In any case, the dower house is far too large for only myself."

In the eternal silence that seemed to punctuate their every conversation, his fingers smoothed over his breeches repeatedly in what she optimistically thought might be a nervous gesture. But if he was nervous, he was certainly good at hiding it. Helen herself felt flushed and breathless as she desperately wondered how much she should tell him.

"Lady Helen, I wish to apologize for my rudeness toward you yesterday. It was uncalled for, and has only served to hamper any friendship that we might have found." His sudden shift in topic startled her, and she stared at his fingers, pressed now into the soft cloth near his knee. "As I said, I know your brother has been disturbed by the lack of news of you. If I can assure him that you are well, and well-provided for, I shall feel as if I have eased his mind greatly."

It had the ring of a practiced speech, which only made her resent that she did not have words at the ready. She looked up sharply. "You must permit me to be skeptical, my lord. My brother has only to ask my solicitor, or indeed even to write to me, which he has not done these four years past."

The dark eyebrows pulled together. "He told me you did not answer his letters."

"His notes – for I would hardly call them letters – did not invite response, and after a short while they stopped entirely." The indignity of Alex's words in those missives would likely never cease to annoy her. He had written of honor, of how he was working to restore the family name, how she should take at least some of the money he had put aside for her dowry to live a quiet but dignified life as far from London as possible. Every word from him was an accusation: it was *her* fault he had to work so hard to restore what *she* had ruined, and to live in anything other than the circumscribed manner he deemed appropriate was further insult.

But she had decided that she could not bear to take anything from him, nor live according to his comfort. If he thought her worthless, then she would not cost him a single shilling. She had taken the amount her grandmother had put into Thompkins' hands for her, only a tiny portion of her dowry sum, and found the solicitor very willing to act on her behalf. Like her ball gowns and silk slippers and bonnets, it was relatively easy to give up the whole of that life. She was different now and, she thought, infinitely less vapid. It was the one point she prided herself on, that she took care of herself and those around her as best she could. The girl she had been would have found it more vital to visit the couterière than a sick or needful neighbor.

Maggie came into the room once again, bearing the tray. "I'll serve, Maggie, thank you." She watched her friend take up the chair at a discreet distance, a move that had been calculated to serve both propriety and Helen's own anxieties.

Now Helen looked to Lord Summerdale as she set the cup in front of him. He had an air about him as though this were a business meeting of sorts, and she wished to know his agenda, so that she could touch upon the topics and have done with it.

"I know there are things you wish to ask me, but I cannot help but remember that you carry my words to my brother. And though I should like there to be some sort of contact with him, I" – here she paused and took a steadying breath – "I would not wish him to believe that I regret my past actions, or that I have waited all these years for a chance to ask his forgiveness."

A taut silence followed these words. She had an absurd desire to laugh at the way he carefully sipped before speaking, acutely aware of how they both considered each word as if a secretary stood by transcribing every statement for posterity. Suddenly Summerdale looked up at her as though he had had the same thought, and a look of frankness came into his features at last.

"I don't wish to report your every word to him. I should only like..." He paused, his eyes straying to her hands. "I should like to be able to tell him, generally, how you manage without his support. And why it is you do not regret your actions, as you have said. I should like, if it is possible and if you do not object to it, to help the two of you to be a family again."

To be a family again. How her heart leapt up at the idea of it. She took a deep breath and prepared herself to return his apparent honesty.

"As for my not being sorry for" – she cast about for a term other than *The Odious Henley* and rushed through saying it – "for the circumstances that ended my betrothal, I have never felt that there was any call for me to regret anything I did, or at least those actions which led to my current situation. I will not speak of those events again in my life, sir. Not to you or anyone." There, that had come out firmly, and well. "But as to how I manage without my brother's support, the answer is quite simple."

So she told him of how Maggie went largely unpaid, and how the dower house brought her a small sum when she rented it out. Explaining how very little it cost to live in Bartle, she told him that she had no need of ball gowns, after all, nor a score of new dresses every season. At this he gave a significant look at her attire, but she distracted him from comment by detailing the bartering system she employed for most of their food. As she spoke, she became aware of the way he had about him of making her feel quite relaxed. It was nothing he did, or said. He had a presence that caused her to feel comfortable, and the words tumbled out of her, regardless of any reserve she had felt only moments before.

"And do you not feel the loss of your former life?" He spoke lightly but his eyes were fixed intently on her, and she felt this was more than simple curiosity. "You don't ever wish for a bit of velvet, or a carriage for travel?"

"I have enough for my needs, my lord, and those are things that I do not need. Even you have survived this last half hour without those imperative goods," she said with a smile.

He gave an answering smile, another burst of warmth. "True enough, I have. And I see that as you said, you do well enough without the wealth to which you were born. I doubt that many others would adjust so easily."

She felt herself blush faintly at the compliment, and the lingering effect of his singular smile. She wanted to ask after her brother's wife, and could not find a way to lead up to it. Well, he wouldn't be tricked into saying anything, nor would he simply not notice her interest, so she must swallow her pride and be prepared to ask it outright.

She rehearsed the words over and over in her head before finally forcing herself to voice them. "And will Lady Whitemarsh be interested in my situation, too?"

Immediately she felt his quick look, the razor-sharp focus that would not fail to note the eagerness in her. *He doesn't miss a thing*, she thought ruefully. But he answered easily.

"She will, yes, though I do not think it wise to tell her I have found you. She might ride through the night to come here and see you with her own eyes, most likely with your brother dragged by the ears."

Gratifying as it was to think of Alex being dragged anywhere by a woman, she could not return his grin.

"She wants so badly to find me, then?" Perhaps she wished to come here and begin a lecture on the grief that had been brought to Alex, to rail at Helen as Alex had, so long ago.

"Lady Whitemarsh has told me that she longs for a sister, someone to tell her about her husband's youth." His voice had taken on a tone of reassurance, and she cursed herself for letting her apprehensions show so clearly. "I have met her only briefly, but she made no secret of her impatience with Lord Whitemarsh in regards to you."

A hundred questions about Lady Whitemarsh began to pile up in her mind immediately. But her pride would not allow her to ask them. She had decided that, given the opportunity, she would ask just one simple question. Now she forced herself not to care how pitiful and grasping it might sound. She could regret it later, as she most likely would regret talking to him at all.

"Will you tell me a little about her?"

He did. At great length, and with the minutest of detail, he described Elizabeth's background, her bearing, and how she had managed to catch Alex's interest (they met at a dinner party at the Duke of Thursby's home, and were bored to tears). It was more than she'd ever hoped to learn, and she did not question why Summerdale spoke so freely. She only relished the warmth in his voice when he related Elizabeth's growing determination that Alex should forgive his errant sister.

When Summerdale left, with a promise to call again on his next pass through the village, Helen was already thinking of the thousand things she would ask him next time. It was not until he was well gone that she realized he had learned more of her than she'd wanted him to and that he was still not to be trusted, no matter how much she may want to talk with him again.

CHAPTER FOUR

"November, your cousin writes, and will give us the exact date in her next letter, just as soon as she may."

They were all three sitting in the kitchen, Maggie and Marie-Anne and herself, as anxious as debutantes invited to the king's ball. It all came to this, everything they had planned for. Marie-Anne's eyes were bright with enthusiasm as she pulled Helen's hands into her own with a broad smile. *Like children with sweets,* thought Helen, feeling a foolish grin split across her face. *You'd think the child were our own.*

Helen had pictured her countless times: a girl with long dark hair and milky white skin. Her features were less defined in Helen's imaginings. She could hardly bear to think of the child's parents, and every attempt to conjure up a family likeness ended in cold sweat and nightmares. Helen had turned her thoughts over the years to the future. Bringing the child here was the first step, and after that she allowed herself to build dream castles, all occupied by the little girl she'd never known.

Katie. The name came to her a hundred times a day this last year, and often enough in the years before that. She would make dinner and wonder if Katie liked fish. She would dress for bed each night and think of the pink flowers she'd embroidered on a little white nightgown, hoping Katie would like them. On a walk through the village, she'd mentally point out every home and tell Katie about who lived where. And she'd saved just enough to get passage for the girl and Maggie's cousin to come across the sea to England, where they could live happily in this quiet village.

This girl and their plans for her had become the center of everything. Now Helen admitted it to herself, how it had slowly become her only reason for waking each day. She kept herself busy, found ways to make herself useful, and enjoyed the company of her friends. But there was no denying that her life had become, since that fateful day six years ago, a rather meaningless existence. What was the point of it all, with no family left to her, and no prospect of making a new one? There *was* no point, a fact that haunted her thoroughly, until she had determined to make Katie the focus of it.

This one thing, she could still do. She could care for an orphaned child, work toward that one purpose: give Katie a life worth living. Let it all have some meaning in the end, her own downfall and banishment and empty days. Only keep the child safe, and bring her here where Helen could watch her grow and thrive and live and love – and her own life would be worth living, too.

Whenever the nightmares came on her and drove

her mad, whenever she found herself living in that worst moment again – smelling the smells, feeling the weight of him, tasting her own terror – it was thoughts of Katie that drove it out and brought her back to her senses. *Katie will come here,* she would chant to herself in the terrible night. *Katie will sit safe here next to me, and I will feed her cakes and watch her laugh. Katie will be with me. Katie will be here.* With each repetition, her heart would slow its wild beating. With each vision of this happy future, the visions of the unspeakable past receded into nothingness, until she was calm again.

Of course, Katie's coming also meant Maggie's leaving, a fact she had not dwelt on until now. Watching her maid gather up her bundle and hastily leave for her day of work at the Hawkins home, Helen tried to imagine a life without her friend. Maggie had always wanted to return to her family, of course. How could she not, having left so precipitously? She wanted to care for her ailing father; she wanted to start a family of her own. So she would take the ferry back there with her cousin, while Katie was safely delivered to Bartle.

Since that long-ago and horror-filled day, Katie had stayed with Maggie's family. With the little bit of money that Helen managed to send for the girl's keep, she liked to think that life was good there. Katie was sickly, she had always been. But she was also a bright girl, according to every report sent by the diligent cousin, and her prospects would be better in England. "Nothing for a girl in Ireland but maid's work, and not even that for a girl that came from a Traveling family," Maggie had said.

All that was enough to convince Helen that it wasn't her selfishness alone that brought the child across the sea. The idea of Katie's dismal prospects paled in comparison to the danger Helen felt the child exposed to. The Odious Henley lived on the nearest estate and was the lord of the manor. He was the law in that place, a fact she had learned most definitely, and explosively. Helen greeted each letter sent for the last six years with a mixture of joy and terror, never knowing if she would be told that Katie was now teething, now walking, now learning her letters, or now discovered by Henley. She knew it was unreasonable to think that he would know of the child, or care anything about her, but reason had no place in her thoughts about Henley.

Marie-Anne's voice held a vast satisfaction. "Jack and Sally have already prepared a room, and if Sally knits one more scarf for the girl, they'll be able to stuff them all in a mattress for an extra bed."

"Do you think we should wait to tell them until we know the date of her arrival? If anything goes wrong or delays them, I don't want their hopes dashed."

Helen would happily have taken Katie in as her own, and they had discussed the possibility of saying it was a cousin, or a niece. But she knew that in spite of her own acceptance in the village, there was enough knowledge of the rumors to leave a cloud of scandal around her. Such a cloud would do no favors to a young girl come to live with her. It was a cold fact, and one that Helen had no choice but to accept: no matter how the villagers cared for her, they would no more forget what she had come from than would the fine lords and ladies in London. She would not have her own ruin follow an innocent girl around for life. Besides that, Katie deserved something of a normal life with a mother and a father, and Jack and

Sally deserved a child.

They all deserved to be happy. Together. Helen was really very happy for them all. Or so she kept telling herself.

"The next letter sent will give us a more precise date, and then we'll tell the happy couple," Marie-Anne suggested. "Jack must be told, so that he can plan to take the trip. And everything will go well, of course! You worry so much, my dear."

"I do, I know, but so many things can go wrong." Helen bit her lip. "I am afraid, I think, mostly because of Lord Summerdale." They had not spoken of him yet, and it seemed to Helen that there was much to discuss. "I wish he had not come now, spying all around, sniffing out the details of my life. What if he should learn of Katie?"

Marie-Anne raised her eyebrows at this. "There is no reason he would, I think, with Jack and Sally in the next village over. And even if he did know, what of it? Besides, he's not likely to come to Bartle often."

Helen stood, agitated. "But he will. I was stupid enough to make him feel welcome to visit again, and he's come expressly to learn more about me, for the purpose of telling my brother how I get along. I don't like it, Marie-Anne!"

Her childish outburst did not ruffle Marie-Anne in the least, who only picked up the bundle of herbs on the table and began methodically to strip the rosemary from the stems. "Do not pretend to me that it doesn't please you to know your brother will learn the extent of your independence. I know the idea of a peer telling him how very much you don't need his help to get along absolutely delights *me*." Marie-Anne had never made a secret of her feelings toward Alex;

she thought him second only to Henley in his barbarous treatment of an innocent girl. "So I think that you must mean you don't like Summerdale himself, though he seems most agreeable to me."

"Agreeable! Indeed, it's his amiability that I dislike most. He will charm you, just as he very nearly charmed me." He had no right whatsoever to inquire into her financial affairs, yet she had been as open with him as she was with her solicitor, all on the strength of his blasted friendliness. "One more smile, and I'd have taken him on a tour of the root cellar to show him how well provisioned I am for the winter."

"Well, there is something in his smile that makes a woman want to give more than she ought," observed Marie-Anne sympathetically, "and show him all sorts of delightful things. In the root cellar indeed." There was a quirk at her lips and a twinkle in her eye that Helen had not quite patience enough to tolerate.

"Oh, do stop being so very Gallic, Marie-Anne." She heard the peevishness in her own voice, and reminded herself that Marie-Anne would always choose to laugh, when she could, and that this was something she should treasure in her friend. "He is handsome, I'll admit, but he uses it well and always to his own advantage. Remember that, if you please, when he calls on you next."

"I look forward to it!" Marie-Anne laughed with delight. But she sobered at the sight of her friend's clear anxiety. "Hélène, you must believe that I will not tell him anything you don't wish me to say. I'll speak to this Summerdale about my Shipley as much as I can, to keep him off the subject of you. But you have not told me how much he already knows. Did he ask about The Odious Henley?"

Helen stiffened only slightly. They had assigned this title to Henley, deciding long ago that he deserved it. Nothing too sinister, so they could speak of him easily. He *was* odious, and so much more than that. But they could turn him into a character out of a bad novel by referring to him thus, and Helen preferred not to think of him as completely real. At least not when she was attempting to have a normal conversation.

"I've refused to speak of it. He did not press me on that, only offered me the chance to change my story. So I believe he must know. Alex will have told him something of it, though God knows what." She smiled grimly. "And the rumors are out there. He would have heard of it in any case."

Marie-Anne made a gratifying noise of disgust. "Rumors, not truth." She flicked her fingers. "What I want to know is what you want me to tell him. Or what it is I should not tell him."

Everything she had spoken about with Lord Summerdale rolled around in her head. Of her finances he need know no more than she had already revealed. It was the news of her new sister-in-law that intrigued her most, and the yet unknown depth of sincerity in her brother. She considered a long time while Marie-Anne waited patiently.

"I think I want to know if Alex really wants me in his life again, or if this is all the design of the new Lady Whitemarsh." She did not try to hide the quaver in her voice that betrayed her emotions. "She sounds wonderful, but she is not my brother. His affections matter to me, not hers. Not really."

It was a hard thing to admit, especially to Marie-Anne, who virtually hated Alex.

Marie-Anne sighed as she scooped the herbs into a bowl. "Well, I shall look on it as an opportunity to seek information from Lord Summerdale, then, and not as an opportunity for him to learn more about you. We shall see if your brother has any good in him at all." She stood up and laid a hand on Helen's shoulder. "I only want to prevent you from suffering more at the hands of this brother, you know. I shall scratch the eyes out of anyone who brings you any more pain," she said in a kind and gentle voice, and Helen did not doubt her every word.

"Now!" Marie-Anne exclaimed cheerily. "Let's talk of happier things, like dear little Katie, and how we will best welcome her when she comes."

Marie-Anne de Vauteuil was no empty-headed debutante, nor was she coldly calculating. What she was, Stephen decided as he sat in her sparsely furnished parlor, was a very good friend and a woman entirely confident of herself and her place in the world. It was a rare thing indeed. It was even rarer to find someone who could so deftly evade his questions.

He put on his most charming smile — she liked it, he could see — and tried again.

"Are you as contented to stay in this little village, madame, as your friend Lady Helen seems to be?"

"Bartle is a lovely village, I find. Small, and very little to entertain a man like you, I think, but the people are kind. Daniel Black is a good man, and pleasant, do you not think?"

"Yes, he was most obliging, and his son as well."

He tried not to sound dismissive of this on his way to forcing the topic back to that person he wished to discuss. "They are both quite taken with Lady Helen. I understand she has been a good friend to them, and to all the villagers?"

She gave him a dazzling smile. "I am most taken with the villagers myself, you know. One can hardly keep from making friends here, if one lives as they do."

She quite obviously wanted to be clear that he could never be seen as anything other than a lord here, and it would forever keep him apart. He hoped he would not be reduced to working in the fields in order to glean information from anyone, and thrust aside the unexpected and uncomfortable notion that he cared at all what common villagers thought of him. He once again forced the conversation back to where he wished it.

"Lady Helen seems to have made many friends here as well, despite the fact that she has not always lived as they have. Was it so difficult for her to find acceptance?"

It didn't surprise him when she ignored the question and picked up a small cake and offered it to him innocently. "Mrs. Gibbons makes the most wonderful cakes. Won't you try one? Do you know, it was a love of French pastry that brought my Richard and me together? He was looking for a chef, and—"

"Madame." He cut her off, thinking that if he heard one more inanity about Richard Shipley, or if he had to parrot the name of Lady Helen Dehaven one more time, it would drive him from the room, as she no doubt depended upon. "I am sorry to speak so plainly—"

"Hardly a thing to apologize for, *monsieur*."

"But I notice that you are determined to avoid speaking of Lady Helen. Yet I feel quite sure she has told you I came here in search of her."

"She has." She acknowledged it with a graceful tilt of her head.

"And will you oblige me with at least an acknowledgement that the woman exists?" he asked with some exasperation.

Her lips curved into a slight smile, a deep dimple appearing at one side of her face. "I will of course admit that she exists, my lord."

"Thank you." His exaggerated gratitude widened her smile. Since they could both talk in circles all afternoon, and had been doing so for the last ten minutes, it was time to come to the point of it before the heavy clouds rolled in from the west and opened up over his road home. But hardly had he determined to speak plainly when Mme de Vauteuil seized the initiative.

"What would you like to know, my lord Summerdale? That she is happy here? She is, I believe. At least as happy as she can be anywhere. Do be sure to tell that to her brother Lord Whitemarsh." She cocked her head at him curiously. "What else would you like to know?"

His mind went utterly blank and, unthinking, he spoke the first thing that came to his mind. "Why does she dislike me so very much?"

Before the amusement around her eyes grew into outright mockery, he continued. "Neither one of you were very hospitable on my last visit to your home, madame. Even before Lady Helen knew who I was and why I had come, she loathed me. Will you tell me what occasioned such a force of feeling?"

She put the plate of pastries down and looked at him directly, all traces of amusement gone. He had the distinct feeling that he had chosen precisely the wrong thing to ask.

"What did my lord Summerdale think of Lady Helen Dehaven, before he even set eyes on her?" Her eyes narrowed. "You don't have to answer, my lord, because it is quite obvious. You hide it better than most, but you are by your nature what Hélène and I think of as 'Them' – not Us, you see. You came here knowing about what society is pleased to call her ruin, and so you came here looking for a ruined woman. Never just a woman, but always one with a scandal attached. Is it any wonder that she would hate a man, so obviously a gentleman, so obviously like all those who whispered and laughed and stared at her before she came here? It is not who you are, but what you are."

He looked at her, and thought he had rarely seen a woman so young who was so sure of her own judgement. It suited her to hide this uncommon acumen behind laughter and wit, but there was no mistaking it, once she chose to reveal it.

"And do you despise me as well, madame? For I am also aware of your past."

She gave a shrug and settled back against her chair. "I am less bothered by such things. Hélène cannot be so sanguine."

"Why is that?"

He had hoped to catch her unawares, to hear a response that was offhand and telling. But her relaxed and frank attitude was not at all a sign of a mind growing careless. She merely plucked an imaginary piece of lint off her skirts and asked idly, "Why do you think, my lord?"

With any luck, she would tell him what she knew of the Henley affair and he could be done with this business. He was not such a fool as to think it would be easy, or to believe that rumors were always true. He was in a unique position to know that they were lies sprung from truth, and his objective was to learn about the initial truth of this gossip.

"I should think the matter most distressing for her. But I am not entirely familiar with the events which led her here."

"Are you not? You do not seem deaf to me, my lord, or cut off from society."

"I know of the rumors, of course. I prefer to hear the whole of the story."

She took a breath, as though considering it. Her gaze rested on a point just to the outside of his left knee.

"It is not my story to tell. Hélène has spoken to me of the time," there was a controlled anger in her voice, "but it is not a tale to share over a cup of tea with a virtual stranger. What her brother heard from her is the truth, and there is nothing new in it now. Do not ask her to repeat it."

He took the warning seriously. She did not seem the kind of woman to be in the habit of taking such a dire tone. Again, he found himself slightly awed by the devotion Helen Dehaven inspired in her friends. He doubted, now that his own brother was dead and gone, whether there was anyone who felt so strongly about his own well-being. But then he rather doubted that many people in this world were ever lucky enough to find one person who wished to protect them, while Lady Helen had a village full of protectors.

"Will you tell me, then, how the..." he faltered, searching for a correct and entirely proper word, "how the incident became so well known?" This part he knew only from common gossip. But he wished to know if Lady Helen had given a different account to her friend.

After a little pause, Madame de Vauteuil gave a little nod. "There were several in the party who went to the– that is, to Lord Henley's estate." She spat out the name like a grape seed caught between her teeth. "It was Mrs. Wilke – not the older Mrs. Wilke, but the detestable young widow Diana – who spread the rumor. She was helped by Anne Pembroke, who I will tell you is a viper."

He did not dispute the vileness of Mrs. Wilke, nor defend Anne Pembroke. They both had acid tongues and no compunction about cutting down anyone who stood in their path to a wealthy match. But neither of them had ever had any designs on Henley that summer so long ago, from what he could deduce. Even if they had had a reason for wanting Helen Dehaven ruined, it did not necessarily mean they had invented the story.

"Did they lie about what they saw?"

"They did not have to. All that was needed was word that Hélène had come out alone from a spot in the woods, and that Henley," again the name was loaded with disgust, "was seen to come from the same place with his clothes as mussed as hers. They were known to have carried on in such a way during the courtship – mooning is the word, I think? Well, that was all it took. That's all it ever takes," she said with an unmistakable bitterness.

She rose from her chair in agitation, gripping the ends of her shawl as she took measured steps across the room. She stopped by the front window, her face in profile to him. On the subject of whatever had happened at that spot in the woods, of whether the presumption of the gossips were true or false, she said not a word.

He had risen when she had and found himself with nothing to do and little to say, his hands clasped behind his back. It was only her unusual gravity that kept him from letting out a sigh. How many times had he listened as someone raged against the evils of gossip? It seemed hardly to matter that a person acted reprehensibly; it only mattered that others heard of it. Looking at Marie-Anne de Vauteuil's pensive features, he felt more sympathy with her than he had ever admitted to himself at moments like these. Rumors had come to sicken him as much as they obviously disgusted her.

Looking out at the gray day, she spoke quietly. "I loved my Shipley, Lord Summerdale, and as you have seen, I will never apologize for the love we shared. But all of society despised us for it, because it pleased them to do so. Just so did it please them to make Hélène suffer, and it pleased her only family to cause her to suffer even more, and all alone." He watched her gather the ends of her shawl together, pulling the cloth around her shoulders tightly as though a sudden chill had swept over her. "I have seen war, and I have seen love, Lord Summerdale. And when I met Hélène and learned of what happened to her, I understood the only difference between the two. Love can be more dangerous, and far more destructive."

He waited in silence after this extraordinary declaration. He saw her swallow and stare hard at his collar, until finally she looked into his face. "She loved her brother. She loves him still, in spite of herself. I would ask you to be honest with me, for her sake. She has been hurt enough, I think. So. Is this notion of forgiveness really his, or is it only your meddling? Or Lady Whitemarsh's?"

He knew he could not look away from her if she was to believe him. He did not pause before committing himself to the course he had chosen.

"Her brother. It is entirely because of his regard for her that I have come here."

In the moment of speaking it, he believed it. The conversation he'd had with Whitemarsh about the potential in a new business venture with Henley of all people – how advisable it was to trust Henley, what the implications of such a partnership would be – all of it was easy to dismiss. Business affairs were only an excuse, he was now sure. He remembered Whitemarsh's face when speaking of his sister, a tangle of love and pride and confusion. He should have immediately seen that above all else, the man wanted his sister back in his life. It was only that he had been loathe to admit it outright, and the only means Whitemarsh could find to approach her while preserving his pride was by appealing to Stephen's business sense.

Stephen had a sinking feeling of inevitability. Of course he had seen only what Whitemarsh had wanted him to see. His own disinclination to refuse a man like Whitemarsh had made him errand boy once again. In the end, Whitemarsh would either have a sister again, or a very sound business deal. There was no advantage to Stephen in a reconciled family, so he was presented with the more profitable reason to act on Whitemarsh's behalf.

He meant it, though. He had not until this moment, but now he did mean it. There was such deep sentiment between brother and sister, and so long denied, that it could not but engage his sympathies. It was for this broken little family that he would continue here, and restore them to one another if he could.

Mme de Vauteuil nodded slowly. "Then I only warn you not to let her brother cause her more pain, or else he will answer to me." She gave him her mischievous smile. "After all, my reputation cannot be worse and I have nothing to lose by taking him to task. I have so much time, too, to dream up marvelous revenges. Do have a cake, my lord, and I shall see you on your way before the road is washed out."

CHAPTER FIVE

Dearest Helen,

How very cryptic you are! And how well you know me, that I can't resist sharing everything I know of someone so fascinating as Lord Summerdale, inasmuch as anyone can know anything of him.

At present, he is considered to be The Man Who Knows, because he seems to know simply everything even before it happens, from the most secretive movements in the government to the affairs of cookshop boys, I vow. He is a friend to Whitemarsh, chiefly in business dealings, so have no reservations on the veracity of that claim. Whispers about some members of his family have been known to be titillating but ultimately benign, and his own reputation is perfectly spotless (horrifically boring). The most recent gossip is vicious, that he has delighted in his brother Edward's death, but no one gives such blather any credence. He is too good.

The only other gossip attached to the man was the affair of Lady Clara van Doran. He and Clara spent much time together, and we all thought it was to be a love match. It was a surprise when she wed the Duke of Bryson's eldest son, no doubt for his superior rank. Then plain Mr. Stephen Hampton became the heir to Summerdale scarcely a month after Clara's wedding. There are no jabs directed at Summerdale for this – impossible to mock the man for inheriting too late to snare a woman who now seems nothing more than a friend to him. In any case, no one dares speak ill of him for fear of his encyclopaedic knowledge of others' sins, and even if one were inclined to slander his name there seems to be nothing at all to be said. He is above reproach.

Discretion is the word most often associated with the man, for he seems to know all the gossip but shares none. To this I add my own opinion, which is that he is so very mannered and accomplished and (overlooking the probability that such a proper gentleman might well be exceedingly dull) everything one would hope in nobility yet never seems to find. I shall also say, in the spirit of thoroughness and in the event you failed to note it, that he is wonderfully handsome.

Now I shall send this off quickly so that you may have an answer to your impudent questions. I am more vexed than ever to know that for the first time in the history of Bartle on the Glen, more exciting things are happening there than in London!

My love to the ladies of Bartle,
Joyce Huntingdon
(Martyr to the infamously Gouty and Twice-damned Baron)

༶

Stephen had tried one last time to write the letter before giving up. A dull ache had lodged just behind his left eye from staring at the blank page every day for more than a week. It was not precisely blank, he scoffed at himself as he led his mount down the path that would take him to Bartle. He had gotten as far as *Dear Lord Whitemarsh* several times, but had stopped there without a single thought on how to continue.

He could tell her brother that the entire undertaking was doomed to fail, as he was now convinced the truth of what had happened to cause Lady Helen to break her engagement so long ago would never come to light. But admitting failure in this, his sole talent, was more difficult than he could have imagined. Besides that, he now firmly believed that whatever had happened was not Whitemarsh's prime concern. Stephen could write: *Your sister is well and refuses to speak of the affair,* but that was hardly informative, nor did it even attempt to address the question of Henley's trustworthiness.

He had tried: *I am offended that you misrepresented your motivations to me, Lord Whitemarsh, for I see now that you have used my interest in healthy commerce to your own quite personal ends in order to reconcile with your sister.* But that would not do either. Aside from risking his friendly relationship with Whitemarsh, which he was not even remotely prepared to do, it was not true. He was not offended. He was rather strangely pleased to be used in such a way. Instead of mucking about in others' affairs for financial or political gain, it was something of a relief to meddle for the sake of reuniting the Dehaven family. Perhaps he should have written so.

Dear Whitemarsh, you would be appalled at the circumstances she lives in.

Dear Whitemarsh, you must forgive your admirable sister, she is worth more than a dozen suppliers of wool.

Dear Whitemarsh, kindly provide me with more excuses to see her.

This thought brought him up short, and he eased into a trot, suddenly realizing he was almost galloping the distance to her tiny village. He wanted to see her again, had thought of little else, and his feeble attempts to compose a letter to her brother were little more than a way to distract himself. She was fascinating, with her interest in radical politics and her mercurial beauty, her dirty fingernails, and the smiles she strove to hide from him. Somehow, at some moment he could not pinpoint, he had stopped caring that she was a woman of few morals.

He scanned the horizon for any signs of foul weather, but it was unseasonably warm and clear. He would invite her to walk with him if the weather held. *I do not ride,* she had said in that small, stifled voice. *She has been hurt enough,* her friend warned – and something had happened to him. It had been careless of him, to overlook the absence of a lady's saddle, and it had caused her embarrassment. If he was more careful with her today, maybe he could coax another soft smile from her. If he had convinced Mme de Vauteuil that he meant Lady Helen no harm, perhaps he would eventually be trusted enough to help bring about some contact between Lord Whitemarsh and his sister, and he would have the pleasure of knowing he'd brought some happiness into her quiet little world.

Or perhaps he should stop agonizing over the girl's happiness and remember what it meant to be acquainted with treacherous ladies. Sobered by the thought of his own several weaknesses, he rode on, and resisted the thought of his very real desire to hear her laugh.

When he reached her home, it appeared abandoned. No one answered at the door, but the sound of a horse's soft whickering reached him. Dismounting, he followed the sound around the side of the house and heard her voice burbling with laughter. His pleasure in the sound died a quick death as he observed that it was a very fine mount. Evidently someone quite wealthy was paying Lady Helen a visit, and causing her no small amount of delight.

Suppressing the childish disappointment that welled up, he scanned a mental catalogue of all the estates within riding distance to divine who her gentleman caller could be. It was at last something to tell her brother, he thought with a twinge of regret.

"It's so very small! I feel almost naked!" he heard her protesting. "And my arms are tired. May I let go the pose now?"

Before he could quite wrap his mind around the image these words presented, he heard the heavily accented tones answer her. "Hélène, it is not a costume for a masquerade," came the stern response. "Let her finish and you can put your arms down."

"You are not using my face, I hope, Emily? Marie-Anne, remind her not to use my likeness."

It was futile to resist the curiosity that overcame him. Holding his horse's lead loosely in one hand, he peered through the trees and around the corner of the house. At first he thought it was a statue standing in the bright sunlight, a beautifully sculpted likeness of Diana at the hunt, complete with bow and arrow. Mme de Vauteuil's voice was indistinct, but whatever she said shattered the stillness of the white-clad figure before him. His breath caught as he realized it was Lady Helen who dropped her head back, her loosely piled hair spilling backward over her bared shoulders, her breasts flexing upwards, her laughter like champagne through his blood. She wore only a light scrap of fabric, loose and falling high on the arc of her thighs, the draped folds secured by a thin cord about her curving waist. His breath came short to know it would only take the slightest nudge to reveal all the lushness beneath. The sight of it, of the soft flesh of her breast where the white of the fabric fell just a little away from her shoulder – all of it paralyzed him, sent fire to the pit of his stomach. He could not possibly move from where he stood. He never wanted to move again.

Even as he watched, she returned to the still pose of an archer, focusing her notched arrow on some unseen target. She held the pose for an indeterminate length of time while he made himself stare at the sweeping curve of her arm, as Marie-Anne's voice chided her to remain in the pose only a moment more. She stood perfectly still, as motionless as he was. She looked like a goddess straight out of Greek mythology, as lithe and voluptuous as any artist could imagine. The vision was all the more tantalizing because it was so different from what he would have suspected. He had thought her figure unremarkable, but this is what she hid from the world – this body that would tempt a saint, concealed beneath the lumpy dresses she wore every day.

When at last she broke the pose, he heard her maid speaking. "Now, now, Miss Helen, you're not thinking you can just go now, do you? It's the arrows we want to see flying, not yourself. Go on and give us some of those Amazon ways."

"It is said the Amazons cut off a breast always to improve the aim, you know," came Marie-Anne's voice.

"Did they now? Does that seem right to you, Miss Helen?"

Helen's bow lifted and she pulled the string tight as though preparing to loose the arrow. But she gave a comical grimace and let her arms fall again. "Perhaps it's because I'm accustomed, but I can't see the advantage in it." She laughed again, the sound of it pouring like honey into his ears. "Unless the Amazons were extremely well endowed."

This was met with laughter from her companions, hidden from his view, and they began once again to insist on a demonstration of her prowess with the bow. "Well, the target is set up anyway, and we must keep Emily entertained. Shall I show you how the archers in Roman times did it?"

At their approval, she pulled arrows from a quiver that was slung on a branch and began burying the tips in the soft ground at her feet until a line of eight stuck straight up from the earth. He forcibly reminded himself to breathe, watching her careless movements.

She lowered herself into a crouch. "Ready for it, Emily?" she asked with a glance toward her unseen friends. Then she released her first arrow. Before the sound of it hitting the target reached him, she had already notched another, and the entire line was rapidly deployed in what seemed to be one long smooth movement. She straightened in the midst of applause and bid her friends to see how well she'd done. They came into view at last, Marie-Anne ducking beneath branches to seek out the target and the maid stopping in front of Helen with a look of sudden look of worry.

"Oh, I've been forgetting to watch out for visitors!" she exclaimed.

Stephen heard no more, instinct and a kind of shame at himself pulling him back from his hiding place. He moved to the front of the house as quickly and quietly as he could. The sound of footsteps rustling through the fallen leaves behind him forced him to re-evaluate his intention to leave altogether. The maid would see him there, dismounted at the corner of the house. He turned as if just arriving and hallooed loudly around the corner. If there was one talent he possessed, it was the ability to act as if he had not heard or seen something that was not meant for him to know.

"Is anyone there? I thought I heard voices," he called.

The maid was wholly surprised at his appearance but bobbed a quick curtsy, keeping her head bowed. He went forward as if to move past her to the back of the house, looping his horse's reins over a stout branch, but the little maid stepped into his path.

"Begging your pardon, milord, but Miss Helen's not taking callers just now," she announced in a loud voice.

He directed a pointed look at the other horse, hobbled and cropping the grass beside her. "It would seem otherwise," and he stepped around her quickly through the screen of trees to see what would await him. In the same way that he had raced down the road to get here, he could not seem to pause in the path that led to her.

Helen Dehaven stood shielded from him, with Mme de Vauteuil spreading a long cloak around her. He saw only her arms raised high and working furiously, he assumed, at her hair. The air of carefree gaiety was gone among the women, replaced by a stifling politeness. Marie-Anne turned to face him, blocking his view of the cloaked figure at her back, with a shocked look that gave way to a tentative but not unwelcoming smile.

"You have come to us again, my lord." She offered her hand for him to bow over briefly, and seemed ready with more of her practiced small talk to distract him from Lady Helen, but he cut her off before she could get started.

"A delight as ever, madame. Is that you, Lady Helen?"

She murmured his name in greeting but came no closer, so that he was forced to walk around Marie-Anne and into the hush that surrounded Helen. Her arm extended automatically to him, a slim whiteness out of the dark cape she held closely about her. He lingered over her hand too long as he tried in vain to forget the little she wore beneath the threadbare cloak, not knowing why he hadn't given her the time she so obviously wanted to compose herself. Her hand was warm in his, delicate. He held it as he looked up at her. He should release her hand; he should. He didn't. The hair that had flowed in bunched waves down her neck was now tightly bound as ever.

She would not look at him, her eyes lowered and her cheeks flaming with color. He felt the fear in her then, the tension, in the way she pulled her hand out of his as she stood frozen for a long moment and breathed shallow, stilted breaths.

"You will excuse me, my lord." She moved quickly away from him to her waiting maid, and disappeared around the corner of the house like a startled doe.

Watching her sudden retreat and feeling suddenly bereft at her absence, he at last noticed the other visitor seated against the side of the cottage. Her riding habit was a rich blue, and the sketchbook in her lap identified her as the resident artist.

Not a gentleman caller. A woman, another of her many friends. She made no move to greet him, only continued to scribble on the pad with a sharpened stick of charcoal. He walked forward with Mme de Vauteuil following alongside him, the other girl not looking up at the sound of their approach.

"This is Emily, a friend," she had time to say before the girl ripped a corner of the page and handed it up to him, smiling. *I am Emily, a niece to the Marquess of Rothebury,* he read. *I cannot hear. Please write me your name so that we are acquainted.*

He was pleased to do so, taking the charcoal she offered and ignoring the protest Marie-Anne was making at his side. "She told you, I'm sure. Emily, you must have a care for your reputation!" Exaggerated facial expressions and much finger wagging accompanied this admonishment. The girl Emily waved her hand eloquently, as though shooing away a fly, and reached for the scrap of paper that now bore his name and a brief message of greeting.

Marie-Anne gave a quick huff. "Her uncle would have the apoplexy if he knew she came here, and she tells you who she is without any thought! You must think us the strangest lot of ladies you have ever met, my lord."

He looked at the women before him, a ruined Frenchwoman and a deaf young woman of noble birth. He thought of the little Irish maid who was clearly pretending to be no more than a servant, who had disappeared into the house with Lady Helen. The target had been pulled forward and a cluster of arrows bristled at its center. Glancing to the sketchbook, he saw it held only a drawing of the trees that surrounded them, no sign of a scantily clad goddess on the open page.

The slow uncurling of some nameless restriction in his chest released a smile across his face.

"On the contrary, madame, I find you all delightful. Really, quite..." he almost laughed at his own understatement, "fascinating."

Upstairs, Maggie buttoned the dress at the back while Helen reached for her stockings. She should have known he would come today, when the skies were clear and the wind not yet crisp. They saw Emily so rarely, though, that she hadn't given much thought to other visitors, only put on the ludicrous costume and posed for her friend.

"Maggie." The maid stopped in the midst of retrieving Helen's shoes. "He did not see me. Did he, Maggie?"

There was no hesitation in the answer. "He was coming round the house, just as I come out from the back. Sure, he didn't see anything, Helen."

She stepped closer and touched Helen's hair in a soothing gesture before pulling out the hastily placed pins and redressing the chignon. The soothing words and the capable hands, engaged in such a practical activity, immediately helped the beating of her heart to subside to a normal pace. Helen closed her eyes briefly and envisioned Katie sat amongst them in the back garden. She would sketch with Emily. She would learn archery. She would laugh with them, be with them. This was what her future, Helen's future, would be.

It worked, as it always did. Now she could breathe easily again, and she opened her eyes. There was nothing to be afraid of. Nothing. The Earl of Summerdale was an honorable man, a gentleman, who had so far shown her only kindness.

When Maggie had finished with her hair, she slipped to the window and reported that Lord Summerdale was writing a conversation with Emily.

"And he's trying to learn her hand signals, I think," observed the maid. Helen felt a resurgence of fear for a moment, before she remembered that discretion was the word most associated with the man. She hoped to God he had not learned Emily's name, else the poor girl would be ruined indeed. As it was, Emily was merely an embarrassment to her family – an unwanted burden, not fit for society because of her supposed inability to communicate. But if she was known to associate with the likes of Helen and Marie-Anne, her horrible uncle would likely lock her in a garret for the rest of her life.

Emily had never been the least concerned with that, Helen was reminded as she stepped outside to join her guests. Lord Summerdale was absorbed in mimicking a familiar gesture, his fingers curled to meet his thumb in a circle before flicking apart like a bursting bubble. He looked thoughtful as he brought the fingers together again and rubbed them lightly against his thumb. Emily's hand waved in front of him and caught his attention as she performed the same gesture more slowly, bringing her hand closely to her ear as though to listen to her fingers rub together.

She looked at him meaningfully until his face brightened with discovery. "Bubble and squeak, is that it?" He bowed to Emily's delighted applause. "Do you mean to tell me it's the bubble and squeak at the pub house that brings you here?"

Just then, Emily spotted Helen and gestured that she should explain. "She loves it, Lord Summerdale, and never misses a plate of it when she comes through town."

He turned to her immediately as she approached the group. There was a pause as he looked to her waistline, where the bunched fabric of the dress thickened her middle. She stood waiting for his frown, but he looked into her eyes and gave a splendid smile, the white of his teeth a flash in his face, stealing her breath for a minute. He was really so very handsome, in a way that she would never have expected to appeal to her. The clean lines of his face held nothing of the artistic beauty that was so prized. He had an almost boyish look to his features, but there was nothing at all boyish about him. When he smiled at her like that, there was an intensity to him – not the dark magnetism that had drawn her to men in her youth, but the intensity of his pleasure, like the sun shining full on her.

Something had changed. He had spoken to Marie-Anne, and now he smiled openly at her with an expression akin to wonder. She struggled to recall what they were speaking about, but thankfully Marie-Anne had caught the thread of conversation and carried on with only a moment's pause.

"It is almost time for luncheon. I shall ask Emily if she plans to leave us in favor of the pub's fare."

Lord Summerdale was still looking at her, the ghost of a smile lingering on his face. "If Lady Helen does not object to my intruding on her plans, might I suggest a picnic?"

She was flustered in the face of his solicitude. There was some bread and hard cheese in the larder, she quickly calculated, but it would barely be enough to feed three of them. As she struggled to find the proper words to inform him that it was impossible, he saved her by smiling in that damnably charming way.

"I've brought a few things in anticipation."

Before Helen could quite recover from the groove in his cheek that had appeared with his grin, Maggie was bustling back to the house to find a cloth to spread on the grass and Summerdale – *Lord* Summerdale, she reminded herself emphatically – was fetching forth a variety of items. The abundance was startling. If he had originally intended to share his lunch only with her, he had wildly over-calculated her capacity. She held back from the little tableau of Maggie spreading cloths on the ground, Marie-Anne clutching the wine, Emily examining the grapes he held up. He suddenly seemed more a part of the group than she. So quickly, so easily, did he become part of her circle that she tried to remember why he should not be welcomed so unreservedly.

He knew everything before it happened, her friend had written, and what was there to know about any of them that was not already old news? They had little to hide in that respect. Emily was the only one of them who...

The unfinished thought brought her forward to Marie-Anne's side. "Marie-Anne, he does not know who Emily's family is, does he?" she queried quickly in French.

The annoyance on Marie-Anne's face was a clear answer, and even as she responded with a quick

"*Oui*," Helen had swung around to the foolish girl in question.

"Why in bleeding *hell* would you tell him?!" she burst out, reaching for the paper to begin a written tirade. Emily's response was a confused stare, and it took Helen only a breath to realize what she'd said. Her hands clapped over her mouth in mortification as she dared a look at Summerdale.

He looked truly shocked – almost as shocked as she was at herself. As she madly began to formulate an apology for her crude language, his expression changed, the grin appearing again. His laughter rumbled out and over her until a warmth spread throughout her. She should not; she told herself she should not. But soon she was laughing with him, Marie-Anne gasping with mirth behind her and Maggie explaining to a baffled Emily precisely what was causing so much amusement.

Helen at last caught her breath enough to say, "Pardon me, my lord, but you cannot expect delicacy if you choose to pass the time with ladies who are *not* ladies, you know."

And with that, he was firmly established as a friend to them all.

꽃

After nearly every scrap of the excellent picnic had been consumed, Helen found herself seated next to him and talking of archery. He was quite impressed with her aim even when she told him the target had not been set as far back as she would have liked, and she protested a further demonstration with the bow. Maggie had gone to her job at the Hawkins, never once abandoning her deferential attitude to Summerdale. Marie-Anne and Emily wrote to one another where they sat a little way off in the shade of a tree.

Several times throughout the afternoon she had felt his gaze rest on her, but each time she raised her eyes to him he was looking elsewhere. Her thoughts revolved almost entirely on what she would do if she caught him in his stare: would she hold it, or look away?

He seemed so different. Each time he came here, he had become more civil, and now he emanated a relaxation and satisfaction that pleased and puzzled her, leaving her filled with an awareness of him that was more acute than ever.

"You appear content to mingle in such questionable company, Lord Summerdale," she observed with what she hoped was a lighthearted tone.

"Will you do me the honor of calling me by my Christian name? My title is most recently inherited and I find it difficult to accustom myself to it." He looked almost sheepish at this admission, keeping his eyes trained on his fingers as they twisted a stem of grass. She forced herself to look away from the line of his jaw where it sloped into the softness of his throat.

"I think it entirely too familiar, my lord." Perhaps he thought she would disregard all rules of society, but she could not relinquish the exacting standards with which she was raised. Not with him.

"Of course." His voice was barely audible, but he carried on as though the breach of formality had never been proposed. "I am content here, as you say. You'll think it fanciful of me, but your household feels rather like something from a storybook," he smiled. "Like an enchanted glade, or a private Avalon. I've never seen the like, and I have seen much."

She gave a huff of laughter at that. "An enchanted glade of the forgotten ones, I suppose." She looked at Emily writing furiously with Marie-Anne watching the pen's movements. A sudden dread for the girl stole over her. "Enchanted glades should remain secret, my lord, don't you agree?"

He looked at Emily, then back at her. "I had heard of the Marquess's niece before. I was given to understand that she was an idiot, incapable of caring for herself. I am delighted to find that report false."

The letter from Joyce flashed before her mind's eye again. "You know many secrets."

"I do. And I keep them, however sordid as they may be. It is no hardship to keep one that would only bring pain in the telling."

It was a promise she believed utterly. She knew something about secrets and pain, and the desire to keep both hidden. He made a motion as though to stand, but she stayed him with a hand on his arm. Snatching her fingers back as he stilled, she looked away from his intense look, curling lingering warmth of him into the palm of her hand to hold it there.

"Wait, please," she almost whispered, desperately flustered by his look and the heat of him tingling on her fingers. "Don't draw their attention to you. Emily is upset over something, you can see by the way she writes. She will finish soon, but not if she is interrupted. Marie-Anne will calm her, I think."

He stayed beside her, and she suddenly felt that she was too close to him. Entirely too close. His voice broke through her nervousness, taking up the teasing tone again. "Are there many more of your social circle I should be aware of? I wouldn't want to look shocked at the wrong moment."

She pressed the smile from her lips. "No, this is all."

"Is it Emily who provides you with your scandalous literature?"

"Ah. That is Georges, a friend of Marie-Anne. He is somewhere in the Iberian Peninsula now. He is rarely in England though, and we never see him anymore." She cleared her throat and bit her lips to keep from laughing, wondering if he could still be shocked. "His sin is to be a bastard, you see. And lover to a German duke."

His eyes widened minutely, but he did not sneer. He only chuckled along with her soft laughter at his reaction as Emily and Marie-Anne approached. "I believe our little party is breaking up," he observed. Emily, lacking her usual cheeriness, was gathering her things together. It would appear that she was distraught over Mr. Tisby, according to Marie-Anne.

Naturally Lord Summerdale would know of the man. Tisby was an excellent sort, a naval officer who had no claim yet to riches, raised not far from here. Emily was completely taken with him. Helen couldn't dream of why they should confide all this to

Summerdale, yet before she could utter a single protest Marie-Anne was twittering on about their romance, explaining to Summerdale about Emily's fear that the dreaded Marquess would never allow a marriage.

"Tisby is away at sea now," she was saying with anxious looks to Emily. "The Marquess becomes angry at every letter from him that arrives. I don't know what to tell her."

"Perhaps I could be of help?" He was all solicitude. "I would be happy to tell her uncle that Tisby is a good and honorable man. I think he can be made to see that he could not hope for a better match."

She could hardly believe the conversation. He and Marie-Anne went on with their scheming while she was enlisted by Emily to write her what exactly was transpiring. She cut in before the whole nonsense got out of hand.

"My lord, I can hardly think that a word from you would solve the matter entirely. The Marquess—"

"I believe I can convince him, Lady Helen, have no fear of that. There would at least be no harm in trying."

He was so confident. She tried to think back to a time when she was ever so sure of the worth of her own words, and failed. Setting her jaw stubbornly, she presented an irrefutable bit of logic. "And how shall you say you know her at all, much less that you know of her romance? It will only make her association with us plain to him, don't you see? You must not forget what we are, and what it means for a respectable girl to be linked to us."

She wanted to bite back the truth in the words, but could not. Emily was attuned to the quick change in mood and tapped Helen's shoulder for an explanation of the embarrassed quiet. The Earl of Summerdale was staring at her without expression, the green of his eyes sparking in the sun.

"We shall say that I met her on a ride through the village, when my horse lost its shoe. It is indirectly true, at least, you must admit." He looked to Marie-Anne now. "I'll invite her to...a dinner party at my home. That's where she will confide in me about Tisby. Will the Marquess make her refuse the invitation?"

"From you, my lord?" Marie-Anne was wildly amused. "He shall push her out the door! And her aunt will escort her. It can work."

"Perfect," he said shortly. "The Marquess's wife is oblivious to scandal, I understand, unless it's announced in the pulpit. You must all come." His boyish grin reappeared. "I can hardly have a dinner party without guests."

He would brook no argument from Helen, hatching a scheme that would convince Emily's aunt that the dinner was to do with a church donation, and the ladies present all active in the parish. Emily was to be vague as to the other women invited, and his coach would call for them Thursday next.

In less than a minute, it was all settled. Marie-Anne was enthusiastic, and Emily delighted. It was only Helen who did not join in the planning, feeling so surly that in the end she put up no protest despite the risk, despite the knowledge that she hadn't a proper dress, and despite the feeling that he had entered her world almost completely and left her in a state somewhere between anxiety and delight.

※

"Such a lovely carriage to carry such a drab specimen," complained Marie-Anne.

Helen shot her a look that said she'd had quite enough of the topic. She had unbent so far as to unearth a dress she had been used to wear for Sunday services. It was a steel gray, and simply cut, perfectly respectable and serviceable, though seven years out of fashion. The shawl Helen had chosen and the alterations that kept the dress from constricting her breath were at fault for offending Marie-Anne's sensibilities. Helen had last worn the dress when she was sixteen, so she'd had to let out the bodice. So long as she was re-working it, she had seen fit to raise the neckline somewhat with the addition of a scarf as trim. It was still too low-cut for her liking, particularly how it almost exposed her shoulders, which is why she'd insisted on the shawl.

"But really, Hélène, you could have worn my pretty pink wrap. This one is..." she wrinkled her nose in distaste. "Ugly. It is the only word. That color!"

"The color is brown, Marie-Anne, and you may take yourself off to Paris if you're so desperate to see well-dressed ladies. Try to remember that we are supposed to be church mice, not peacocks."

"Her looks will do, if that's what you're carping on," Maggie interjected in English.

The rest of the ride was spent in extolling the inherent taste of the French in all sartorial pursuits, as opposed to the ignorance of the frumpy Irish. Helen left them to it and set her mind to the task ahead. It was foolish, this plan. There was no reason for such a preposterously elaborate ruse. Surely someone like the Earl of Summerdale could have found better reason to approach the Marquess on behalf of Emily's romantic hopes. With each passing mile, she felt more and more trapped, hemmed in by the velvet hangings of his coach. Emily and her aunt were to meet them at Lord Summerdale's home.

Somewhere between Maggie's impassioned defense of Irish wool and Marie-Anne's reminiscence of her favorite Parisian milliner, they pulled into a curving drive lined with stately oaks. As the manor lights came blazing into view, Helen's hand clenched on the rug across her knees. She would have gladly spent the next few hours digging in the garden or cleaning the chimney. Even scrubbing the laundry would have been better than this excursion into polite society.

Lord Summerdale was waiting for them in the entry foyer. The sight of him in his formal, midnight blue coat made her want to flee into the night, but still stay to look at him. He extended a hand to her, bowing over it and once again holding on for just a second more than he should. But she did not pull away. He seemed the only thing that was stable in her swaying world. She watched him greet Maggie as an honored guest "representative of the local churchgoer" instead of the housemaid he knew she was. The farce came to him quite easily, she thought, though it was kind of him to include them all.

"Miss Emily has not yet arrived. I would usually give you a brief tour of the house, but I'm afraid most of the rooms are being re-furbished, and there is little to see but drop-cloths and pails of varnish," he explained as he led them further in. "I fear I have made the worst possible choice for the main salon, so I will spare you the sight of it even half-finished."

"A gentleman always needs the help of a lady in such things," Marie-Anne sniffed. "Come, Maggie, we will advise Lord Summerdale, and see if you have more talent for décor than for gowns."

He did not object, only requested that Helen come with him to await Emily while the others were shown on their way by the butler. Again, she had the feeling of being trapped by design as she followed him. He led her past the dining room, saying nothing as she walked hesitantly behind him.

When he opened the door, it took every ounce of energy she possessed not to let out a gasp of delight. It was the library, stocked floor to ceiling with books. She said nothing to him, only walked over to the nearest shelves to examine the leather-bound volumes. Her hand hovered over Shakespeare's sonnets, then moved to a work by Shelley, before resting idly on Keats.

"It would seem you are a romantic, my lord. I should have guessed, the way you contrived this evening for Emily." She slid her eyes over to him and was amazed to see he looked abashed.

"You have only seen the poetry. I assure you, there is a wide variety of all kinds of literature." He waved his hand vaguely. "You may find something to interest you on these shelves."

She crossed over to them, a pamphlet between the books catching her eye. She pulled it out and turned to him with eyebrows raised. "A treatise opposing the Corn Laws? An upstanding subject of the Crown as you are? I am shocked, sir."

He shrugged with a smile. "There is a treatise supporting them as well, you'll find. And arguments for constitutional monarchy, and against. Slavery and anti-slavery, federalism and anti-federalism – that debate is old but continues. I thought you may have an interest in them particularly, with your sympathy for the Americans."

"Well, you are not one to choose sides, are you? Interested in all arguments but not advocating one over another." Her back was to him as she searched through the books for the essays. When he did not respond, she thought she had offended him. "I did not mean to imply that... Well, I don't know what I meant," she apologized over her shoulder.

A smile quirked at the corner of his mouth as he looked down at the floor. "Your brother said you were perceptive," he said thoughtfully, as though to himself. "It's true I don't enter the public debate in politics. Or in much else. My beliefs on such things remain private when possible, which I consider vitally important."

She had obviously intruded into that privacy by speaking of it. She turned back to the shelves and wished madly that he did not look so elegant. It was terribly uncomfortable, being in this house where the carpets were so thick and the fires roared with huge logs. He probably never considered the cost of fuel, or the damage a stray spark could do to the expensive Aubusson silk. She felt small and awkward among the opulence of the furnishings.

If only she had met him years ago, anywhere else, in any other circumstance. He could have drawn her attention across a ballroom and asked for a dance. They could have taken a jaunt through Hyde Park, or viewed the gardens together on a pleasant afternoon.

He should have known her before, when she was not swallowed up in fear and regret.

She stood lost in that thought, her eyes unseeing until he came up closely behind her and reached slowly over her shoulder.

"I think this is what you're looking for, Lady Helen," he said softly, pulling a book from the shelf.

He was only inches away from her. She looked at his hand holding the book, powerless to reach out and take it from him casually, the quiet moment spinning into an eternity. He was staring at her again. She knew it without looking but she kept her eyes trained on his fingers, afraid to see what was in his face when her heart was stuttering in such a way. She felt like a coward – she could not remove her gaze from the book, his hand, the crisp white of his cuff. Very slowly, he tilted the volume toward her and she reached up to take it, telling herself all the while that she should move away from him. Away from his heat and the thin cushion of charged air between them.

But she didn't move away. She only gathered herself with a shallow breath, determined to take the strangeness out of the moment, and looked up to find his eyes fixed on her lips.

For a moment, she let herself feel the excitement of it – the light falling on his face, the sharp focus of his gaze on her mouth – until she remembered and stepped back from him. She turned back to the shelves, blinking repeatedly, and looked down at the book she held. She stared blindly at it and murmured, "Thank you," as she began riffling through the pages in search of something interesting enough to discuss. If only Emily would come.

He at last stepped back a pace. "I thought perhaps," he cleared his throat lightly, "that perhaps you might like to borrow something that interests you. Anything at all. You have only to choose it. The Greek philosophers are especially well represented."

The spell at last broken, she gratefully wandered over to an armchair and was pulled out of her distraction by the open book she found there. "Simonde de Sismondi? Are you reading this now?" she asked with a false brightness. "I would not deprive you of it, but I have heard it is most fascinating."

"I have recently finished it. You are welcome to it, of course, but are you sure it's what you prefer?" He looked at her as if she had said she had a preference for a dessert of sawdust.

She lifted her shoulder casually. "Indeed I am. The study of economic theories has become interesting to me over the years. There is little enough to occupy my mind, so I have passed the time with what most people would say are unusual interests." She was chattering on senselessly again. "I may choose during dinner to make an argument against the Corn Laws, and you can support them, and we shall bore Emily's aunt to tedium. We'll have her snoring before the soup is cleared and she'll be none the wiser. An excellent plan, wouldn't you say?"

"Most excellent," he smiled.

"But this isn't a translation. It's the original French?"

"It's too recent to have in English, but I am assured by Madame de Vauteuil that you are proficient in French."

"And she assures me that you are not." She looked at him curiously. Why hide such a thing? Unless he had thought to catch them off guard, to hear something that he could pretend not to understand. It might be one of his tricks for learning everything about everyone, discreetly.

She folded her arms and gave him a critical look. "Well, well. You talk of enchanted glens. You read romantic poets but turn the topic toward politics and economics. You know French, but pretend you do not. What am I to make of that, my lord?"

He straightened his shoulders and spoke with mock dignity. "You are to make nothing of it, of course."

"Am I not?"

"No. It's all supposed to add to my charm, you know," he confided.

"*Most* charming."

"Always keep them guessing, I say."

"You've done quite well at that. I daresay no one knows what to make of you, concealed as your true abilities and intentions are." She was not quite joking anymore. It was disturbing to realize how little she knew of him, and all that she did know was conflicting. He adjusted quickly to her shift in tone, making her wonder if he was, in addition to everything else, a mind-reader.

"You have observed that I do not choose sides, and it's true to a certain extent. I prepare myself for every conceivable eventuality. But there is always only one side I take, in all conflicts," he said seriously. "My true motivation, Lady Helen, is to advocate understanding between both parties, no matter the nature of the contention."

He was speaking of her brother. He wanted to bring them together again, despite his disapproval of what had caused the rift. That in itself was a romantic notion, that he could achieve such a thing.

She didn't want to speak of it, did not even want to think of Alex right now. She never wanted to think of the events that had caused the conflict between them. She only wanted, with a desperation that frightened her, to believe in the quiet strength of this man who seemed so very capable. She wanted to trust his vision of the world as it could be. She wanted... oh, the things she wanted.

He stood quietly, waiting for any response she might give him, but she could think of nothing. In the middle of his comfortable home, with his presence surrounding her, she felt heavy and weightless at once. She could let go of everything in her past, just let it fall away and step fully into his world, if only her feet would obey. She felt like she'd been lost, and here in this quiet library, could be found again. Everything in the past had been a fiction, like the dark wood in a fairy tale. It only wanted the golden key, the magic word, and she would come out safe on the other side.

But these were fantasies, she knew, even before she was startled out of them by the butler announcing Emily's arrival. Soon they were caught up in introductions and glasses of sherry and the ongoing debate between Marie-Anne's preference for red in the salon and Maggie's staunch defense of cream.

The evening wore on, the ridiculous charade played out quietly over dinner. It was over the pheasant that the question of the mythical church charity was finally raised. He handled it well, solemnly declaring that repairs must be made to certain nearby churches, and the pious aunt was eating from the palm of his hand within minutes. Helen gave him a sharp look, wondering how far he was willing to perjure himself.

"And which will be repaired first, my lord?" Helen couldn't resist needling him. It was too wicked of him, to pretend to give a large amount to a good cause for the sake of this charade.

He looked back at her, full of innocence. "I had hoped for guidance from you. The vicars of all three are in receipt of the money, but the workmen are too few to mount an assault on all of them at once. The water damage to the refectory in Hemmerton is most severe, but it may be more prudent to repair the roof before winter sets in."

She had nothing to respond to that. Emily's aunt was not so reserved, handing out advice for the next quarter hour as Helen stared speechless at her plate. He had truly made the donations. She wanted to laugh at her own misjudgment of him, at the lengths he had gone to for Emily's little romance. She suppressed her amusement at how neatly he had turned her goading of him into a jab at her own ignorant assumptions. It was like the time when she, as a child, had invented tales against her brother, only to have the nursemaid present her with incontrovertible evidence that she was lying, the shards of the broken vase in question tangled in her own hair as proof against her wild stories.

She bit her lips together to contain her mirth, and then made the terrible mistake of looking up at Lord Summerdale. He could sense her hilarity, she knew, for he scowled quite a stern warning in her direction. It only made her want to laugh more, but she controlled herself by taking a few breaths and focusing on the candelabra. It was not funny. It wasn't. Not even remotely, she scolded herself.

Composed at last, she looked at him again. He appeared absorbed in the conversation. He waited a moment – perfectly timed to set her off again – then slanted a mischievous glance her way, the soft green of his eyes touching her through the glow of candlelight.

She supposed, really, that there was nothing to stop her becoming someone's mistress.

The unexpected notion, and the little surge of excitement it engendered, rushed in upon her and utterly eclipsed all other thought. She had never considered it, never thought to want it, but there it was: her status afforded her that freedom. She thought of this, that she was a fallen woman, and all the reasons for that, at the same time that an involuntary vision of his hands on her came to mind – and turned immediately into something else. The thought of soft caresses becoming a bruising grip and moist breath hot in her face, and the muscles in her thighs pulled tight, pressing her legs down hard on her chair.

She stared at the pheasant on her plate and fought down the queasiness that lodged in her throat, a legion of squirming eels in her belly, her breath coming short and inadequate. It was always like this, coming swiftly and irrevocably into her mind, a force she could not defend against when she least expected it. *Think of Katie,* she told herself as she always did. *I will feed Katie little cakes. Marie-Anne will teach her to make lace. Katie will be here. Katie will be with me, like a daughter to me. Katie will be here.*

Now she could think more clearly and breathe normally, but the sick anger did not abate, not even when the footman came to clear her plate. She leaned away from the servant, stiff in every limb, and concentrated fiercely on the clean white linen of the tablecloth before her. She did not belong here, among the crystal and silver and silk chintz. She wanted to go home, right now, even if only nightmares awaited her.

But the evening continued relentlessly, and they were in the drawing room as Marie-Anne played the pianoforte with the frail old woman listening intently and Summerdale scribbling with Emily in a corner. It was all going according to plan, and they would be on their way home soon. She listened to him affect a tone of surprise, saying that he knew Tisby. She watched as he promised to call on the Marquess soon. She was glad when he paid her no more attention than he did the other women.

When finally it was time to leave, he handed them into the carriage himself. Maggie was praised for carrying off her role and Marie-Anne was thanked for her ability to twist a conversation any which way. As he took Helen's hand, he asked if she felt quite well, and she murmured that she had a touch of the headache. He did not inquire further, only silently pressed a book into her hands and closed the door of the carriage. They rode off into the night, an elegant coach full of fraudulent ladies, she chief among them.

CHAPTER SIX

They spoke of books. Of political trends on the continent and faraway places and anything else the conversation turned to, but never of London. A thousand times he steered the discussion away from the past, hers or his own. The doings, inclinations and thoughts of the upper classes were of no interest to him, as long as he was with her. She never asked what the current rage was, nor even gave him a hint that she cared to know the talk of the town.

In that, she reminded him a bit of Clara. Ridiculous, really, to associate the two women. Clara the fair, so lively and stylish and a delightful addition to any garden party or soirée. Helen, named for the face that launched a thousand ships, only to be left shipwrecked and stranded in Bartle-on-the-Glen. He could not imagine Clara here any more than he could imagine Helen at her ease in a London ballroom. He could certainly never have dreamed of spending an entire afternoon with Clara discussing economics without ever once hearing mention of who was at Lady Carrington's most recent ridotto.

Not that Clara was empty-headed. Far from it. She had never been one to gossip in his presence, most likely because she knew as much as anyone else about the latest scandals. She never burned to know who had designed the Princess of Wales' gown, because she herself was modishly outfitted by the best of couturiers. She was tasteful, elegant, knew when to be reserved and how to be coy. There was nothing at all outrageous about her, except for her beauty. She was a perfect lady. And she was married. Quite perfectly married.

Helen was none of those things: not coy, not flirtatious, not stylish. Not a perfect lady.

But he turned his thoughts away from that, determined to do nothing to jeopardize his continued welcome. He could not shake the feeling that the time spent with her was enchanted. She wove a spell about him simply by virtue of being far removed from the self-importance of the city. He had come to think of her home as something of a refuge, where he could find respite from his thoughts of Clara, the scorn of his family, and the secret machinations of the social whirl. Carefully, at each meeting, he paid out bits of information about her brother like a rope, slowly letting go another measured length and waiting for a slight tug from her before feeding the line again. He knew he should be gathering information about her, trying to uncover her past. But she resisted each tentative inquiry and he could never seem to remind himself that he had been sent to discover the reason behind her actions so long ago.

She stood now in front of him, only half an arm's

length away, aiming the arrow at a target hung from a branch.

"I'll have to re-fletch some old arrows if we are to continue this exercise in future. It's not my greatest talent, and I'll have to send Danny searching for feathers, but there's little else to be done," she said, before letting go the bowstring. As ever, she found her mark.

"I had almost forgotten," he said. "I've brought some new ones for you."

He had not yet recovered from the lunacy that had driven him to transport his books from London, only for the sake of putting a library at her disposal, before he had searched out the best arrows for her sport. She seemed about to protest, but he forestalled her with a grimace. "It's the least I can do, after I have put so many into the tree."

She smiled easily, and he thrilled once again to see it. How comfortable she was with him, sometimes.

"In that case, I shall accept them as reparation. But your aim has improved greatly since last week, and one can hardly call it a fault that you are possessed of such a very strong arm."

A fetching blush and downward sweep of the eyes followed, a heartbeat behind this last statement. It was not practiced or artful. She was truly embarrassed to have said it. There was no time to question her on it, or even to put her at her ease with an offhand comment on the weather, for Maggie came around the corner of the house and drew her away with no more than a wave of her hand.

"Pray excuse me, my lord. That will be the post. I'll not be long."

When she had gone, he mused over her apparent

fascination with correspondence as he shot the last few arrows into the target. Twice before on his visits, he had been present when the post arrived, and both times she had excused herself to peruse whatever had come. She was only ever absent for a minute, but today she was gone for much longer. He waited outside, noting the unmistakable onset of winter. He had stayed away from London, from his life, for as long as he had originally planned to do. He had written Whitemarsh only that he'd made contact with Lady Helen, and hoped to further gain her trust. He should mention something about Henley, at least, as a decision on that must be reached before spring. There was no reason he should not urge Alex to attempt a reconciliation already, except that it was really Stephen's sole purpose for being anywhere near her.

Whether it was the mystery of her, or the relief of being so far removed from the whispers and deceptions that filled his other life, he did not want to leave. Only this morning, he had made arrangements to stay through the end of the year, purposely stalling work on the manor house and sending messengers to London with letters and contracts so that his business affairs would not stagnate. The weather was growing colder every day, and soon he would have no reason to offer for riding out to her in the wind and sleet. No reason but the truth. They were friends. She did not object to his company. She even seemed to like him for himself.

For the first time he could remember, he belonged. He was not shut out here.

He walked round the house to retrieve the bundle of fresh arrows from his saddle, pushing aside the unworthy thought that she hid the less admirable bits of her character from him. Her refusal to speak of Henley bothered him; the only reason he could imagine she would not wish to tell her side of the story was because all the rumors had been true, and she did not wish to hear his censure. He wished he had pressed her brother for a more clear description of her account so long ago. *Wild tales*, Whitemarsh had said vaguely, dismissively. He said that she had refused to speak at all, and then when she did, she was plainly inventing the story on the spot, stuttering and searching for words, producing a far-fetched story that made no sense whatsoever.

It was hard to imagine that version of her, as she seemed so sensible and level-headed to Stephen. He would like to hear the truth of it, once and for all, even if it reflected poorly on her.

From the corner of his eye, he perceived a movement in the front window. Helen stood, clutching Maggie to her, both of them smiling and jumping excitedly like children. She spoke to the maid, and though he could not hear her words through the open crack of the window, there was no mistaking the joy in her voice. He immediately started to the back of the house again, before they noticed him.

It was intrusive, to watch them and wonder what caused their happiness. It was childish, to become sullen over the knowledge that it was not he who had provoked such a smile. Ridiculous to resent that they shared something with each other, something he had no part of. He picked up the bow and listened with satisfaction to the loud whistle and thunk of his arrows meeting the target with more force than was strictly necessary.

When she came back to him, she was subdued. It pierced his heart to know that she would not confide her good news to him, that he must pretend not to know of it. There was a light in her eyes that was not fully diminished.

"Why, Lady Helen, I believe you're glowing," he announced to her, with as much gallantry he could muster. "Whatever could account for it, I wonder?"

"These arrows, of course. They are so fine!" she said with a delight that mollified him somewhat. She picked up an arrow by the shaft and examined it closely. "Indeed far too fine for practice. One would think they were meant to fight a war. Where did you find them?"

"A Welshman. His family's made them for generations, and still use them for the hunt." Her expression was one of great surprise. When she spoke, it would be to draw attention to the expense or the impracticality of the purchase, he was certain, so he spoke before she could. "It seemed practical to find arrows of a quality that they might last through many seasons of continuous use. And to send to London for more common ones would have taken just as much time and trouble. It was much more convenient this way." Protesting too much was a clear indicator of deceit, and he rushed on before she noticed his defensiveness. "Try them. You'll find they fly wonderfully."

He watched her hesitation with suspended breath. When finally she picked up the bow and hit the target, he saw with regret the cool blankness on her face that had replaced the earlier joy. She avoided looking at him, holding another arrow in her hand and rolling it between her fingers thoughtfully.

"Well," she sighed. "It would seem I am in your debt. You kindly provide me with these, and lend me a new book each time you come, and I can only ever offer you a cup of tea. It does not seem much."

He stopped himself from saying that the debt was repaid a thousand times over with each smile she bestowed on him. He really was growing appallingly romantic.

"Each time you offer me your hospitality, Lady Helen, you give me a great gift." He found himself saying something of the truth that was in his heart. "I am not used to being so free with others. I suppose I am rather lacking in companionship."

He didn't know why he said it. He shouldn't have, he was sure. Since Edward had died, he had been so very alone, and there was no one who knew of that loneliness. Except Clara. And now Helen knew, and he suddenly felt it was idiotic of him to have told her. She might make light of it, or use it to mock him, and he couldn't bear the thought of it.

But she said nothing, only running her fingers along the white feathers of the arrow she held, and he felt his whole body grow taut as it had when she stood in his library. He had only to reach out to her, break through the invisible barrier of reserve that she wore like a cloak, and she would – what? What would she do, if he were to touch her? He closed his eyes, thinking of the possibilities. He did not trust himself to look at any part of her. Not yet.

It was she who moved first, taking up the bow and planting more arrows in the far-off target. When he felt safe enough to look at her again, he saw the contentedness on her features and knew the dangerous moment had passed.

"They are excellent, and I thank you for them. As I thank you for your friendship," she said quietly. Then she returned easily to her cheerful manner, another cloak she put on for him sometimes. "But you'll never loan me anything again if I forget to return that novel to you. I finished it days ago, so you must remember to take it with you today."

"And the Sismondi? Have you finished it?"

"I put it aside for the novel. Really, I couldn't resist a good story, but I am nearly finished. It's fascinating, and it was most difficult to stop reading last night when the sun went down."

"Why did you? I thought you voracious in your reading habits. I would've expected you to burn the lamp all night," he teased.

"I would have, if only there were more oil for the lamp, or more than a few tallow candles to see us through to next quarter." She said it with a matter-of-fact attitude that seemed a tragedy to him. "The days are growing shorter."

He wanted to know what she thought of it. Her observations on the unlikely topic of economics were, like everything else about her, novel and startling and engrossing. Her lack of lamp oil was sure to haunt him, as much as the sight of her stroking a white feather would fill his thoughts for days.

"If you wish to visit the marquess today, you must leave soon," she was saying. "You think your first meeting went well enough? Is there such a need to see him again?"

"Most definitely. We are very close to victory for Emily and her Tisby. I won't let her cause languish. Her uncle is quite close to consenting to the match, so now is the time to press the matter."

She pursed her lips. "It's remarkable, the way he has heeded you. A pretty trick, and most intriguing. I should like to learn how to give my own words a power like that."

"Ah well, years of practice, you know. I shall be glad to teach you." He grinned but she gave him only a distracted quirk of her mouth in answer.

"There is no time for years of practice, if you are to call on the marquess." She gave him the stern look of a schoolmaster. "I expect a full report of how you fare when next you visit me."

"And I shall be pleased to deliver it."

"See that you are. Tuesday?"

He nodded. "Tuesday. And see that you're prepared to report to me on the matter of Sismondi."

She smiled. "I make no promises. But don't let that stop you from coming."

"Oh, no," he said, keeping his voice light. "It would take much more than that to keep me away."

※

Helen watched him leave. He made no sense. Their friendship made no sense. All of it was foolish, without merit or motivation. Every time he rode up to her little home, she expected him to keep riding past her door. Every time he left, she asked herself why he wanted to come at all. All the benefit was hers. She gained his conversation, borrowed his books, took advantage of his expansive knowledge of the world. He entertained her.

For his trouble, he received nothing but a few cups of tea and her amateurish opinions on foreign policy.

A few times, she had felt the tension between

them, her body aware of his, the space they shared full of a buzzing energy. She did not know if it was her imagination, or if he felt it too. But he always, gently, smoothed it over and made the moment normal again. Never with words but with the quiet way he had, of controlling the atmosphere of any given situation. And she was left with scattered thoughts and a sensation of emptiness, trying to acknowledge neither in favor of making coherent conversation.

It surprised her, whenever she would reflect upon it later and alone, that this physical awareness of him was miraculously free of the sort of fear and disgust she would have expected. It only felt warm and pleasant, a little thrilling, to hope that he might embrace her. She rather thought she might like it, if he did. For some reason, the thought did not fill her with dread, or bring back the unwanted memories and sensations which always required her to calm herself with visions of a happy, safe, growing Katie.

It was unfair to think he had some ulterior motive for becoming a regular caller. He had never offered her insult, not in all the weeks she had known him. He seemed to be everything Joyce had described: mannered, accomplished, everything one would hope for. And marvelously handsome. There was that. It was what worried her most, that he was a handsome nobleman, cultivating a friendship with a woman notorious for her questionable morals. On the surface, it was extremely suspect. But he never even hinted at more than friendship, and so she had assumed he already had a mistress, or else he was wed to propriety itself.

That was the most likely explanation. He treated

her, all of them, with a kindness and respect that was as gratifying as it was unexpected. She had come to think of him as taking a small holiday away from a rigid morality, enough of a respite to treat them as ladies, but not enough to forget she was still untouchable. It left her with only a persistent suspicion that he was not all that he seemed, that his reasons for befriending her were not entirely benevolent, and it was impossible to know what he really wanted out of it all.

All of her intuition told her he wanted something from her, and for all her hours of speculation, she was no closer to understanding what it could be.

The sight of Maggie coming toward her lightened her mood considerably. She looked askance at the new arrows Helen had gathered up and then gave a shrug.

"Has he left, then?" She asked in an exaggerated whisper.

Helen nodded. "He's off to Emily's uncle, to seal Tisby's fate. I believe he'll be successful, if confidence has anything to do with it. Let's go inside, and you can tell me all about your visit to Jack and Sally."

Once inside, Helen went straight to the letter, which held the momentous date in black and white. At the end of November, Katie would arrive in Holyhead, and Maggie would sail to Ireland.

"Let us hope the roads are fine." Helen worried at her lip with her teeth. "If Katie is as sickly as your cousin says, it's a bad time of year for travel."

The letter said that Katie was very unwell lately, which accounted for the late date of their crossing. The ferry would not run but a few times in December, and the departure had been delayed to almost the last minute in the hopes of the child becoming stronger.

"She's a poor judge of health, my cousin. She said my father was dying even a month after he started recovering, you know," Maggie snorted. "And the tickets are as good as bought already, with the money in her hands."

"Yes, I suppose so," answered Helen, thinking of the expense. In a fit of guilty indulgence for taking the child away from the only life she had known, she had sent her last shilling so that they could secure a cabin. Now there was almost nothing left until the next quarter. It was an extravagant gesture for only a six hour crossing, but she felt vindicated when she read of Katie's failing health. The picture of a sick child in the cold rain for so long, battered by the waves, was enough motivation to empty her purse of what little she had in the hopes of offering comfort.

"Four days for the journey," Helen frowned. "And there's enough money and provisions for that long on the road, I think, in case of bad weather. I hope we're not forgetting anything." The coach fare, inns, meals... Her mind revolved around all the expenses she had counted on, and those that might crop up.

Maggie silently took Helen's hand in hers, looking down and speaking in that comforting way she had. "You can't be worrying yourself all the time, Helen. Not everything that starts out as a promise ends up broken."

It was only ever Maggie who could speak to her this way. Only Maggie who understood the depths of Helen's disillusionment with promises. She had been there when the world came crashing down, and saw the change it had wrought in Helen. Marie-Anne knew, but couldn't understand it completely. Alex knew, and didn't believe. But Maggie was the one who saw what had died inside of Helen. Without ever really speaking of it, Maggie had years ago guessed rightly that Helen believed in no one, ever watchful for the lies she was certain must lurk in every man.

And Maggie would be leaving. It was like losing the best part of herself.

"Oh, Maggie," she laughed at her own tears, "How will I ever live without you?"

"You'll do well enough," Maggie said, with a little squeeze of Helen's hand. "There'll be Katie to keep you busy, and Marie-Anne to keep you laughing. And that Lord Summerdale to bring your brother back to his senses. He's a good man, that one."

"Do you think so, Maggie?"

Maggie gave her a patient look. "I do, as far as any man is good. I know you don't trust him, and it's smart enough to be cautious, wicked as all gentlemen can be. But I've the feeling he's to be trusted."

That was reassuring, as they'd already trusted him to enter their lives. But Helen had already determined not to trust him with any knowledge of Katie. The fact that the girl came from Ireland could pique his curiosity, and she felt certain the questions he'd held back would flow forth. Or he could investigate through his secret ways, and somehow discover Helen had been Katie's patron for years. He would sense some subterfuge, and question her about it. She would not suffer any inquiry into her Irish ties, when they had begun, why she cared so deeply. The subject of Katie, in his hands, would open a door that she wished to keep firmly closed, and locked. Even, or perhaps especially, to him.

The package came the next day, delivered by one of Summerdale's servants to her door. The servant said nothing, only gave her a bow and handed her a note before stepping up onto the carriage again. They did not leave in the direction from which they'd arrived, but headed into the village.

Helen looked at the box suspiciously. Breaking the seal on the parchment, she read his missive in disbelief.

Lady Helen,

To celebrate the upcoming nuptials of Miss Emily and Mr. Tisby, I present you with a humble gift. Our triumph in the realm of matchmaking deserves to be marked with some gesture. Besides, it is entirely selfish of me, and can be rightly seen as a gift to myself. My desire for an intelligent discussion of Mssr Sismondi requires that you accept.

-S

She returned her scrutiny to the package at her door. Perhaps it was an innocent gift. He could have given her any number of things that would be welcome, but she couldn't imagine a single thing that would be proper. Champagne, maybe, to toast the couple on his next visit? But that did not explain his note. Despite her suspicions, she trusted his natural inclination to propriety, so she decided she must at least look.

It took some time, necessitating a thorough search of the house for an implement to pry out the nails. When at last it was opened, she was trapped somewhere between laughter and outrage. Half the crate was packed with beeswax tapers, the other half with lamp oil.

He knew she had none, and that it interfered with her reading. And so this was his solution, to provide a bounty so that they may be able to discuss his books, or so he said. He did not appeal to her vanity, or her sensibilities as a lady. Instead he appealed to her practicality. He knew her that well, and it filled her with a commingled sense of fondness and dread.

Worse than anything, he presented her with a necessity that was beyond her ability to provide for herself. A snap of his fingers, and he provided enough to light her home through next summer, never thinking of the cost. He probably burned this much in a single evening of entertainment, and she had seven tallow candles to see her through the new year. He might just as well have given her jewels.

She could not accept it. It was every bit as presumptuous as if he *had* sent jewels, and that thought sent her over to ask Danny if he would run to the pub and see if the Summerdale's carriage was there. It was, his servants partaking of the famous bubble and squeak.

When they reappeared at her door, she explained they must take it back. The servant looked doubtful when she told him that the box was not meant for her, but she insisted it was to be returned to his master with all haste.

She should have sent a note explaining herself, but had been unable to find the words for the offense she took. As she sat in the dark by the meager fire that night, she tried to think of a way to tell him that the things he did for her – the arrows, the books, the candles, all of it — only made her think the worst of him. It made her feel even more impoverished, more outcast. More like he wanted something in return.

She never expected him to come the next day. She was sitting at the desk, spurred by his gift and this month's added expenses to reckon her finances until next quarter. It was quite dismal. They had nothing but the stocked cellars and the kindness of their neighbors to see them through. She was chewing at the pen in consternation when he arrived at her door.

Maggie showed him into the house and then left them there, being late for her job at the Huxley's. He was ready with a smile, as always, and Helen felt the familiar jolt at the sight of him. That he should be comfortable here, that he always seemed pleased to see her, never failed to amaze her. Weeks ago, after the dinner at his home, he had begun dressing more simply, in subdued colors, foregoing any kind of embellishment. It had put her at ease until now, when she recognized it as one more way he had subtly made himself part of her world, to what ends she did not know.

"Lady Helen." He bowed to her when she did not offer her hand.

"Lord Summerdale," she nodded. "I congratulate you on your work with the Marquess. Emily must be ecstatic."

"Yes," he said warily, eyeing her as though expecting an outburst.

"I thought you were not to come again until Tuesday."

"I hope my coming today doesn't inconvenience you. It seemed there were things we should discuss."

She supposed he was giving her the upper hand by

allowing her to bring the subject forth. Well, there was no use pretending. She shrugged. "If you mean my refusal of your gift, there is nothing to discuss. I cannot accept it. It would not be proper."

He raised his brows. "Come, Lady Helen, it's not as if I presented you with a petticoat. As I wrote, it was an act of selfishness. I only wished you to be able to read more."

His gentle exasperation did nothing to soothe her agitation. She stood looking at the ashes in the hearth, stiff with pride.

"It seems to me like a gift of charity, my lord. I know that you likely spend more on candles in a day than I spend all year, but it is a gift of great value in my estimation. I know little enough of economics, sir, but the notion of comparative wealth is something I understand. A box of lamp oil is the same as diamond earbobs to someone in my situation."

He spread his hands before him, as though to ward off the onslaught of her words. "Do you mean to say that beeswax and oil are as presumptuous as jewels?" He let out a disbelieving laugh. "I shudder to think what you would have done had I sent the Welsh longbow I found in my armory."

"I would have sent it back even more quickly, I assure you!" He did not take her seriously. He thought it harmless to shower gifts on her, only because their cost was a mere pittance to him. "Do you not see? It would be like...like..." she struggled for an apt analogy. "Like the czar of Russia giving you half his kingdom, only because he could do it easily, and because you had no lands there. Could you believe that such a gift would come with no expectations of you?"

"Expectations?" He looked nonplussed, almost angry. "Do you think I expect anything more than your friendship?"

"I don't mean to imply that you intended an insult to me. Not in that way, not *that* kind of expectation." She was flustered at the thought, dancing around the topic without naming it. "Nevertheless, I do take insult. I want no charity."

He was staring at the toe of his boot, as if understanding were etched there. "So I can't convince you to accept something as harmless as a box of candles?"

"I cannot. Your gifts – the arrows I should never have accepted, save that you so cleverly presented them as replacement. And your books, your visits, your notion of repairing my relationship with my brother…" Words failed her as she perceived the number of his kindnesses. There was so much, and his reasons for it all were obscured to her.

He crossed to her, suddenly and swiftly, his frown deepening. "Am I to pretend that it does not affect me, to see you living in poverty?" he asked. "I come here and I see how you live, with no help from anyone, and I know what you were born to. Not this," he waved his hand around the room, "this imitation. I have seen that you are worth more, Helen. I see it every time I call."

"You are wrong!" She was spurred to anger by his blithe mention of her former station in life. "You forget that the world has judged my worth, and found it wanting. It is *your* world, my lord, and you should be familiar enough with its requirements."

"It is your pride that keeps you poor," he persisted stubbornly. "Your brother would give you adequate means to live here or anywhere, but you will not accept it from him. Just as you will not accept a humble gift from me."

"My pride is all I have!" She was breathing heavily. It was all tumbling out now, the things they had scrupulously avoided for weeks, all the feelings she had held so close for so long. "I will not accept anything from him so long as he doesn't accept *me*, do you understand? And I will not accept anything from you, because it will only prove that I am what everyone believes." She should not speak of it. It would only lead to questions she didn't ever want to answer again. "I am nothing more than a villager here, with an unusual lineage. That is all I wish to be."

"You are more than that, I know it." He stepped closer to her, speaking earnestly. "You cannot hide your worth from me."

She felt his fingers touching softly on her elbow, where she knew the fabric was ragged and in need of repair. With him so close, staring down at her arm, she could see the fine lines beside his eyes, left from years of smiling in the way that took her breath. But he was not smiling now.

"How can I believe that you are no more than what you pretend to be?" he asked, as though he truly hoped she had an answer to it.

She had no answers at all. She could not think clearly when he stood so close. It was as if all else had fallen away, and all the candles in the world were snuffed, leaving them in smoky silence.

"I suppose," she found herself whispering, "I suppose I could have accepted *one*. But a whole box seemed too ... extravagant," she offered weakly.

But he was not looking at her. He seemed not to

be listening to her defense, staring instead at a place below her ear where she felt a curl of her hair falling out of its binding, coming to rest against her neck. He looked like he had just discovered something, there in the strands that tickled her skin. She should pull away, at least disengage her elbow, but she seemed unable to move. It felt amazing, miraculous, to be so close that she could feel the warmth of him. There was something in his face, something she almost recognized, but she could not fix her thoughts on what it was before his hand rose.

He brushed the back of his fingers along her cheek to her temple, watching the movement intently. Not knowing why she did it, she tilted her face slightly against his hand, feeling close to tears at his tenderness. He made her feel that she would like to move closer to him, to feel his arms strong about her, as if he could shield her from the world and all the things that frightened her. He could protect her with only a word from anything that threatened.

When his lips brushed gently across hers, she was surprised and not surprised at the warmth that blossomed deep inside her. His mouth barely touched hers, moving softly, waiting for her hand to come up to the stark line of his jaw, the hard smoothness of his skin filling some aching place inside her. He pulled away slightly, looking down at her with the heightened intensity she had felt in him before. But this time it was stronger, and he did nothing to move them back to safer ground.

Her heart stopped as she realized she did not want him to move away. He needed no words to interpret her mood. He never needed words, this mysterious man, who looked at her lips parting and answered her with his touch, spreading his fingers across her cheek and pressing his lips to hers. She had not been kissed in years, and she had never been kissed like this – like he meant to give as much as he took, even when his tongue parted her lips, a hot invasion that set her heart to beating again with a vengeance.

She returned the kiss with a passion she had thought dead in her. When he pulled her closer she did not resist as she would have expected of herself, but leaned against him and relished the feel of him. She could not think past the sweet pleasure of his kiss, the way he moved his lips now over her cheeks, her forehead, and back again to her waiting mouth. It was like a drink of water after years of wandering in the desert.

When his hands curved around her ribcage, his thumbs meeting just beneath her breasts, she slackened her hold on him. It was a struggle to think why she should not be doing this, why it was wrong. The space between their faces was a magnetic field, pulling her back when she told herself to turn away. She tried to find her breath as his hands rested there, so close to her breasts. It was her response to his touch, the heavy yearning that filled her, that brought her back to reality.

She knew this feeling, this painful need to be close to him, how the earth stopped spinning when he walked into a room, the way her body strained closer when her mind told her to keep a distance. She knew it, and it frightened her more than his touch.

She pushed back from him abruptly. Her back met the stone of the fireplace and she stared at him, staring at her. Both of them were breathing raggedly, and he looked... dazed, which frightened her so much that she feared she'd never breathe properly again. Just so, Henley had looked on that day so long ago. It set her mind racing. How could she defend herself? Maggie was gone, and the nearest house was not in shouting distance. She began a frenzied search of the room without moving from the spot, feeling the panic rise up in her. Why, *why* had she ever fallen out of the habit of identifying possible weapons in every room she entered? She used to always do so, but had stopped sometime, because she was silly and stupid and she never protected herself when she should.

There, the poker. It was just inside her reach. She moved in front of it, gulping air to still the frantic pounding of her heart as her hand closed about the cold metal behind her back.

"Go. You must go, please." It was a plea when she wanted to scream at him to leave.

"Helen—"

"Please!" He was not Henley, she told herself. She knew he wasn't, but all rational thought had fled with the realization of what she'd done and how he'd touched her, of the thousand terrible things he could be. Her mind fixed again on how little she really knew of him. "Leave me! I will not see you anymore. Go and never come back!"

He looked bewildered. "Never come back? When this is the only place I wish to be?"

"I don't want your gifts or your kisses or your romantic notions!" she cried wildly. "You make no sense! I want you gone from here. Go bother someone else. Seduce your way into someone else's life, you must leave me be. You have no *place* here."

She must calm herself. There was no reason to be so vehement. He had not moved since she'd pushed away from him, and the look that flashed across his face at her words stirred a regret that wrenched at her heart. But it was better to make him leave now, before she came to care more deeply or to depend on him. Katie would be here soon, and she tried to soothe herself with that thought as she always did. *Katie will come. I will have Katie. We will be happy like a family. That will be my life, that is my life. Katie will be here.*

It did not calm her. It only reminded her that she could not risk his suspicions if he knew about the girl. He must never come back. If ever he touched her again, she did not know what would happen.

The confused haze in his features faded, replaced with a kind of determination.

"What of the romantic notion that your brother might forgive you?" He spoke it quietly enough, with no inflection. But a kind of madness in her grasped at his words, pulling them apart until she found a focus at last for the suspicion that had plagued her.

"Is this all part of your plan for my brother and me?" she demanded, the thought coming full-blown into her mind and taking immediate hold. "Did you think to come here, and kiss me, and see if I would yield so you could tell Alex I am the whore he thinks me?"

It echoed in the room, the vulgar word that no proper lady would use. *Whore.* An hour ago, she would have never thought to insult him so, but now she wanted him gone. When she said the words, it seemed the likeliest reason behind his intent. He would never want her for himself. His disdain of her at their first meeting forced its way back into her consciousness as she watched him standing silently before her.

"I was right that first day, when I said you had come to judge me," she said. The blankness in his face was all the answer she needed. She felt suddenly very tired. "So go, then. Go back to my brother and tell him what you have learned. Just leave me."

He still did not move, but seemed to draw himself up.

"Is that what keeps you from trusting me? I'll tell you, then." His was a controlled anger, betrayed only by the tightness of his words. "I came to discover the truth of why you threw Henley over, even after you had given him your virtue and knew it would be your ruin."

Trying not to betray her thoughts on that, and all that it implied, she lifted her shoulder. The cold was stealing over her limbs, exhaustion making her flippant in the hopes of his departure. "It's as everyone says, of course. That I did not like the sound of Helen Henley for my married name."

"I find I am not in the mood for humor, Lady Helen. Tell me this and I will leave you. I see I have been a fool to think that we could be friends." There was nothing of the man she had come to know in him. He was hard, and cold, more disdain in his voice than he had ever revealed to her. "I'll not plague you with my romantic ideas or my unwanted affections any longer. Only tell me. Was it because you loved another?"

She actually found it in her to laugh at that. "Oh, no. Not that."

"They said you were an excellent match. That you seemed to care deeply for one another."

"You should know as well as I, Lord Summerdale, that they say anything at all which pleases them."

He was silent for the longest time. She made herself return his stare in spite of the burning dryness in her eyes. At least they had come to the truth. She found no happiness in knowing she had been right, that he had hidden his true purpose. For weeks, he lay in wait, cajoling her into relaxing her defenses to hear her pointless story. As if Alex's version of it was not enough for him. That she had been such a fool as to believe in his friendship for an instant made her want to weep, to tear her hair out and berate herself for having learned nothing in the course of her life.

"Is that it, then?" He looked hard at her. "You never loved him?"

She looked away from him, her fingers curling around the poker at her back. "On the contrary," she said with soft conviction, "I was foolish with love for him. We argued, and I was foolish, and that is all you need to know."

He stared at her a long time before he picked up his coat and hat. Without a word, he left her, closing the door softly behind him while she wondered what possible construction he could have put on her words. She didn't really care, so long as he didn't come back.

He didn't.

CHAPTER SEVEN

My dearest Stephen,

I do not believe you when you say that your country manor wants improving, that this is what keeps you from Town. How long will you rusticate?

Life goes on without you, days dragging by. His Grace occupies himself with his mistress and I occupy myself with nothing at all. I spend much time composing letters that I never send to you, knowing as I do how impatient you would be to see page after page filled with descriptions of your every virtue. Or to read how sorry I am, how foolish I was to refuse you, how I would give up everything to go back to the time when our thoughts were as one.

But you hide yourself away from me. You never write me anything of importance, and that so infrequently and in such distant tones that you make me believe everything between us was only a dream. If you stood here before me, I might know if that depth of feeling was only my imagining. Do you wish to forget me? You cannot. I will not let you. Say you will come before Spring. Say that we are still friends. My heart aches to think that you distance yourself from me.

Do not make me beg to hear from you. This is a cheerless existence (of my own doing and by choice, no one is more mindful of this than I am) and a word from you brightens even the darkest day. Write to me.

Ever Yours,
Clara

It had taken hours of searching among the dusty boxes, but they had found the three remaining dresses of Helen's trousseau. The gowns lay on Marie-Anne's sofa, undergoing a strict evaluation of their worth and usefulness.

"The pink is most appropriate for such a young girl, I think." Marie-Anne stroked what was left of the gray riding habit before pronouncing her agreement with Helen, that it would make the most practical dress for daily wear. Her hand then moved to the green gown. "It is a shame not to use this for something, even if not for Katie. So lovely. But perhaps when she is older."

Helen agreed completely. It had been her favorite dress: an emerald green made of silk with a shimmering lace-trimmed overlay, delicately puffed short sleeves, the neckline dipping low in a way that was out of fashion now. There had been a hat to match it, and gloves too, both sacrificed years ago to pay for the services of Katie's doctor. Helen had never worn the dress in public, but had spent months dreaming of how she would wear it as a married woman, at the first ball they would attend together after the wedding. Now the memory filled her with disgust for herself, for the Odious Henley, for the modiste who had designed the dress with immodesty in mind, and most of all for childish dreams.

But she did not hate the dress. It was beautiful, and she had been beautiful in it, once, standing in front of the cheval glass, marveling at how adult she had become. She had had other dresses that were much more valuable, and even the pink gown had undergone the salvaging that the others had. But the green gown remained whole, and perfect, and Helen was afraid to question her own motives in keeping it thus.

"Well, we should set to work on the gray first," Helen declared. "We can guess at her size well enough to begin on it, anyway."

"Hard to believe she will be here so soon," Marie-Anne muttered as she pulled the scissors from her pocket. "Even more difficult to believe that Maggie will be leaving us."

Helen occupied herself with packing the green gown away, trying to hide the sadness that overcame her. She could scarcely think of Maggie's leaving without becoming teary-eyed. She did not know how to take leave of Maggie, how to put into words what she felt at this parting, much less what she felt for Maggie herself. She had the hysterical idea that she would collapse beneath the weight of her gratitude and love in the midst of trying to express it, or in trying *not* to express the lonely self-pity that consumed her when she considered the impending absence of that love.

"Maggie will stay in touch," she said instead, struggling as always to focus on the positive. "We'll miss her of course, but we cannot grow maudlin over it. One loses friends over the course of time. It's only natural."

She sat across from Marie-Anne on her customary chair and began to remove the piping from the sleeves of the riding habit. They worked in silence for a while, until Marie-Anne at last spoke.

"Hélène, I do not wish to upset you, but I must ask. Will we never see Lord Summerdale again?" She was so carefully casual, in how she asked it. "It has been so long, and he never said goodbye. At least, not to me."

It had been a month since he had walked out her door, and Helen had never offered a reason to Marie-Anne or Maggie for his sudden absence. She found it too difficult to lie to her friends, and so much more difficult to tell the truth of the matter. If she were brave, she would say: *He frightens me, Marie-Anne.* But she couldn't say it; it was too upsetting in either language. Instead, she sought to find the words to imply as much to her friend.

"He said goodbye to me. I'm sure he regrets being unable to say so to you." She hesitated, then plunged ahead. "But he left at my request, and I asked him not to visit here again."

Marie-Anne showed no surprise at her words. "Why did you do that?" she asked mildly.

"I..." Helen could feel the flush creeping up her neck. "He insulted me." Even if she had not said it in such a tentative way, it would still have sounded unlikely reason. Lord Summerdale was not the insulting type. His courtesy was too well known.

Her friend still did not look up, but answered quite normally, as though it were the most natural thing in the world to say, "So he must have shown you how he feels for you, no? Perhaps he told you of his affection, or even dared to kiss you?"

Helen's mouth fell open. Her mind was utterly blank, incapable of forming a response to this unexpected insight. She gaped at her friend until she managed to choke out, "He *told* you?!"

Marie-Anne at last looked up and laughed outright at Helen's expression. "Oh, no, *ma chère*, he has told me nothing. Do you think anyone needed to tell me? Recover yourself, Hélène, or your eyes will come right out of your head." She had stopped laughing now, settling into a quiet amusement as she spoke. "I am very Gallic, as you tell me, and see these things even when they are more subtle. It was plain to me he wanted you from the moment he saw you."

An instant denial was on Helen's lips, but she did not give voice to it. She had seen nothing in Summerdale when they'd met, except the threat he presented. She had only felt his censure, his disgust. It was impossible that there was more than that, and she said so to Marie-Anne, cautiously. But all her arguments were dismissed with an impatient flick of the hand.

"I saw the look on him when you met, and again every time you were in front of him. Many times he looked at you with more than courtesy or friendship, so don't pretend to me that you never saw it."

Helen thought back to the dinner at his house, his eyes alight with a mischievous flirtation as he slid his glance in her direction through the candlelight. No, she couldn't pretend she didn't know that look, or the many others he had given her. She had told herself that it was his way, that he enjoyed the challenge of making her laugh, purely for the sake of friendship.

But she knew those looks, and what they really

were, and had hidden their meaning from herself. It had been pleasant to indulge in a light flirtation; she never dreamed it was anything other than perfectly safe, like sighing over the gallantry of Sir Galahad when she was a girl. Fictional knights didn't lament her poverty while standing in her home, though. They didn't look at her like he had. They certainly never leaned out of the picture book and kissed her.

"I suppose," she admitted slowly, "that I saw it, but did not recognize it. And when I did, I told him to leave."

"Only because he desired you? He would never act without encouragement, from what I have seen of him. You blush, Hélène! There is nothing in this to be ashamed of, so it must be..." She stared hard, almost squinting at Helen, and a look crossed her face – amusement, chagrin, delight and incredulity all at once. "It must be that *you* desire *him*!"

Helen stood abruptly, trailing the gray material behind her as she walked a few paces toward the window. "It is not a joke, if you please, Marie-Anne."

"I'm sorry, *ma chère*, I know it is not," she answered. Instead of teasing, her voice took on a gentle, maternal tone. "But I thought you understood that it is nothing but natural."

She had told Helen, long ago, that what had happened in Ireland was a perversion of love. That it was not like that, truly, between those who cared for one another. Even if she had not said so, Helen would have understood it only by seeing the look that came over Marie-Anne when she spoke of her Shipley. There was no discomfort there, or anger, or fear. Through a combination of fate and her own stupidity, Helen had experienced the twisted version of passion, and Marie-Anne had made it clear that it need not always be so. She didn't know whether to be grateful for the knowledge, or even more furious to learn the extent of what she had lost that day.

"I understand that, Marie-Anne. I suppose I do. In my mind, at least, if not in the rest of me." She fought her way past the usual desolation that filled her thoughts when she turned her mind to her own feelings about Summerdale. "And though I doubt it, perhaps I could have invited him back one day, if it were only that which had upset me. But he told me why he really came here."

"This sounds ominous," Marie-Anne said cautiously.

"Indeed. He sought me out only to know the truth of why I broke my engagement. He is not our friend; he was only after any sordid details which Alex may have left out." She closed her eyes and spoke past the pain of the admission. "He is sent here as judge, my virtue once more on trial, so that Alex may learn if I am any less a whore than he has believed."

Marie-Anne did not speak at first, absorbing this news that no doubt came as much of an unpleasant surprise as it had to Helen. Finally, she gave a deep sigh. "Well, that is disappointing, and I wouldn't have thought it of him. You were right to send him away, then, if you won't tell the tale."

Helen gave a snort. "Why should I try again to tell it? It's no different than what Alex already knows, and I doubt I could give any better rendition of it now. God knows it's as unbelievable now as it was six years ago, so I won't open myself to Summerdale's scorn over the affair."

She picked up the scissors again and blindly

attacked the fabric, nearly slicing her thumb. Ignoring the tears that threatened and the hard lump of injustice that swelled inside her, she took a deep breath and thought of Katie. This dress was to be for the girl. She must be calm.

"I think he would not scorn, my friend. He is a better man than your brother." Marie-Anne picked at the thread to pull a seam apart, her head down and her voice mild. "But it is your story to tell, and yours to never tell again if you don't wish it."

Helen frowned at this, suddenly doubting. "Do you think I did wrong to refuse?"

Marie-Anne looked up swiftly, and spoke firmly. "There is no wrong or right in this. It is in your power to choose what you will or will not share, and that is the only thing of consequence. It is you who made the choice," she shrugged, "and that is good."

She and Marie-Anne did not talk of it anymore, turning their attention to the preparations for Katie's arrival. They took the ruins of the gown and bent all their concentration on making something new and beautiful out of it, salvaging the tattered remnants of the past to piece together a different, less magnificent but perfectly presentable future. They were both quite practiced at it.

She dreamt of Lord Summerdale that night, of him standing below her with his arms outstretched, waiting for her to fall from a great height.

She always did fall, in the dream, and he always caught her in strong arms before tumbling backwards with her, laughing and kissing her soundly. She was never afraid in the dream. It was only when she awoke that she became filled with a shivering fear, and the face and mouth in her mind changed to another's, leaving her awake and terrified until the gray dawn lit the room.

※

In the end, when it was time for Maggie to leave, Helen did not even attempt to express her feelings at losing her dearest friend. They only held hands as the cart pulled away, letting the distance pull their arms straight before the grasp was broken. Helen kept her arm outstretched, the emptiness of her hand saying all the things that she could not voice.

She walked back to the empty house, and the door closed behind her in an echoing boom. She leaned her back against the door and slid down to sit on the floor with her knees drawn up beneath her chin. She stayed that way for the rest of the afternoon and into the evening, sobbing as she had not let herself do for years.

In the five days that followed, she had taken to walking. Even though it was gray and cold, and the cloak she wore was barely worthy of the name, she found comfort in the monotony of lifting one foot after another. She told herself she was seeking distraction from her thoughts, but in truth she only allowed herself to sink more deeply into melancholy. She saw the years stretch before her, without Maggie's companionship: she and Marie-Anne would be a silly pair of spinsters, playing the role of doting aunties to Katie, who would be Jack and Sally's child. It would be different, all of it.

She quickened her step, frustrated with her self-pity. So it would not be perfect, but whatever in life was? There was no call for this ridiculous moping about. All of it, from the empty days in front of her to the penniless days behind her, would be worth it. There was only one goal: to see Katie safe and grown. Helen would give it all again, would give the rest of her days or anything else it cost, to take care of the child. It was the only task left to her, and she would pour everything of herself into it.

Determined to turn her thoughts to anything other than Maggie's absence, she finally forced herself to think of what she had avoided in all her days of walking. She would never see her brother again. He did not believe her, and was not more inclined to believe her, or forgive her, or care about her at all. Perhaps she should have lied. Truth seemed to matter very little. Easy enough to say she regretted her flighty youthfulness, or some other nonsense that would lay the blame at her own feet.

But it galled her to think of playing a charade, when the truth was all she'd ever had. Her own truth, no matter what anyone else believed. It was hers, as Marie-Anne had said. All of the pain and injustice and anger, the whole experience, belonged to her, and she would not change it for her brother's peace of mind. Even if she could it would not mollify him, as there was no way to reverse time and honor her betrothal. And no matter how it had happened, she had lost her vaunted virginity. She could change that no more than she could change the course of the stars in the sky.

And the stars would be out soon, she realized, as she noticed that the sun was sinking. She didn't at first hear the sound of her name being called across the fields.

Shading her eyes from the low slant of the sun and trying to quell her alarm at the note of panic in the voice that called to her, she began to walk towards him. She couldn't imagine who it was, or how he'd gotten there, until she came close enough to see his face.

"Jack! What's happened? What's wrong?" Her legs had almost given out beneath her when she saw it was him. He was supposed to be on the road from Holyhead, with Katie in tow, in a hired coach. But he stood before her, panting and holding his side.

"Is it Katie? Is she all right? What's happened?" She was beginning to breathe as harshly as Jack was, her eyes watering in panic as she imagined the worst.

"Miss Helen, it's all gone wrong something terrible and I'm sorry for it. The girl's fine for now, I think. Miss Maggie and her cousin are with her. I came as fast I could, I didn't know what else to do." He caught his breath finally and straightened, worry in every line of his face.

Maggie was always better in situations like these, and Helen calmed minutely as she took in the news that whatever had happened, the resourceful Irishwoman had the situation in hand. She consciously adopted the practical tone and mannerisms of Maggie, ignoring the dread inside her, and told Jack to walk with her to the house and tell her what he could on the way.

"The cousin," Jack began. "When we got to the port, the cousin – Janet's her name. She was nowhere to be found, nor Katie. So Miss Maggie and I, we asked around everywhere and one of the men working the ferry told us they was bein' held in the harbormaster's jail."

"Jail!" It seemed to call for more outrage than Jack had voiced, which only filled Helen with apprehension that whatever happened next was even worse. "Why on earth would she be in a jail? And Katie with her?"

"The shipmaster said they hadn't paid their way, and not a soul would listen to Janet. She paid the porter for the cabin, as she told me and anyone else would listen, and paid him before they ever left out of Dublin. But that porter's a nasty type, and so I said when I saw him. He kept the coin for himself, and no one to believe Janet or even Maggie, though she near took the head off the lot of 'em. She's wicked in a temper, is our Maggie."

Helen felt a violent surge of pride and love. "Our Maggie's made of iron, Jack, and no one better to be with Katie. Here, now, come in to sit in the kitchen and I'll bring you something to drink. Did she get them out of the jail?"

"That she did, though she had to pay both fares again – and they raised the price, and then pay the fine, says the harbormaster." He slammed a fist onto the table in his anger, rattling the cup before him. "It's a rare port town that's not dirty and greedy, I'm always hearin', but had to see it with my own eyes to believe. Maggie spent more than she had for her own fare to get them out, and then more of all she had to find them a room at the inn."

"But why didn't she send Katie back with you? Why waste money on an inn, when there's so little for anything at all?"

Jack took a deep drink of the water before he answered. When he faced Helen, his face was grave, sending waves of fear through her.

"Because the little one shouldn't travel just yet. That's what the doctor said. She was sick all the way over the water, and a day and night in that jail hole only made her worse."

Helen sank slowly into the chair, clutching the cloak she still wore about her as though it could protect her from what she was hearing. "The doctor. You said there was a doctor?"

He nodded. "Maggie took one look at the girl and run off for a doctor. That's what took the most of her money, after the bleedin' harbormaster. But she said you'd want it and she wouldn't be leaving the girl unless she was safe and whole, and the doctor says she done right. So I took part of the money what you gave me for coming back to Bartle and gave the rest to Miss Maggie to pay for the room." For the first time since he'd run into town, his face lost its grimness and took on a pained expression.

Helen stared at the tabletop, seeing nothing. "How much is left, Jack?"

She thought the big man might actually cry. "Two shillings, nothin' but that little. And Maggie and her cousin on the coast without fare for the crossing, and Katie with no way here, and us with no way to get back there. None of us knew what to do. But Maggie said, sure as anything, she says to me, go right to Miss Helen and she'll fix it."

She kept staring at the boards of the table, looking for the answer there. She had no idea how long she sat, unmoving, as Jack waited patiently beside her. When she finally looked up, she felt the kind of sure and solid strength that she imagined Maggie must feel every day of her life.

"I'll take care of it, Jack. I will. Go home to Sally, and tell her not to worry. I'll bring our Katie to you soon."

"Hélène, can we be sure there is no other way? You look pale as death at the very notion."

She sat in Marie-Anne's bedroom, in front of the dressing table. It was a conscious effort not to ravage her hair with the brush, and she watched her hands tremble a little as she took gentle strokes over the strands. It would be no use to show up at his door looking as sick and terrified as she actually felt.

"If you have another suggestion, I'll be more than happy to consider it, but we have been through it all. We've nothing more than a few pence between us, and the cost of a trip to and from Anglesey to conjure from it. Daniel's horse will not take me even as far as Gloucester, and there's nowhere else to sell anything, even had we anything worth so much as we need." She experienced an equal amount of desperation and relief in laying out the situation logically. "Unless I am there within the week with the funds we need, Maggie and her cousin will miss the last ferry of the season to Ireland, not to mention being tossed out of the inn, so that leaves out a London trip to appeal to the solicitor, or to Alex. I am desperate enough for that, even. But there is no time for a trip to London. So you tell me, Marie-Anne, where else do I find such a sum within the next twelve hours?"

Her friend paused in her agitated fumblings with the green gown. It wanted only the tiniest bit of slack in the bodice to fit Helen as perfectly as it had six years ago, and Marie-Anne was quick with the needle, her hands far steadier than Helen's. Only imagining the gown slipping over her head was enough to impart a sense of vertigo.

"The moon is bright, and I can find my way there easily. Jack has said that the roads were good all the way to Holyhead, so if I can obtain the money tonight, I can be well on my way in the morning and at the port in a few days."

She made herself look in the glass and consider her hair, pulling at it to twist it up on her head in an attempt to guess what she could make of it. She had only a few hairpins at her disposal, so it would be nothing elaborate even had she the skill.

Marie-Anne watched her from her seat on the bed, meeting Helen's eyes in the mirror. "He will give you the money, I am sure," she declared.

"I am sure of it, too. That is not in question. What is unknown is what he will ask in return."

Her usually composed friend wore an almost comical expression of outrage and confusion upon hearing these last words. Helen saw her turn her face down to snip the thread quickly before she looked up again and insisted, "But, no. It is not in his character. He is not one to treat a friend so!"

Helen dug the tip of a sharp hairpin into the pad of her thumb. "We are no longer friends, he and I. We parted...badly. I no longer hold his respect, Marie-Anne, it was clear. I will ask him for the money as a loan. If he does not agree, I will offer anything else I have of value, from scrubbing his floors to darning his stockings, though I doubt he has need of a maid."

They had both carefully avoided naming the only other thing of value she possessed. At least she still assumed it held some value for Lord Summerdale, and covering it in silk and lace would not hurt her cause. There was need to look a beggar, she supposed, although she had no illusions that she was exactly that.

"What if he is not there? If he has left this manor and gone to another?"

"Daniel spoke with one of the grooms when he returned the book for me weeks ago. Lord Summerdale will stay in Herefordshire through the winter. Luckily for us."

"I could go."

"Marie-Anne," she said as calmly as she could. "You are the one who has said he wanted me. And that may be our only advantage."

Marie-Anne picked up the dress and stood. Letting go of her hair to let it fall down her back, Helen walked briskly over to the bed. It had turned out to be a good thing that she had kept the dress, after all. And a good thing she had not been wealthy enough to gain any weight over the years, though she had never been slight-boned. If only she could manage to draw a complete breath, she might have a chance of putting the thing on without falling to the floor. She closed her eyes as Marie-Anne slid it over her head, then ran her hands along the smooth silk while it was fastened.

Giving into an impulse of modesty, she reached into a drawer of the dressing table to pull out a filmy white scarf and laid it over the bared skin of her chest. Marie-Anne said nothing, but helped to tuck in the ends, her face solemn. It made Helen smile. There was no one better than a Frenchwoman to arrange a scarf.

"Well!" said Marie-Anne with an obvious attempt at normalcy. "We have only to decide what is to be done with your hair, and you shall be ready." She hesitated. "You look very lovely, Hélène. You can charm him with appearance alone, and if you can give him a smile, well, what man can say no to a pretty woman in need? Men love to play hero to the damsel in distress, and he has enough money to give you a thousand times what you ask, so I think you will not have to make any great sacrifice."

The upward break of her voice on this last statement betrayed Marie-Anne's doubts. Helen knew less of men and their proclivities than her friend did, but even she knew it was wishful thinking that she would escape so easily. It was worth it, no matter what she might be forced to give. The vision of Katie lying sick sustained her. She twirled the ends of her hair and turned to the mirror.

She did look well, she supposed, if one discounted her pallor. The green emphasized the dark richness of her hair, glossy waves that spilled down almost to her waist. She looked a stranger to herself.

"We won't waste time in trying to dress my hair." She heard herself make a sound somewhere between a cynical laugh and a sob. "I'll leave it loose. Like my character, I suppose."

Marie-Anne gave a twist of her mouth in response to that, and then crinkled her nose. "To leave it hanging free is not so much wanton as it is vulgar."

Helen picked up the cloak where she had left it on the bed. If she left now, she could be there just after dinnertime. "Then it's quite fitting. What could be more vulgar than this?"

CHAPTER EIGHT

Stephen thought he must have heard the butler wrong. She would not come here, at night. Alone. At all. He shoved his papers into the desk and stood in preparation for whatever would walk through the door.

It took a moment to realize that it was her. He saw little more than the gown she wore as she stepped into the room, a gleam of silk in the candlelight. He felt all the air go out of his lungs as he recognized the curves revealed by the cut of the dress, curves she had hidden so very well. He felt lightheaded as his gaze traveled up to her face, taking in the sight of her unbound hair.

A month. It had been only a month, and he'd forgotten what it was like to look at her. He felt the familiar tightness in his throat, the sudden urge to smile at her like an imbecile. She only stared at the fire, immobile as stone. Finally, she gave a slight curtsy, lowering her head and spreading her skirt with one ungloved hand, as if they were about to begin a country dance.

"Lord Summerdale, I hope I have not disrupted your evening beyond forgiveness," she said into the hush, and the sound of her voice broke over him like water on dry shore. He did not answer, only watching the play of light on her hair.

She looked up at him. "I went to the servant's entrance and made sure you had no guests before I approached your door."

"Looking to preserve your tattered reputation?" It came out sullen and spiteful, because he could not hide the hostility that sprang to life inside him. It lived alongside the longing for her.

"No," she answered quite civilly, as if she had expected his contempt. "I was looking to protect your own quite excellent reputation, and those of any guests you might have had. I am sorry if my presence here offends you."

It offended him. It upset him and unsettled him. It made him want to go down on his knees and beg her to stay, to pull her tight against him and push his hands through her hair, to feel her lips seeking his again. But he took refuge in derision and indifference, pulling his shoulder up in a shrug.

"Do you intend to tell me why you've come? Or will you hang about the doorway all evening and distract me from matters of importance?"

He had no hopes that she was here to tell him at last about her broken engagement. There was too much pride in the set of her shoulders to indicate that she was willing to divulge any secrets. But what else she could possibly have come to him for eluded him. He opened his hand in a gesture toward the chair across from the desk, but she looked instead to the decanters on the table nearby.

"Can I impose upon your hospitality for a drink? It was a long ride, and I am grown unaccustomed to being in the saddle."

He gave no hint of surprise at the irregularity of her request. Expect no delicacy from a lady who was not a lady at all, she had once said with laughter on her lips.

"Do help yourself, Lady Helen. Will you take whiskey or port, I wonder?"

He was glad she did not look up as she poured and drank, for he could not have helped but betray his amused surprise at her choice of whiskey. It was a singular experience to see her take a healthy swallow without turning a hair.

"It meets with your approval, I hope," he said.

She nodded and moved to take the chair before his desk, but said not a word even after he sat and looked expectantly at her. He allowed the silence for long enough to observe the determined set of her features. She was as beautiful and as ordinary as she had always been, the clothes and her hair falling freely about her shoulders doing nothing to change the truth of her appearance. Where the fire lighted the left side of her face, she seemed as unremarkable as he had first thought her. But where the candlelight touched on her right side, he saw again the depths of her eyes and the heartbreaking loveliness of her face. She was only beautiful in moments, at certain angles and in certain moods, her features arresting one minute and common the next. Her body was another matter entirely, and he resolutely focused on her fire-brightened face.

"To what do I owe your unexpected appearance at my door, Lady Helen? Come to browse the library?" Her calm upset him, while he could only feel the familiar burn of the anger he had felt in the weeks since he'd seen her last. "Or perhaps to have a look at that longbow I mentioned?"

"No, on both counts, my lord."

"Wondering about the progress of our little church charity?"

"No."

"Perhaps you are afraid I might undo all my good work with Emily. You hardly need bother, the marriage contracts are signed and in order."

"I never thought you would interfere with that."

"Then I confess myself at a loss, madame." She would not be drawn into an argument, and she was evidently impervious to mockery. "Will you enlighten me as to why you should so suddenly appear at my door?"

She nodded stiffly, setting her glass on the table beside her. Placing her hands on the arms of her chair, she faced him squarely and addressed herself to a point just below his eyes.

"I am come to ask a favor of you, my lord. As you must understand, you are the only one who can help me or else I would not be here." He watched as she gathered herself, no doubt swallowing her precious pride so that she was able to look into his wary gaze. "I need to borrow some money, and you are the only one I know of who is capable of providing such a sum quickly. I have no time to waste. If you can lend it to me tonight, I can promise to have my solicitor reimburse the funds within the month."

He let his eyes fall away from her and rest on the

desk, where he played idly with a pen in his hands. He dimly thought that he should be happy, to know that in her distress she turned to him. But he could not be happy.

A loan. She came to him for money. If he had thought it impossible that she could hurt him any more than when she had shouted at him to take himself and his assumed seduction out of her life forever, he found he had been sadly mistaken. He should hardly be surprised she saw him as a bag full of coins. Her brother, and everyone else he knew, after all, apparently saw him only as a source of valuable information. How idiotic, to have hoped for a moment that he was anything more than whatever he could contribute to someone else's plans.

"What could you possibly need so urgently, to lower yourself to walk through my door?"

"I cannot answer that. I will not."

Her tone was definite, without hesitancy. He had come to know her well enough to recognize instantly that she would not give him any reason for her request.

"You need it badly enough to approach me, yet not badly enough to offer explanation," he said thoughtfully, as though considering. "I am not in the habit of making investments blindly, Lady Helen. Nor am I in the habit of making loans when I do not know where the money goes. It would seem we are at an impasse."

He saw her tighten her grip on the chair. "Then you refuse me?"

Her calm evaporated, her entire demeanor changing to one of utter desperation. It sharpened his curiosity into alarm. It could not be some simple everyday expense, to send her into such obvious despair. She may be determined to hide the reasons for her sudden need of ready cash, but he was suddenly just as determined to know the truth.

"I refuse your terms. That is all I refuse, Lady Helen."

"I know I was rude to you at our last meeting, for which I can only offer my apology. But if you cannot accept it, if you wish to see me humiliated in return for that rudeness, I will spend the rest of my life as your charwoman." She really was desperate, more so than he had realized. Her voice was rising almost to a plea, and he doubted there was any humiliation he could mete out to equal what she must feel at this moment. "Or I can sell you the dower house, or repay you twice what you give me, with interest. Given some time, I can do it, I swear."

He hardened himself against the pity at seeing her reduced to this. He reminded himself that she had done this to herself. She'd refused to marry her lover and now she paid the consequences. It was simple, and cruel, and the way of the world. He told himself again, as he had done so many times since meeting her, that it was not his responsibility to help her out of the poverty into which she had so recklessly thrown herself.

Advantage and opportunity, that's how he must see this. It always came from moments such as this, desperate people confiding their sad situation to him. If he could know the truth of why she was in such need, perhaps he could take the information to her brother and salvage something out of this ludicrous venture after all. It should mean nothing to him if she looked pale as a wraith. Nothing.

"I'm not looking to purchase a house in godforsaken Bartle-on-the-Glen. I am not in need of a scullery maid. And you'd have to ask for a far greater sum than I suspect you need in order to make a double repayment even remotely interesting to me." He let his contempt and impatience have full reign over his words, attempting to enjoy the sight of her flinch.

"So," he continued slowly, anticipating the moment when she caved in and told him, against her will, what it was that drove her to this. "What can you offer me that I could possibly want, Lady Helen?"

She remained as she had been, sitting poker-straight on the edge of the chair, but he saw the change come over her. The grasping desperation in her expression faded away, but did not leave her entirely, settling instead into a resigned determination. In fact, her face took on a perfect blankness, with only a shadow of uneasiness lingering there. Without looking directly at him, she reached up with one hand, slowly, and pulled away the scarf that was tucked around her neckline.

Had he not been seated, he might have stumbled in shock at this gesture. As it was, he felt close to falling out of his chair at the sight of her deliberate motions. The dress swooped down from the shoulders, exposing the full length of her collarbone before revealing the swelling curve of her breasts. Next to the dark emerald silk, her skin was a field of white, gently interrupted by slopes and valleys that were illuminated and shadowed by the changing light.

He had thought that the glimpse he'd had of her body, months ago, had been a dream. So quickly did she change from moment to moment, so well did she hide any sign of womanly curves, that he'd convinced himself he had imagined it. It had been no dream, he now knew. It all came back to him: how she had smiled, lifting her arms, laughing, unconsciously revealing more of herself with each slight motion. The difference between that and what was now before him struck him. Then, she had been unknowingly caught in a solitary moment, all unaware of the effect her body was having. Now she bared herself to his eyes, inviting him with purposeful movements.

Without conscious thought of moving, he stood up from his chair. He felt lightheaded again, drifting slowly around the desk, coming to stand in front of her, staring at her skin. The same impetus drove him as ever, the need to be close to her, the unknown force drawing him inexorably to wherever she was. She had not moved, not even to take a breath, since she had pulled the scarf away.

His voice was faint. "What are you doing, Helen?"

She immediately began breathing again. Her throat tightened in a convulsive swallow, leaving him staring at the pulse point in the inviting hollow at the base of her neck.

"You asked what I could offer you," she said, sounding infinitely calmer than he felt.

It took a long time for him to translate the sounds of her words into a meaning. When at last he understood her, the force of it pressed his hands into a tighter grasp on the desk. He had forgotten, in gawking at her like a schoolboy, that she saw him as a bankbook. Disgust washed over him – at her, and at himself for still wanting her even in the midst of his revulsion.

"You offer me yourself, in return for money." It was not a question. It must be said outright, so that there could be no confusion. So that he might remind himself that she wanted payment for her body. That she did not want him, but whatever amount of shillings and pence she required for her secretive purpose. He kept his voice carefully controlled. "Even knowing that I will tell your brother of this conduct?"

Her face did not change, but her eyes lost their sharp focus on his collar and stared somewhere in the middle distance between them. She blinked once and nodded. "Even knowing that, my lord," she answered. Her voice was quite steady. She meant it. She was prepared to do it.

So the little fantasy that he'd held so dear – his Avalon, away from the sordidness of society, a place where he was fully welcomed – was truly crushed. She left him not even the memory of it. She smashed everything to pieces with this degrading display. It hardened him to her, made him want to be cruel.

"It's good of you to show me the wares for sale. I thank you," he murmured. It would be interesting, not to say enlightening, to see how prepared she really was.

He leaned forward, lifting his hand to her forehead and gently catching a thick strand of her hair. She did not flinch away, staring into the nothingness between them, as his fingers followed the fall of her hair beside her face. He hesitated a moment when his hand came to rest briefly on her shoulder, vividly remembering the way a curl had found its way out of its tight knot to fall on the side of her neck, seizing his heart in his chest seconds before he had kissed her. He looked for it again, among the dark tresses that spilled down her back, but it was lost in the silken curtain, and he could not bring himself to search out the soft place where it had come to rest against her skin. It was as if it had never existed, never happened, and was better forgotten.

He let his hand trail down to the upper curve of her breast where this strand ended in an upward curl. Hardly able to stop himself, he pressed a finger to the curl, separating the strands, fanning them out over her heart. Then he shifted his hand to her neckline, his fingertips slowly following the sweep of it down from one shoulder to where the shadowed declivity between her breasts made him involuntarily pause. The warmth of her skin made it hard to think, to remember why she was here. He only knew and cared that she was in front of him, letting him touch her. He pulled air into his chest with an effort, and found himself moving closer to her. To keep himself from giving in to the temptation to kiss her, he looked down.

Her hands were locked on the chair in a death grip, her knuckles white as bone, whiter even than the scarf she still held. She radiated tension, still as a statue. He flicked his glance up to her face and found her staring, wide-eyed, somewhere in the vicinity of his chin. Now he moved deliberately, closing the distance that separated her lips from his, until his mouth hovered over hers.

When her lips parted, letting go a little rush of air, he spoke. "As tempting as it is, Helen, I decline your services."

She seemed not to have heard him for a second, staying still and staring at his mouth. Then, as if coming slowly out of a dream, her eyes did a rapid scan of his face and she drew back quickly in her chair. He pushed away and stood upright, looking down at her.

He gave her a sympathetic look. "If I wanted a whore, I would hire one in town, you see," he apologized.

A strange mixture of relief and outrage transformed her face before the blank wall took over her features. It, too, was quickly replaced with chagrin and the earlier echo of despair. He watched it all play across her face, waiting in vain for her to voice any of it. But she did not speak.

He frowned a little. "I suppose I might still be enticed. Tell me, my dear, how much are you asking?"

She blinked rapidly and turned her gaze once more to his collar. "Ten pounds," she breathed.

He laughed. "Ten *pounds?* Good God, I could keep myself in London professionals day and night for a week at that price."

"I can lower it to as much as eight," she said without emotion. "And you can have me for at least a fortnight, but no more than a month. The entire arrangement is under the condition that I have the money immediately, and that I leave tomorrow morning. I can be back in your service a week hence."

She had obviously considered all the terms before she'd ever come to his door. It was the most appalling proposition he'd ever heard.

"I doubt I'd want you for more than a night," he lied quite easily. "And why would I bother paying so much for something you are known to have freely given?"

He did not think it was possible for her to grow more pale, but she did, drawing in a swift breath as though he had slapped her. Her hands went tighter on the chair, and he had the distinct impression that she was fighting down an attack of nausea.

"Of course. How...stupid of me. And here I thought I was selling myself cheaply." She paused, her nose flaring delicately as if she smelled something foul. When she at last spoke again, it was with a controlled anger that mirrored his own.

"You asked what I have that you would want, Lord Summerdale. If it is not this, nor anything else that I have offered, I ask you to tell me now if there is any way you will help me."

He waited until she met his eyes, gauging the depth of her need. She could be brought no lower than this, he knew. Her begging and pleading and willingness to sell herself plainly indicated that he could ask anything.

"The truth," he announced.

She stiffened, but did not look away. "You want to know about my engagement?"

"No, Lady Helen. If I had any doubts that the rumors were true, you have laid them to rest tonight."

"Then what?" she demanded, a hiss between her teeth.

"What this money is for. That is my price – to know what you could want so badly. And don't tell me it's some trivial household need, unless that is the truth. I must ask to see for myself what you purchase."

Her jaw worked. He thought she might balk, but she only closed her eyes for a minute, fighting some internal battle.

"You're sure you wouldn't prefer to buy me?" she asked with a kind of hopeless sarcasm.

"Quite sure."

She slumped back in the chair with a shrug, as if she had suddenly become indifferent. "Very well. But if you care to see this... *purchase*, it will take quite some effort on your part."

Her mouth curled up in a humorless smile as he allowed his confusion to show. "You see," she explained, "you will have to leave with me immediately and be prepared to travel for a few days. The required sum will be much less, if we can take your carriage and move with haste. If you have a servant who knows the road to Holyhead, that would also be helpful."

"Holyhead," he echoed.

"Yes, in Anglesey. I'm quite sure you've heard of it."

Lady Helen Dehaven wasted no time or breath on explanations. Obviously, she trusted him to find the truth at the end of their road. In Holyhead, of all places. She sat expectantly, and he saw the mocking challenge in the upward tilt of her chin.

He pushed himself off the desk, propelled by a stronger curiosity than he could ever recall experiencing. "Let's go."

CHAPTER NINE

It was madness to start out in the dead of night, but he was loath to forfeit her wordless challenge when he'd dared to suggest they wait. She had not spoken since she'd come from changing her dress, except to inform Thomas, the sole Welshman among his staff, that a speedy route was of paramount importance before climbing into the carriage to fall silent.

She ignored him completely, which suited him well. It was more difficult to work up the proper scorn when she was dressed once more in her more usual modest, drab gown. He did not question his impulsiveness in agreeing to this. There were letters to be written and decisions to be made. He could ill afford a week rambling through the countryside. Yet here he was, flaunting all propriety in favor of being in Helen Dehaven's presence.

The decision to remain in Hereford had been a simple one, and filled with cowardice. It had seemed the easiest thing to do, in order to avoid the temptation Clara offered. Her letters might reach him here, but she could not. Every time he thought he'd managed to forget her, another letter would arrive bearing sentiments that stirred up the memory of their time together and reminders of her loveless marriage, tender appeals to his still vulnerable heart. He feared she had only to speak the word and he would be as helplessly in love with her – more deeply, even, than he had been when she unexpectedly married her duke.

Treacherous women. One sat before him, as fickle now as she had been in her youth, staring out the carriage window. He still didn't know whether he had truly stayed in Herefordshire in the hopes of avoiding Clara and London, or if it was because he'd only wanted the chance to see Helen's smile again. A foolish wish, it turned out, as he'd seen nothing but anxiety from the moment she'd appeared. He felt a strange sympathy with Henley. If ever he met the man, they might commiserate over the changeability of women in love. He had thought it bad enough to love Clara, to have her admit even now to loving him, though she belonged to another. But poor Henley most likely had it worse, to have Helen love him and go so far as to give herself completely, yet still refuse to marry. It must have driven the man mad.

Anyone who dared care about her would easily be driven mad, with her penchant for keeping everything within her a secret. It was that way sometimes, he had noticed it in a few others he'd known. They kept everything close, determined not to give the tiniest truth away, even when the telling of it presented no threat whatsoever. It had never mattered so much to him to force the truth out, until he met her.

He thought he was likely to fall asleep in the dark

silence. The swaying of the coach lulled him into a stupor that he tried to wipe away with some kind of useful conversation.

"Tell me, Lady Helen, what would you have done had I refused to help you?" he asked, hiding his intense interest in her answer by employing a tone of idle curiosity.

She looked mildly annoyed at the distraction. Apparently pitch black was fascinating to her. "I did not have another plan," she responded with a shrug.

"No other plan?" he echoed, raising his brows. "As desperate as you seem to be, and yet you gambled all on my willingness to aid you? I thought you more practical."

"Everything was at stake anyway. It was not such a gamble." She glanced toward him after a moment, studying his face briefly in the little moonlight that filtered in. "Oh, very well. I see you are not satisfied with that answer. I would have taken the horse as far along the road to London as possible before he dropped dead of exertion, then I would have begged or stolen a purse for coach fare, or else stolen a more robust mount to carry me. Failing that, I would have walked or crawled on my hands and knees until I reached my solicitor or Alex and debased myself however necessary. In short, sir, I would do anything. Does *that* satisfy you?" she asked testily.

"I suppose it must, though I can't imagine why you would not make your way to London in the first place."

"Because I have already told you," she said impatiently as she glared out the window. "There is no time."

"And haste is quite obviously more desirable than

any kind of honor," he returned.

"Honor," she all but sneered. It was amazing, to watch her well-bred manners fall away like this to reveal so much of what she felt. "May God preserve me from men and their notions of what is honorable and what is not. I see plainly that you and my brother are cut from the same cloth. But at least he would not have asked so much as you have."

He gave a disbelieving grunt at this. "I have asked only the truth." Something that he'd never had to demand before this, allowing time and trust and human nature to do the trick. It was the only thing at which he excelled, to take the measure of another and eventually, but always, learn the truth. "But I can see how preferable it is to you to sell yourself."

She did not say anything for a while, looking out the window as the darkness sped by. The scant moonlight outlined the curve of her cheek, the only corner of her he could see in the darkness. When finally she spoke, it was to ask him a question.

"How old are you, my lord?"

All the fight had gone out of her, and she sounded tired. Indeed, she must be exhausted after riding to his home and hours now in the carriage. "How old?" he asked, wondering if he'd heard her right, and if the sadness he heard in her was imagined.

"Yes. I would guess twenty-nine years, perhaps."

There was a kind of wistful melancholy in her voice. "Thirty-one, just barely," he replied.

"And in thirty-one years, have you never had one thing you would protect above all else, for which you'd forsake honor?"

He stared at the little bit of her that was illuminated, her eyelashes fanned out on her white cheek. The image of her pulling her scarf away in the firelight assailed him; the memory of her kiss pressed on his lips.

"Thirty-one years, and you think the truth is so easy to give away." She paused, then gave a slight huff of weary laughter. "But then, you do not ask me to give it. You buy it from me. My body is not enough of a prize. You are not satisfied unless you can have access to my very soul."

He felt the pull of her in the dark interior of the carriage. He knew without seeing it, the bitterness and sadness in her face, the lines of exhaustion around her eyes. "Is that where we go, Helen?" he asked quietly, not wishing to demand too much when she seemed like she might speak at last. "Is it your soul that lies at the end of our road?"

She did not move, did not even blink. "It is," she whispered, and there was such an anguish in her voice that he could not make himself push for more.

"How old are you, Helen?" he asked, though he was aware of her age. It was only something to say.

"Old." She leaned her forehead against the wall of the carriage, pressing her eyes shut. "As old as the earth. And quite as trod upon."

He did not inquire further. She sounded as if she might shatter with another word, a prospect he found unbearable. At the next stopping point, he got out and instructed the coachman to hire fresh horses, no matter the expense, so that they could travel quickly and without pause.

※

She followed the barmaid up the stairs to a small

room. At least the inn looked clean and comfortable, which set her mind at ease instantly. She felt Lord Summerdale's presence behind her, but for the first time since she'd gone to his home she was less afraid of him than she was of what awaited her here in Holyhead. Anything could have happened – Katie could be at death's door after such a rough crossing over the sea and confinement in a prison. But Maggie would be here, the serving girl had said so. That braced her for whatever else she might find.

In the room, Maggie was smoothing blankets over the little lump in the bed that could only be Katie. Helen felt a kind of unhinged elation to see proof at last of the child, even though there were only a few black curls lying across the coverlet to confirm Katie's presence.

"Maggie," she whispered, hearing the quaver in her voice. "Maggie, I've come."

The relief on Maggie's face when she looked up spoke volumes about what she must have been through since they'd said goodbye. She said nothing, only coming to Helen and embracing her warmly, holding her in her arms as Helen bit her lip and tried to stop the trembling that had begun inside her.

"There, and I knew you'd come," she said simply, the Irish lilt in her voice doing its best to reduce Helen to tears.

"Oh, you did, did you?" she asked with a shaky laugh. "I had no idea if I would manage to come or not. But I suppose you have the gift of seeing into the future, Maggie Conway?"

"No, that I don't. But I have the gift of seeing you as you are. It's only the devil himself could keep you from coming." She tilted her head back and gave

Helen's hair one last stroke with her hand before breaking away and glancing toward the door. "I hope it's not the devil you've had to pay to get here, though," she muttered.

Helen did not deign to look in Lord Summerdale's direction. Two nights and a full day in that carriage, filled with only silence while he looked at her as if she were a particularly fascinating insect. But he was the least important thing in the world to her right now. Later, when she needed his cursed money, she would take notice. For the moment, she walked quietly to the bedside, and Maggie followed.

"Cousin Janet's gone to fetch some water. The doctor promised he'd come back tonight, so you've come at the right time."

Helen looked down at the girl in the bed, still seeing no more than a pile of curls. She knelt down on the floorboards and leaned over, pulling the blanket slightly down so she could see Katie's face. The child was flushed, bright spots of pink on her cheeks, but she did not look feverish. She had strong features — straight dark brows set in a rectangular face, sharp cheekbones that jutted out becomingly, a square chin and perfectly straight nose. So this was Katie.

"Hullo," whispered Helen, stroking one soft curl away from a delicate pink ear, to pick it up and press her lips against it as she settled more comfortably on the floor. "Hello, Katie." And she laid her head against the bed, not far from the pillow, and tried not to think of lost things.

How long she stayed that way, she could not guess. When she looked up again, Lord Summerdale and Maggie were gone, and a woman who could only be Cousin Janet sat silently by the door. Helen met Janet's eyes, only to be rewarded with a shake of the head and a gesture toward the door.

"I won't let the child alone for long," she said stoutly once they stepped into the hall. "I only wanted to say that I'm sorry for the troubles. I've helped to look after the girl since she came to us, and it's a shame to me that I let such a thing happen. I've spoken with the owner here and he'll let me work for wages so I can make me way back to Ireland."

Helen's mouth nearly fell open at this speech. The woman had the air of a penitent servant. "But, Miss Janet..." She shook her head, hoping to clear some of the fuzziness. She had not slept, and her brain was slow to think. "There's no need, of course. You shall leave with Maggie on the next available ferry. Please don't worry yourself over money."

"Indeed, that is my task." Lord Summerdale stepped forward from where he'd been hiding in the shadows with Maggie. He glanced dismissively, though not unkindly, at Janet, and nodded at the closed door. "Stay with the child, if you please. I must speak with Lady Helen."

Janet wasted no time in obeying him, and Maggie hastened to follow. Helen caught her eye as she passed, and was given a miniscule shake of the head in response to her silent question. Maggie had not told Summerdale who Katie was. Thank heavens.

"Well, Lady Helen," he began as she turned to him with a sigh. "Maggie tells me the child is recovering and the next ferry is tomorrow noon. There is a bill waiting to be paid downstairs for tonight's lodging, fares to be bought, and I've no doubt the doctor will want to be paid for his visit tonight. There is no need to look at me so, I will pay them all and any other expenses that arise. But I am waiting."

She barely had the strength to summon any emotion other than a vague suspicion. "Waiting for what, my lord?"

"For an explanation, of course," he replied coldly. "That was our agreement."

"Was it? As I recall, I asked you for the necessary sum in exchange for allowing you to see what your money would buy. You see for yourself how your coin is put to use. I have no memory of offering you any explanations. You must judge for yourself and find meaning in my actions as you may."

Something about speaking to him made her feel stronger, even though she could see he was angry. She only raised her brows at him, knowing she had succeeded in frustrating him thoroughly. But she was tired, and short-tempered, and it was none of his affair.

He narrowed his eyes at her. "What would it cost me for an explanation?"

"That is not for sale, my lord."

He looked ready to press the matter, but before he could open his mouth, the doctor was at the top of the stairs. Helen went to the man immediately, waylaying him with questions about Katie as Lord Summerdale turned on his heel and left them in favor of the common room.

༺❀༻

Katie slept the night through, and half the morning. It would have worried Helen more, if it was a restless sleep, but the girl seemed perfectly peaceful.

After several wakeful nights filled with a racking cough and uneasy breathing, the doctor insisted that Katie only needed sleep to recover properly. Sleep and a warmer climate, he said, and since they could not change the climate they let her sleep on.

The barmaid offered to oversee Katie's breakfast while Helen went downstairs with Maggie to see her off again. Summerdale was nowhere in evidence, having left the inn last night for more luxurious lodgings. No doubt he resented waiting for instructions, but he had at least sent his servant to see to any needs they might have.

"The girl thinks you're a wonder of the world, you know, Helen," said Maggie. "They've told her about you over the years. It's a fairy godmother you are to her."

"I only hope I can live up to such a reputation." She watched Cousin Janet instruct the footmen in the matter of the baggage. "I do not know – I have never really known, how to do this without you."

"What, help to raise the child? I've no more experience at it than you."

"But you are so much more capable than me, Maggie, and so much stronger."

She gave a huff of indignation. "Helen Dehaven, you're the strongest person I ever knew or may lightning strike me down." Maggie shook her head, an impatient dismissal. "Now, the doctor says you can leave today without worry and if she's kept warm, it's just as well as staying here. She'll be traveling in style, she will, thanks to his lordship."

"He asked nothing but to come here and see for himself what was so important to me, you know," she told Maggie, as they had not spoken of it. "Strange man. Well, it's done no harm, I think, and now his carriage awaits you, Lady Maggie."

She swept a deep curtsy to Maggie, hoping to hide the wrenching sadness at having to say goodbye once again. Straightening up with a bright smile, she saw Maggie holding out a hand to her. "Shall I kiss it then, Queen Margaret?"

"Loyal subject, that's what you are," sniffed Maggie. "They'll say I put on airs when I get home."

The thought of Maggie at home, surrounded by people Helen had never known, sobered her mood. She took Maggie's hand.

"I've not said to you, Maggie, ever. I have never said–" She pressed her lips together. "You have been the greatest friend – and it's too small a word..." She gave it up and looked in her friend's eyes through a blur of tears.

Maggie looked as she always had: infinitely capable, manifestly good. Her face was filled with the same combination of practicality and compassion that Helen had last seen at another inn, as her newfound savior had wiped away ugly smears of blood from her legs.

The thought of it closed her throat up, and she reached for Maggie, hugging her tightly. Maggie only held her a moment, speaking softly in her ear. "I only did what was right. There is kindness in this world, Helen, and you should be believing in it, sometimes."

Those were the words Maggie left her with, not even adding a goodbye to this last bit of wisdom, a parting gift to her friend.

They left for Herefordshire that afternoon, Helen taking great pains to see the child comfortably settled. He'd watched her speaking with the driver, witnessing for the first time the extraordinary charm she exerted when she wished to ingratiate herself. She had a way of giving orders while at the same time deferring authority to the servants. They were perfectly pleased at the same high-handed manner that grated on Stephen. Then again, she had done nothing to make him feel the equal even of his own footman, dictating what she needed and when she needed it, making no pretense that he was in any way valued above his service to her needs.

He climbed into the carriage after her, handing her the cloak he'd been compelled to buy for the child. Helen looked at it for a moment, but did not comment on the richness of it, wrapping it around the girl without touching the thick fur lining. The little one stared out the window with wide eyes for the first hour of the journey, asking Helen occasionally about things they saw along the road and darting shy looks at Stephen before she settled back and dropped off to sleep. She looked quite well, only a slight darkness around her eyes indicating that she had been ill.

He had no idea what to make of it. Everything in the way Helen acted toward the child... She had begged and pleaded, debased herself for this little urchin, but it was obviously the first time they'd ever met. She fought like a lion for the girl, and it was clear that nothing on this earth was more precious to her. She *must* be the girl's mother, it was the only answer to the riddle. But why would she have refused Henley, if she loved him so much and had been pregnant as well? And why on earth have the child in England, send it off to Ireland, and bring her back now? He didn't even think the girl knew Helen was her mother – she addressed her as "miss", but there was awe in her eyes when she caught sight of Helen. Exactly as one might expect from a child upon meeting its mother for the first time.

It gave him a raging headache to think of it, and he understood quite well that she would not solve the puzzle for him. Nor would she answer any questions about the child, he knew, unless he could corner her alone, and probably not even then.

There was less disgust in him than he would have expected. Very well, she'd had a bastard and hidden it from the world. What he found unconscionable was that she would hide the truth of it from a daughter she obviously adored, and that she would continue to refuse her brother's financial support when this child depended on her.

She sat now with her arms around the child, leaning back in a corner opposite him with the girl resting against her. Such a maternal pose.

"What was your own mother like, Lady Helen?" he asked, searching for a roundabout way to force her to impart some information.

She looked up from her deep contemplation of the sleeping child, her hand flexing protectively on the little back as though to shield it from some danger. She had obviously been deep in a troubled thought and had not heard him, tensing when he spoke. She looked at him as wildly as she had after he had kissed her, a fear such as he'd never seen directed at him as she spread her hands over the child's back.

"I... my mother?" she asked, the fear dissolving in the moment she met his gaze.

"Yes," he continued, ignoring the strangeness of her mood. "I think she must have been quite a forceful character, if your own bullying is anything to judge by."

"A bully? You think I bully her?" She turned her eyes back to the bundle at her side with a frown of concern.

"No, not the child. I rather meant myself, and that doctor at the inn. You are adept at giving orders, you know," he informed her ruefully. "I thought your competence in such matters might have been inherited."

A slow curve of her lips revealed her amusement, transfixing him with the soft pliability of her mouth. "Not quite inherited, no. My mother had little to do with me, as a rule. If you find me at all dictatorial, the blame must be laid at the feet of a series of stern governesses. And Maggie's example, too."

"Your parents..." He hesitated, but she seemed to speak of them quite easily. "They died when you were quite young, did they not?"

"When I was fourteen. I did not know them well. My father was ill for some months, and my mother attended his sickbed but did not wish me there. In the end, she died before him, an accident. She was with child, and she took a fall down the stairs." She spoke as if in a trance. She had probably not slept much, which accounted for her sudden willingness to confide in him. "My mother died after the baby was stillborn. It was...very bloody. I detest blood. My father died not two weeks later. There was nothing for him after my mother died. Alex and I were..." She shrugged with nonchalance. "We were not enough. We were always excluded from the little world they'd made together. We distracted them from their grand romance, and there is no greater sin to two people so in love."

"It sounds a lonely childhood," he observed, hoping her mood would last. He tried not to think of her own grand romance with Henley, but failed.

"I had Alex, though. We made our own little world to counter theirs. But ours was a child's world, with games to play and tricks on each other. He had a fondness for putting toads in my bed," she smiled. Her face lost the glow of reminiscence and became sad as she said, "We looked after each other, once."

Like Edward and me, but for entirely different reasons. He felt a sudden wave of loneliness, seeing her arm around the child as she spoke of her beloved brother. Even in her downfall and banishment, she had more than he'd ever had.

No one. He had no one at all in his life, a fact he'd always avoided admitting fully to himself until now. His brother, a cautious ally in the wars of their family throughout their childhood, had become his friend as an adult, only to die too young. Clara was the only other person to teach him anything of love, how to open himself to another, to feel as if his life were more than a desert wasteland. And she was gone from him.

He wanted to ask Helen if she understood her own good fortune. She had her villagers, her tight circle of friends, this lovely frail daughter. She could never know what it meant to be utterly alone, with no one to turn to, or the fathomless depths of loneliness that could rise up in the dark of a carriage containing a woman and child who were no part of him.

He had not realized the depths of it himself, until

she had let him into her life, and then turned him out into the cold again.

"And you, my lord? Shall we exchange life stories in the absence of other entertainment? Tell me what your family is like."

He contemplated telling her about the endless mockery of his mother, his father's criticism, how they played their children off one another. How his skin was never quite thick enough to resist being pricked by their barbs. How he was a disappointing bore to them all.

"I had a brother once, too," he surprised himself by saying. "He died not long ago. He was..." He shook his head lightly. "My father died earlier this year. I have two younger sisters. I'm sorry, it reads more like a laundry list than a family. What of the girl? Katie is her name? Does she have siblings?"

That seemed to have disarmed her. Her eyes became unfocused and she tightened her grip on the child again, turning to look at the mountains in the distance.

"No, she doesn't."

She fell silent until evening came, when they stopped at an inn. Even then, she only thanked the coachman for keeping to a smooth road before she bundled her charge up to the private rooms Stephen procured for her. He went to his own room, leaving her to her child, remembering the smile that touched her lips, and how they had moved beneath his, feeling the sting of isolation as acutely as a starving man shut out from a feast.

In the late morning of the third day, they arrived in her sleepy village. They had spoken little on the journey, the girl consuming her attention even though she slept most of the time. Helen said that the girl did not sleep the nights well because of the coughing, and often as the child slept on the ride she woke up sweating, becoming slightly feverish.

He watched Helen grow more concerned over the days of their journey, sleeping in the coach next to the child. It was a sight that he had grown to both love and envy at once. But she virtually ignored him, polite to the point of indifference. He supposed she was filled with thoughts of her former lover, the child's father, whom she had so impetuously turned from. If Henley was the father. If Helen was the mother. Unlikely as it might seem, he could not deny that she acted the mother and that there was no alternative explanation.

She directed the carriage to the blacksmith's house instead of her own. He descended after her and watched in amazement as she settled the child in with the family, in a cozy little room. She acted as if he were not there at all, which incensed him. He would talk to her. The need for answers grew increasingly more urgent as he understood she meant the child to stay here, and not with her.

Stephen waited impatiently for a moment when he could speak to Helen alone. When at last he realized that an opportunity would not present itself, he walked over to her and commanded her attention through the simple expedient of remaining by her side and staring silently. She could not ignore him for long, and at last she excused herself and followed him out of the house.

"Well?" she demanded impatiently. "What is it? You are quite welcome to leave, my lord. You have given what you promised and I will disturb you no more."

"It has gone far past the point where you can dismiss me from this business at your whim," he bit out, infuriated that this was to be all between them, that she would allow nothing else.

"You have made it clear that you will not explain the child to me, but you don't have to. What I should like to know, Helen, is how you can have such a fondness for the girl and yet continue to lie to her."

Her brows drew together in outraged confusion. "What are you talking about? How have I lied to her?"

He reached out and grasped her wrist, jerking her closer to him so that he would not need to shout. She resisted, twisting her arm to be released, but he would not let go. He clenched his teeth and hissed in a furious whisper.

"You allow her to be raised by others, and when you bring her to you, it's so that others will care for her once more. She has no idea, does she?" he demanded. "I suppose you intend to be a friend to her, but you do her ill to conceal the truth and deny whatever support your brother may give."

She stilled, shock coming into her face. "You think she's mine, don't you?" She stared at him a moment, then her lips gave a faint twitch of amusement. "I should have guessed it, but I thought you more astute than that."

"You give me no other explanation, so I am forced to come to my own conclusions." Her mockery of him and denial of her relationship to the child made him grip her wrist harder, when what he really wanted was to shake her until she was forced to acknowledge that he had some part in her life. "Maggie told me the girl is six years old. It's rather too much of a coincidence, don't you agree? And you loved Henley. What I cannot understand is why you would have the child here and then sent away to Ireland, if you cared for her and her father so much."

She stared at him blankly. She gave one tiny shake of her head in denial, but he would have none of it. Her secrets drove him mad, to the point of desperation. He must have the truth, and in the next moment he asked the questions that had been haunting him for days.

"Does Henley know? You keep contact with him?" He bit down hard on what he really wanted to know – if they were still lovers; if ever they contrived to meet. He told himself he was outraged, but still could not shake the feeling that it was jealousy – sharp, mortifying, uncivilized jealousy – that surged inside him and forced the questions out.

Her look was cold, her voice scathing. "You are a fool. Leave us now."

"I shall go nowhere, madame, until I learn the truth."

He did not pull her closer, but she did not pull away. They were locked in this pose, glaring at one another, when the blacksmith came upon them and summoned her inside quickly, the urgency and fear in his voice breaking through to them.

Helen swept into the house the moment he released her. He could not leave her, would not, uncaring that she wished him gone. In the bright little room, the child sat up in the bed with a cloth pressed to her mouth as she coughed. It was a desperate sound, too loud and violent to come from so small a child. The noise of it made it easy to understand the fear in the blacksmith's face. Helen stroked the girl's forehead until she calmed again. It took a very long time and when it was over, it was plain that the girl was feverish.

Helen looked to the smith who stood waiting, and gave a nod which sent the man off at a run. He must have gone for the doctor. Helen stayed sitting, her hand on the child's forehead, looking utterly defeated. He thought she must have feared this, and that now she feared even worse.

"Miss Helen," said the girl with a shy eagerness, her eyes bright with the fever. "I wanted to ask you something before you go. May I?"

Helen's helpless gaze reached across the room to him, her hand crushing the handkerchief she held. She looked bewildered, as though she could not imagine that she must answer. But after a moment she turned back to the girl, her face relaxing into a kind of dazed acceptance.

"You may ask me anything you like."

Stephen considered leaving, but could not bring himself to break away from the scene. He felt his breath come short in anticipation. The truth was coming. He recognized it, smelled it seeping into the air like smoke from under a door.

"They told me you knew my mother and father." She stopped speaking at the emotion that flashed briefly across Helen's face.

"You would like to know about them," Helen said, regaining her calm. "Turn away a bit, so I can pull your hair back. There. I only met them the once, the day they died. The day we found you. I can't tell you much."

The child's fingers plucked at the blanket covering her legs. "Oh. Then they really are dead, miss?"

Helen stared at the child's head, smoothing her hair in a mechanical gesture. "Yes. You may call me Helen, if you like. I saw them when... Your father had hair like yours, black and curly. Not a big man. He had a kind face." Her voice was dream-like, the words floating through the room like feathers in the wind.

"And my mother?"

"Black hair, too, but straight. And blue eyes. Pretty hands. Your face is like hers, strong-featured."

He was intruding. He knew this conversation was private and none of his affair. But he knew equally well that Helen Dehaven was at last telling the unadulterated truth about some piece of her past. He recognized it immediately, the shame of misjudging her smothering him, immobilizing his limbs.

"I'm sorry, I never saw her face," she was saying now, in a voice that trembled. "Or knew her name."

As if to distract herself, Helen brought out a packet from beneath her cloak, carefully unfolding a square of cloth to reveal brightly colored ribbons. They were neatly pressed, as if they had been prepared far in advance of this moment. Seeing them, the girl's flushed face lit in delight. "They're so pretty!"

He watched Helen and felt something inside of him give way, break loose and attach itself to her as tears began to fall from her eyes. She hid it well from Katie, whose back was to her. She reached around to where the child held the ribbons, taking up a green one and gathering black curls in her hand.

"You've been so good to me, both of you," said Katie, looking skittishly at Stephen as he schooled his features to show nothing. "You bought me the nice cloak and everything else. I never had such nice things before." She held the ribbons up. "I hope they didn't cost too much," she said sleepily.

A spasm of grief crossed Helen's face, a quick creasing of her features as her tears slipped silently down.

"They came quite dear. But the expense does not signify. I bought them long ago." She managed to hide the sound of her tears as she spoke, tying the ribbon around the girl's hair and biting her lips together as she laid a hand on Katie's head. Her whisper caught at him as he slipped out of the room, and she unmistakably spoke to herself as much as the child.

"Never again think of the cost. It does not matter now. Not anymore."

CHAPTER TEN

Whitemarsh,

I write to you briefly and deliver an unequivocal message: Have no dealings with Henley, in business or otherwise. I ask you to trust me in this judgment, without giving you cause to do so. I can only hope that my reputation speaks to the worth of this advice.

In the matter of your sister I leave all judgment to you. I have come to know her better, but I find myself reluctant to speak to the terms of your reconciliation, if indeed you should wish such a thing. If you care to find her, she can be found and I will venture to say that she may well like for her brother to find her. I will say no more on the topic.

As for myself, I will not treat with Henley on any matter. I hope that we may continue as partners in business dealings and together keep the enterprise viable, but if you choose to associate with him I must regrettably retract my backing of the shipping venture. If I have in any way offended you with these words, accept my sincere apologies.

My regards to Lady Whitemarsh.
Summerdale

He hired a doctor, the best he could find, sending the man off to Bartle to see to the child and asking for daily reports of her progress, if there was any. The path from his manor to her house was worn down with the passing of messengers and the hooves of his own mount. He visited every other day, to see if anything was needed.

He supplied whatever was called for, without being asked. On his first visit, he brought a new cloak for Helen to replace the ragged one she wore. When she looked about to protest, he told her it was ridiculous to care for the child but not for the caretaker – it was getting colder every day, after all – and she seemed too tired to argue it. He brought a book each time he called, something that would amuse a child, or so he hoped, and sat back to listen as Helen read by the bedside. Always looking around him for anything missing, anything at all he could provide, not knowing if he did it for Helen, or for Katie, or for his own conscience which still smarted with guilt over his accusations against her.

"If the child is to recover properly," said the doctor, "she must remove to a warmer clime. I do not hold out hope that her lungs will ever be strong."

So Stephen spoke to Jack, the blacksmith who already considered the girl his own. It had become evident that he and his wife had anticipated Katie's coming for so long that they already felt for her as much as any natural parents might.

"I've a cousin in Sussex, a place called Eastbourne," said Jack. He looked toward his wife, who had joined them in the little kitchen while Helen sat with the girl. "Like a brother to me, when we were boys. He says to me the sun shines all the time there, and the doctor says the sea air will do her good."

Stephen nodded. "You are assured will find a welcome with your relations there?" If not, there was the Gildredge family, who owned half the land around Eastbourne. They would give whatever modest help might be needed for the family to establish themselves, if he put it in their minds to do so.

Jack was sure they would find a place with his cousin. "But," he said, with a look at his wife, "He's had the idea in his mind for a time now, to make his way to America. And I'm thinking it may be even better for her there, when she's strong enough to make the trip."

This became the new, carefully introduced topic of much discussion over the next week. The doctor endorsed the move to Eastbourne and thought it advisable, if the girl was stronger after some months there, to consider a move to the Carolinas. It was a strange and sudden turn for them all, especially for a child who had only lately left Ireland, and he said as much to Jack.

"It's in her blood, as I understand," was his mysterious rejoinder. But though Stephen questioned him, he would say no more about it. He pled ignorance, his face closing up in that way all the villagers had with outsiders. Stephen was still an outsider and always would be, he knew.

When moments later, Helen came into the kitchen and heard of this proposal, she fell utterly silent. When asked what she thought, she did not respond. Jack listed the undeniable advantages to the girl's health, and she only stared at the hearth and nodded faintly. It was only after the mention of emigration to America that she looked up at last. She seemed as bewildered as a child.

"She won't be here. With me. She won't..." Her voice trailed off as though she had not more breath to speak. Then her eyes focused on Jack and she spoke in a voice that seemed to Stephen to throb with suppressed resentment and grief. "She will be with you. Away from me. It will be better for her."

Jack looked unsure of how to respond. He looked to Stephen, then back at her, and just as he opened his mouth to speak, she turned and walked with a purpose back to Katie's room. Everything in her manner seemed to indicate that she would not speak of it with them.

At first the idea of their leaving seemed only to be a kind of theoretical musing. But after the child's fever broke and she began to recover, it became more real. They began to talk about going immediately, to enjoy a milder winter in the south. Helen let them talk, and never participated in the conversation, as though she put all consideration of it into their hands. So Stephen took it in hand entirely. He wrote to acquaintances in London to make discreet inquiries into the most promising places to emigrate in America, where the weather was warm and the prospects good. He spoke with the doctor and with Jack, and he made all the necessary arrangements as they were needed.

And all the while, he watched Helen pretend as though it was not breaking her heart. She smiled as Katie grew stronger, and happily told the girl about the adventures to be had in places so exciting as

Eastbourne.

"How lucky I shall be," she said one day when Katie was strong enough to take a walk down the lane, "if I should have a friend in America. You must learn your lessons well, so that you can write pages and pages to me, all about everything you will see and do there."

The girl chattered happily in response, roses blooming in her cheeks, unaware of the emotion that was so plain to Stephen. Such a sadness came from Helen that he could not bear to look at her, sure as he was that she might burst into tears at the thought that she would never see the girl again. He looked instead to Marie-Anne, who walked alongside and quietly slipped her hand into her friend's hand, and who looked almost as forlorn.

When he came to visit, it was to Helen's house that he rode. She always met him at the door, and they walked together to see Katie, who now breathed so well and ate so heartily that the decision was made to leave at once, before winter set in. The date was set and Jack and Sally prepared to pack up their home. They were anxious with the hastiness of it and fretted that Katie would not do well on the journey, but it was Helen for whom Stephen worried.

She barely spoke anymore, except to Katie. She seemed to become more frail and distant with each passing day. He thought that she was only waiting for the little family to leave Bartle, and then he could not imagine what she might do except to fall into a thousand pieces. Even the doctor noticed it, as Stephen discovered when he took the man aside one day and noted her pallor.

"Melancholy," the doctor said, after some

hesitation over whether he should even speak of it, as he had not been engaged to care for Helen. "Without examining her, I cannot say with any real certainty. But if it is as you say and this is not her usual disposition, then I daresay you can expect her spirits to improve with sufficient sleep and adequate nourishment. See that she rests, and eats more, or else it will grow into a chronic condition, my lord."

So he watched her. He came to visit even when he knew there was no more for him to do once he had arranged the most comfortable and swift transportation to Eastbourne, once the doctor had declared Katie fit for travel. But still he came to see Helen, to assure himself that her spirits were not even more downcast.

On the day before Katie and her new family were to depart, Helen did not answer his knock. He turned back to the road but heard a dull thud that carried through the crisp air, a sound he followed to its source.

He found her behind the house, a veritable forest of arrows at her feet where she had worked the tips into the earth. As he watched, she jerked one from the ground and notched it, pulling back the bowstring violently and letting go with a soft grunt. Even from this distance, he could see the target was nothing more than a battered piece of wood now. Helen shot arrows as if possessed, yanking them from the ground and letting fly with barely a glance at the target. But she never missed her shot.

As he watched, she ran out of arrows and stalked over to the target, pulling the shafts free with a savage twist of her arm. When she turned back to begin the whole process over again, she saw him.

Gone was the sadness that had seeped from her for so long, replaced with a fury. Her anger had always been, in the few times he'd felt it, a cold and controlled scorn. But now she seemed in a rage, and his presence served as a focus for it. She glared at him almost menacingly, half-running toward him and stopping a few paces away.

"Well, my lord? Why have you come?" Her voice was low, filled with a sullen accusation. "To announce you have found a place for them in Abyssinia, no doubt."

Her pale face showed exhaustion, her body rigid with tension. It caused a wave of affection to spring up in him, to see her so unhappy. Her anger was a thing he welcomed, relieved at last to see that she would show something of the truth of her feelings. But he could also see beneath it, to what caused it, and could not help himself. He raised a hand to her forehead.

"I come to see that you are well, Helen. To see if this furrow in your brow has become permanent." He stroked the lines on her forehead with the back of his hand, gratified to see the tension ease a bit.

It only lasted a heartbeat before she pulled back from him, jerking away from his touch as though it burned.

"Don't. I cannot bear your kindness." She looked down, gathering her hands into tight fists at her side, recovering her anger after that instant of vulnerability. He could almost hear her reminding herself to hate and distrust him. "You come here to see me weep. To see me broken, so that you may enjoy the sight of it."

He did not bother to defend himself against this accusation, but only stood where he was, waiting for more. He remembered, vividly, how he had longed to shout like this when his brother lay dying. There had been no one there to shout at when he realized how great his loss would be, and that was the worst part of it all. If he could be here for her in this, perhaps he could make himself something other than just a means to an end. Perhaps she might allow him to become her friend once more, a more permanent part of her world.

His stillness only seemed to infuriate her. She stepped closer and pushed at his shoulders, nearly knocking him down with the force of her feeling.

"Don't you see?" she cried. "It is all for nothing! All the time and expense and the planning – for years, do you understand? It was all for her, but it was for *me*, too. It was for *me*. That I might have something for myself. I am that selfish."

She whirled away from him, showing him her back. "Nothing I can do will make it what I thought it would be. Not even you, not even the Earl of Summerdale. Everything you know, and how you know it – they say you know everything that happens, ever. But the best it can give her is a life far from here. Far from *me*." Her voice grew harsh, hoarse with emotion. "And she should be far from me, I know it. She will have a family, she will be safe. But I can only think how it was all meant to be different, how hard I worked for a future I will never see. You cannot imagine how much I hate myself for thinking it."

The bitterness in her voice cut at him, so many words after so long a silence. It made him picture the future she had thought to build for herself, tucked away in this quiet village where she might have something like a family again. How much she must have needed the comfort and the promise of it, and now she must watch that promise ride away from her forever.

"You must not hate yourself when it is only natural to feel such a loss keenly."

She turned back, her anger swinging back to him. "Leave me. Why are you still here? They will be gone and there will be no more need for you to come here. You will go soon anyway, so go *now*."

"I will not leave you, Helen," he said calmly into her anger, knowing he was powerless to help her. He could only stay with her, which was the only thing he'd wanted to do from the moment he had first seen her.

"Puppet of the gods," she said suddenly. "Like Helen of Troy. Hah! How appropriate! No choice and no control over *anything!*" She turned her face up to the sky as though to make the gods hear her.

She came to him, shoving at him again. "Go! I am useless, don't you see? I was useless then and I am useless now and so are you, so just go. Go, go, *go!*" she cried, with a shove to his chest with each repetition.

He did nothing but watch her silently as she continued pushing at him until the movement gradually lost force, her anger spending itself. Finally she let her hands drop and made a despairing sound. "I was going to feed her little cakes," she said with a hollow laugh, looking as though she would mock herself if only she were not so close to tears.

He lifted his hands to her shoulders, pulling her unresistingly forward until her head was beneath his chin. She trembled there. He felt it like an ache.

"I will be no one," came her whisper. "I will be

nothing."

He turned his head down, closing his eyes to better smell the sweetness of her hair, willing her pain away. He pressed his face against her hair, rocking her gently and spoke softly.

"You are everything," he breathed, and did not know if she heard him above her own quiet sob.

※

He did not come to see the little family off on their journey. He bade them farewell the day before their departure, knowing that Marie-Anne would be next to Helen as they said their goodbyes to the girl. He knew it was cowardice that kept him away from the scene, a fear that they would not want him there.

It was perhaps a groundless fear, he found, as he happened upon Marie-Anne outside the bakeshop in Bartle a day later. He had debated all afternoon whether he should visit Helen, only to find himself lingering in the village on the cusp of nightfall. In his uncertainty, it had grown too late to call on her. But her friend had a warm greeting at the ready.

"Is it usual for the ovens to be fired so late in the day?" he asked, noticing the steam that rose from the little basket of buns she held. There seemed to be quite a variety.

She tucked a cloth over them and let her hand linger over the warmth as she answered.

"Not usual, no, but Mr. Higgins is very accommodating," she said with a glance toward the bakeshop. The baker was closing his door for the evening, nodding to her and giving her a look that seemed to say a lot more than a simple good evening.

"Is he indeed?" Stephen felt himself fighting against the first smile in days. "I suspect he is most accommodating when *you* wish him to be."

The arch look she gave him made it even harder not to smile.

"We each of us use the advantages we have, my lord." She gave him an irresistible smile, her eyes sparkling with mischief. "I may not have wealth and title, but I am not altogether powerless to help my friends, I find."

"Ah," he observed. "The basket is for a friend, then."

"It is for Hélène," she said, and her face grew serious. "I hope to tempt her to eat."

He held out his arm and offered to escort her to her home, which she graciously accepted. When she said no more about Helen, he decided to be straightforward with his concerns. "Do you think she makes herself ill in her distress?"

"She is heartsick, my lord," she answered with some reserve.

"As you are, I am sure."

"Yes, but it is different for me. We are very different, she and I, though we are the dearest of friends." She frowned a little. "I am satisfied here, in this little village with my little life. I am happy with my memories. To bring Katie here was charity and a pleasant amusement for me. But it was much more than that for Hélène."

He struggled to understand her meaning. "What was it, then?"

She stopped walking and looked up at him. Her face was so very thoughtful, considering him, that he began to worry what she might say, what judgment she might be about to deliver. With the air of having made a decision, she let go his arm.

"Perhaps you will ask her." She held out the little basket of bread to him. "Perhaps she will tell you."

"Now?" He found himself holding the basket, caught between protesting the impropriety and fulfilling his wish to see her.

Marie-Anne only looked at him, drawing all his attention to her in her gravity. "Go to her, my lord. Give her bread, and let her speak. I think you may learn many things you have not understood."

She turned and began to walk away in the failing light, and stopped when he spoke.

"But she was angry." He felt like an awkward boy, standing with a basket of bread and his heart in his mouth while the perfectly poised Frenchwoman looked patiently at him. "When I last saw her, it made her... angry, to see me. I would not wish to add to her distress."

"I hope I know what is best for my friend," she declared, clearly in no doubt at all about what was best. "For *our* friend." She tugged on her gloves a little and pulled her thick shawl tight around her shoulders.

He stared down at the napkin that covered the bread, hesitating. The word rolled about in his mind: *friend*. It seemed possible, if only he knew what he might do for her.

But Marie-Anne de Vauteuil knew, and repeated it for him. "Go to her now. Give her bread. Let her speak. I am not mistaken in you."

She left, the darkness gathering around him as he wondered in what way she was not mistaken.

She waited upstairs in her bedroom, the house empty all around her. She knew he would come eventually. He always came, and she only had to wait.

It was morbid, she knew, and childish, to let it affect her this way. There would be a happy ending for Katie, after that terrible beginning, and that should be enough. But there was that spoiled child within Helen, the stupid, silly girl who she thought she'd stamped out, who would not be satisfied. What was it for, what had that suffering been *for* if she could not say that at least it gave her this one good thing?

And what would she tell herself now, when the memories came? There was no more promise. There were no more visions of a rosy future to pull her out of the terrible past. She would wake from nightmares the rest of her life, and would no longer be able to calm herself with the vision of a happily growing girl. A girl who would be safe. A girl who would grow up and have an ordinary life, with ordinary pleasures and sorrows.

It would still happen, of course. Katie would have those things. But Helen would not be part of them. She would never see it.

She stared at the empty hearth and heard his knocking at the door, his voice calling. The unseasonable storm that had threatened all day would break loose and soak him if she did not open her door to him, but she did not move from the spot. Let him come all the way. Let him find her in her hiding place, as he always had. She was too tired to meet him halfway.

His boots sounded on the stairs. Another minute

and he stopped in front of her bedroom, searching into the gloom to see her where she huddled on the floor, wearing only her nightgown covered by the thick cloak he'd given her.

"Helen," he said. The warmth of his voice was like a sliver of life, but she resisted it even as he came to stand above her. He stooped down and she kept her eyes forward, refusing to meet his gaze.

He went around the room lighting the lamps by the bed and above the mantel, scowling down at the empty fireplace. He built a fire quickly, stoking the flames high until she could feel the warmth from where she sat on the cold floor. Within minutes the room was warm and welcoming, a refuge from the thunderstorm that had broken loose outside. He had gotten wet in the rain, she saw. Drops glistened on his hair and soaked his shirt. His coat, lying across the chair by the door, dripped water into a pool on the floor.

She let him urge her to her feet, off the cold floor, until she sat at the foot of the bed in front of the fire. He pulled a chair forward to sit in front of her, holding out a basket of buns that smelled like heaven. It nearly brought her to tears, that smell.

"Eat," he said, and she took one.

He must have taken care to keep it dry, in this rain. That thought, and the freshness of the bread in her mouth, brought a lump to her throat. She made herself swallow past it again and again, until it was finished and she took another from his outstretched hand. Halfway through the second bun, she thought how there should be tea and she should be properly dressed. They should not be sitting in her bedroom, with her in her stocking feet. But all that seemed too much to care about.

"I would have brought the doctor to you, if you refused to eat. Are you comfortable? Warm enough?" he asked.

Her bones were like ice inside her, and she thought she might never truly feel warm again. But he accepted the nod she gave, and they both fell silent, staring into the flames and listening to the thunder that crashed and rumbled outside

She felt stronger, now that he was here, his quiet strength close enough to touch, never demanding speech but somehow always making her feel that she could say anything at all. She wondered if she could tell him how she had held the promise of Katie like a talisman to her heart. She wondered what he would say if she told him that sometimes the memories came on her in such a way that she was frenzied, panicked, living in the awful moment again – and that she was only made sane again by assuring herself that Katie would be here. He would think her mad, and she wondered if that was worse than being thought a whore. She found that she didn't really care anymore, if she was mad, or a whore. Nothing mattered anymore, except that he had come to her. Against all propriety and though she had shouted at him and wept, he came to her.

It struck her finally that he didn't know anything, that she had concealed all the truth that she could from him. He had helped care for Katie, never knowing who she really was. He gave her comfort now, never knowing what grieved her most.

All her reasons for concealment no longer mattered to her. It was all protection that was not needed, she could see now. And so she suddenly wanted to tell him, to make him understand, but didn't know how to begin. She had never known. Even the thought of speaking of it acted like a fist around her throat, squeezing off every word she thought to say. It all swirled around her, inside her head, confusing her into a state where she could only feel the anger and shock and fear all over again.

It always happened like that. What was unreasonable was that she had expected it to be any different this time. She stared dumbfounded into the fire, staying silent until words burst forth from her.

"I told you once that I had no regrets."

He looked up at her sharply, a wary expression coming over his features. It was obvious that he had not expected this, had not come here expecting to hear about her past or her regrets. She looked away, her eyes roaming restlessly around the room. She could not look at him, not if she was to tell him anything.

"I lied," she continued. "I have nothing but regrets. A whole life filled with them." She felt the pressure begin in her chest, crushing the breath from her lungs. "I hate him." Her voice came out thin, barely a whisper. "He killed them."

She sensed the change in him, his whole body going still as if poised for something, attentive.

"Who?"

"Katie, her family," she said, already faltering. "He had to kill them all, and I was too late." It was wrong. She was telling it all wrong again, like always. But she could only take the words as they came, tangled up in her breath, never sounding real. "If I could keep her safe, I thought – I told myself it would be worth it. If it gave me Katie."

She should stop. She was not making sense. But she couldn't shake the mood, the need to tell him. He was trying to catch her eye, but she could only look at him in a glancing pass of her gaze.

"Who killed them, Helen?" He said it patiently, sensibly. As if she were not trembling and incoherent.

She pushed past the constriction in her chest, the force that clamped her lips shut and stole her words. "Him. I hate him...the...Henley."

She watched his face go blank, and spoke immediately, not choosing her words but saying anything, anything at all, to forestall the denial he was sure to make.

"It's simple. It's a simple story. I went to the woods. To see him. To kiss him." She swallowed past the lump of nausea that rose up. "I loved him. I was so stupid. And they... Oh God, I *loved* him. And he was dead already, on the ground." Her voice was so thin that she could barely hear herself. "The man was, I mean. And then the pistol – the woman. She was holding the little girl. Katie's sister, but I never knew her name. And he shot them, through both of them and..."

Her mouth dried up, and she searched his face. She knew she must look wild, must sound mad, her eyes skittering continually across his face, panting as though she had been struck a blow to the stomach. But he did not look confused at anything she said. He looked appalled, horrified.

"You saw this? You saw him kill her family, is that what you're saying?" he asked, as if he could not believe he'd heard her correctly. She nodded at him, staring, as a realization slowly came to her.

"Alex," she said, more strongly. "He didn't – he

never told you? What I told him, he never—"

A sharp and violent shake of his head cut her off. He stood abruptly, sending the chair scraping back, turning to pace the floor in front of her.

"He said it did not bear repeating. He said you were incoherent!" His open fist slapped against the wall, startling her. But he checked himself suddenly, visibly, and turned back to her. She felt rather than saw him studying her, controlling his sudden burst of anger. "But you... it is not easy for you to tell. Do you know why he would do it?"

She shrugged helplessly. "He had drunk much. I think. They were on his land." It made her remember his face then, in that moment when she had found him, startled by the sound of shots. With a horrified little laugh she said, "He had a new pistol. He wanted to test it. I think."

"Did you go to the authorities?"

"*He* is the authority there. Anyone else of any power over him is his friend," she said, and knew he would understand how a peer could be so protected by his station. "And no one cares if a few Travelers are murdered in Ireland. Who cares for gypsies, anywhere? No one. Except Maggie, and me."

He stood by the wall for a long time, saying nothing as the storm outside grew louder. She waited, bracing himself for more questions that she would be unable to answer with any sense. But he did not. He only stayed silent and pensive for the longest time until he finally came to sit next to her on the bed, not touching her, looking into the fire. It seemed impossible that he had not known the story of that day. Or the story of the day after it. But she refused to think of that, pushing it out of her mind, knowing she would break into a thousand babbling pieces if she attempted to tell that part of it, too.

"And so you refused to marry him, and took care of Katie."

She gave a nod, and now it hurt a little less to think of Katie, happy and safe and far away with a new family.

"Do you..." she trailed off, looking at how the firelight played on his face. "Do you believe me?" He could not believe her. It was unbelievable.

His face turned quickly to hers, a line between his brows showing confusion. "Of course I believe you. How could I not?" he asked almost angrily.

He believed her. Her mind could not comprehend it, that he would understand it so quickly, in so few muddled words, and know it as truth. She shook her head slightly, relief flooding through her.

"Alex didn't believe me." She gritted her teeth, refusing to cry. "And I lost him, too. And then Maggie, and now Katie. I am alone," she said, hating the self-pity that she could not hide. "I have nothing left, can't you see? He ruined me, in every way. An empty house and years alone. He took everything from me."

She felt his hand on her face, caressing her cheek, pushing the hair behind her ear before falling away to clasp her trembling fingers. Oh, God. He believed her.

"Your brother is a fool. Henley cannot hurt you anymore."

He said it like he said everything, with such simple confidence. She reached up to him, putting her hands on his head, sliding them down to hold his face. She leaned into him, letting her forehead fall against his.

She wanted him there, wanted him closer, loving him for not asking her more.

He believed her, and he was here. She was not alone.

"Don't leave," she whispered.

All at once she was angry at being afraid, defiant in the face of this fear that had gripped at her heart for years. Not allowing herself time to think of what she did, she pressed her lips to his, twining her fingers in his hair to hold him tightly against her mouth.

He didn't move, didn't return the kiss. She felt the shock in him, in his quick intake of breath, the way his hands came up to her shoulders to push her slightly away. But she resisted it, denied him escape by holding him to her. She reached out to the loneliness she had felt in him, moving her lips across his until he gave a short groan and opened his mouth to her, pulling him to her.

It felt like life. Like sunlight and laughter and joy. All the energy she had spent evading the heat in him, shying away from the oblivion in his kiss — she surrendered all of it, wanting to feel his hunger for her obliterate the words she had spoken, the images she had evoked with her pitiful story. Her tongue slid against his, taking the strength and heat he offered. She did not want to think, did not want to feel anything but this, ever again, his hands winding through her hair and his lips on hers, their breath mingling.

They fell back on the bed, his body pressed against hers, side by side. She smoothed her hand over his shoulder, feeling the warm flesh beneath flexing under her touch.

"You are not yourself, Helen." He pulled back,

breathing heavily, his eyes searching hers. "You don't want this," he said against her lips, and she heard the question in it, the doubt.

She stretched her body against the length of his, curling her hips up to press against his thigh. "Don't tell me what I want," she whispered. In truth, she had no name for what she wanted. She only knew that she would turn into a block of ice if he left her now, if he did not kiss her and hold her, and drive the ghosts from her mind.

A cold wind whipped around the house, rattling a window downstairs. But it was safe here, with him. She dropped her head to his throat and, nuzzling the curve of his shoulder, breathed deep to take in the scent of him. It excited him. She could feel it in the tension of his arms, in the stirring hardness on her belly. She opened her mouth on his hot neck, pressed her teeth to his skin and sucked gently, then tasted him with her tongue.

His reaction was instant, turning her beneath him and gripping her waist. Now that she was here - on her back, on the bed, all of his power hanging over her - she felt the first hint of fear. That he could unleash all his strength, overwhelm her and hurt her, she had no doubt.

But she was tired, so very tired of being afraid. Tired of worrying over the things he might be, of what he might hide. He was not Henley. He was not. Oh, how glad she was that he was so very different. How astonishing, to feel this curiosity about his touch, about what it might be like.

She didn't give him time to consider his morals and propriety. She wanted all of him, not the polished veneer he gave to the world. She pulled on the ribbon that closed the neck of her night rail, reached down and grasped his hand, laying his fingers across her breast. Her body arched up, filling his palm, kindling flames all along the surface of her skin and burning away doubt and fear.

She watched his face, resisting the urge to close her eyes, wanting to see that it was him and no one else who touched her, who firmed his clasp on her breast and lowered his head to her bared body. It made her want to weep, the tenderness and hunger in his touch. Her hands gathered the fabric of his shirt, pulling it off and away until nothing between them.

It overwhelmed her, his bare skin next to hers, his mouth at her breast. She didn't know, had never imagined, that she could feel this way. Hot and lascivious. Wanton. His fingers were inside her, wringing a gasp from her as she parted her legs further, opening herself to him without hesitation. His legs shifted, his boots falling to the floor with a thud. The urgent intent in his movements surged around her and brought back unwanted memories that she fought off with the sight of him. His lips came to hers again, a fierce possession of her mouth while he worked to free himself of the breeches.

She helped him, furiously beating down the nervousness that fluttered in her stomach. She was not afraid. She would not let herself be afraid of him, of anything, ever again. He kicked free of the last of his clothing and lay fully on her, his weight pressing her into the bed. He let out an explosive breath and dropped his cheek to hers. She felt the restraint in him, how rigidly he held himself, but he must move now or her courage would be lost. She slid her hands down his back, to the place where soft flesh curved into the hard muscle of his thighs. She gripped him there, pulling him to her desperately, her whole body straining toward him.

His head came up again, looking into her eyes. She felt the slide of his belly on hers as he shifted and stopped, staring at her as though seeing her clearly for the first time. His eyes gained focus, looking to the very depth of her, and he began to move, her eyes fixed on him as he pushed forward, filling her slowly.

It did not hurt. He would never hurt her, she knew that, never with his body. She felt the catch in his breath against her lips, but she didn't want him to hold back. She wanted the power in him unleashed inside her. This once, she wanted him to lose himself and forget what was expected of him. And he knew — he always knew what she needed, even when she did not. He moved in answer to it, driving to the center of her, the wild pleasure growing with each second. Everything she touched or felt or saw, the very air she breathed, was him.

She watched his face change, heard the sounds she made, each exhalation of breath carrying a little panting moan as the sensations rippled through her. But she stubbornly refused to succumb to the urge to close her eyes, not wanting to know what images awaited her in the dark behind her eyelids. Let him lose himself. Let her see it. She felt him fight against it, but urged him on with her hands until he gasped against her mouth, his eyes squeezing shut as he drove deep once more, a harsh groan through his teeth, and then he stilled above her.

She lay panting beneath him, still throbbing. He did not open his eyes, but after a long, long moment, he dropped his head to the curve of her neck and relaxed in her arms. She lifted herself up again, tentatively, looking to ease the excited tension she still felt.

It was in that moment, her body still yearning and his face hidden from her, that she realized what she had done. The enormity of it engulfed her in a wave of dismay.

To pull him to her, to press against him like this. To become in truth what everyone, what he himself, believed her to be. Her head jerked in denial of it, staring blindly at the ceiling. At the same moment, she remembered what she had stubbornly fought against: the smell of wet grass in the forest, the bruising grip holding her down. It made her stomach lurch.

But still her body moved against his, wanting more.

The shock of it hit her like cold water, full in the face. She finally understood, after all this time. She understood the Odious Henley, what drove him, what had motivated him that day. A lust as pure as the one she felt now, with no regard for anything else.

She pushed him away, feeling the shaking in her gut, squirming out from under him until she reached the edge of the bed. She rolled off, landing on her knees and groping under the bed for the chamber pot, where she heaved up everything inside of her – all of the desire and disgust, vomited into the painted white porcelain.

CHAPTER ELEVEN

"You were ill? You lost your supper?"

"Marie-Anne, it isn't at all funny!"

They sat together in chairs pulled close to the fire, shoes off and feet curled under them.

"Of course it is! Oh-ho! You vomited, and it was" – Marie-Anne could not contain her laughter – "immediately after?"

"Yes," said Helen, catching her friend's hilarity and struggling to speak through a fit of giggles. "I– I fell off the bed and g-grabbed the ch-chamberpot!"

Marie-Anne fairly whooped with laughter.

"Oh, the poor man!" she said, wiping away tears. "What on earth did he do, Hélène? What did he say?"

"He was very solicitous, of course," said Helen, who now felt herself blushing even as she continued giggling at the memory. "And then he said he thought himself experienced, but that he'd certainly never experienced *that*!"

This proved entirely too much for Marie-Anne,

who slipped to the floor, clutching her sides. "Hah! *Mon dieu*, help me off the floor. No, don't – I'll only fall off again if this gets any better. He never experienced such a thing! I would hope not. It was very...very original of you, Hélène!"

"You must stop, my sides hurt! I wanted to talk to you seriously, and now you have me laughing like a lunatic. Oh God," she said, mortification returning, "How very original indeed."

"But then what? What happened next?"

"He wrapped a blanket around me, and tucked me in the bed like I was a child. It was better than I deserved, I'm sure. And when I woke this morning, he was gone."

"But he stayed by you through the night," said Marie-Anne, who apparently thought this noteworthy.

Helen lowered herself to the hearth rug to sit next to her friend. "And he left without a word. I fear I may have driven him off for good."

Marie-Anne snorted at this. "You will have to work much harder to achieve that. But tell me, *mon amie*," she looked closely at Helen. "Why do you blush? What else happened?"

"It's just that I was the one – I mean, it was I who initiated everything. I didn't mean to. I just wanted... And you know how very proper he is."

"You think he's more disgusted by you wanting him? For God's sake, Hélène, don't hide your face, you wanted to talk of this. And I know that you didn't repel him by *desiring* him."

"How can you be so sure?"

Marie-Anne shrugged as though it were the most obvious thing. "He is male."

"I defer to your wisdom, Marie-Anne. But I must

have driven him off with something. I suppose I must seem terribly difficult – hiding everything, then shouting at him, then telling him the truth, and then–"

"And then making love to him and vomiting! It's priceless!"

"Stop!" But she could not help joining in Marie-Anne's renewed laughter. "Oh good Lord, I am absurd. It's all absurd, isn't it?"

Marie-Anne wiggled closer, an impish grin on her face as she slanted a knowing look at Helen. "But did you not like it? You must have, now you turn almost purple!"

"Don't tease, Marie-Anne. It was... He was lovely."

"Yes, those broad shoulders of his," said Marie-Anne appreciatively, almost dreamy. "And he has marvelous big hands."

"Wicked woman," admonished Helen, laughing at little. "I can hardly say what it was like, except that it was... what you have previously given me to understand it might be like." She shrugged, suddenly shy about putting words to it.

"Patient and tender?" Marie-Anne asked gently, putting a hand over hers. Helen nodded. "And exciting and delicious?" Another nod and yet more fierce blushing, which elicited a warm smile of satisfaction from Marie-Anne. "I knew I was not mistaken in him. And now *you* know, ma chère, and your body knows. This is good, I think."

Helen could not be quite as categorical as that. "But now he's gone and I may never see him again. I don't know what comes next."

Marie-Anne waited, her brow furrowed in thought, and then simply asked, "What do you want to happen?"

She looked into the fire and pulled her knees up to her chin, wrapping her arms around her legs and considering all the possible outcomes.

"I don't... I honestly don't know."

※

He rode through the mud until he reached the stream that marked the midway point between his home and Helen's. It was more than a stream now, flooding over the sides and swollen to twice its normal width, the waters roiling around fallen branches. It would be difficult to cross.

It stopped him. Why go home anyway? He could just as well curse Alex Dehaven, Earl of Whitemarsh and bloody son of a bitch right here on a muddy bank in the middle of absolutely nowhere. Where the bastard had banished his perfectly coherent sister for the horrific crime of objecting to a marriage with a murderous blackguard. Where the admirable Lord Whitemarsh sent the ever-willing, never-indiscreet, always noncommittal, base animal who had bedded a woman in despair. A woman who had obviously not been herself. A woman who sighed most sweetly, and at all the right moments. Who had told him not to assume he knew what she wanted.

What she wanted. He couldn't guess at that. He hoped she wanted him to find her brother, or Henley, and beat both of them to a bloody pulp. He could do it quite easily in this mood, ride straight to London and find her precious brother and horsewhip him for being such a monster. Henley may have ruined her, but it was her brother who had assured her downfall.

Stephen had known it, had been resenting the fact for months. The injustice was nothing to the utter cruelty of it – to abandon Helen Dehaven entirely only because of an ugly rumor. When rumors were nothing, he realized now, to the truth of her. That her brother professed to have been so close to her, and her only protection in the world... It was heartless. A more direct wound than the one Henley had inflicted on her.

Only seventeen years old. She had only been seventeen, blithe enough to give herself to the man she loved and had planned to wed, but strong enough to recognize her mistake. She had stood up to Society, to her brother, and to Henley himself – and refused to go through with it, even knowing the ruin that awaited her. It was really rather awe-inspiring.

But the honorable Lord Whitemarsh had not seen that, had chosen not to believe her and left her to her own devices. Stephen had thought it went against good sense, not to mention all that was proper, to stand by her and aid her these past weeks. He had told himself he was still looking for the truth, was looking for a way to do what her brother had not. A gently bred noblewoman should not have to live so, he'd rationalized countless times. He had hoped to fill the void left by her brother, to step in like a knight in shining armor and quietly, privately, do the decent and humane thing by helping her. He had agreed to do so, in exchange for the truth.

The truth. There was little comfort in it. How long ago had he learned not to ask for it, if he did not like it when it finally came? He had hated the first truth she had given him, that she'd loved Henley. He'd been blind, bending her words to his own experience, stupidly likening her to Clara. Clara, who loved him and left him for no other reason than that she'd wanted a duke. And Helen, who'd loved Henley and left him for being a murderer. They were nothing alike. Nothing at all.

He gripped the riding crop and slashed viciously across the branches of the nearest tree over and over again, thinking of the other truth she had given him. Henley. How far to the coast? How far would he have to ride until he reached the water, so that he could swim across the Irish Sea and mete out some sort of revenge? He felt like an animal, a savage in the jungle, howling for blood.

It was Helen who did that to him, brought out the primitive beast that he'd never known lived inside him. She wept and trembled, and he became a faithful hound. She told him the truth, and he dreamt of bloody vengeance against anyone who dared to hurt her. She kissed him, and he became a rutting beast. No matter that she'd wanted it, that she'd pulled him to her, that he'd given her a thousand chances to stop him. No matter that he thought he might live a thousand years and never forget the way her eyes turned dark and deep, capturing him, drowning him, urging the animal in him to be unleashed.

It was outside his experience. He had known love – thought he had known it, anyway, with Clara. But he had never known a potent lust like this. Already he wanted her again, to take the path back and find her in her warm bed. He stared at the ground, feeling drunk, imagining her there waiting for him. There was nothing civilized at all in what he wanted, what he had always wanted with her. She would regret it, of course, all of it: telling him the truth, when it was evident that she did not ever want to think of it; reaching out to him for comfort, only to be used by him as all men wanted to use a woman of her reputation. He vacillated between the conviction that it was what she'd wanted, and the fear that she would never want it again.

That should be obvious enough, he thought sourly. Not five seconds after, she'd retched up her dinner. Better evidence of instant regret, he'd never seen. Methodically, he stripped the twigs from the nearest branch, cursing himself for taking what she'd offered in her distress. He was a gentleman, he reasoned, as little as he'd acted like it last night. Or he was supposed to be, anyway. Hadn't he spent his whole life proving it, putting himself above all those shameless others? He'd been quite successful at leading a spotless life. Until now. Until Helen Dehaven had burst into his life and shown him what honor really meant.

He wanted her, but it was nothing next to what he wanted for her. The hunger for her body was mixed in with the desperate need to hear her laughter once more, to be the one who made her happy, to shield her, to protect her. He would not disappoint her as Henley had. He would not abandon her, never, as her lout of a brother had done.

For the whole of his miserable life he had avoided clinging to anything – to any person, any idea, any belief. But now he believed in Helen. Believed that she deserved the image of shining perfection he'd managed to make himself, the security and comfort that image afforded. No more would he hedge his bets, remain safe by refusing to define his convictions. Never had he come down strongly on the side of anything. It was time for that to end. It had been ending for months, from when he had begun wanting her.

He turned his horse south, a necessary detour in the path that led forever back to her, more sure of his course than ever he had been.

⁌⁍

"You are mad."

She hadn't meant to say it, but it rolled out of her mouth. It was the only explanation. He must be mad. Or his brain was addled or he was ill. Upright and proper Stephen Hampton, Earl of Summerdale, the very symbol of all that was untarnished and virtuous, proposing such a thing. To even let it be known that he willingly socialized with her on any level would drag him down. At least somewhat. It was not in keeping with his reputation. People would find a welcome reason to mock him at last.

She had thought about it for hours, laying in the sheets that still smelled of him, and of them together, thinking she would never be able to sleep. She had slept, though – a dreamless sleep that had held her in its grip until he'd come knocking at her door again, bringing the same breathlessness and scattered wits as he always did. She was utterly unprepared for his mere presence, much less what he had come to say.

But this of all things, she had never imagined. She could not imagine it even now. Her face was numb, all the sensation drained out of her.

His grin – that horrible, wonderful smile – spread across his face as he watched her confusion. "Not mad. Or perhaps a little, but only in the best way. The most sane way."

She felt completely dumbfounded. Mad but sane, he said, while he wore that smile. Of course it must be a joke, and she found herself angry, offended that he would amuse himself at her expense when she was turned every which way.

"You mock me," she said stiffly, taking comfort in being able to at least show offense. Anything other than this swaying softness that had lodged in her hips at the very sight of him.

The smile immediately disappeared. His expression was serious, growing more so by the second.

"I would not mock you, Helen. Not now or ever. And never about this."

"But how am I to take this in anything but jest?" she demanded, feeling rather embarrassed by the whole thing. "Marriage, my lord! The very fact that you could speak the word together with my name suggests that you have lost your senses." She stared at him helplessly, but his smile did not return. She heard Maggie's voice in her head – *Jesus, Mary and Joseph*. He was dead serious, and determined. "What possible advantage would you gain by marrying me?"

He flinched slightly, but did not hesitate in his answer. "Unlike so many of my acquaintance, I do not always take an action for the advantage in it. There is such a thing as honor," he said gently, carefully, "though I know you have seen little of it in the men you have known. Including myself."

She shook her head vigorously. "You have always treated me honorably, even when I did not deserve it," she protested. How could he think otherwise?

"Not always," he corrected her.

And suddenly it was in the air between them,

unavoidable. He had named it, the thing that created the air of reserve and restraint in the room. His kisses and her nakedness. Clutching him to herself. Him lying beside her all the night through. She stared down at her feet, feeling the blood rise to her cheeks, wishing it was as easy to speak about now as it had been yesterday with Marie-Anne.

"Oh. That."

"Yes," he confirmed. "That."

"But—" She hesitated before forcing the words out in a rush. "You did not act without my... permission." Her insistence, really, but she did not say it. "The blame is not yours."

He looked ashamed, angry with himself. "Indeed it is. I am perfectly capable of mastering myself, yet I did not." He cleared his throat. "There are consequences to such actions, and it is you who will be adversely affected. I seek to rectify that circumstance."

His business-like tone was worse than his smiling. It was hardly the kind of marriage proposal she would have expected from a secret romantic, or from someone who had held her as he had. Then again, it was in perfect keeping with his beloved propriety, wasn't it? Of course. He would want to make up for the terrible breach in etiquette, the ridiculous man. It was really too much.

"Lord Summerdale," she began in her most practical tone. She might at least try to match his tone. Perhaps it would help to overcome the inexplicable awkwardness she felt. "It is very admirable of you want to follow the social graces, but there is hardly a need. You'll have noticed you cannot save me from ruin. Any adverse effects you would hope to circumvent have already been visited upon me."

He looked at her strangely, a kind of eager pensiveness in his expression, like she spoke a foreign language that he knew only minimally. She rolled her eyes and lifted her hands in a helpless gesture, striving to ease her embarrassment with a touch of humor. Marie-Anne would laugh herself silly, if she could see.

"A marriage under these circumstances, solely for the sake of saving a woman's reputation, is pointless in my case." She watched a frown of concentration spread over his features. Ridiculous man, refusing to understand and offering to ruin himself. For her. "Why must you cling to this notion of doing the honorable thing?"

"Why do you not want to marry me?"

The question flustered her even further. She could tell him that she had lived so long without hope of a husband that the idea was alien to her. Or that she did not need him, having managed so long on her own. *Because you will come to resent what this does to your impeccable reputation, and hate me, and I don't want you to hate me.*

That was it. He believed her, she knew. But if one day that belief ran dry, he would turn on her as Alex had. All his attentiveness and concern would trickle away into indifference, and she would be left cold, after coming to depend on him.

Or it could be worse than that. What other terrible things could he be, that might be revealed to her too late?

But she could not say that to him, not all of it, no more than she could tell him how she felt infinitely better and yet a hundred times worse that he had come back to her. That he did not abandon her.

"I never said I didn't *want* to marry you," she countered feebly. It was so very difficult, when he looked at her like that, to marshal the myriad reasons why she resisted. All the disjointed objections raced through her mind like birds, dashing themselves uselessly against his insistence, falling stunned to the ground. It caused quite a ruckus in her head.

"It seems to me that is exactly what you're saying, and it makes no sense. All the advantage is yours, yet you do not take it. I offer my name to you, my home – everything I have, because you deserve it. And not just because of what has happened between us." He paused, looking down at the gloves he twisted in his hand. "You deserve whatever I can give you because of who you are. You have been wronged, Helen, and I can do everything in my power to set it right. Not that it will ever be right, what you have suffered."

All the thoughts whirring in her head stopped suddenly, leaving her silent. No, it could never be set to rights. She had always known that. He held so much of the secret now, in his two hands. She had given it to him, exposing more of herself than she had ever wanted, and it had not been erased with the telling of it. It would never be erased, not with his belief, or his kisses, or just because she wanted it gone from her.

But he, with his romantic notions, wanted to make it better. To be the agent of her salvation, rescuing her from a life of loneliness and obscurity. Did he think they would write an epic poem to celebrate his great sacrifice?

"I will never be acceptable to Society," she stated baldly, reduced to pointing out the obvious.

He shrugged, as if it were an insignificant detail. "That doesn't concern me in the least."

"It would ruin your good standing! And you would become as unacceptable as me. You know quite well how it goes," she insisted. "You could not take your wife with you to any gatherings, affairs and such—"

He suddenly closed the distance between them, cutting off her words by kissing her. It drove out all thought of what she had meant to say, replacing her argument with the coaxing of his lips. An excellent argument, she thought. Oh, really... rather... *wonderful*, this line of reasoning. He took the resistance out of her as easily as he stole her breath, reminding her quite forcefully that the night between them had been real. As real as this notion of marriage.

He dragged his lips away and stared hard into her eyes. "Say yes, Helen. And promise me that you will always be with me," he said. "I want you beside me, in all things. If we cannot be somewhere together, then we shall not go at all, and society can go hang."

His intensity took her aback as much as his kiss. It was so important to him, though she could not fathom why. Still, she couldn't promise him the kind of wife he wanted when she was still reeling from the fact that he wanted her to be his wife at all. It was too sweet a dream to indulge in, these kisses every day. It frightened her, to want something so much, and she pulled away to a safer distance.

"If you took me to wife, then it would seem we'd spend much time *out* of society altogether, under that condition."

The idea seemed to please him, adding to her complete bafflement.

"Yes, it would," he said with a faint and satisfied

smile. "Although I would prefer not to call it a condition of marriage. Only a very strong preference." He looked at her, piercing through the remnants of her resolve with the depth of his sincerity. "I feel the need to be near you, you see. Constantly. And I abhor the notion of a typical society marriage."

"I hardly think a marriage between us could be that," she said tartly, but her resistance was flagging. She knew what he meant. One could barely know who was married to whom in high society much of the time. Keeping separate homes, separate social schedules, dallying with whomever they pleased.

"That is all I would ask of you, as my wife." The early morning light from the parlor room window sparked his eyes as he looked again at the side of her neck. Exactly as he had before he kissed her that first time, though her hair was severely pulled back now. No loose strands to distract him, but still he stared at the spot with that faint half-smile until her skin grew warm. He wanted to be near her. Constantly. She could have said the words herself, so true were they to her own feelings.

She blinked, not knowing if she wanted him to kiss her again. She stared at his hair, remembering how it felt between her fingers. "I have not said I will be your wife. It's such a..." *bad idea*, she thought, but said: "a very strange idea."

His lashes lifted, a dreamer half-waking. "Is there any particular expectation you have of a husband? So long as we are stating our preferences." He said it hesitantly, as though worried he would not measure up.

"I want never to be spared the truth."

The words had come out of her instantly, without thought. It was something about the way he looked at her, so openly and honestly, hiding nothing. It made her think how desperately she wanted him to look at her like that, always. Hiding nothing.

"Even–" She took a breath. No matter what their relationship turned out to be, it was vital. "Even when it would hurt me, never hide the truth of what you are."

He must know why she said it, of course. The discovery of her last suitor's true nature had brought them to this moment, after all – had brought her to this life – and she saw him make the connection immediately, quick as ever to understand what lay behind her every word. She broke his look, letting her eyes slide to the window and feeling as though she stood on the edge of a precipice, staring down at the earth from a great height with her heart in her throat. She gave him no time to answer her.

"You think to spare me some kind of disgrace by offering marriage, but you have given me no satisfactory reason why you would do this," she continued stubbornly. "It is senseless to throw yourselves to the wolves for my sake." He didn't know what it was like when people whispered and stared and laughed. He could have no idea what it might be like.

"Do you have any idea how much you have changed me?" His voice came to her as she stared out at the bare trees, the mud. "I have come to know what integrity is, because of you. I have come to understand how wrong I have been, how empty..."

He trailed off, and she turned to him. It was true. He had changed. She could see it plainly. When he had first appeared at Marie-Anne's so many months ago he had not been the kind of man who would do this, offer to ruin himself to save a ruined woman, who could look at her as he did now with open admiration and respect shining in his eyes. She felt at a loss. What on earth had he found to admire in her?

The silence stretched between them. She looked hard at the floorboards, thinking how they needed scrubbing, how she would put on her apron and do that just as soon as he left. Because he would leave. Naturally, he would.

"You want to know why, yet you find fault with my reasoning." He did not sound like the Earl of Summerdale at all, not like the man who could change the world with a word. He sounded lost. "Because I want to marry you, Helen. Because I want you."

She felt something like a hairline fracture in the casing of her heart. Oh, he could not want her. No one wanted her, ever. No one but The Odious Henley had ever wanted her, and look what had come of that. Better to be undesirable.

She did not answer; she could not, and his mood changed back to the businessman when she went so long without speaking. He stepped back from her.

"Shall I give you a reason that you will understand, then? One that appeals to your practicality?" He slapped the gloves in his hand, a sharp snap that brought her instantly to attention. "I have certain responsibilities and duties that I've neglected. And I won't have the next Earl of Summerdale raised a bastard in this village, and his mother called a lewd and abandoned woman by the locals."

He cut right to the heart of the matter mercilessly, voicing the one problem that she had been unable to dismiss in all her tossing and turning of the last twenty-four hours. Of course it had come into her mind. Of course it had. But to think of his rights in the matter had not occurred to her, nor had she allowed herself to contemplate what it would really mean to her own life. The whole subject was so frightening that she preferred to think of anything else. And now he took away her ability to think past it. She needed time to think, and he would not let her.

But he was right. He was more right than he knew. She felt it like a great gaping hole growing inside her. The villagers whom she so loved would never treat her quite the same. She thought she might be able to live through it, herself, but to willfully put a child into that life was nothing but cruel. Now he offered the way out, a means to make it acceptable.

And would she refuse him and regret it later, regrets and misgivings piling up on one another like stones on a cairn until she finally suffocated?

"We could wait," she suggested. "We could wait and see."

He came closer to her again, close enough to touch, his nearness rescuing her from the panic that she fought down. "You've asked me not to spare you the truth, no matter how harsh," he said gently. "It will be difficult enough to squelch rumors even if a child is born within nine months. If we wait, it will be impossible."

The air was thin, the earth falling away from her feet to leave her suspended. He was right. As always. Thinking it through would not make it any less true. It was a sickening feeling, her vision going black at the edges, dizziness threatening to engulf her. But he was there, like he always was. As unmovable and real as the truth he spoke, everything inside of her clamoring toward him.

"Yes," she whispered, flinging herself to solid ground, his presence pulling her back from the abyss. She looked into his face, to convince herself he was real. A child of his – to have his child, to have him look at her every day of her life as he looked at her now. To have the protection of his name, to make a family of her own and so much more: to have some kind of a life again, one where she did not dread the empty days and nights.

"Yes."

He raised his hands to her face, a look of relief and certainty softening the line of his mouth, spreading into a smile. He did not disappoint, pulling her mouth to his and kissing her soundly, thoroughly, until stars swam behind her eyes. He caught her, saved her from the long fall, just like in her dreams.

***

She stood at the top of the stairs with Marie-Anne, wondering if she would wake up eventually. She had not thought it would happen so soon. She had barely finished agreeing to marry him when suddenly everything had been put into motion.

It would seem that her bridegroom, so soon to be her husband – a word that slithered around in her head, alive with implications – had planned everything in the day they had been apart, before ever proposing to her. The minister, it turned out, together with the license and a few Summerdale servants, had waited in carriages just outside her door. It drew half the village, fortunately including Marie-Anne.

Her friend had hastened inside, leaving Summerdale – *Stephen*, she thought, with a bit of a shock to realize that she might use his given name now – to sort out the arrangements while Helen was bustled upstairs with a maid. It had been only an hour since she'd given herself over to the preparations, and now they waited for her below. He waited. To be her husband. It was all quite overwhelming, to say the least.

"Yellow suits you wonderfully, in that shade," Marie-Anne announced.

Helen looked down at the dress. It was a soft white with yellow trim, and came from the depths of Marie-Anne's wardrobe. It was a summery thing and two inches too short on Helen, but with the donation of Mrs. Linney's new yellow Spencer jacket (which fit Helen perfectly) and matching wide ribbon (which was easily added to the hem), it was quite lovely. It was all done so efficiently that she suspected Marie-Anne might have been planning out a contingency wardrobe in case of a hasty wedding.

The maid had done wonderfully with her hair, as well, pulling it up and wrapping it in yellow and white ribbons, arranging thick strands to cascade from her crown to her nape. Marie-Anne looked inordinately pleased with it.

"You must be thrilled to see me out of my dregs, as you call them." Helen attempted a smile, but found her mood unequal to the task. Her palms were beginning to sweat, and she felt just a little bit of hysteria coming on.

"No more rags for you, *ma chère*, or dregs, or anything else that is not suitable to someone of your station," she said with a twinkle in her eye.

"I'm ousted from the ranks of the Fallen, am I?"

"You'll always be an honorary member, of course," she grinned. "But come now! They are waiting for you."

Helen gripped the banister, suddenly certain she would tumble down the stairs in a heap. It was all happening too quickly, and too fantastical to believe.

"It's mad, isn't it?" she asked, disbelieving. "It's completely mad. However will it work? What on earth will happen?"

Marie-Anne gave her a shrewd look. "You will go downstairs and be married to a very good and honorable man. More than most women get in life, I don't have to tell you."

But then her expression softened, and she closed a hand comfortingly around Helen's arm. "I will tell you, Hélène, that I have always worried since I have known you, that you will never have a chance for happiness. After Ireland, and... all that, I thought you would never be close to any man. To be physically close, I mean."

Helen blushed, her widened eyes lowering at the idea that Marie-Anne had ever taken the time to consider such a thing. But her friend reached out to her, tipping her chin up so she could not hide her face.

"You don't have your mother, Hélène, and on your wedding day you should have someone to speak to you. Lucky that I am French," she continued with her most devilish grin, "and that we talk of these things more easily than you English. It's been difficult to find acceptable euphemisms, you know!"

Helen felt the smile on her own face, in spite of her attempts to remain impervious to Marie-Anne's humor. "Well," Helen took a breath, steeling herself. "What do you think I should know, then?"

Marie-Anne laughed. "There is not time now for all that you should know, but I don't doubt your husband shall be an excellent teacher." Then her smile faded and she continued, more sober. "All you should know is that he is a good man, and you need not be afraid of him. But I see you have learned that already. Really, if you want to be happy — and I mean truly happy, as I think you have a chance to be — then you must not be afraid of yourself. Or more precisely, of what you feel when you are with him. It is yours, this body, and it will never be another's, no matter how you may feel in certain moments."

Helen felt the familiar and sudden queasiness, how the muscles of her legs pulled tight and her knees drew together. *I will not think of it,* she said to herself. Not of Ireland, not of Henley, not of everything he had taken away from her. He had only taken that part of her for a moment, but it was hers again now, just as Marie-Anne said.

She gave a small nod, acknowledging Marie-Anne's advice. "Thank you," she said, and leaned forward to kiss her friend's cheek. "It's all very frightening, you know."

Marie-Anne gave a quivery smile, tears beginning to brim in her eyes. But she blinked them away and said, "Well, that is because it is life. So now go and join the living again, *ma chère*. It is only what you deserve. And I shall keep in mind," she giggled, the gleam returning to her eye, "that if ever I want out of Bartle, I need only seduce a man and become violently ill. An excellent scheme."

And that was how, tripping down the stairs into

the parlor where Stephen waited, Helen came laughing to her wedding.

CHAPTER TWELVE

An hour or more in the carriage, and still she had found nothing to say. She stared down at the ring on her hand and wondered, if she blinked hard enough, whether it would disappear. The sense of unreality was as much due to her complete ignorance of what lay ahead as it was the swiftness of the day's events. This morning she had woken ruined and penniless, and now the sunset saw her married to the most thoroughly respectable man in the country, making their way through the muddy roads to his home.

"Will we live here, in Herefordshire?" she asked, knowing she would never be so lucky. He had told her once that his lands here were insignificant, and that he had never thought to stay long.

"Only tonight," he answered softly, as if to reassure. But something in his face told her there was little comfort to be found. "Tomorrow we'll travel to the estate in Bedfordshire."

"Oh," she said, as steadily as she could. "Not to

London, then?"

"Not yet, though I cannot hide forever." He seemed to go away into himself a bit, thinking deeply, as though absorbing the idea. Contemplating a return to London didn't put him in any good humor.

She stared out at the bare trees and setting sun. It would do no good to tell him she had warned him of this, as little as he had taken heed of her words. His standing in society was important to him. Now he sat across from her, likely saying a silent farewell to the life he had known. Perhaps it would be better if they did hide forever.

"Tell me about your estate," she prompted, hoping to divert him. "Why do we go there so soon?"

His mouth curled up in a humorless smile. "Why, to show my wife her new family, of course. My mother will be there, and my youngest sister as well. Better to go now, and have you well established before winter lets out."

"Is that important?"

"It will make things easier, I think. Our marriage will not be fresh news when the Season starts, if we spread word of it now. And once the household has a good opinion of the new Lady Summerdale, it will go easier." He noted her confusion. "The servants will talk, and if they have favorable things to say about you to other servants they meet in London, it can only be to the good."

She took a deep breath at this novel way of thinking, and let out a sigh. "They do say you know everything. I am beginning to understand why, if you concern yourself with servants' gossip. It's very clever of you." She concentrated on not wringing her hands. "And if your servants do not like me?"

He brightened at that. "Impossible," he smiled. "You have a way about you. Don't let it worry you overmuch, it's only an idea."

He laid a hand over hers. The warmth and sureness of his touch both comforted and unsettled her. It was unreasonable to be so nervous about her wedding night, after what had already passed between them. But she was nervous. For all her joking with Marie-Anne, for all her resolve to leave the past in the past, she had no assurances that the fear would not overcome her in the end. It was horrible, a living thing inside her that she could not completely subdue. She did not know if her will was strong enough to control the sick fear that so unexpectedly gripped her at times.

His hand moved on hers, clasping her fingers tightly. "I can protect you in Society, Helen, at least from being jeered at openly. But there will always be talk." He ran his thumb across her palm, his brows lowering in concern. "If I could spare you from it, I would. But I cannot make miracles. It will call for a great deal of strength from you."

She bit her lip. Still, he thought only of her. Never of himself, of what this might cost him in the end. She forced a humorous indifference, for his sake. "Pish-tosh, it is nothing to me what they think. I have as much strength in my little finger as it will need," she said lightly.

She watched the frown on his face disappear, replaced with a slow-growing grin. It set her heart to beating fast, caused a warmth to grow in her belly. But the fear was there, just beneath the excitement. *Tell him*, she thought. *Tell him now.* He should know the true extent of it. Her nervousness would seem odd to him, and the notion that he believed her to be a woman of experience made her take the air into her lungs too fast. He was her husband now. He should know.

"You have twice as much strength in one eyelash as ten men would ever need in their lives," he corrected with a smile.

But she knew he was serious, that he thought she was fearless. She proved him wrong, remaining silent on the matter, looking at his hand in hers and thanking God that he had more courage than she could ever hope to possess. She was sure he would need it, having chosen this path.

※

He stared at the stack of letters waiting for him. It would be difficult, going home, but at least it was not so removed from things as this part of the world.

Home. The word seemed not to apply, now that Edward was dead. He should have warned Helen. He still should, but he did not want to give up these hours they had together and alone, away from it. There was no sense in putting it off, but they could have tonight.

"Ah. Jackson." He shook himself to awareness as the butler came to the door. "Lady Summerdale has her bath?"

"Yes, my lord. I have taken the liberty of assigning her a lady's maid. Will you be taking dinner in the dining room this evening?"

Stephen gave a grimace. He couldn't possibly think of eating, stuffed as he was from the wedding lunch the villagers had hastily prepared. "If it is agreeable to

Lady Summerdale, I would prefer to forego dinner. If she wants anything, have it brought to our room."

She would be waiting for him, fresh from her bath. She was his wife. It was impossible to think she could be his, that she could belong to anyone but herself. Her dark will, so forceful and determined, forbade entry to that secret world she kept inside. But she had let him in, or at least had given him a glimpse of what lay within her. And now, she would be there, waiting for him.

Jackson interrupted his thoughts. "The correspondence from London arrived this morning after your departure, my lord. The messenger indicated that there were matters of importance that should not be delayed."

"Yes, well, when isn't there?" Best to look at them now, and ignore the vague dread that settled around him. "Thank you, Jackson." But the butler was already closing the doors as Stephen sifted through the correspondence. Near the bottom of the stack of papers, he found what he knew he'd been expecting.

The handwriting was elegant. His fingers traced over the sweeping curve of the S, the upward slant of the script causing a familiar ache. Inside, there would be words of love and regret, invitation and desire — everything he'd ever wanted from her, neatly written down and contained in a page or two. His hand hovered over it, tempted to read it even now, with Helen waiting upstairs. But he thrust it into the drawer. Later. He would face it later.

The last envelope awaited, likely some boring business detail. He didn't recognize the hand. He would open it, and then he could go to Helen. Or perhaps it was too early. There was a reserve about her, a shyness that had come as something of a surprise. After using all the persuasion he possessed to convince her to marry him, everything had moved very quickly, as he'd wanted it to do. But she had clearly not expected it and was a little dazed by it all. Not the best politics, then, to barge in on her while she still bathed.

He picked up the last letter to distract himself, and nearly threw it to the fire once it had been opened.

Lord Summerdale,

Though we are not personally acquainted, I am obliged to introduce myself by letter in the hopes of appealing to your sense of Honor, which is well known and esteemed by all. I pray that you will be so kind as to read these pages, and if a natural Sympathy induces you to aid me I will be forever grateful.

You are aware, I am sure, that the Earl of Whitemarsh has for some time proposed to contract with me for the purchase of my finest wool. The agreement was made, as the enclosed letter from him will attest. However Whitemarsh has declined to sign the Contracts that would bind the deal (also enclosed for your examination) without enlightening me as to why such a sudden reversal should occur.

I appeal to your sense of honor, sir. I took Whitemarsh on his word as a Gentleman that the exchange would take place. There is some devilry here, I fear and I am forced to observe that he has proven unreliable in the matter of legal commitments in the past. I trusted him to deal fairly with me but am disappointed in him once again. But I am reassured that his partner is a most upstanding Gentleman, who is perhaps unaware of this breach of faith and I appeal to you to judge the circumstance with temperate wisdom, and to the benefit of your own interests.

*Respectfully,
Henley*

He stared at the signature as outrage surged up from the pit of his stomach. He would appeal to a sense of honor, would he? Alex had misrepresented the matter and had proven himself once again "unreliable in the matter of legal commitments"! Stephen knew well that Henley referred to the breaking of a marriage contract, so many years ago. As if losing Helen was akin to losing a business deal.

He thought of Helen's face as she told him the truth, how she could barely breathe, barely speak. As though the shock of it was still fresh and she saw a family lying dead and bloody before her on her bedroom floor. Her voice haunted him. It had sounded like the words had been dragged from the very depths of her, from a dark universe of terror and loathing and despair.

So long as Henley stayed in Ireland, so long as his injury to her stayed in the past, there was little he could do. It was the most infuriating part of it all, that it had happened to her years before Stephen ever knew her name, that it was now too late to stop it or even to exact some form of revenge. The dog skulked in Ireland, out of his reach — safe, where no weapon could touch him. No weapon save one.

Words were all Stephen had ever had. Secrets were power, but it was a power he had always shied from, doing no harm and only reaping the rewards of discretion. A closed mouth and open eye, action taken only as a result of the information gained, but never using the information directly. He knew he could ruin a hundred of London's finest citizens in a day's time with only a word, but he had never taken the power in his own two hands. Just as he had never, before two nights ago, held Helen's hand as she asked him if he believed her.

He turned the documents over in his hands, resisting the urge to rip the letter to shreds. Control. It would call for the utmost control and calculation, if he meant for it to work.

He sat down at the desk again, sharpening his quill until the point was a dangerous edge, and began to write.

❧

When he entered the room where she waited in the firelight, his breath caught at the sight. Her hair was pulled up in a multitude of pins, above a sleek rose-colored robe that opened to show a glimpse of her gleaming white leg. She was curled on the chair by the fire, bent over a book, but his entrance startled her and made her drop it into her lap and look up at him – a quick blaze of awareness, her eyes skipping across his face before she looked demurely down at her folded hands.

He leaned back against the door. The aura of reserve was around her, making her unapproachable, as though she lived in another world and he must find just the right words, the right attitude, if he wanted to gain admittance. He stood there, taking in the sight of her hands calmly folded on her lap, her eyes turned down, the tension in her shoulders. It was decidedly awkward to come to her, knowing that he would spend the night at her side, that he wanted it more than the air he breathed, and yet still unable to break the silence.

At last she stood, laying the book aside and darting a glance around the room. She seemed to be trying very hard to act normally.

"I suppose I shall have to become used to such luxuries again," she said. "It is strange to have a hot bath and a generous fire, not to mention the wealth of literature your home affords."

"Our home. It is ours, for tonight."

"Yes. Of course. I only mean that I feel a bit out of my element." She sighed. "It will take some time before I am completely comfortable."

If he had taken any other woman as his wife, he would have understood that as his cue to leave, to offer her time to adjust while he gallantly installed himself in other quarters for the night. But he had not married another woman. He had married her, and she stood in front of him with all her curves outlined in the thin robe.

"You wanted no dinner?" he asked as he sat on the bed and pulled off his shoes. "You could have it sent here, if you like."

"No, I am not hungry, thank you, my lord."

She had turned away from him to look into the fire, every line of her body rigid. He saw the narrow margin of skin at her nape where the tender wisps of hair curled. He crossed slowly to her, removing his shirt along the way.

"Did I tell you," he asked softly when he stood close behind her, close enough to take in her fragrance, "that you looked very beautiful today?"

She didn't move, her back to him. "I...thank you, my lord."

His hand found her back, the tips of his fingers moving lightly over her shoulder blades and the cool silk of her robe. "Will you call me by my name?" he whispered.

Her chin came up, but still she looked straight ahead, some of the tension going out of her. "Stephen," she said quietly, his name like a vow, an affirmation. "Thank you, Stephen, for today. For everything."

He was determined to chase the shadows from her, to see her smile again as she had when she came to marry him. She so often hid her laughter from him, her smiles so careful and reserved.

He raised his hands to the pins in her hair, slowly removing them. "It is your friends I would like to thank, for arranging your gown and dressing your hair. I have imagined you many times, with your hair swept up. Of course," his voice lowered confidentially, "you must think me inconsistent, intent as I am on seeing it down now."

He did not mention how intent he'd been to have the dress off her as soon as it was on, either, contenting himself with watching her hair fall down to her shoulders. He thought he could see just barely, from the angle at which she held her face, a faint curve to her mouth. Looking more and more hopeful.

"And I would have preferred to see you in anything other than that lumpy brown monstrosity." A slight twitch, as if she held in a laugh. Better and better. "Though it was nothing at all to that travesty in black you so often wear. I wonder, did it serve you well in cleaning out the chimney? I'm sure such a coarse fabric filed the stones down to satisfactory shine."

She ducked her head and let out a small sound. She was laughing now, quietly, little huffs of air. "I rather wondered if you were more appalled by the dress or the apron."

"If I had to choose, I would rather see you in the apron," he answered as he rested his hands lightly on her waist and brought his face closer to her hair. "Just the apron itself, of course, but eventually it would be dispatched as well."

A vivid vision of it burst into his mind, making him slightly weak at the knees. But he saw at once that she reacted differently, standing up straighter even as his hands slipped around to the tie of her robe and rested there, just beneath her breasts. She was jittery, as if they had never been together before.

"No doubt I would be dispatched with all haste by one of your villagers, if they knew I had such thoughts." He buried his face in her still-damp hair, inhaling the scent of lavender. "I'm surprised they didn't run after me with pitchforks and torches when they saw I intended to spirit their beloved Miss Helen away."

She placed a tentative pair of hands on his arms around her waist, a soft touch that changed the slow burn in him to a leaping flame.

"They would not, you know," she told him. "They have come to trust you."

"Oh, you say that now, when I am safe from the mob. I saw the look on the baker's face. I'll do well to stay out of Bartle for a time." Her hands came over his and she laced her fingers with his, leaning back into him. "Next time I ride through town, they'll heave week-old bread at me, and break my skull."

Her full smile encouraged him, and his hands moved to untie her robe. She did nothing to stop him. It fell open, revealing a river of flesh that he could see over her shoulder, the firelight dancing on the skin exposed at her throat, between her breasts and her belly. He briefly closed his eyes at the beauty of her, breathing deeply. Before, it had been impulsive, impetuous, unexpected. But now he had the luxury of seeing her, of watching as she grew languid in his arms and gave herself up to the slow seduction of his hands running lightly along her sides.

"Mr. Higgins is more likely to use his rolling pin as a weapon, I think," she said breathlessly. "Or to call on his wife. She has a reputation for a heavy fist." He could feel her all along the front of his body, how she made an effort to divert herself with humor and fought against the desire to hide herself.

"Mr. Higgins is more likely to call in the blacksmith, and I would find myself dodging a flying anvil," he contested, watching her bare stomach tighten with the little laugh she gave out. "Word would get out that you resisted the notion of marriage, and they'd rise to take you back. Danny would harness me to his father's cart for my trouble and I'd be covered in bruises from sturdy boots and sides of rotten beef."

She was fighting the laughter now, only a thin core of resistance left in her. "Well, it's not as elaborate as the Trojan horse, but they do what they can."

He smoothed his hands over her hips, pulling her back against his hardness, letting her feel his hunger, hearing her soft gasp that was not at all nervousness. "As do you with your arrows," he murmured, gazing at the curve of her neck. The sweetest curve there, just behind her delicate jaw, sloping down beneath her ear. "Your aim is always true." And he pressed his lips to the place he had fallen in love with her.

She relaxed against him at last, but only for an instant. Then she pulled back, all her nervousness reviving just at the moment when she had begun to lose herself in the heat of their bodies. He put his hands on her shoulders and gently turned her to face him, seeing the look he never wanted to see on her again. Fear. Something in this frightened her. She wouldn't look at him, her eyes beginning to skip across the room just as they had when she told him of Henley's treachery.

Of course, she must be thinking of him now. Of how she had given herself to him then, the regrets she had. There was no mistaking her mood.

"Stephen," she said haltingly. "I should tell you – I should explain..."

But she seemed to lose the words. He let them slip away, wanting her to forget everything that had happened before. She would look to her past and the sadness it carried, always, if he did not stop her now.

He forced her chin up. "Look at me, Helen." She did, her eyes finding his and staying locked in his gaze. "I don't care," he told her. "Do you believe me? I don't care about the mistakes you may have made in your past. I understand what it means to give yourself to love."

She looked as if she might cry. "Love?" she said faintly.

He held her face in his hands, feeling the ache of his heart. "If you were in love, and you gave yourself, could I condemn you for that? I don't care, Helen. I have tried very hard to care, since I met you." A ragged breath of amusement escaped him at the thought of his own folly. "But it doesn't matter what the world thinks of you. It only matters that you're with me now."

He had found them somehow, the words that stole the tension away from her. Suddenly, she was in his arms, embracing him, pressing their bodies close together with no fear. She kissed him, her mouth coming up to his with a hunger that made him hold her more tightly as he backed her toward the bed. When they reached it, he could not resist pulling her down with him, spreading her body over the coverlet, kissing every inch of her, from the toes up.

He followed the line of her legs up and opened his mouth over the heart of her. Her scent enveloped him, the feel of her legs falling apart, her damp warmth, a honey glide on the tongue. He learned the textures of her skin with his mouth until she was as excited as he, raising herself urgently to meet his caress. Drawing away to lay his head on her thigh, he looked up across the vista of her belly and breasts spread out above him, and found her looking at him.

Her eyes were dark moons that called to him, inviting him to bring his body over hers. She was so different — her look holding him, panting breathlessly, all shyness in her gone. And he went to her, gave her what her eyes and her body asked of him, sinking into her with a sigh, the scope of his life beginning and ending in her. She never looked away, capturing him with eyes as vast and beautiful as the night sky until he was only dimly aware of his own movements. There was nothing but the sound of her rising agitation and the feel of her moving beneath him, her stare steadily demanding until he gave in to her will at last, losing himself.

He lay next to her, dragging air into his lungs, listening to her immoderate breathing. Never had he felt like this before, as he felt with her. Any kind of control or self-possession was only a myth, when she gave herself to him.

He watched her as he regained his breath, and after a while he reached out a hand to lay on her stomach. She looked at him, and he cocked a brow at her, affecting a mock concern.

"You feel well?" he inquired. Her brow creased in confusion. "I can have a powder sent up," he offered with a grin. "It was a rather large lunch."

Her eyes went wide with embarrassment. She turned and buried her face in the pillows. After a moment, her whole body began to shake, and she pulled her head up to look at him. Her girlish giggles turned into uncontrollable laughter, grew to unladylike guffaws. It shook the mattress, her smile as bright and wide as the future he imagined for them.

He had not known, not until now, how very much he had wanted this: Helen, her glorious body stretched out next to him in his bed, the sound of her joy filling the empty corners of his life.

CHAPTER THIRTEEN

It was a huge house, even larger than her brother's estate. It was most impressive, especially with the staff smartly turned out in the Summerdale livery, lined up to welcome their lord home and to be inspected by the new countess. If only the new countess could tear her eyes from her new mother-in-law. Helen felt perhaps her first duty as lady of this place would be to ask a footman to retrieve the woman's jaw from the ground.

Stephen seemed to find nothing at all unusual in his mother's gaping. But Helen found it almost as disconcerting as Lady Caroline's laughter. The girl was fairly shrieking with it.

His hand was firm on her elbow, though, and she would not give into the urge to turn tail and disgrace him as his family was so blithely doing. Good God, in front of the *servants*. She had imagined, if his family was anything at all like Stephen, that she would be met with grave disapproval. She had been preparing herself for it all day, but she'd thought it would be delivered in private. She had no idea what to do when one's new sister-in-law was helpless with laughter, and one's mother-in-law looked on the verge of an apoplexy upon introduction.

Stephen, though, seemed to know precisely what to do. His voice was withering and his look positively glacial, as he flicked a negligent glance at his sister and spoke to his mother.

"Shall we take this spectacle inside, mother? You look in need of a swooning couch."

At that, the dowager countess's mouth snapped shut and she looked at her son as though he were a curious nuisance, her gaze flicking up and down him. It seemed as though his sarcasm came as a bit of a surprise, for even his sister's raucous laughter died down to a chuckle.

"Oh, fiddle, Stephen!" said Lady Caroline with a mock severity. "You've ruined my fun. Who would ever have thought our dear Mama could be shocked? And by *you*? I was quite enjoying the sight."

Their mother looked annoyed at both of them, but silenced her daughter with a dismissive wave of her hand and returned her full attention to Helen. "Is it true then? You're really Helen Dehaven?" Something like amusement mixed with admiration began to light her face as Helen nodded. "And *he* married *you*?!"

She said it with a scandalized delight that left Helen at a loss. It was Stephen beside her, quiet and cold, that made her find her voice at last.

"Indeed he did, my lady," she said, with as much quiet composure as she could find. "I think it would be best if I made acquaintance with the staff, and then we can get inside out of the cold. I should very much like to speak with you in more private circumstances."

Leaving the dowager countess and Lady Caroline goggling behind them, she allowed Stephen to steer her to where the butler and housekeeper stood. He did not take advantage of the brief moment to speak to her, but gave her elbow an encouraging squeeze.

She managed the introductions as well as she could, considering how very mortified she was. She had thought the staring and mockery could be avoided for a while, at least until they were forced into Society. But here they were married barely a day, and already he had to come face to face with behavior that he could expect for the rest of his life. She hoped he did not feel too keen a regret.

She thanked the housekeeper Mrs. Bates for preparing their rooms on such hasty notice, and requested that tea be made available. "I'm afraid I don't know the best room for such a conference as this," she confided to the stout woman. No point in pretending as if their reception was in any way normal, when the servants had eyes and ears as good as anyone's. "Where would you suggest, Mrs. Bates?"

"The yellow salon, my lady, unless you would prefer the library?"

"The yellow salon will do nicely," Helen responded, with a glance back at her in-laws. "I think the Dowager Lady Summerdale will require the tea be as strong as you can make it, if you will."

It was impertinent of her, really, and inappropriate to speak to the servants in such a way, but she could not see them as faceless nobodies. They rather reminded her of the villagers back home. Mrs. Bates seemed to find nothing wrong with it, though, and Helen had the distinct impression the woman wanted to smile.

"Right away, my lady," she bobbed. "Some salts won't be amiss, either." And she turned to one of the maids behind her to see to it.

She did her best with the butler, and turned back to Stephen, who gave her an approving smile before his features turned grim once more. He led her inside, and she quickly lifted her chin in the hope of mustering a bit of spirit as Stephen guided her to a lovely yellow room where a fire cheerily blazed in the hearth.

His mother and sister followed them into the room, but he waited for the footman to take Helen's cloak before he leaned against the fireplace and looked to his mother expectantly.

"Well?" he inquired. "Haven't you more to say? I'd rather have it out now so that dinner might be a shade less purgatorial."

The dowager countess, though, was still looking curiously at Helen with an unmistakable gleam of malice in her eyes. Helen braced herself, knowing there was little defense against it. It was nothing she hadn't encountered before.

"You are Helen Dehaven," she said with a touch of wonder. "Oh but pardon me, I must remember to call you Lady Summerdale, mustn't I? Though I doubt I shall ever become accustomed to the idea that my son could be so very daring as to marry someone like you." She cocked her head thoughtfully, as though remembering. "I must say, my dear, no one ever thought to see you again. I remember the scandal plainly. Told this one she'd do well to wait until *after* marriage to run off into the woods with a lover, not as though she were in danger of acquiring one," she sniffed, inclining her head to Lady Caroline.

Helen stiffened at the delight in the woman's voice. *They are only words,* she told herself. She turned herself into ice, unable to conjure any other defense.

"But to surface as wife to this old nun," she turned her gaze to Stephen, who stood like a marble statue, expressionless. "I dare to think there's some hope for you yet, my boy. I can't imagine you'd raise a scandal for my amusement. Can it be possible that you couldn't resist, fell into her bed, and felt compelled to marry her?"

As she watched, Stephen held his mother's stare and allowed a meaningful pause before he spoke. The air of menace in the room heightened in the silence.

"I suggest," he said in a soft and dangerous tone that Helen had never heard from him, "that you assume nothing, and that you guard your poisonous tongue when speaking of my wife."

His mother raised a brow. "I do believe that was a threat. My, my, quite an unprecedented day when Stephen takes a trollop to wife and actually threatens his mother. It won't fly, you know. I know you too well."

"Then you know I can cut off your allowance tomorrow, though perhaps you think that I won't." He took two steps forward until he stood within an inch of his mother, his voice still soft and deadly. "I will. Nothing would give me greater pleasure, so you'd best think twice before speaking such filth again."

There was no sound but the tick of the mantel clock. Helen had no idea what to do, or if she should do anything at all. She was clearly watching the latest skirmish in a long and bloody war, and she had no desire to stumble further onto the battlefield. Her husband seemed quite an experienced veteran.

As she watched, her mother-in-law narrowed her eyes and observed, "Another first. I believe you actually mean it."

Stephen didn't answer, but his sister had kept silent long enough. "I believe he does, Mama, and I shouldn't be surprised if he saw fit to cut the tongue out of your mouth." She spoke idly, as though this were nothing unusual, and sat down to her embroidery. "Now, Lady Summerdale – may I call you Helen? Will you tell me the truth of why you cried off your engagement? No one seems to have ever known why, not even Anne Pembroke, though she's always had other things to say about you."

Helen fought to stay quiet at this. One would think it had happened only yesterday, instead of six years ago. Did people actually still speak of it? And did Anne Pembroke, that viper, really still bother to speak of her at all? No doubt she must, so long as there were vicious gossips such as Lady Caroline to listen.

"Miss Pembroke is no friend of mine," she said through stiff lips, wishing that she were back in her empty little house in Bartle, that Stephen were no more than a humble hostler, and that they could be free of scenes like this.

Just then the tea arrived, saving her from having to address Lady Caroline's interest in her past. Helen would have offered to pour, had she thought she could do so without spilling the entire pot, or dashing it into the girl's face. Her hands were trembling, rage and humiliation coursing through her. She had expected to be mocked even by his family, though she'd assumed it would not come so soon or so openly. But that they would treat *him* so horribly, and that they obviously always had, made her want to reach for the nearest vase and smash it over his mother's head.

She looked up as his sister poured and his mother sat. He stood stock still, staring straight ahead, a hint of the brooding frown about his mouth. When he looked up at her, his features lightened somewhat. She raised her chin and sent him a look that contained all the loyalty she could put into it. She was grateful that he'd chosen to see this through now instead of waiting until she had rested or been shown her rooms. It only confirmed how much he understood her, and how she much preferred to have it over with.

Lady Caroline seemed eager to continue a discussion of the past. "There now, Summerdale, I shan't insult your bride as our darling mother has done. In fact, I must say that she's far more interesting than that girl you had your eye on before."

"Clara," broke in the dowager countess. "A boring fribble if ever there was one. Much more suited to your tastes, I thought, but she slipped away, didn't she? She replaced you with a duke, and you replace her with this—"

"Oh, but she was so *dull* and this is absolutely delightful!" crowed Caroline. "Just wait until I write to Miss Pembroke and tell her that Saint Stephen has lost a duchess and married a—" She cleared her throat with a sideways glance at Helen. "That is, a woman whose character was formerly in question."

"You will inform no one, Caroline," he said sternly. "I shall tell our acquaintances myself, and have already begun to do so."

Helen felt a little jolt of fear at his words,

wondering what he would tell her brother. But suddenly the thought of her brother and all the disapproval he'd heaped on her seemed like the sweetest sugar next to Stephen's relations. She made a mental note to write a message to her brother's wife at last. And to look over Joyce's letter from months ago. She had mentioned this woman, Clara van Doren. *A friend*, she had written. Only a friend, now. And safely married to a duke.

"And I'll thank you not to question my wife's reputation, whether now or in the past," he continued. He came around the settee to stand behind Helen, placing one firm hand on her shoulder. There was no mistaking the warning in his words or his gesture. She lowered her face and sipped her tea.

"Don't get your back up, Summerdale," returned his sister irritably. "I was rather more concerned for your coveted ability to hold your perfection over the rest of us. However will you manage to look down your nose at me now that you've gone and joined the rest of us down in the muck, I wonder?"

"No more than I wonder what could have motivated you," interjected his mother. She looked at him keenly, then at Helen. When neither of them bothered to answer her, she gave a resigned sigh and stood. Helen almost wanted to laugh, so eager were they both to know and so badly did they hide it. They could hardly hope to mystify the rest of Society as much as they had managed to confound his mother.

"I'm going to dress for dinner. You'll want to see your rooms, Lady Summerdale," she said with a tug on the bell-pull and a chuckle. "Ah, a new Lady Summerdale. This will be delightful, I think." And she swept out of the room, just as a footman appeared.

"Come," Stephen said softly to Helen once his mother had gone. "It's been a long journey, and you'll want to rest before dinner."

"No doubt," replied Helen, giving a nod to Lady Caroline as she prepared to leave. "Once more unto the breach, and all that."

He quirked a smile at her as she turned to follow the footman. She heard his sister speaking to him as she reached the salon doors.

"My dear Saint Stephen," she drawled in an amused voice. "I'd solve the mystery for our mother if it wouldn't give her such satisfaction. Let her think you've decided to become scandalous, but I can see the truth of it." Her laughter followed Helen as she stepped out the doors. "My cold fish of a brother has married for love. How very unlikely!"

Helen paused outside the doors, waiting in the hall, unseen by any save the footman who stopped with her.

"Very unlikely," came his reply, and she hurried on, unwilling to hear more, at least not with the servants about.

※

Dinner proved even worse, which Helen would have sworn was impossible. She found herself wishing for Marie-Anne's quick wit a thousand times. Apparently the rest of the world might hesitate before speaking ill of Stephen, but his family had no such scruples. It was unbelievable that any people could speak to each other in such a way. To think that Stephen had endured an entire lifetime of such venom made her heart ache for him.

No wonder he had led a spotless life. She couldn't bear to imagine what cruelty they would heap upon him if he had given them legitimate cause for scorn. With a shock, she realized that he had done just that, simply by marrying her, and yet he had done it willingly, had insisted upon it.

"How long until you go to London and shock the masses?" his mother asked over the soup.

"You wish to be deprived of your sport?" asked Stephen. "I thought to stay and torment you as long as possible."

"But you do not torment me, my boy, you delight me," she replied with relish. "If only we had some guests about to liven things up further. It's really very rewarding, my dear Lady Helen, to see you here in the vaunted ancestral home."

Lady Caroline leaned closer to Helen. "Mama has been in agony since my brother inherited. You've saved the family from becoming dead boring."

"Yes, we couldn't have that," Stephen cut in. "Nothing is quite so unforgivable to my mother as an absence of eccentricity. I've been sadly lacking."

It galled Helen to be the one through whom the dowager countess's dearest dreams were fulfilled. She looked at Stephen from the corner of her eye, but he was utterly composed. He never seemed to rise to their baiting. She had the idea that Lady Caroline was her mother's pet, a partner in vexing Stephen. But any notion that the two were a united front was dashed somewhere between the salmon and the roast beef.

"Perhaps I shall create a scandal myself," mused Lady Caroline. "I'll set my sights on that Lord Granville, who is still suspected of poisoning his last wife. You'd tell me, wouldn't you Summerdale, if he really was a murderer?"

But Stephen didn't have a chance to answer. His mother was too quick.

"Granville would never look twice at you. No man with any self-respect would. There are more attractive dung heaps in London, my girl; I thought you understood that."

The most telling part of it all was that Lady Caroline did not even turn a hair at such abuse. Plainly it was nothing new; she only became quiet and turned her attention to her meal. It was appalling. Helen found herself actually admiring her own parents' indifference.

It was just before dessert that the situation grew worse. Stephen had been quiet for the most part, refusing to take part in the conversation even when they spoke most rudely of him. Helen counted eight times that she held herself back from throwing the candelabra at the women, but he remained unruffled until they brought up his brother.

"I wonder would Papa have approved of this match?" posed Lady Caroline, evidently finding the proceedings far too tame. "No, that's an obvious answer. He'd have disapproved only because you did it, of course. What I really wonder is what Edward would have thought."

Stephen went very still, fixing his sister in a stare that made her squirm and look down at the table uncomfortably. But his mother was not so faint of heart.

"Yes, what would he have thought, Summerdale?" she asked. Helen gripped her napkin tightly in fear of what the horrible woman would say next. "Did he whisper on his deathbed that you would never make a proper earl unless you could equal him in his whoring? This marriage is an excellent first step but you've a long way to go until you can outdo him in that regard. And you can't possibly surpass his parentage."

The tension in the room grew so thick that the servants seemed to have become statues along the walls in order to escape notice. Helen watched him grip his wine glass hard enough that she feared it might shatter, and desperately tried to think of something, anything, to divert the explosion she felt must come at any moment. She did not know exactly what his mother meant but she had obviously spoken what was, to Stephen, the unspeakable.

"My *brother*," he said slowly, staring daggers at his mother, "had a civil tongue in his mouth, a trait which was obviously not inherited."

"Inherited from his parents, my dear?" His mother gave a complacent smile. "Which parents are those?"

Stephen stood abruptly, the chair skidding back into the waiting hands of a footman. He looked ready to lunge across the table, but Helen suddenly found her voice.

"My lord, I have no taste for dessert. I am sure it is excellent, as everything has been. But I have a number of things to see to, if you'll be so kind as to escort me to our rooms."

Her voice was overloud, but he almost seemed not to hear her in his fury. She had never seen him in such extremity. She laid a hand on his arm and he looked at her, his features softening minutely.

"It has been quite a fatiguing day, my lord," she said. "Let us retire, and you can advise me in my letter to Lady Whitemarsh."

Still he did not move, and the table was silent. Helen feared his mother was waiting in delicious anticipation for an outburst, and knew absolutely that Stephen would regret losing his temper. And gradually — ever so gradually, she felt the subtle shift in the air, the silent and secret way he had of gaining control over the mood. He slid a hand over hers, his fingers tightening slightly.

He turned back to the table. "Good night then," he said flatly. He took her arm and led her from the room, as though nothing untoward had happened at all.

◈

"It could have been worse, you know," he said sleepily as they lay together hours later.

"Worse?" She tried to keep the shock out of her tone. "How so?"

He gave a half-laugh with no humor in it. "My father could still be alive."

His hand traced a lazy circle in the light sweat on her bare hip. She was tired, really she was, but when he touched her like that... She would have nestled even closer and kissed that tempting spot at the base of his throat, but he sounded exhausted.

"He never knew for sure. None of us has ever known the truth of it, except my mother, and it's impossible to say if she invented it only to bedevil my father."

"Did it drive him mad?" she asked, lacing her fingers through his.

"He didn't let it," he answered, dropping a kiss on the top of her head and settling deeper into the pillows. "But it drove Edward mad, not knowing, being constantly mocked in his own family because of it. And it drives me mad, because I'm sure it's a lie."

Her eyelids felt very heavy. "Well, then, it is a lie, I'm sure," she said through a yawn.

"Flatterer."

"No," she mumbled blearily. "I mean it. You have a marvelous instinct for such things. You are always right. That's what infuriates them."

He seemed to come more awake at that, his arms tightening around her. But she was slipping deeper into sleep.

"Always right. Except when it came to you."

It felt so good and companionable to lay here with him. So, rather than to think of the ways he had been wrong and right about her, she let herself slip into sleep.

CHAPTER FOURTEEN

He was afraid that he would lose her. There was nothing he could point to in justification of the fear, only an instinct he had learned to ignore at his peril.

Three nights of the last seven, he had woken to the sounds of her nightmares, little whimpering moans or even shouts that woke her too. One time she had turned to him and curled up in his arms, falling asleep without ever telling him what she had dreamt. The other times, she moved away from him and wrapped a blanket around herself to go and sit in the window seat. She had touched his face lightly and said his name before retreating, but it was clear she did not want him to follow. It was clear to him that she did not wish to be touched. So he watched her sit in the moonlight, her face turned from him, her breath visible in the cold night air. She seemed to prefer it to the warmth of his bed, sometimes. And he let her be, grateful that she allowed him onto the fringes of her internal world, happy to keep stay away from any topic that might bring her pain.

But it haunted him, the feeling that she could go. That she *would* go, if given sufficient provocation. Each time he woke to find her next to him, he felt immense relief that she was still there. When she still wanted him even after hearing what his mother and sister had to say of him, he wanted to thank her. When he touched her, he felt as though his hands only skimmed over the illusion of her, that she waited to dance out of his reach.

It was something about how very competent she was. She did not need him, not truly, to survive. It was a fact she had proven every day for the last six years. If she tired of him, of this life, what was to prevent her leaving him? He could not imagine that he could hold her.

Even now when she sat across from him chattering on about household affairs, she did not seem entirely real. He felt no permanence, as though at any moment she would stand and walk out the door, and keep walking until the horizon swallowed her up.

To prevent it, he strove to remove anything disagreeable. He'd found it easy enough to persuade his mother to visit her lover. Not that he said it outright, but he made no hesitation to put the notion into her head, knowing she couldn't resist the chance to mock him within hearing of more sympathetic ears. His sister was much more manageable, and avoidable. He took great pains to be sure Helen did not have to endure any more scenes such as those on their arrival.

He wished he could spend more time with her, but there was work to be done. He spent hours in his office and would look up to find her gliding into the room in the afternoon, bringing the tea tray with her. They sat together as she told him of her latest conquests among the staff.

"Foster's sister is expecting," she said. "She lives down in the village, and she had a hard time with the last child. He tells me the midwife passed on last year and there's been no suitable replacement."

He was unsure exactly what he should make of this. "Foster? The first footman?" It had always seemed enough to know the man's name, that he came from Surrey and felt somewhat out of place here. He knew this Foster was one of those servants who was unsympathetic to his mother, loyal to the memory of his brother – and that's all Stephen had felt the need to know. But now Helen gave him a life, complete with a sister and concerns about childbirth.

"Yes, Stephen, the first footman," she laughed softly. "But I speak of his sister, and more importantly of the need for a new midwife in the village. Chambermaid Susan tells me her mother was a midwife and taught her well. Shall I give her leave to attend births from now on?"

As he'd been unaware until this moment that there was indeed a chambermaid named Susan, he gave his wife a smile and permission to do whatever she liked. She had taken it to heart, the idea of winning over the servants. He had no doubt that soon enough they would love her as well as everyone back in Bartle had done.

Nevertheless, there were shadows under her eyes. Spring was coming, and the inevitable return to London. She had sent the carefully composed note to her new sister-in-law, and soon enough an answer came.

He went to find her in the midst of her meeting with the groundskeeper. She was diplomatically imparting her disapproval of rhododendrons when Stephen entered.

"Are you very attached to the rhododendrons, my lord?" she asked with an anxious frown when she saw his gravity.

"I'm far more attached to you," he replied with a smile, trying to remain calm and congenial, for her sake. "Do whatever you like with them, but come with me now. We have visitors."

The blood drained from her face, but she gave a nod to the groundskeeper as she moved toward Stephen. She paused outside the door facing him, her face set.

"Who?" The one word held a wealth of anxiety.

"Your brother and his wife." He waited, standing quietly beside her as she froze. It reminded him of the first time they had met, when he had mentioned her brother and everything in her went still.

"Helen, if you do not want to see him, I will send him away." But not without first telling Whitemarsh to his face how wrong he had been, how he was all that was dishonorable and unfeeling.

"No, I–" She stopped, looking down at her dress. It was the steel gray, serviceable and plain but not tattered. "I only want to look less – well, I should like to change if Lady Whitemarsh has come. At least one of the new gowns must be ready by this time. I'll be down again soon."

He caught her hand before she could escape. She was trembling. "I will be there," he said as he held her hand. "I'll stay beside you all the while, unless you wish to be alone."

She bit her lip. "Of course you will," she said, giving his hand a tight squeeze and then letting go to hurry up the stairs.

It would give him time to speak to her brother. He made his way to the drawing room where the butler had shown them, feeling the anger surge in him like a tidal wave.

They were waiting quietly, Lady Whitemarsh seated on the divan while Alex stood with his back to the door and staring at a porcelain figure on the mantel. The frozen tableau was shattered when the door closed behind him. Alex did not turn, but raised his head suddenly and gripped his hands into fists as his wife jumped up and stared with round eyes at Stephen.

"Oh. Lord Summerdale," she said with some disappointment. He came to her and took her hand, bowing quickly.

"I should like a word in private with your husband." He was unable to keep the anger from coloring his tone. Alex had turned to him now, relief in his expression as though he thought Stephen would be any more forgiving than Helen.

Lady Whitemarsh cut into his thoughts in a stern voice. "I prefer to stay, my lord. Neither you nor my husband will prevent me from meeting Lady Summerdale." She shot a peevish and distinctly mutinous look at Alex.

Stephen forced his thoughts away from the too-appealing vision of a duel with his wife's brother. "I would venture to say that Lady Summerdale feels the same, and I think it unwise to test my strength against the both of you. All the same, I ask only a moment with your husband. My wife will be down shortly."

"Your wife," echoed Alex. He looked as if he didn't believe it. "You've married her, then, it wasn't one of her wild tales. And tell me, what could possibly have induced our noble Lord Summerdale to marry a pariah? I'd dearly love to know, sir!"

Absolutely astonishing. The fool was actually angry with him. Stephen would have laughed at him, had he been capable of feeling anything but outrage.

"Wild tales!" Stephen fairly shouted at the man. "And do you defend her now, my lord? How do you *dare* to think you have the right to judge anything that concerns her well-being when her wild tales are all true?" His voice had risen, but he did not care. If Lady Whitemarsh would not leave, he could only give vent to his fury by shouting it. "Incoherent, you said! Let me tell you, she was perfectly coherent, every last damned word was clear as crystal. And you – her beloved brother, the only one who could defend and protect her – the *only* one! But you chose to believe anything else, didn't you?"

He was breathing heavily, the disgust and rage battering against reason and forethought. Alex stood still, looking at him blankly, not even bothering with excuses or protests.

"You believe the likes of Mrs. Wilke and Anne Pembroke, but you do not believe your perfectly rational sister's story."

"They were not the only ones, those two!" Alex burst out, his volume if not his anger matching Stephen's. "And she was not perfectly rational. You cannot know."

"I know that no young girl can be expected to be composed when forced to speak of such savagery. I know that it was *you* who ruined her. It was you who took what life remained to her when you turned your back."

"I could not risk being seen to approve of her, not when her actions brought such discredit to the Whitemarsh name," cried Alex, a hunted look on his face. "It hardly matters *what* the truth is, you know that."

This defense deprived Stephen of words for a long moment. "Hardly matters?" he asked in disbelief.

Alex held up a hand. "I did not mean it in that way, damn you, I only meant that what was believed of her would ruin her no matter what I might wish to believe, and no matter what the truth was."

"You betrayed her. You sent me there to learn what you already knew but did not believe! And why?" He stopped, gathering the remnants of his control as his shout echoed in the room, trying to find some satisfaction in the embarrassed flush that had stolen over Alex's face.

"Tell me why," he said tightly. "Why were you so quick to dismiss her words, to dismiss her entire worth?"

There was silence as Alex merely stared at him. He shifted his gaze to his wife, but Lady Whitemarsh shook her head slightly.

"I will not defend you in this, Alex," she said quietly. "I never have."

He looked ready to collapse into tears. His shame was evident, flooding into the room and slowly filling every corner until at last he licked his lips and spoke hoarsely.

"I was so young," he said faintly and with a humorless laugh. "So young and stupid. And she always loved to invent tales as a child, to get herself out of mischief..."

"Mischief!" Stephen could not believe this. Had not Lady Whitemarsh been there, he would have gladly lunged for the man's throat. "You call it mischief when she has the audacity to refuse marriage with a monster?"

Alex winced at the word and closed his eyes briefly. That he could be so willfully blind, that he could stand here now and make the whole thing out to be a terrible misjudgment, was insupportable. "Answer me, damn you," he insisted.

"I did not want to believe it!" Alex shouted. And here at last was the truth, obvious in the way that Alex was appalled at his own words. He seemed smaller, as if he had been deflated in the discovery his own cowardice. He looked up at Stephen, who watched him lose the struggle for composure.

"I didn't want to believe it," he repeated, his voice small now. "I still don't, that such a thing could happen to her. That I could not protect her from it, and that she ever had to endure such things. I didn't want it to be true, Summerdale. It was easier to believe that she was a liar than it was to believe that he had... done such a thing."

Stephen looked at him, wordless. He found it impossible to believe they were brother and sister, when he was so weak and she so strong. The man was a fool, how had he not seen it before? But he dimly heard the voice of his own conscience, the memory of all the things he himself had believed of her. And he could not forget, ever, the terror on her face when she had told him what had happened. It was understandable, if not excusable, to prefer the lie.

The sound of her footsteps on the stairs came to

him, and he became forcefully aware that it was not his place to forgive, or to judge. It was hers, as much as he might resent the fact. He did not dare move closer to Alex for fear that the urge to strike him was still too strong to resist. But he spoke from where he stood, softly enough so that she would not hear but loud enough that Whitemarsh would not misunderstand.

"I will kill you if you hurt her again."

And then she was there in the doorway, standing erect with her chin level. Like a soldier going to battle. But when she finally looked up and her eyes went straight to Alex, she lost the combative pose.

She stared at him, and he stared back at her, both of them looking not a little lost as she walked slowly toward her brother. She stopped a pace away from him, her eyes drifting over his face.

"You've got gray hair," she observed in a whisper, her eyes resting on the patches of silver at his temples.

Alex's lips twitched, a smile that died before it was born. "And you've taken to wearing shoes."

She lifted a hand and lightly touched the hair that fell on his forehead. It suddenly seemed quite natural, like the most obvious thing in the world, that these two should still love each other. That their bond had not been completely broken. Stephen felt like an intruder once again, witnessing things that he should not, his anger ebbing away at what he saw.

Alex made a choked sound, hanging his head. Helen watched her brother as his knees buckled and he sank to the floor. His weeping was only the sound of wasted years and broken promises to Stephen, but he saw it stir compassion in her. She knelt next to him on the carpet and took his hand, and he knew without a doubt that they should be alone.

Stephen took Lady Whitemarsh by the elbow and steered her away from the scene. He could not bear to watch as his wife – unbelievably, incredibly – comforted her sobbing brother over his guilt. He closed the door behind them and left her to fight her own battles in whatever way she chose.

§

"It was true, then, all of it," said Alex. She could see from the horror in his face that he was imagining the details. "God forgive me, it is all true."

"It's no use to dwell on it. It is impossible to live at all if you think of nothing else. I have learned that."

She had an arm around him as they knelt together on the floor. It felt strange, that she would not be angry with him or feel any vindication. Perhaps she would, later. For now she could only think of the pain Henley had caused to so many people, and that included her brother. It gave her no joy to think that the guilt and helplessness might dog him all his days. She quelled the urge to apologize for carrying this thing with her wherever she went, this memory that would not go away. It contaminated everything. She contaminated everything.

But she was determined she would not lose another thing she loved. Not even her brother and all his faithless suspicions.

"Can you ever forgive me?" he asked, pulling away from her. "I'll go. You cannot possibly ever forgive me. What have I been thinking?"

She looked down at her hands, still after days of

trembling. "I don't even know what forgiveness is anymore, Alex. I cannot forget it, and I cannot love you again with a carefree heart." She gave a sad shrug, tired of years wasted in thinking of what forgiveness meant. She felt the tears swell in her throat and threaten to spill. "But you are my brother. I have tried and failed, to stop loving you."

"I am unworthy of it." He wiped his hand roughly across his face. "I'll find him and kill him. That's what I'll do."

"You'll do no such thing!" she snapped in alarm, tears forgotten. It terrified her even to think of anyone she cared about putting themselves in Henley's path. And Alex now wore the look of a man ready to do murder, or worse. "I will not lose another thing to him, do you hear me?" She shook him. "Do you? *That* is something I would never forgive you."

She watched him acknowledge this, that she truly meant it. He gave her a resigned look. "Then I'm sure your new husband will be pleased to flay me alive."

"Well, you won't oblige him, please."

"But you – when..." He closed his eyes tightly as though to hide from his own words. "It hurt. Henley. He hurt you badly. What he did to you, I mean."

"It is the past, Alex." He would think of it, picture it, and she couldn't stand the thought of her brother imagining her violation over and over again for the rest of his life. Just as Stephen would picture it, if he knew. She gave him a more severe look than ever she had given him. "You will leave it in the past, as I have. I will not suffer talk of it." She took a deep breath and blew it out. "It happened, it's done, and I am well. Now tell me about your wife."

He stared at her, and she thought he must be

trying to reconcile his memories of her younger frivolous self with the resolve he saw before him.

"She was here, but..." he said, distracted. "But I want to know about you and Summerdale. I do not intend it as insult, but really — how did he come to wed you?"

She couldn't resist smiling at his eager curiosity. *My brother,* she thought as a warm glow spread to her fingertips. *I have my brother again.* And in the same moment, she reminded herself that she must not invest too much hope in him. He had failed her, and she forgot that at her own peril. Still, it was wonderful, to have a brother to talk with and tease once more.

"He asked me. He was really rather insistent, you know." She laughed at the astonishment on his face. "I actually tried to talk him out of it, if you can imagine. It fairly boggles the mind."

"Well, he's an excellent man," Alex murmured, obviously trying to overcome his confusion. He looked keenly at her, catching her lighthearted air with a tentative smile. "Of course he would come to care for you. He is no fool, and only a fool would fail to love you instantly."

"Oh, thank you very much," she laughed at this extravagance. "I vow, I do enjoy a repentant brother."

"But what about you? Did you marry him for love, then? Are you happy as you deserve to be?"

She avoided answering all of it, knowing better than to admit anything as dangerous as love. She gave her brother a smile and responded with the one answer she was sure of.

"I'm happy."

The next few days passed in a kind of daydream for Helen. Her brother was there, and her new sister-in-law, and the manor became like home at last. They promised to come again and stay for a longer visit. "Next time at your invitation, of course," said Lady Whitemarsh, who did not apologize for dragging Alex and Helen into each other's presence. Lady Whitemarsh was keen to hear about Alex as a child, and Helen was most pleased to oblige her with tales that made Alex blush and bluster.

The second day, when Alex and Stephen had closeted themselves in the office to discuss business affairs, she took Lady Whitemarsh out onto the grounds for a quick stroll. It was under the pretense of asking her opinion on the gardens, but Helen really wanted the opportunity to speak to her out of the servants' hearing.

"I hope this business our husbands are so intent to discuss is not too dire," Helen said. "Lord Summerdale seemed rather tense about it. There is ill-feeling between them," she observed. Stephen had been coldly polite to her brother all through the evening meal.

Lady Whitemarsh pursed her lips. "Well, I dare say there would be ill feelings. I'll tell you honestly, Lady Helen, that I care deeply for your brother. But the one thing I have always found despicable is that he refused to believe you. I very nearly refused to marry him because of it. I only agreed on the condition that he would speak to you again."

Helen resisted the smile that came to her lips. Oh, she liked this new sister. It was most pleasant to have a woman to speak to. She was beginning to miss Marie-Anne desperately, and though of course she was irreplaceable, she thought her friend would approve of her brother's wife.

"Yes," she granted with a nod. "That must be the cause of the animosity, but I should hate to come between them. It is the past." And she was determined to think only of the future. She would not be afraid and she would forget and be happy. "At least business affairs seem to force them together. I can hope that whatever they're discussing will heal the breach."

"I hope you are correct in that," said Lady Whitemarsh with a frown.

Helen wanted no frowns, or any talk about the past. "I believe this fountain is visible from the office window," she tried. "Perhaps I'll ask Lord Summerdale if he objects to pulling out these shrubs."

And they were launched into a discussion of gardening until the cold drove them inside. Their husbands did not appear until dinner was served, both of them looking in much better humor. Whatever they had discussed had eased the tension between them, though Helen couldn't hope to understand how simple business affairs had managed it.

Her brother and Lady Whitemarsh left the next day. They had avoided asking if they would all meet up again in London soon, but Stephen alluded to it briefly. "In the spring," he said, and it was clear he meant they would go then.

London in the spring. The season. Helen dreaded it, not only for herself, but because Stephen seemed very grim whenever London was mentioned. She wished they could stay hidden here, or perhaps somewhere else where his family would not come. That would be a perfect world.

Even this was wonderful, with his mother gone. It was easy enough to avoid Lady Caroline and her thinly veiled threats to invite "friends" to visit. Helen had no doubt about which friends she alluded to. If ever it bothered her, if ever she found herself growing uneasy, Stephen set her fears aside by his mere presence.

She sat composing a letter to Joyce, wondering whether or not she should tell her that they would be in London soon, the anxiety building at the thought. And Stephen would suddenly be there, grinning in the way that made her forget everything else. She had dresses made, feeling the apprehension swell inside her until her husband looked at the finished gowns and made her laugh by saying that Marie-Anne would insist on more flounces, that she was too modest in her tastes to appease the French sensibility. Life with him was like slipping into a dream, and she gave herself to it willingly.

It would be a rude awakening when they went to London and saw his friends, his associates. But she found that she did not have to wait so long as that for the harsh reality to shatter her happiness.

She went to his office one day while he was out riding, meeting with some tenants to discuss the planting. She had only wanted to find some wax to seal a letter to Emily. Not wishing to call Foster, she went to the office – a room she normally avoided in preference of the library – and searched the side drawer of Stephen's desk. There she found a stack of letters.

She would not have taken notice of them had they not been bundled together with a blue silk ribbon. It was a sense of foreboding, a horrible feeling that she should have known about this, that made her pick up the letters and examine them more closely. It was vile, really, to pry into his private correspondence. No, she wouldn't do that. But she couldn't resist taking note of how thick the stack was. Hundreds of letters, a woman's writing on each. The same woman. A woman who evidently sprinkled her parchment with perfume, and who had written most recently by the stink of it.

She told herself not to look almost as many times as she told herself to look further. It felt like being possessed of two entirely different minds: one wanting to act as if she had never seen it, and one wanting to rip them open and read whatever lay in wait. She had felt it before, this rejection of what was before her eyes and the dawning realization that she couldn't deny it. Just as she couldn't deny that she had seen Stephen hide his correspondence from her more than once. *Oh, the terrible things he might hide,* whispered that voice which had been born in her six years before.

"Silly girl," she admonished herself.

She let neither impulse win out. She only set the bundle on the desk very gently, as if it would explode at any minute, and prepared to wake up from the dream.

§

Stephen stayed outdoors far longer than he should have, discussing crops and cattle with tenants who seemed more eager to talk about the new countess and how she had kindly solved the problem of a midwife in addition to making a favorable impression on everyone in the village when she had visited a few days ago. He could not stop the smile that crept across his face every time she was mentioned. There seemed to be no detail too small for her to involve herself in, and no reason to fear that she was not happy to make her home here, with him.

And so he told himself as he strolled into the house, smiling broadly because he knew he would see her soon. But there was no sign of her in the library, or in the salon when he looked there.

"Collins," he said to the butler as he spotted the servant on the stair. "I'm late for dinner, am I?"

"Lady Summerdale has requested the meal wait for your arrival, my lord. I have alerted the kitchen to your return."

There was something like reproach in the butler's look. He must be imagining it.

"Very well, then. We may wish to take dinner *en suite* this evening," he said, heading toward the stairs, expecting to find her in their rooms.

"As you wish, my lord." The look on the butler's face as he said it stopped him. If Stephen did not know him better, he would say the expression was sly. But the butler gave a slight bow and said, "I believe your secretary has sent some rather important documents. You will find them in your office."

Stephen was not expecting any important documents. That, coupled with the cunning look on Collins' face, was enough to alarm him. If Alex had written, if Helen had seen their correspondence and her eye had been drawn to Henley's name on the page... He wanted to shield her from anything having to do with Henley. And if she knew that they worked now against him, he was sure she would try to stop them. He did not wish to be stopped. He did not wish to debate it with her, when it would require them to speak of her past. With a growing sense of dread, he made his way to the office to dispose of any telltale scraps having to do with Henley. The he would seek out Helen to find if any damage had been done.

It was too late. She was there, sitting on the small divan before the fire, no other light in the room. She made no acknowledgement of his entrance. He had the feeling she'd been there all day, and a cold weight settled in the pit of his stomach when she did not turn to him. Even when he came to stand behind her and kiss her head in greeting, she stared down at the table in front of her, stiff and silent.

"I'm late," he said softly. "You've been waiting. I'm sorry."

Silence was the only response. She was as remote to him as she had been on their first meeting, the distance so great and difficult to traverse that it felt like they were strangers. Finally she spoke, with such polite detachment that he thought he had dreamed everything since he'd first seen her.

"You need not apologize," she said with a pleasantness that chilled him to the bone. "I have no wish to take your time or attention away from your business affairs. Or your personal affairs, either."

He concentrated on drawing air into his lungs. "What do you mean by that?" he asked with what he hoped was indifferent curiosity. "And why are you here in my office? I've become used to finding you in the library."

And then his eye fell on the table before her, the ribbon that held Clara's letters gleaming in the firelight. He felt it like a silent explosion in his chest, a weakness that spread throughout him and made him want to shout a denial. He stood there for an eternity listening to his world crumble.

"I didn't know what to do," she said steadily. "I was looking for sealing wax." She gave a little flip of her hand, as though to dismiss the unimportance of it. "I thought I could either pretend not to see it, or I could read every one of them. But in the end I couldn't decide, so I stayed here. I didn't want to...touch them again, but it seemed impolite to leave them sitting here."

"Helen," he began. Then he stopped, not having any other words to say in the midst of the emotion that seized him. Fear and embarrassment, but also a childish resentment. He had no right to be angry, but he was. Angry at her for finding them, for being there at all where she didn't belong. His affairs, his office, his correspondence — what business did she have looking through his desk? And he, idiot that he was, had left them there, so easy to find and so obvious in what they were, condemnation bundled in a cool blue ribbon.

The sudden realization that he had to choose between them angered him in a way he had never expected. So many secrets he had learned and kept in his life, but Clara was the only one of them he had cherished. The only thing that was his own, the pain and joy of her neatly contained in this damning stack of paper. He had given Helen everything it was in his power to give: thrown his principles to the wind, made her his wife, had chosen her and her protection over the life he knew, would gladly endure the mockery of all his acquaintance for her sake. And still it was not enough.

It was this that would make him lose her, and the pain of it kept him frozen where he stood. She had not moved at all, a sculpture in ice as he stood dying slowly behind her. It was her indifference, her apparent resignation and acceptance that made him shut his eyes and take a deep breath. He didn't allow himself to think as he walked around to the table in carefully measured steps.

He looked down at them, at the ribbon that he remembered tied around Clara's hair on that night when they had last met. He had woken the next morning to read that she was engaged to her duke, as if the kisses and avowals of love between them had never happened. There near the top of the stack was her letter of condolence that had come to him upon Edward's death. Above it was a year's worth of love letters; below it was everything since, filled with more love and friendship and promise, his only buffer against solitude.

He picked them up, Helen's silence at his back threatening to rip him into pieces, and set them in the fire.

He regretted it instantly, even as he took the poker and pushed them deeper into the coals. The ribbon burst into flame immediately; the edges of parchment curled up and turning to black dust before his eyes. He leaned against the mantel, feeling nothing but the ashes of incinerated love blowing through him, knowing he could not turn around to face Helen yet. The surge of resentment was too fresh, the loss of what little of Clara was left to him like a blade in his heart.

He watched it burn in the quiet of the room until he could not stand another moment of it, wondering if it would be enough or if he would lose his wife no matter what he gave up to keep her.

It seemed like a lifetime before she broke the silence.

"You didn't have to do that."

He gave a bitter laugh. "Didn't I? Or is it not enough unless I throw myself in the fire?"

"I meant that you are entitled to keep your...friends. Please do not think that I wish to make any demands of you in that way."

He whirled on her. "No, you never make demands, do you?" His vehemence startled her, and himself. He stopped himself from saying more. She made no claim on him; she never had, and it drove him to desperation. Only in the night, when he held her and buried himself in her did she ever demand anything, and then it was total surrender of his body and soul, while she held herself back from him.

She recovered her composure, folding her hands tightly on her lap. "The only thing I have ever asked of you is that you will not spare me the truth, no matter how painful. You have changed your life for me quite enough already. I can have no objection to you keeping your mistress."

"She is not my mistress. She was never my mistress." He would give her that much of the truth, but moved quickly to interrupt whatever nonsense she would spout next. "And am I to allow you the same liberty? Do you hope to find satisfaction with someone else?" Stupid. *Don't bring it up, you ass.* He could not stand to lose both of them in one night.

"Because you can abandon that notion right now. I will not share you, as much as you seem willing to share me."

She stood with a look of disgusted offense contorting her lovely face. "I did not say that, stop putting words into my mouth!" She strode to the desk and back, stopping at the end of the room furthest from him. "I am not blind to everything you have done for me, Stephen, and how little I have deserved any of it. And it will only be worse when we go to London. But I cannot possibly face it if you do not tell me what to expect! I only want to know if I will be followed by the whispers of my own past, or if there will be talk of some other woman in your life that I must contend with."

"There will be no talk about me for you to contend with," was all he managed to say. That's all she cared about. The idea of a mistress she would willingly live with, but God forbid she be bothered with the senseless gossip of London. It was hard to believe he had actually loved her practicality. He would give everything for even the hint of jealousy from her, some sign that it mattered to her at all.

She gave a brisk nod of her head as if that settled everything, frustrating him further, and he found his voice again.

"All I have asked from you, Helen, is a promise that you be my wife. That we not have the kind of marriage I have watched my parents and so many others play out. Have you forgotten it so soon that you would propose I keep a mistress?" he demanded, unable to control the way his voice rose.

Her face was carefully blank. "I have not forgotten."

She turned away to face the door, and the sight of it drained the anger from him in a sickening swoop. She would walk out. She could keep walking forever and he would lose the last thing that meant anything to him. The certainty of it left him hollow.

But she did not leave. She hesitated, stayed on the spot for an indeterminate length of time while his life waited in the balance. Finally she gave a little stamp of her foot, like a child in a temper tantrum. All her cool composure was gone, and her emotion released a warm flood of relief inside him.

"I don't want to care for you so much!" she cried. "Not if you will hide your heart from me. Can you not understand that?"

He understood it. They only wanted the same thing, after all – to keep her safe and happy. He crossed to her and put his hands on her arms, leaning his chest against her back, glad to feel her soften against him.

"It's not hidden from you," he said. This was one pure truth he could admit without hesitation. He reached forward and took her unresisting hands in his, running his fingers along her open palms. "It's right here."

And he turned her to him and kissed her, laid her down on the carpet and took her in the firelight, knowing it was not enough to bind her completely, but praying it would keep her with him for another night.

CHAPTER FIFTEEN

Chère Hélène,

I give you the village business quickly, so that I can move on to what is more important. The Huxleys have acquired an enormous bull that frightens everyone from here to Hillside, little Agnes blushes whenever John Turner steps into the pub, and Mrs. Gibbons stunned us all by making a cake fit for a king to bring to The Reverend's annual picnic. Voilà. I am sure you're reeling with the excitement of it all. Fetch some salts and read on.

I will be in London to collect my quarterly allowance in a few weeks — is this soon enough? I don't like this writing to each other, you are too good at hiding things on paper. What is wrong, my dear friend? Except you say that nothing is wrong. I am supposed to think you want me to tell you stories of my darling Shipley? As if you have not heard them all a thousand times! You are worse than the Sphinx.

But you sound happy and it brings me joy to know it. Whatever else there is that you do not say, it worries you and takes away from the content you have found. I will not allow this. How I can help, I do not know, but I shall come to you (with discretion, of course). I will not object to seeing your handsome lord husband, as Bartle is become dismal without his devilish grin.

I hope that you are well settled by now. The townhouse sounds marvelous, will I have a room? Ooh, and servants! I'll do my best not to be outrageous.

Bisous,
Marie-Anne

~~~

They had been in London only two weeks when it happened. Much of the country staff had traveled with them to the city, and Helen was grateful that she didn't have to adjust to any new names and faces. No need to explain to a new cook that Helen occasionally enjoyed looking in on the kitchen sometimes, or to insist to yet another butler that she disliked being doted on continually.

The butler, Collins, was one of her greatest conquests. He had been stiff and formal when they'd met at the country estate, a faint but recognizable gleam of judgment in his eye that told her instantly he knew of her past. But he had thawed at the first evidence that Helen had a strong aversion to her mother-in-law, and she had found in their ensuing alliance that he made an excellent friend.

She teased him mercilessly over his penchant for gossip, which he never hesitated to share with her if he thought it could be useful. Lady Cashley had been the first to call at the townhouse only a week ago. When Collins brought the calling card to her and saw her blanch at the impending first foray into good society, he informed her she need not worry. Lady Cashley was indebted to Lord Summerdale for some service about which the butler remained tight-lipped, and she would not have come calling to cause trouble.

It went well, as did other visits. Stephen was with her through most of them, but left her increasingly on her own after the first week. The London season was not yet in full swing, and the real test would come later. For now the trickle of visitors were her husband's nearest associates, who would share an interest in welcoming her into society without reserve.

She had been thinking that perhaps it would not be so terrible. Perhaps, despite everything she had learned from life, they could manage to succeed in escaping the jaws of her past.

Silly girl. In one blinding moment, she finally understood that there could be no escape. It was a monster from the deep, dedicated to pulling her down into the depths and smothering her.

Collins had the day off, over his own protestations. Helen had insisted he must have one day to himself before the season was upon them, had insisted it for most of the staff. Stephen would be back in time for tea and any visitors that may come, and there were enough servants left to tend to their needs.

But it seemed there were early visitors, from the sounds issuing from the entry hall. Helen sent her maid to tell Foster to show the visitor into the salon. It must be that kind-faced American woman calling; she'd have no notion that it was far too early, but Helen didn't mind. Only yesterday she'd received a letter from Jack, saying that Katie had improved beyond anything and they now considered emigrating.

She could hope the American lady would know something of Wilmington, where they proposed settling.

She made her way down the stairs, her mind filling with all the questions she had. Passing by Foster's slight scowl, she gave a roll of her eyes to show her acknowledgement and acceptance of the irregularity of it.

"Send for tea, please, and don't worry," she murmured as she approached the drawing room. "It's only a social call."

She turned with a bright smile of welcome prepared on her face, her hands outstretched in greeting, straight into a nightmare made flesh and blood. It spoke her name and robbed her balance and laid waste to six years of freezing calm.

Through the silence that pounded on her ears, she heard her own voice, sounding as though she had never spoken in her adult life, creaking with rust and disuse. It escaped from numb lips with the one word she wished never to say again.

"Henley."

It seemed impossible to think beyond the sound of his name. Impossible that he was here, in this home where she had thought herself safe, impossible that he looked precisely the same. In the instant she looked in his face, she experienced the strangest sensation – as though all the evil in him were only a dream, that such darkness could never exist behind his handsome face and bright blond hair.

But it was gone in a flash when her own words came back to her. They came to her like a haunting, like no time had elapsed at all and they only continued where they had left off. The last words she had spoken to him, as she pressed the miraculously found blade against his throat: *Get out of me.*

The echo of them erased the unreality of it all and replaced it with a tidal wave of terror. *Do not turn your back on him.* The command came clear to her mind, stopping her from whirling around to the door when her legs strained to flee.

She stood rooted to the spot, petrified, a rabbit going still in the grass as it tried to escape the notice of a greater and more cunning creature. She could not find a scrap of courage. She was distantly amazed that she had ever screamed at him, refused him, defied him – that she had ever thought she could win against him.

She felt a sharp pang of grief for the girl she had been, the girl she had chastised as silly and stupid, who had not been afraid and had suffered for it.

"It pleases me to see you have done well for yourself, Helen," he said with apparent sincerity.

He gazed at her, and the blue of his eyes was the color of lies, brimming with affection. It made everything real again, reminded her that he had truly loved her, had been frantic at losing her. And she had loved him to desperation. All of it... it had all happened, and he stood in her drawing room as if he were greeting an old friend.

"Why are you here?" she choked out, the weakness of her voice betraying her terror. "Leave. Leave now, and I will not tell my husband you have come."

He raised an eyebrow, the arrogance of his expression ushering in a host of forgotten memories. "But it is your husband I have come to discuss, my dear."

The anger came so quickly that she could not stop

the waspishness of her words. "I am not your dear!" She pulled in a breath as her mind began at last to function. A weapon, something, she must find something in case he came too close. *But do not turn your back to him.* She edged toward the writing desk.

"Leave. You are not welcome here." She tried to speak it in a low warning, tried to summon the protective rage, but it came out tremulous and thin. She felt shamefully close to tears. He reduced her to a cringing child.

"Helen, please, I must speak to you. You must hear me!" He looked to her with a longing that she recognized well but reminded herself was poison. Everything about him was a lie, from the coaxing in his voice to the air of harmlessness about him. She reached the edge of the desk, but did not look down.

"Please. I know we parted horribly, but I do not deserve this treatment. If ever you cared for me before I so recklessly lost you, I beg you to help me." He reached up, and she gave a start before she realized he was only running a hand through his hair. "They are ruining me, Helen. The bankers will not act on my behalf. No one will extend me credit." He looked hunted, hungry for understanding.

"Leave!"

God, would her voice never gain strength? It was imperative that she not listen to him, inconceivable that he would be imploring her for help. He could dismiss it all as parting badly, and she knew herself susceptible to the delusion, knew that she wanted nothing so much as to pretend it had never happened. But she could not. Her panic would not let her.

She nervously ran her hand over the desk behind her, closed her fingers in a death grip around the paper knife at last, and opened her mouth to let out six years of hatred.

"Why did you kill them? *Why?* They did nothing to you!" Katie's face rose up in her mind, a reminder of the child he had killed. The solid handle of the paper knife in her hand was a reminder of the blade she had held so long ago, giving her courage. "They had nothing. They were not poaching on your lands, you fool, but you *knew* that. And you killed them anyway, only because you could! How many others have you killed?" The rage kept her afloat now, pounding through her, uncontrollable. "How many?" she shouted.

"Helen–"

"Keep my name out of your mouth!" she screeched. She dragged in a ragged breath, feeling hysterical fury flooding her. "It was a child. Just a little girl!"

"What do you know of it!" he burst out impatiently, resentment curdling his features. "They were nothing to anyone. Nothing. They are the filthiest beggars, I will not suffer them to live and breed like a pestilence on my land. And you left me for it. For that diseased rubbish! It was none of your business."

"Murderer!" It was nothing more than a frightened yelp, the depth of his depravity renewing her fear. "It was my business not to marry a murderer!" She wanted to close her eyes and shut out his face, to collapse on the floor and give in to the shaking nausea and fear and exhaustion. "I don't care why you came here. Whatever was between us is over and past. I want nothing more to do with you."

"I return the sentiment in full, I assure you," he

said with a glower. "But the past has come back to you for a reason, Helen."

She heard nothing beyond that. Whatever else he said was lost as she understood that she would never be allowed to escape him. She watched his lips move in a litany of grievances that she did not bother attempting to understand, feeling the weight of her past bear down on her.

Unbelievable that he would come. But of course he would return to her life. Of course the past could not be buried, no matter if she bent herself to the task every moment of every day. She could not, she knew at last, steep the ugliness of it in the happiness she had found, expecting the stain to dissolve and disappear.

But she could use it, she saw now. If it would never leave her, then she could claim it as her own. If she was well and truly ruined, then let it serve her.

She gripped her fingers around the knife and looked inside herself for the thing she feared most. Her own violence, so deep and long denied, was waiting there. It had come to life only once before, in a flash of brilliance that she had sworn would never be resurrected.

When he stepped forward and put a hand on her shoulder, the sudden and vivid memory of leaves rustling beneath her nearly choked her. It came fast and furious, as it always did – the feel of his leg hard and insistent between hers, the uncomfortable weight of her skirts bunched around her hips, the sharp something on the ground scraping behind her knee.

Things she had forgotten, or never remembered. They all rose up as a lump in her throat, strangling her, carried there by his hand lifting to her shoulder, concentrated in her grip on the knife.

※

Foster seemed almost frantically relieved when Stephen walked through the door.

"A visitor, my lord," he said before Stephen had time to strip off his gloves. "He's in with Lady Summerdale. Come."

It marked the first time he had ever been ordered about by a servant, and the sudden lack of deference spurred him to action. He followed Foster down the hall. "Who is it?"

"He gave his name as Duncan, my lord. She wants him gone, but he does not leave."

They had reached the salon. A maid stood outside the door, holding a tea tray and staring into the room as though watching a crucifixion. As Stephen ran through a mental inventory of names, searching in vain for any Duncan he knew, the scene burst into view. A man held Helen's shoulder, giving her a little shake as he tried to break the look of ice calm that she wore.

"What must I do to convince you I do not come here to hurt you, Helen?" He was pleading in earnest. "I loved you!"

This is when he should have said something, done something. But at the mention of love, he could not help looking to his wife, whose face became a mask of disgust and loathing.

"Were you loving me more when you forced my skirts up and covered my screams, or when I held the razor to your throat to stop you?"

Her voice was little more than a whisper, low and

deadly. But Stephen heard it. It stopped him where he stood next to the maid, mired him in stunned confusion. There was no time to absorb what she had said, to allow anything more than the bare fact to register. There was only the sharp reality of what it meant, and that Henley stood before him.

In three long strides he was across the room, propelled by an animal rage. It was the work of a moment, to rip the man's hand from Helen's shoulder, to knock him to the floor and watch with satisfaction as he cringed away. But he would not let him get away, hauling him up so that he could deliver blow after blow to Henley's face, elated when he felt the nose shatter under his fist. Above the blood pounding in his ears, he heard himself let out a bellow. He struck Henley again and again – once for having ever touched Helen, again for the nightmares he had given her, again for putting the shadows beneath her eyes. Over and over again, for the unspeakable horror that Stephen could not bear to think about.

He felt blood trickling over his fists and found an unholy pleasure in it. It drowned out the sounds of other voices that called for him to stop, to control himself. But he had controlled himself forever, and he would not stop now, not when Henley gasped and bled and begged to the rhythm of the blows.

He begged for his life, which made Stephen want to choke it out of him. He wrapped his hands around Henley's throat, watched the face turn purple and swollen, ignored the hands pulling at his arms. He only squeezed harder, waiting. When Henley's eyes lost focus and rolled back in his head, Stephen let go.

He stared down at the gagging heap at his feet. It

had been too quick, too sudden. He felt outside himself, unreal. Slowly, he became aware of Foster standing beside him, speaking his name fearfully. He turned around, gulping air, and caught sight of Helen. He had forgotten her entirely.

She sat on the floor in front of the desk. She had absolutely no expression on her face as she stared at Henley. The maid was less composed, weeping and grasping at Helen while she gaped at the scene. Stephen blinked, trying to regain coherent thought as the tumult of rage died down to a simmer. He motioned to Foster.

"Send for Lord Whitemarsh," he rasped, as quietly as he could so that Helen would not hear. "Tell him what has happened. Remove this...filth. Keep him in the stables and take Lord Whitemarsh to him."

It was the only thing he could think of. Let Whitemarsh deal with what was left of Henley. Stephen could not bring himself to leave Helen's side. She was white and lifeless, sitting there in a heap.

He crossed to her and dropped to his knees as Foster moved to do his bidding. Stephen stopped the maid's hysterics with a sharp word and sent her to the kitchens. Still Helen didn't move. When he reached out to her, she gave a little jump and stared at his hands moving to embrace her. But she backed away, scooted just out of his reach on the floor.

He looked down at himself. He still wore his coat and gloves, and they were covered in blood. He could smell it with each ragged breath of air he brought into his chest. Dimly, he remembered her voice speaking to him on a night that seemed a lifetime ago. *I detest blood*, she had said.

He sat there wordless, unable to reach out to her,

only capable of saying her name. But she didn't respond, didn't move. She hardly seemed to breathe as she stared at the floor. He waited for her to come back to him, to show anything at all, even if it were only to scream or cry. She was like a shadow of herself, a lifeless statue.

The servants came and dragged Henley out, coughing and wheezing. Stephen had them bring a basin of water and cleaned himself, cutting the slick buttons off his gloves with a paper knife that had fallen to the floor. He felt bruised inside, devoid of any thought except that he must not come to her with blood on his hands.

When he was clean, he looked at her again to find that she had not moved.

"Why—" His voice caught on an unexpected sob. He pressed mouth shut to stop it, squeezed his eyes closed to block out the vision of what was becoming clear to him. "Why didn't you tell me?"

Her voice came as a whisper, the ghost of words riding on an exhalation of air. "It wasn't so important." She looked up at him, still without expression, tilting her chin a little. "He didn't kill me."

His arms lifted to her, but she pulled away again, moving across the floor in tiny increments as he followed her on his knees. She reached the wall and slumped against it, blinking at him.

He looked at his outstretched hands, shaking between them. He let them fall, looking at her helplessly. His knuckles were throbbing, and he dropped his gaze from hers as he sat back on his heels. She didn't want him. How could she ever want anyone to touch her? He had thought she was only reticent, that she capriciously chose to let someone in or keep them out in the cold. That it only wanted time to breech the walls she built around herself. It should come as no surprise that he would fail, that he would be left outside. As he always had been.

But she surprised him, as she so often did. He felt her hands close around his, felt a shiver in her grow from a fluttering to an uncontrollable shaking.

"I'm tired, Stephen." She sounded like a child. She bit her lips and looked at him as if she didn't understand herself. "I'm so tired."

And she let him put his arms around her and carry her upstairs to their bed. He laid her down, wrapped her in a blanket as he had the first night they were together, and stretched out next to her in silence.

She did not sleep. She lay shaking against him and stared as the shadows lengthened in the room while he stroked her hair and accepted defeat. The one thing he'd ever taken pride in, knowing the truth. Understanding the nature of a complicated situation, when no one else could. Seeing what others could not.

And when it mattered the most, when all the signs were there, he failed. His family turned out to be right after all. He was useless and dull, nothing more than a cunning illusion of power. Destined to live outside the circle of warm life he felt in Helen, that he would give anything to be made a part of. She did not hold herself back from him in the night because she was selfish or timid or cold, as he had told himself a hundred times. It was because of this – of the pain and fear and violence she had known. In his colossal blindness, he had blamed her.

Finally, when night came, she turned in his arms, a quick movement that startled him after her hours of immobility. Her arms wrapped around him and he saw she was close to sleep. She spoke against his throat, a soft murmuring that reached deep inside, past the bleak sorrow, and left him floundering in a sea of hope.

"I only want an ordinary life," she breathed. "I can have that, can't I?" He felt her tears slide down his neck, a warm tickle that broke his heart because he had no way to stop them.

"I want it." She rubbed her face against him. "With you."

And they lay in silence as she drifted to sleep.

CHAPTER SIXTEEN

Nearly two weeks, and still he had not touched her with anything other than brotherly affection. They went on, day to day, and he showed the same tender concern as he always had, but he never came to her bed at night. He disappeared into the dressing room that adjoined the chamber they had shared, and slept on the little cot there, with the door closed between them. Helen thought she would weep for the loss of him.

Perhaps she disgusted him. Perhaps it was acceptable for a woman to give her body out of love, but to have been forced was something that made her untouchable. She didn't know, and she couldn't bring herself to ask him why he kept his distance. At first, in the day that followed Henley's appearance, she was happy Stephen did not try to kiss her or touch her in any intimate way. She had been exhausted from it, and it had taken some time until she felt quite herself again. But she was herself again, so as the days went by and he left her to sleep alone, she began to worry that it would never be the same between them.

She had asked him, fearfully, what would become of Henley, and he had been quick to reassure her. Alex had taken care of things, he said, though Helen knew her husband must have played some part in it. If Henley ever stepped foot in England again, he would be thrown in the nearest prison barge – if he lived that long – and Alex and Stephen had been sure to make that plain to him.

"He'll not come near you again, my love," Stephen had said, delivering a chaste kiss to her forehead.

After that, he had set about charming her, trying to make her forget any sadness or fear. There was never a moment she was with him that she was not laughing at some jest or drawn into some engrossing conversation. It was like when he first came to her little village and wedged his way into her life, only now there was no hint of seriousness beneath his bantering. It was a gentle flirtation without the promise of something more.

But he seemed more protective of her than ever, she was reminded as they sat in the Duke of Thursby's cavernous dining room. She had not wanted to come to the dinner party, knowing that the Duke was famous for choosing his guests with an eye to entertainment. He mixed and matched members of society, often producing a volatile blend of personalities. Occasionally, the mixture produced nothing but sheer boredom. Helen was hoping for even that, for anything other than another night sitting with only Stephen at the table as she tried not to think of the cold bed that awaited her.

Unfortunately, Thursby's dinner was eventful in a

way she would never have wished. There was the celebrated violinist and the actress who was his mistress, both of whom sat across from Helen. A viscount and his wife, whom the Duke had introduced with a gleam in his eye. She thought perhaps the viscount and Stephen had some bad blood between them, from the hopeful look on the Duke's face. Among the assorted others was a debutante who was all the rage this season, a Mr. Niles known for his business acumen and gambling habit, a parson who spoke twelve languages fluently, and a handful more of London's most fascinating citizens. And Anne Pembroke. Of course.

Stephen had stayed unfashionably by Helen's side before dinner, steering her away from Miss Pembroke after a brief hello. He seemed to know that the one thing this disparate company had in common was that each one was fully informed and positively gleeful about the scandal that had shaped Helen's life. But he did not shy in the face of it, as Helen would have done had he not been by her side. He greeted each of them pleasantly, introduced his wife with a note of quiet pride and implicit challenge, and they made it through dinner without a hitch. That was in no small part due to his own stature, and his ability to subtly direct the conversation among the diners. He had them discussing the price of grain and the fear of revolt among the workers, drawing the viscount into a defense of the protective laws on imports.

He was clever. It was a topic that sparked lively conversation among them all. No one was unaffected by it, and everyone had an opinion to impart. Everyone, she reminded herself, but Stephen, who only observed them all and prompted the debate by politely inquiring after the flaws in each of their arguments. He carefully preserved his neutrality, and she began to understand that it was more important to him than his reputation.

The Duke, who had been casting disappointed looks at Stephen throughout the dinner, looked hopeful again as the ladies withdrew to the salon and the men stayed for port. Now was the real test. She must sit with the ladies, without Stephen to protect her from whatever they may choose to say to her. Or about her.

She spent the better half of the time talking to the actress, Miss Avery, the only one of the women who did not hesitate to speak to Helen. The debutante looked at both of them as if they carried a disease she was afraid to catch. But though the other ladies kept a carefully polite distance, they were civil enough. Anne Pembroke, it would seem, was biding her time. She found her opportunity after Miss Avery had finished a song, slipping up behind Helen to speak in a too-sweet tone.

"She's quite a celebrated talent," Anne observed, "both on and off the stage, I believe. Before she was occupied with her violinist, the Duke of Varley was quite taken with her."

"Is that so?" It was all Helen could think to say, in the absence of any way to stem the tide of her gossip. "I understand Varley's a sponsor of the expedition to Africa to take place later this year," she groped, remembering something she had read in the papers. Anything was more interesting than discussing Miss Avery's lovers, and Africa was far more intriguing than Anne Pembroke's idea of suitable topics.

"Africa? My, but you have such *unique* interests.

Indeed, I would say your preference of acquaintance is unique, if you were anyone else," she said with a nod to the actress as the other ladies gathered around. "But knowing what I do about you," she continued, with a malicious little smile, "it is rather more predictable."

Such disapprobation, only because Helen had dared speak with Miss Avery. She could not help but feel a little sorry for this young woman. Poor Anne Pembroke. All these years of scheming and conniving, and still she had not bagged a rich husband. Instead, she chose to pass her time in making remarks about Helen's past.

With that thought, the pity was gone. She might not have Marie-Anne or Maggie at her side, but she knew exactly what they might say about this dreadful woman. The thought of it gave her heart.

"I have found that predictability has its advantages, Miss Pembroke," she said calmly. "Are we not kindred spirits in that regard?" She watched Anne work herself into confused offense. "I mean, of course, that you are predictably still Miss Pembroke, and have not stirred things up by doing anything so bold as taking a husband. It's quite admirable."

The debutante let out a horrified little giggle, and the rest of the ladies looked delightfully appalled. Only Miss Avery looked directly at Helen, an admiring grin on her face as she mimed applause in Helen's direction.

Helen was suddenly ashamed of herself for rising to the bait. Anne Pembroke looked as if she might like to scratch her eyes out. *Oh, please God do not tell me Anne Pembroke can in any way make trouble for Stephen,* she prayed. As if her thoughts had the power to summon him, she realized that the men were entering the room. But Anne had rallied.

"I am not fooled by you," hissed Anne, apparently unaware of the new arrivals. "You are every bit the hussy you were six years ago, no matter that you've married the Earl of Summerdale himself."

"Do I hear my name?" Stephen asked, moving smoothly to the little party and taking Helen's arm. He looked at Anne as if he had only just noticed she were there, giving her a little gracious bow and a smile that did not quite reach his eyes. "My thanks for your good wishes on our recent wedding, Miss Pembroke. And give my regards to your cousin."

Helen had time to notice Anne's sudden pallor as Stephen pulled her away. "My cousin?" she asked, and Stephen hesitated.

"Yes," he replied with an easy grin. "I believe he'll be back from the... country in another year or so. Would you care to tell me how he's faring?"

There was something in it the way he said it, and the look of horror on Anne Pembroke's face, that changed the seemingly harmless statement into something much more. Miss Pembroke fluttered her hands as though she could shoo the topic away, but she was unable to disguise her agitation.

"No," said Stephen quietly, with a meaningful look at her. "I didn't think that you would wish to speak of him." With another slight bow, an acknowledgement of Anne's quick nod, he steered Helen across the room to where the viscount stood.

"Her cousin?" Helen whispered as they moved.

Stephen brought his fist up to his mouth, clearing his throat. "Debtor's prison," he responded under cover of his concealing hand.

It continued that way for the rest of the night. Anne Pembroke's outspokenness had brought forth the topic, and though she did not pursue it, the others now considered it open season on Helen. When the viscount slyly congratulated Stephen on the swiftness and secrecy of his wedding, Stephen thanked him politely and made some inquiry about the opium trade that left the other man speechless. The others were not quite so outspoken, but it only needed the hint that Helen was the target of the next comment for Stephen to introduce a subject that was outwardly innocuous, yet somehow powerful enough to de-fang one of the guests in an instant.

Helen could not guess what lay behind his comments that made the others become practically servile in response. Even the parson, when he seemed reluctant to speak to Helen, changed in a blink after Stephen merely mentioned Coventry.

She watched him change, in a single evening, from a neutral bystander to a dangerous foe. Every last person was intimidated – scared stiff, she would even say – by the time he was through. And she was certain he did it only for her. He gave up the noncommittal air that he had carefully cultivated for the sole reason that he did not want her to suffer the sting of condescension and mockery. She looked at him, feeling a wave of tenderness as he challenged the Duke with a question about the artwork on the walls.

The Duke gasped like a fish out of water at that seemingly innocent inquiry, but Helen could only see the sweep of her husband's lashes as he reached for a glass. *I love him. God help me, but I love him more than myself.*

She felt it like an arrow through her heart,

knowing how much of himself he gave up for her. She'd rather put herself up for public mockery than see him become the very thing she well knew he loathed, but he did not give her the chance. Almost, in that moment when the brooding set of his mouth caused her to drop her eyes for fear that all could see her feelings, she nearly reached for his hand on the glass. They were so strong, so beautiful, and it had been so long since she had felt them on her.

When they returned home, he went directly to his office, leaving her to crawl into bed alone again. It was her, not him. It had always been some fault of hers that now made it easy for him to sleep elsewhere. He had made her a part of his life, and he did nothing but suffer for it. The demands of her past had come to haunt his home, and now his reputation changed from perfect gentleman to active player in the game he despised.

When she thought of it, she could not fault him for staying away. She didn't even want to sleep with herself anymore.

"A visitor to see you, my lady."

Helen looked up from the silver serving spoons she was polishing. The staff still found it odd that she sometimes helped with household chores, but they were quick to indulge her in it. During her years with Maggie, she had learned from her friend how useful these monotonous tasks could be when she was upset. It helped in sorting her thoughts. Just now, she was carefully rubbing tiny circles on the silver, watching the surface shine while asking herself over and over again if it was wise to be so in love with her husband, who was courteous and kind and handsome, and had hired workers to renovate the room next to hers. It used to be a nursery, and now it would become his bedroom.

He had announced it casually last night, as if it were of no more importance than purchasing new curtains for the drawing room. Her fork had clattered to the plate as she stared in shocked misery at her uneaten dinner. She mumbled something inane, unable to bring herself to demand that he come to her bed, or kiss her just once with desire on his lips. Instead, she said she'd been unaware that he was looking to improve the townhouse.

"It's quite a bit of trouble to go to," she had murmured.

"No trouble at all," he replied smoothly, and she gathered herself to look at him. It seemed as if he expected her to be pleased.

"Stephen," she said timidly, feeling herself blush to her roots. But she had to say something. "There is no reason you should remove to your own rooms." Her eyes roved over the place settings in mortification at having to speak so plainly. "You are welcome – that is I mean, more than welcome, to..." her voice died to a whisper, "to sleep with me."

He did not answer, and when she looked to him again it was to see a look of such tender pity on his face that she thought she would burst into tears. He might have said more; in fact she had the feeling that he wanted to speak to her of the matter explicitly, uncomfortable as it was. But the footman had come forward with the dessert and the matter was dropped. He had gone out for the evening and left her to contemplate that pitying look all night, not returning until long after she had fallen into a fitful slumber.

It was awful. If he thought this was what she'd meant when she voiced her desire for an ordinary life with him, then she must find some way to make him understand. She doubted her ability to speak of such a thing in bold terms, which was why she'd come to polish silver and think of the proper words.

She pulled off the gloves and set them aside with the polish. A visitor was welcome. No matter who it was, she could use some diversion from her thoughts.

"A Mrs. Navire to see you, my lady," Foster informed her with an anxious look. He was still contrite over the matter of Henley's appearance that fateful day. He hovered about now whenever there was a visitor.

"Navire?" she asked. It was an odd name, and one she didn't recognize, but she stepped into the salon with Foster at her heels to see a petite woman clad in black, as though in mourning. She wore a heavy veil draped over her bonnet that concealed her face completely. As Helen approached, the woman turned around and lifted the veil in a playful gesture.

"*Cou-cou!*" she cried, her eyes twinkling merrily.

Helen clasped her hand over her mouth to hide the sudden smile that was absurdly close to tears. "Oh, Marie-Anne, what a silly disguise!" She fell into her friend's arms with just enough presence of mind to gesture Foster out of the room.

"My dear Hélène, whatever can be wrong?" Marie-Anne asked with concern. "I knew I should have come sooner. Don't weep like that, *ma chère*, you must tell me what can be so terrible."

Helen wiped the senseless tears away with a sad

giggle. "Well, Mrs. Navire – and there is no need to be so discreet that you must play games with your name. 'Shipley' does not translate very well, it sounds very awkward."

"I said I would try not to be outrageous, and so I am awkward instead." Marie-Anne waved this topic away and looked with determination at Helen. "I will not be distracted, my friend, from these tears that have greeted me."

"I am only relieved to see you." She took a breath and settled herself on the sofa, determined to speak rationally. "Oh, how perfect that you have come, and at exactly the moment I need you."

※

An hour later, Marie-Anne had heard the story of Henley's return. She seemed utterly thrilled at Helen's nod affirming that Stephen had assaulted him.

"Marvelous," Marie-Anne declared. "I told you your husband was a good man. Too good to kill the odious beast, unfortunately, or to keep him about long enough for me to spit on him." She gave a delicate shudder. "But this was two weeks ago. Are you still so upset by it, Hélène, that you weep?"

"Oh," said Helen in a small voice, anticipating the conversation ahead. "No, it's not that. It was upsetting, of course, and to see Stephen act so very savagely was disturbing. But it is over now, and it has affected me in a way I never thought to expect."

"It has made you more ready to weep?"

"No, quite the opposite." She struggled to frame her thoughts. It was not easy to explain even to herself. "I feel a kind of freedom because of it. It's as if it is all finished finally, that entire chapter of my life. And now I am free to live as I want to."

"Good," said Marie-Anne with a warm smile that lit up her face. "Life is for the living, and it's time you stop cringing at shadows. But then why did you cry? You are more emotional today than I have ever seen."

Helen stared at her hands gripped in her lap. "It seems to have changed Stephen somehow, to know about... everything."

She stumbled through a description of Stephen's behavior since that day. Marie-Anne stayed mostly silent, listening intently as Helen searched for words. Her eyes widened slightly to hear of the new bedroom he would be moving into.

"But, *mon amie*," she said with a small frown when Helen had finished. "You sent for me even before all this happened."

"Yes." Helen sighed and resigned herself to being embarrassed for the rest of the afternoon. "I think there may be something terribly wrong between us. I thought perhaps you could help me. Because I am so inexperienced, you know, and I'm not quite familiar with..." she forced the words out, "with matters relating to the marriage bed."

Marie-Anne let out an amused sigh. "Having never been married, I don't know that I can help you. Especially if you drop dead of mortification. You are a lovely shade of aubergine."

"I'll try." Helen took a deep breath. "I will, and you know what I mean. You are more experienced than I in these matters."

"*Bien*, it is true I am difficult to shock. What is the problem? I mean before now, when you wrote to me."

"But that's just it. I have been perfectly happy with it. Yet there still seems to be a problem. I think that Stephen was unhappy with me, long before this."

Marie-Anne raised her eyebrows. "Absurd. He is besotted with you. And are you satisfied when you come from his bed?"

"Yes, of course." She felt the heat in her face.

"And you leave him in no doubt of your satisfaction?"

Helen shrugged. "Well, yes, I suppose so."

"You *suppose* so?" Marie-Anne looked as if it was the most inappropriate answer possible. "You only suppose? Very well, I must ask more plainly," she said, with a speculative look. "Do you show him what you like, do you tell him? In the moment of release, I mean."

"Release?" said Helen, mystified. "Should I?"

After a series of questions, each more embarrassing than the last — which Helen answered with painful honesty — Marie-Anne cast her a hard look.

"I'm tempted to say that you are very selfish, Hélène. You take without giving." It was the harshest thing Marie-Anne had ever said to her. "It sounds to me as if you are quite controlling, that you never for a moment relinquish control of yourself, and of course it makes your husband unhappy. He knows what he is doing, and it sounds as if he does it very well. But you hide your pleasure from him. You keep it all to yourself, in the very moment you should abandon all this restraint."

The Frenchwoman looked as though she were prepared to grumble at length about the repressed nature of the English aristocracy, which Helen would have enjoyed under other circumstances. But now she could not be amused by it.

"I know it's my failing," she said. She thought of the countless times she had held herself rigid beneath him as the pleasure came, the very opposite of the word Marie-Anne had used: release. How it must have felt to him, to be closed off in that moment, every time. "I know it, and so does he. But I don't know – oh, Marie-Anne, I don't know any other way. I don't know what's wrong, and I don't know how to fix it," she whispered, fighting tears.

Marie-Anne's face lost the look of reproof. She reached out to take Helen's hand. "It's only normal, I think, because of what you have been through in your past," she said carefully.

Helen looked up at her, suddenly apprehensive. "Do you think that something in me is... That I was damaged in some way, and it cannot be repaired?"

Her friend blinked back tears. "Oh, Hélène..."

For a horrified moment, she thought Marie-Anne might actually burst into weeping. But the emotion was overcome quickly. She straightened her shoulders abruptly and took on a practical tone.

"If that were true, I'd sail to Ireland today and kill Henley myself. No, it can be repaired, it only takes some willingness on your part, to let go of this control which I promise you do not need anymore. But first we must find a way for your husband to stop pitying you, for it's obvious he does. And that's because you let him."

"But I–"

"Your husband cannot be happy unless you are satisfied, and thank God there are men such as him in this world," Marie-Anne said fervently, with a popish gesture that perfectly astonished Helen. "So I will tell you what it is you are missing. See if you aren't willing to try anything to achieve it, after you hear what it can be like. Then," she continued, as if they were drawing up a plan for battle, "some practical advice, which I hope will not shock you into a swoon. We must take some of the English out of you."

It sounded like rather a lot to achieve in an afternoon. Helen took a deep breath. "I'll ring for tea."

Marie-Anne let out a peal of delicious laughter. "Something stronger than tea, Hélène," she giggled. "Have them bring wine, or whiskey. You will need it."

※

For the thousandth time, Helen doubted her ability to even think of the details she had learned, much less act on them. There seemed so much to remember among the suggestions put forth. She told herself to focus on the most important things, the most salient points. Do not be afraid to lose yourself, that was one of them. Do not be ashamed of wanting him, was another. Most important of it all was not to think. *Do not think. Only feel.*

There was something else. She racked her brain, suddenly panicking. What was it? Oh, yes – a drink. That was considered imperative if she was to eradicate the enemy inhibitions, as Marie-Anne put it.

She reached for the wine, afraid that if the situation continued much longer, she would become a drunkard. *Put your brain between your legs and keep it there throughout,* Marie-Anne had said, and Helen had started on the whiskey in the hopes of thinking rationally after such a declaration. But now it was the next day, her friend was gone, and it was time to act before she lost all nerve. And before the blasted builders came.

She could have acted more herself by simply saying to him that they had a duty to try for an heir. But it was cold and practical, not at all true to what she felt nor even the half of what she wanted to tell him. It said nothing about how she did not fear his touch, or how he had brought her to life in a new and cherished way. She had begun to realize, in the course of the long and immodest conversation with Marie-Anne, that she could say all of this with her body. If only she could come to him unashamed.

The first step was to go to him at all. She hovered at the door of the dressing room where he slept. The moonlight shone brightly, showing her his sleeping form. She swallowed down her nervousness, glad of the warmth in her belly that the wine provided, and sat tentatively on the bed next to him. His head rested on his arm, his hair tousled against the pillow and across his forehead. She loved looking at him as he slept. She had spent hours examining his face as he lay next to her in their bed, memorizing the curve of his lips, the fine lines etched around his eyes, the line of his chin.

His chest, his strong broad shoulders rose up out of the blanket, bared to her touch. She did what she had never done before: touched him leisurely, taking a slow and lazy pleasure in the feel and sight of him. She leaned forward and kissed his skin, her lips tingling with the taste of the wine and the fine dark hair that covered his chest. His heart beat slow and steady, and she put her ear against it to listen to his life. Still he did not wake, and she smoothed her hand down his torso, slowly dragging the blanket down over his hip.

He came awake quietly, only the lurch of his heart and the slight tensing of his body announcing his awareness. She lifted her head, letting the moonlight fall on her face as she continued the slow exploration. It was like a dream, the way the tension left him, how she could feel him watching her while she learned him with her hands. A dream when, slowly, he turned onto his back and she felt the rush of excitement shoot through her, a bolt of lightning that awakened her to the possibilities afforded by his offering himself.

She pulled the blankets away, a recklessness stealing over her. He would want this, she reminded herself. That's what she must trust.

Her palm curved around him as her lips played over his chest and down his stomach to where the dark hair curled. *Do you see that I am not afraid?* she wanted to ask, but chose instead to show him what she felt by pressing a kiss to the hardened flesh in her hand. He gasped, and she felt a warm flush that was not embarrassment at all. She opened her lips and took him into her mouth, her tongue stroking – only for a moment, just a moment, because the sound he made filled her with a panting desire. It overwhelmed her, as it had always done when they were together, but this time she let it take her. She let herself be an abandoned woman.

She dragged her tongue up a straight path over his body, quicker than his intake of breath, from stomach to chest to throat and she was there, her open mouth hovering over his. He leaned up to capture her lips, and she shifted to bring her leg across to straddle him. His hands moved over her and she felt his mouth on her chin, her throat. It caused the heat in her to leap up, until she was wild with it, with him. She lowered her hips, bringing the liquid burn between her thighs down to trap his hardness on his belly, rubbing herself along the length of him, feeding the fire.

Stephen gripped her hips, wondering if it were possible to die of pleasure. She rose above him, a dream made flesh. He leaned forward in an agony of lust to lick the trickle of perspiration that ran between her breasts, his resolve to leave her in peace sacrificed at her first touch. She paused in her movement, her breath coming harsh as she held his mouth against her. Then she shifted and sank down on him, taking him into her. He watched her head drop back, her hair streaming down, her mouth as she gasped his name and moved atop him. How did he ever think he could live without this?

When his thumb slipped forward to caress her, there where he was embedded in her, she bucked against him and gasped. Instead of restraint and a fierce control, she smiled and gave a low moan. Instead of her dark intensity below, pulling him in, her exultant joy burst forth above him, showering down all around him. Her hand came down and tangled with his on her hip as she stared at the place they were joined, little whimpering moans rising in her throat as she moved faster. Her body clenched around him, delicious and tight, as she cried out in wordless pleasure.

It seemed to take him a long time to come to his senses. When he did, she was still gulping for air, a disbelieving wonder in her face, leaning down to put her lips against his. She kissed him fiercely, and he answered her in kind, his tongue gathering the dark sweetness and drinking it in greedily as she sagged against him. He turned on his side, taking her with him on the tiny bed that was never meant for two people, and pulled the blanket up over them both. Her eyes were drifting closed, looking at him with gentle astonishment.

"Don't let the builders come," she said drowsily.

If there were an ounce of strength left in his sublimely limp muscles, he would have laughed. "You make a splendid case against them," he muttered as she slipped into slumber. He tucked her against his chest like a precious treasure he could hoard all for himself, and lay awake for a long time, marveling that somehow she was his.

He had just woken and was lost in tracing the pink tips of her fingers, listening to her breathing as she slept, when the valet made his entrance. Stephen had just enough time to cover her with his body, knowing how modest she was, how carefully she hid herself behind high collars even when they dined alone.

"Good morning, my lord," said James, not even sparing a glance toward the bed as he strode to open the curtains fully. He went swiftly about his business as usual while Stephen recovered from the blow his wife had unwittingly struck him in the ribs when she was so rudely awakened.

"Good morning, James," he began, and stopped because Helen had buried her face in his chest and squinted against the sunlight. He had been meaning to say something to the servant, but suddenly preferred to concentrate on the feel of her soft curves pressed into him.

"Would my lord prefer his coffee served here?" James asked, his back toward them as he gathered Stephen's discarded clothes from yesterday. "The carpenters have arrived early as you requested, and await your convenience."

Helen made a small sound, burrowing deeper into him. He pulled the blanket tight to her shoulder.

"Tell them I will not be down for some time, please, James," he said slowly. He dropped a kiss on Helen's hair. "Have Collins inform them their commission has changed, and show them to the nursery with an eye toward refurbishment, instead of renovation. And get you gone from here now, will you?"

The servant's look of surprise changed to satisfaction as he spied Helen's dark hair spilling from under the blanket.

"Immediately, my lord," he bowed, clearly suppressing a happy smile.

As soon as the door was closed behind him, Stephen leapt up to pull the curtains closed. He thought the glare disturbed his wife, but when he turned back to watch the shadows close on her skin, she was watching him, staring at his nakedness.

"Good morning," he smiled, still holding the curtain open. She immediately turned shy, turning over to hide her face in the pillows. It left the sinuous curve of her back bathed in morning light. She mumbled something from the pillows that sounded like "Good morning."

"You're exceptionally beautiful this morning." He

found he was in an irrepressibly good mood.

"Thank you," came her muted response from the depths of the bed.

"Shall we stay in bed all morning? All afternoon, even. Though I'm rather torn between throwing myself into bed and staying here to look at your lovely back."

She made a reflexive movement, reaching for the blanket around her hips. But she seemed to reconsider, stopping herself from pulling it up. Instead, she pushed her arms up and out, stretching like a cat in sunlight. He felt the image sear into his heart, and made a mental note to keep the memory near. If ever he doubted his love for her, he could pull it out and call himself a fool.

"I'd much prefer you to spend the time over here," she said in an endearingly timid voice, her face still turned from him.

"Now that I think of it," he replied, the memory of her earlier abandon making his blood race, "so would I."

He slipped into the little bed facing her, ducking in amidst her heavy hair, the tousled sleepy scent of her, to find her lips and ravage them with a deep kiss. She slid a leg over his hip and strained closer.

"After all," he said between kisses, "we'll soon have a new nursery to fill." And they set themselves to the task with enthusiasm.

CHAPTER SEVENTEEN

"Smitten," was the word he overheard the servants using a few days later, and it made him smile. "It's a fine thing to serve a love-struck lord, I'm finding," whispered one of them, clearly unaware that the lord in question was within earshot. He proved them right by ignoring it, instead of giving a stern look and having a word with the butler about gossiping servants.

It was only the teasing glint in the butler's eye that kept him from protesting when Helen said she'd be spending the afternoon with Joyce, her one friend in London. He knew it was selfish to want her at his side day and night, but he couldn't help himself. The world felt right when she was beside him, and when she wasn't, he could think of little but her return. He spent the time planning how he would greet her, finding new ways to bring about her now-frequent laughter.

Stephen had wanted to invite himself along when

she announced that Marie-Anne would be there too. A reconstruction of his Avalon was much preferable to an afternoon at Whitehall, where the gentlemen now avoided him. Where once he was sought out for advice he was now evaded as though he carried a plague, no doubt because of his performance at Thursby's. He told himself he didn't care, that he had been hoping for just such a thing — to leave the whispering deceptions behind.

But he found to his exasperation that he was upset by it. At least he had had a purpose, something he was good at, which hadn't been handed to him by an accident of birth. Perhaps Helen's practicality was rubbing off, along with her sense of social equilibrium. It was impossible not to see the world through her eyes, to think of the baker in her little town when some bewigged lord argued to raise the tariff on imported grain, or to remember Katie's delight in a handful of cheap ribbons whenever a coach full of ladies splattered mud on the street urchins as it passed. And now he was left useless in the world he had despised, holding a bag of tricks that would only backfire if he used them in the way they could do most good.

However much he might be feared, the invitations poured in. They were afraid of offending him. He politely declined most of them, but occasionally they would make an appearance if he felt it was important, or if Helen showed an interest.

"Shall we go to Chisholm's weekend party?" she asked after Marie-Anne had returned to Bartle. "Alex and Elizabeth are to go, and I would like to spend some time with my sister-in-law."

So they went, because she seemed to want to and

because Stephen knew the Chisholms were perfectly harmless, as their other guests would be. It proved the only time he was ever wrong about such a thing.

They arrived in time for dinner, hastily dressing and presenting themselves moments before the meal was served. He took Helen's arm to escort her into the dining room and experienced a moment of unreality as he spied Clara ahead of him. She was here with her duke – a runt of a man who was more occupied with ogling Lady Chisholm's bosom than he was in noticing any of the guests. Clara was seated across from Stephen, Helen at his side, though he did not think the arrangement was made with any malicious intent. The world knew he and Clara were good friends; they had taken pains to appear as though there had never been anything more than friendship between them.

He had never spoken her name to Helen, had never told her who the author of his love letters was. But he knew she would guess in an instant if he let any of his emotions show. Clara looked at him as he sat, a polite smile and nod that he returned, but he felt the urgency in it. She wanted to talk to him. He knew at once, with absolute clarity, that he had to speak to her one last time, to make sure she understood that there was no possibility of a liaison. She must know that he would not answer her letters, that what had been between them was over now.

He watched her husband ignore her in favor of the young Miss Elston's charms and contemplated what it would do to her to hear that there was no hope of finding love outside her marriage. *At least not with me,* he thought. He turned to his wife in an attempt to enjoy the evening, refusing to brood on the annoyance he felt toward Clara's husband for neglecting her. How anyone could fail to be captivated by her was a mystery. Aside from her beauty, Clara had always been beguiling in so many ways: an excellent conversationalist, comfortable in every situation, attentive and intelligent. She deserved better of her husband than tactless indifference.

But she had chosen this. She had done it quite willingly. He wished, in a wistful kind of way, that Clara could know a little of the happiness he had found. She had married her precious duke, and couldn't know what it was like to make love in the sunlight, to kiss the sleepy and smiling mouth of someone who made life worth living. He was sorry for her, but suddenly found himself wanting Helen now, to confirm that he belonged to her, to drive out the sadness that the sight of Clara had stirred in him.

As soon as dinner was done, he did just that. They pled fatigue from the journey and went to their room, barely allowing the door to close behind them before he pulled her clothes off in a rush of passion and replaced all thought with the feel of her excitement. He gathered the sound and the scent of her, the feel of her skin against his – a talisman, protection against temptation.

"Open to me," he whispered, and she did, a miracle that never ceased to amaze him in its tenderness. She wrapped her body around him and took him into her again and again, the only place where he belonged.

※

"The grounds are lovely," said Lady Whitemarsh.

"I thought you might like to see the little orchard. It's not far. You might get some ideas for your own estate."

They were strolling through Lady Chisholm's celebrated gardens. It was a perfect day. Helen was happy to be with her brother's wife, and out of the city. Though anywhere she was with Stephen was beautiful, she thought as she bent to examine the flowers. She spent her days giddy as a schoolgirl, catching her breath whenever she saw him. He could do something as simple as hold his hand out to her, and she was lost in the thought of what he looked like beneath the fine coat, his muscles moving smoothly as he reached for her. He would speak a polite greeting to an acquaintance, and she would feel her heart rise in excited knowledge of who he was beneath the polished manners.

She blushed even now, thinking of how he had been last night. He made her foolish in love with his smile, her heart filled with tenderness at the thought of him.

"I have been thinking of starting a rose garden," she said to Lady Whitemarsh. "I'll ask Summerdale if he likes the idea."

Elizabeth smiled widely. "I have the feeling he won't refuse you anything. It's easy to see the affection he has for you, if you will pardon my impertinence in observing it."

Helen smiled back at her. "I think we have the love of our husbands in common. My brother is obviously devoted to you," she said warmly. She thought of last summer, before she had known Stephen. She had not known Elizabeth, or anything about her, had never hoped to know her brother again or the kind of happiness that she now enjoyed.

"But I won't take it for granted that I may change anything on the estate without his approval," she continued. "We ladies must at least pretend to give our husbands the upper hand sometimes."

"Take me at my word," laughed Elizabeth. "If you mention a rose garden, he'll carpet at least ten acres with rosebuds. Alex even remembered some silly little baubles I admired in a shop window long before we were wed. No, they are both quite willing at the moment to do whatever we ask in order to get in our good graces again."

"Good graces?" asked Helen with a slight frown. "I hadn't realized they were out of favor."

Elizabeth slid her a cautious glance, hesitating. "Well, I don't like to bring it up, but surely you know I mean that business with Henley. I fairly skinned Alex alive when he told me what they were up to."

Helen lost her smile at the mention of Henley, but forced herself to listen carefully. There was something here that she had missed, and she searched for it in Elizabeth's next words.

"After all, I was still angry with him for sending Summerdale to you in that little village where you lived, instead of going himself. I couldn't know, of course, how well it would turn out. Still, the idea that Alex would refuse to speak to you for so many years, and then the only thing that could induce him to contact you was Summerdale's business affairs, and only because it involved Lord Henley! My ridiculous husband needed something as insignificant as wool exports to spur him along the path to forgiveness. Men can be such a foolish lot."

Helen stopped walking as the words sank in. She

sat on a stone bench beside the path and fought against the feeling that she had been horribly deceived. Her brother had done business with Henley. So had Stephen. And he had lied to her, never telling her why he wished to learn of her past, except that her brother wanted to be reconciled. Why had he never told her? She didn't know if it would have made a difference in her feelings toward her brother. She would never know, because Stephen had taken the choice away from her, concealing the one element that belied her brother's affection.

A business deal. That was what had mattered so much, not herself. She closed her eyes against the pain of it.

Lady Whitemarsh was distressed. "My dear, you're so pale! I'm so sorry! You did not know about that, did you?" She looked like she might cry. "I've spoken out of turn. It's I who am foolish. Oh, how can I be so thoughtless?"

Helen raised a hand to stop her. "Please, sit with me."

She composed herself, knowing that it didn't matter so much now. What had brought Stephen to her, and had brought her brother into her life again – it didn't matter. But still she wanted to know.

"You have not spoken out of turn," she assured her sister-in-law. "It's something I should have known, so please tell me all of it."

Elizabeth sat next to her and obliged her by explained it all. How she had spent months trying to convince Alex to contact Helen, but how he only relented when he needed Henley for some business deal which involved Stephen as well. "He didn't want to seem to approve of Henley when it would cut you so deeply, and make him lose any chance of knowing you again."

Helen nodded. "Well, men have a way of suddenly caring more deeply when their fortunes are involved," she observed. She did not quite manage to keep the disgust out of her voice.

"Yes, that's exactly what Alex said to me before that horrible man came to London," Elizabeth said with distaste. "I told him, as I'm sure you told Lord Summerdale, that it was dangerous to threaten Henley's livelihood in some crack-brained notion of revenge. But no, he thought your husband's scheme was an excellent one. And all their vengeful work only brought Henley to your door. Alex has been quite contrite since then, hoping to placate me with his little gifts. Still, I wonder how repentant he truly is over the affair. He took a real joy in ruining that man, and we must admit it was deserved."

Helen opened her mouth to tell Elizabeth that she was wrong, that she was confused or had imagined it. The image of Henley in London choked off the words before they were spoken. He had asked her, begged her for help. What had he said?

They are ruining me.
The past has come back to you for a reason.
It is your husband I have come to discuss.

She stared at the azaleas before her, a cold spring of fear bubbling up inside her. Oh god, how could she have blinded herself to it? Stephen had hidden his intent when he first came to her. He hid it even now, never telling her that he had come to Bartle in the interests of business. So easy for him to hide a little thing like that. Of course he would hide something far more objectionable.

"I told him never to hide himself from me," she said, vaguely aware that Elizabeth was still next to her and expecting some kind of response. The sun was suddenly too hot, but not hot enough to thaw the chill that shook her. "It was the only thing that was important."

But her husband thought revenge more important. And he'd brought Henley to her because of it. She felt anger and betrayal like a beast inside her, clawing to be let out. She couldn't look at Elizabeth; she could see nothing at all beyond the deep blush of the flower at which she stared, swaying in the breeze.

He wouldn't have done it to hurt her. He wouldn't. He had only thought to protect her. But her anger at being protected grew until it threatened to overwhelm her reason. She knew Henley as no one else did, could have guessed in an instant that if her husband set about ruining him, Henley would have come to her to appeal to her better nature. And he *had* come to her, remembering her as a compassionate and sympathetic fool.

She thought of Stephen in his rage as he beat Henley into the ground, the blood on his hands as he reached for her, a nightmare vision. He'd gotten his revenge, hadn't he? No matter the cost to her. His love letters and his vengeful task he hid from her, anger and violence cloaked beneath perfect manners and liberal charm.

And worse, oh so much worse – what else did he hide from her? The old chant began again, a refrain she had shut out in the weeks of loving him. *The thousand terrible things he could be.*

"Helen, you look ill." Elizabeth's concern broke in on her anguished thoughts. "Come, you should rest before tea. I shouldn't have mentioned that horrible man."

Helen shook off her hand as politely as she could manage. "No, really, please... I think I will go in alone."

She felt unsteady on her feet, dangerously close to sobbing. Poor Elizabeth looked no better. *What does she have to be upset about,* Helen thought peevishly. *Her husband tells her things.*

But that was unfair. It was all unfair. She must speak to Stephen when they had a moment alone, so that he could explain. He deserved that. She would not lose him over this, only because she was oversuspicious and he was secretive. For now, she had to calm herself and think.

"Please stay and enjoy the weather," she said as steadily as she could manage. "I can find my room." She walked quickly away, looking neither left nor right at the bright flowers. The celebrated gardens seemed to have become nothing but paint on pasteboard, somehow. Nothing but a pretty painting surrounding her, and she could see nothing but the rough canvas and boards beneath.

※

"Duchess," he bowed over her gloved hand. Having stumbled across her in the library, Stephen had determined to speak with her now and get it over with. "I had not expected to see you here."

"I suspect you mean here at Chisholm's estate, and not here in the library, though you know I've never been bookish." She seemed shy, embarrassed as she plucked at her lavender silk skirt. "You wouldn't have come if you knew I'd be here, I'm sure. Months in London, and you've managed to avoid me completely," she said with a nervous little laugh.

He pulled his gaze away from her. She looked ineffably sad, as though marriage did not agree with her. She did not sparkle as brightly as she had once done. "We do not frequent the same circles anymore, Your Grace. I prefer to move less among Society."

"Yes, I've noticed." She looked at him, her pale blue eyes scanning his face. "Marriage has changed you. For the better, I think. I've not had a chance to congratulate you," she said with an unnaturally bright smile. "May you find every happiness, my lord."

It was depressing to keep up a pretense of polite conversation. They were friends, or they had been. Aside from his wife, no one knew him at all except for Clara. And he knew her equally well – enough to know that she was sincere in her well wishes, yet sad that she had chosen this life. He couldn't stand pretending as though they meant nothing to each other.

"I have already found every happiness, Clara," he told her. It was true. If he found a scrap more of it, he would burst.

She gave a little laugh, her mouth collapsing as she strove against tears. "I can see that. It's the talk of London, how you are ever at your wife's side. You must be an excellent husband, to have your wife look at you with such affection."

He fought against the need to talk to her as he used to. *Do you really think she loves me?* he wanted to ask. But it would be unfair to cultivate her friendship again – unfair to her and to Helen.

He shrugged. "I cannot take all the credit. She is an

excellent wife."

"Well, that's good," Clara sighed. "I would hate to see you with anyone less than excellent." She reached out and laid a hand over his. "Summerdale, I wanted to tell you. You must believe I would never have written you had I known that you were married. Well," she amended with a twist of her mouth, "at least not if I had known you were happily married. But I do miss you."

He took her hand. "I miss you sometimes, too," he admitted. "But that cannot be between us."

It was not so difficult to say as he had thought it would be, not so hard to give her up. He looked at the corner of her mouth, where he had spent countless hours staring and dreaming of kissing her. She was still beautiful, blindingly so. Yet he did not crave her laughter, nor live to see those lips curl in a smile. It was something of a shock to feel released from it, to truly look at her as nothing more than a dear friend.

"Your husband is a bastard, you know," he said, shifting the mood.

"Yes, he's out chasing Miss Elston around the garden, I believe."

"No, I meant that he really is a bastard, aside from that. The former Duke of Bryson was unable to father children." Clara gave a shocked laugh, staring at him. "I thought you might like to fling it at him from time to time, to get his attention," he grinned at her.

"I see you've forsworn discretion as well as the possibility of illicit liaisons," she said. "Thank you for that tidbit. I won't ask if you have any more of them hidden away."

"Perhaps I'll sell them," he mused. "It would make

quite a profit. Shall we go find the illustrious duke? I'll make him squirm with talk about the South Seas."

"It's kind of you to offer, though I'm not sure what that means," she said, stepping back from his offered arm. Her smile faded away to a more serious look. "You mean it, don't you, Stephen? That there will never be anything between us, I mean. Not even friendship. Not really."

He looked down at her bowed head, remembering how much he had wanted her, how inconsolable he'd been when she'd left him. But it was nothing to what he felt for his wife. Without Clara, he had been lonely. Without Helen, his heart would not be alive. Yet if Clara had never taught him what it meant to open his heart, he would never have known how to love Helen so fully.

He put a hand under her chin to make her look at him. "No, not even friends." He could not allow that, knowing it would make her hope for more. He watched the hope die in her eyes. "I think it would be best if we forgot whatever was between us."

She nodded, and he saw the reluctance in it. "I will not indulge myself anymore in dreams of what I cannot have," she said, tears filling her eyes. "But I will always regret that I did not choose you. And I won't forget," she said fervently. "I won't."

She leaned up on her toes, softly pressing her lips briefly to his. He knew it was coming, but did nothing to stop it, recognizing it as a fond farewell. She drew away even before he thought of stepping back, looking up at him with a sad smile.

"For goodbye," she whispered to him.

He could let her have that, a kiss goodbye for all the warmth she had given him in that cold and lonely time. It was she who now lived in wintry isolation, and he could not save her from it. He chucked her under the chin and gave her his charming grin, the one that always produced a smile. "Naughty of you," he chided. "Flirting with a married man."

He reached for her arm to escort her out to the other guests in the garden, thinking how strange it was that they had come to this parting, strange how easy and natural it was, and looked up to see his wife standing at the door, staring at them.

※

She was gone before he could wrench himself away from the guilty shock of the moment. He shouted abuse at himself inside his head after he finally gathered himself to follow her. He had just stood there, long after she was gone, looking guilty as sin and clutching Clara's arm in reflex. As if she could protect him from whatever Helen had seen or heard.

She was nowhere in the hall, nor on the stairs. It was almost as if she'd vanished into thin air, as he'd always feared she would. One misstep and she would go — walk away and keep walking to a place he could not follow. He was caught in a diabolical dream, turning everywhere to find her gone, just out of his grasp, leaving only the image of her face in that last moment: disbelief and confusion, turned to sudden embarrassment before she hastily made her exit.

He forced himself to follow his reasoning mind upstairs to their room instead of tearing out the front door to chase after the image of her leaving. She could not go. He would not let her. What could he say to make her understand that it was nothing?

Upset, he thought as he strode to their room. Of course she would be upset, but she would see reason. He would make her see it.

He opened the door to see her maid fastening the buttons on the traveling gown Helen now wore. So quickly. She had managed it so quickly, without a moment's hesitation.

The door closed behind him with a sharp thud, but she looked up at him without surprise, smoothing her skirts as the maid finished her task.

"There you are," she stated calmly. "You're always there, aren't you, Stephen?" She turned to the maid. "Thank you, Gladys. I will finish here, if you'll talk to the coachman."

The girl scurried out the door. Helen turned immediately to the bed where her case was laid out and reached for the nearest dress, quickly folding it and packing it away. She was reaching for another when he finally found his voice amid the panic.

"Where do you think you're going?"

"I'm not sure yet. I may call on some friends I have neglected," she answered vaguely, all the while gathering her belongings and neatly packing them away. "I trust you'll make my excuses to our hosts."

He leaned back against the door, trying to believe this was only a little argument, silly jealousy that he could dispel with the right words. "I will not. If you wish to leave, I'll accompany you."

"There is no need." Still she spoke in that maddeningly calm tone. "I don't believe you'll be welcome wherever it is I decide to go."

He chose to misunderstand her. "I thought we agreed that if we were not welcome somewhere together, then we would not go there at all."

She looked at him over her shoulder briefly before going back to her work. "Yes, well, we said many things. We agreed that you would not hide the truth from me." Her voice for a moment lost its certainty, began to waver. "You were not to hide the truth of what you are. Do you remember that?"

He saw the fire swallow Clara's letters, bright yellow flames consuming everything he'd thought he'd wanted. "I remember."

"It seems only right to me that if you do not keep your promises, then neither should I be held to mine," she answered, placing the last garment on the top of the pile.

"No." He shook off the lethargic disbelief that held him, seeking for something to crack the solid wall of ice she so easily erected. "No, you cannot believe that I feel that way about Clara. Listen to me." He reached for her arm as she latched the case. "I don't know what you saw, what you think you saw—"

"It doesn't matter," she said quietly, looking down at where his hand gripped her. "I saw how much you care for each other. I won't stand in the way of it. You should have what you want."

"I want you," he said, an edge of despair on his words. "It was farewell. Only that."

She was still beneath his hand, and he felt it – the little tremor inside her that heralded her acquiescence. He lowered his head, following instinct, tasting the corner of her mouth. "How could I want anything other than you?" he asked huskily. "Sweet wife... I love you. Only you."

Almost, her mouth turned to his. Almost. But she reached up and pushed herself away from him. "Stop it," she said faintly. Her hands went up to her ears as if to block out his words while she stepped further back from him. "Stop! I will not listen to pretty words and explanations." She gave a little moan and shook her head, dropping her hands, composing herself in the blink of an eye. "I'm leaving."

He nearly choked at the calm determination in her stance, but asked the question he dreaded, and steeled himself for the answer. "Are you leaving this house, or leaving me altogether?"

She didn't speak, only looked at him. It was answer enough.

"Only because of this?"

Her eyes lowered slowly, roaming across his shirtfront, considering. "It's not just one thing," she said finally, and he knew it for the truth, knew it was not some petty misunderstanding that pulled her away from him. Her words were the familiar sound of someone isolating him completely. He recognized it with sickening clarity, felt the solitude close in around him like an old and hated companion.

But he fought against it, refusing to be cut out. He could not let her slip away like everything else in his life.

"What, then?" Whatever it was, whatever the obstacle in his path to her, he would cut it down. He must.

"Alex sent you to me because of a business deal," she said flatly. "You never told me."

He stared at her in blank incomprehension, unwilling to believe that she could leave him over so insignificant a detail. It was like fighting a shadow — there was no way to change what had gone on before, and no way dispel the darkness it cast between them. He clenched his jaw, furious with her stubborn reasoning.

"Does it matter so much that you will dishonor the vows you made? Can't you see—"

"I see that I have been blind," she exploded, suddenly vehement. "I see that I am a silly girl, believing in you, believing in this romantic little world you made for me, and I will not believe it anymore! I knew better. I was taught long ago, and I let myself forget." She pressed her fist to her mouth as though to suppress her emotion. "Silly girl, silly girl. I let myself love you..." she moaned, turning the words he had longed to hear into a lament, leaving a charred ruin where his heart once stood whole.

Her instant of grief was swiftly controlled. Of course, her damned control, what a master of restraint she was. Her voice was ice once more. "And who are you to preach to me about dishonoring our vows? Who will I find in your arms next? How many other parts of yourself have you hidden from me?" She walked to the bureau and picked up her gloves.

"I have told myself time and again that it was fate that would not let my past die out." She looked at him, her dark eyes as fathomless as the sea, cold depths he could not enter. "But it was you, Stephen. It came back with you. Because you brought him back, right into our home." She nodded at his sign of denial, relentless. "I could have told you he would come, but I don't even know if that would have stopped you. I don't know anything anymore."

He watched her move toward the door, fear closing like a fist around his throat. He made a gesture as though to stop her, too small to withstand the force of her will.

"I would have killed him, you know." Already she

was gone from him, her voice sounding from miles away, an infinite distance in the calmness with which she spoke. "I would have. I was an instant from it. You would have given me that to live with as well."

It was all his worst fears come to life: her back turning to him, her hand reaching for the door, her step sure and unwavering. He could not let it happen. He swallowed the guilt that washed over him, guilt that had been drowning him since he'd found Henley with her, and forced himself to move before it was too late. He pushed closed the door she had begun to open, slamming it shut as he took her by the arms.

"I won't lose you," he said. He held her fast as she tried to squirm away. "I won't let you leave, do you understand?"

She stopped trying to escape, staring at the door behind him, refusing to meet his gaze. "What will you do to stop me? Beat me bloody, maybe." Her breaths were quick and shallow. Her eyes watered. "Or take a leaf from Henley's book, and throw me on the bed."

He let go as if she burned him. She meant it. She stood like a statue of fear and courage, the two opposing emotions captured in her bloodless face, her rigid body. It called to mind an image of her that had haunted him, of what it must have been like when she was trapped and defenseless, so long ago when he was not there to protect her.

"You really believe that of me," he said, amazed.

She blinked. "I don't know what to believe of you."

And that, he understood, was the point of it.

They stood apart, unmoving until the knock came at the door. "The carriage is ready, mum," came the maid's voice.

A FALLEN LADY

There was no way to fight it, no weapon to defend against her fear of him. Let her go. Words were all he had, and they were not enough. Nothing could stand against her will – so strong, so invulnerable – and he was nothing to it. To her.

He watched in silence as they took her case – small, so small to contain so great a weight, the whole of their shared life. Watched as she stepped out the door, the beautiful plainness of her face in profile to him, as she pulled on her gloves and looked at him with her eyes wide open.

He watched as she calmly said, "Goodbye," and he refused to say the word. From the window, he watched as she stepped into the carriage, as she never looked back, as it carried her away and left him alone in the familiar emptiness.

CHAPTER EIGHTEEN

Emily was so good about it, thinking an unexpected visitor on her doorstep come for an indefinite stay was a perfect delight. Her face when she greeted Helen was full of happy welcome, the more so because her darling Tisby was off at sea again.

Helen didn't avoid Bartle because she knew Stephen could find her there, but because she knew what she would have to endure: Marie-Anne's censure, the gentle curiosity of the villagers, and worst of all the memories of him that dwelled there. With Emily she could live in silence for a while; conversation could never be as detailed or probing when it must be written out, and Emily's open fascination with nearly any topic made it easy to divert discussion away from whatever Helen wished to keep to herself.

Will you stay through the summer? Emily wrote one afternoon when Helen had been there for nearly a month.

I don't know, Helen wrote back. She stared at the ink on the page. She had wanted to use the silence of this house to gather her thoughts, to contemplate what came next in her marriage. Instead, she slept too much, lazily dozing the mornings away, only ever forcing herself out of bed when inevitably she began to imagine the warm pressure of Stephen's body curled against her back, the feel of his knees behind hers so real she thought she would weep.

She could leave at any time, if she would only decide where to go or what to do.

I don't want to overstay my welcome, she began, but Emily stopped her pen from scratching further and gave her a look that plainly said Helen was not in danger of being asked to leave anytime soon.

Still, she must think of it. It was strange to find the world open to her once more. It was so different than when she had left before, in so many ways. There was no fear of going hungry. There was no hatred or injustice to propel her through the day. And worst of all, worse than anything, there was no Maggie to tell her if she was right or wrong. No Maggie to say there was nothing to be afraid of anymore. There was only the dull ache, the inability to stop loving him.

Until yesterday, she had worried that he would seek her out. He could find her easily, if he bothered to spare a thought for her, and apparently he had. He'd sent her solicitor to her, to discuss the terms of their separation, if an informal arrangement was her preference or if she wanted a legal separation. And, quite carefully, to hint at the question of divorce.

She had stared numbly at the kindly old solicitor who had tried to hide his concern for her, his disapproval. Divorce. She'd had no thought of it, but it was the only way if he truly wanted to be free to marry again. She blinked back tears and told the solicitor that she would not stand in the way of it. His reputation had been so damaged by marrying her, yet he was willing to suffer the scandal of divorce to be completely rid of her. *I am difficult.* She hugged her arms around herself. *Of course he would want to be free of me. I weep and cringe and push him away and beg him to stay and I insult him and leave him.*

He wanted a wife who would stay by his side. And she wanted to forget Clara's lips on his, the smile he had given her. Such a smile. And the exquisite Clara was the center of it, with her golden hair and stunning beauty and her obvious, deep affection for Stephen.

A light tapping alerted her to Emily's impatience. She had written something.

Yesterday. It was bad news?

Emily frowned at her when Helen did not pick up the pen to respond. Try as she might, she couldn't divert the topic. Emily wanted to know, and Helen supposed she should tell her something.

Not good news. Though maybe it was good news, that he would not insist on her return. She had left him, after all. Had wanted to leave, and still did not want to go back.

You've left him, haven't you?

Helen didn't bother denying it. Emily was deaf, not stupid. She nodded.

Why?

What could she say? That he would be happier without her, though he didn't know it yet. That he was mistaken to have married her. That even the smallest of lies from him crushed her, suffocated her, turned her into someone she could not bear to be.

But all of that was the easy surface things, the shape and not the substance. It was something better to tell herself than the deeper truth. Maggie would know. Maggie would understand it, as she always had. Maggie was not an illusion of goodness, and she would know what Helen meant when she said that she was afraid of being happy with him, afraid of what might come of it. But Maggie was gone back to Ireland.

She dipped the pen. *I'm not strong enough for that life.*

Emily looked at the words, trying to make sense of them. But there was no sense in it, none at all. It had nothing to do with being rational. It was what Helen's life had taught her, that the best and most wonderful of people could turn out to be the devil himself. That the more bright and promising someone was, the more carefully one must guard against them and beware of the lie that they were sure to be. And with Stephen, she was weaker than she had ever been, turning and turning away from all the warnings of what he might be.

Emily at last looked up from the paper, giving Helen a determined look before writing.

The strongest people in this world never believe they are strong, she wrote. *You are strong enough for any life, if you want it. Do you want it? Want that life?*

Helen watched the pen tap insistently on the words for emphasis. *Tap, tap, tap!* Each time the pen struck was like a pinprick to her heart, puncturing the numbness she'd wrapped around herself for weeks.

The words blurred on the page until she could only see the blood on Stephen's hands reaching for her, until she could feel nothing but his head against hers, holding her in her grief as she revealed her fear that she was nothing, would never be anything.

An ordinary life. With him. And she was too terrified to have it.

※

Her nightmares increased. They came almost every night now, after she had become accustomed to their fading. They had never left her but now they were more vivid, and different. Stephen was in them.

She would dream she was walking with him, waiting for a kiss she knew would come when suddenly Katie was there in the road. She looked at Helen and beckoned her away, into a stand of trees at the side of the busy thoroughfare. Helen followed, though she knew Stephen didn't want her to. He yelled at her, shouting that she could not leave him. But she did, turning her back on him and following Katie to the trees where Henley waited. She felt Stephen watch as Henley greeted her, held her in his arms and gave her the kiss that should have been from Stephen.

She opened her eyes, thinking they had played a trick and switched places with each other. But they hadn't. It was Henley who had kissed her so sweetly. Stephen stood watching as Henley took her down on the ground and she screamed. She saw blood wash over Stephen's shoes as he watched, holding Katie, her little face buried in the warm curve of his neck. Helen fought in the dream as she had not in life, but Henley was too strong. No matter how much she screamed and begged, he would not let her up and Stephen would not help. He only watched, his face white as chalk as he tried, and failed, to protect

Katie's little back.

When it was over, Henley lying dead on top of her, a knife inexplicably in his throat. Stephen looked at her accusingly. *You wouldn't let me stop him*, he said.

That was when she woke, the pillow beneath her cheek sodden with tears.

※

"My wife is convinced you despise her," said Whitemarsh as he shuffled the papers on the desk. "Can't convince her that Helen has a mind of her own and would do as she pleased no matter what was said."

Stephen barely glanced up from the accounts he was examining. "Bring her for dinner tonight. I'll be at my most charming."

It would be a pleasant ending to their business. The shipping venture was on its way to solvency, and there was no reason to meet with Whitemarsh so often to discuss it. He supposed they could see each other socially, if Stephen ever bothered to go into society again. But he was done with it, once and for all – done with the whispers and lies that had so shaped him that he was unaware of the danger in concealment. A poisonous atmosphere, was the London he inhabited. He had always known it, but had not realized how it had made him like all those he hated until it lost him his wife.

"I don't know that I want your charm released in the same room with my wife," replied Whitemarsh. "She's feeling sorry for you and I'm not entirely forgiven. Dangerous combination."

Stephen turned the page of the ledger book, afraid

to look up and see Alex's half-smile, so like Helen's.

"She won't come back to me." He said it as if it were written on the page before him. "Will she?"

Alex shifted uncomfortably in his chair. They had not spoken of it, except briefly at Chisholm's estate, and then only long enough for Stephen to tell a weeping Elizabeth that Helen had indeed left him. He didn't want to speak of it, but somehow words were leaking out of him. Like a brick stolen from a dam, the hole in his vaunted discretion grew, sending a web of cracks throughout the structure, words and thoughts seeping through until one day there would be a deluge.

"Will you be coming to Everley's ball tomorrow night?" asked Alex, instead of answering him. "You can ask Elizabeth to dance, that should take care of it."

"At the risk of sounding unchivalrous, I'm more concerned about my wife than yours." He heard the drip of his words trickling out, impossible to stop.

"Then stop drinking yourself into a stupor and do something about it," Alex snapped, referring to the state he'd found him in last week. Stephen felt he could hardly be faulted for that little scene. He had just learned his wife did not object to divorce.

He rolled his eyes. "A man takes too much brandy once and is called a drunkard forevermore."

Alex stood. "It was before lunch," he pointed out. Well yes, it was an admittedly unprecedented bit of debauchery, but he did not say so. "And how the hell should I know if she will come back to you? She didn't come back to me, and you told me yourself it was because I made it easy for her to stay away."

Stephen felt the anger rise to the surface, just

under his skin. "You compare your situation to mine?" he asked carefully.

"How can I, when I barely know what your situation is?"

That was fair enough. Stephen barely knew it himself. It was not the same. Her brother had not believed her, but Stephen had done nothing but believe in her. And still he lost her. And she wanted to be lost, as her willingness to divorce indicated.

"Look here," said Alex firmly, clearly in preparation of an exit. "Here's what I know about Helen. She has a wild imagination. She can take care of herself, even when maybe she should let someone else. And I know firsthand that she's the forgiving type." His mouth twisted, clamping shut against whatever else he might have said about forgiveness. "But give her enough time and space and she'll lock herself away. She's always been that way."

He picked up his papers and moved toward the door, where he turned back to Stephen. "If you go to her, you might have a chance, that's all I know. Can't you bother to try?"

Stephen saw his hands held out to her, following her across the floor as she moved away. It didn't matter how much he reached out, how far he extended himself. She only put her hands in his when she was ready to.

"I did try," he answered. "I tried from the moment I met her until the moment she walked out the door."

"Then try again." Alex opened the door. "One more thing I know about her, Summerdale: she's worth it."

Marie-Anne sat across from him in the back parlor. She was quite put out.

"But why would she go to Emily and not me?" She gave Stephen an arch look. "I don't believe she's left you. She has given herself to you completely. There must be more to it than you tell me."

No point in arguing. She *had* given herself completely, for a time, and he had gathered her joy to him, her release and sweet openness. But it was over now; she'd already made up her mind. His teacup clattered on the saucer.

"Eventually, she will go back to Bartle," he said, because he knew she would. "And you can hear about it from her." He lifted his mouth in a wry smile. "Tell her about the day I first came, that I pulled the shoe off my horse as an excuse to stop at your door."

"Why would I tell her that?"

"Because it's the only other thing I can think of that I kept from her. It's the last thing she can use to accuse me of being false."

"*Le diable*," Marie-Anne snorted. She folded her arms across her chest and gave him a critical look. "I told you not to hurt her. I told you she has suffered enough."

He fought the urge to whine like a wronged child, that he had never meant to hurt her. "I cannot hurt her anymore," he said instead.

"Perhaps you should," Marie-Anne said thoughtfully. "Maggie would know this with certainty, but I am unsure."

He pushed the tea away abruptly. "I am sick of cryptic comments, madame. It is done. Will you stay to dinner?" He hoped she wouldn't. He could hear

A FALLEN LADY

Helen in her laughter.

"Will you go to her?"

It angered him that she would not let it drop.

"Must I always go to her on my knees?" He didn't want to say it, but there it was. No way to seal the leak in the dam.

"But of course you must!" She smiled broadly, as though she had uncovered a delightful answer. "It is love, *non? Je t'ai parlé de l'amour*," she said, inexplicably slipping into French. "*De la guerre.*"

"So you did," he answered impatiently. "I don't care to speak of love and war now, if you please, nor of my wife." The words pushed through his teeth. "If she continues to be my wife, that is."

Marie-Anne stood and came to him, putting a hand on his arm.

"It is the answer, Maggie would say. Who knows better than Hélène that love is the more destructive thing?"

He would not stand here and listen to the second-hand wisdom of an Irish maid. He knew what Helen was afraid of, and it made no difference whether those fears were real or imagined. He looked at her friend's delicate features as they softened to see the emotion he could not hide. It was over, and he was a fraud fighting tears. There was no power left in his words, no way to bring her back.

"I know it," he answered her. "She taught me all about it.

CHAPTER NINETEEN

Helen couldn't seem to hit the target. In truth, she barely tried. She listlessly shot arrows, one after the other, taking comfort in the monotony of motion. Her aim had become formidable because she'd always imagined Henley as the target, taken a vicious joy in sending arrows through his imagined body. But now she could not focus on her hatred when she thought so continuously of Stephen, and the arrows flew wide.

She went to retrieve them from where they had fallen behind the tree. Emily had been with her earlier, sketching the summer flowers, but had gone inside when she saw how unsociable Helen was today. It was better to be alone. It was no easier to forget, but there was no need to act normal as she tried to tear the love out of her heart. Tried and failed, over and over again.

She brought the arrows back and shot again at the target, missing eleven in quick succession. The warmth of the day suddenly reached her as she notched the last arrow, the sun warming the chill that had permanently set in. She knew, without turning around to look, that Stephen was there. She closed her eyes. Of course he would come to her. He always came to her.

The arrow was loosed, and she opened her eyes, amazed at the sound of it hitting the target.

Lowering the bow, she turned and saw him where she'd known he would be sitting on the garden bench. But he had no charming grin for her, as she'd expected, no easy manner that soothed the moment. He only sat, looking at her, with an expression like the one he wore as his mother hurled abuse at him.

"Your aim is not what it used to be."

"No." She tried to mimic his flippant tone. "I'm thinking of taking up another sport."

Something flickered in the green eyes. "Marry someone and rip his heart to shreds," he suggested. "It's all the rage." He jerked his head minutely, as though he could catch back the words.

She absorbed that cut, letting it go deep. But still it didn't stop the flow of tenderness that leaked from her, that clutched at her chest and smarted behind her eyes. Knowing it was dangerous, knowing it could topple the fortress of numbness she had carefully erected in the weeks of silence, she walked slowly to the bench and sat next to him. They looked out at the bright flowers together.

He made no move to come closer, his features set in a careful mask. *I am here,* that look said. *And this is as far as I will come.* She pulled the gloves from her hands.

"You've come to discuss divorce," she said. She stared at the gloves, lying like dead things in her hands.

"Have I?" He sounded curious. "I was wondering why I came."

"You told me the kind of marriage you wanted, and it did not include separation." There was no controlling the waver in her voice. "You'll be free to have someone else."

"I also told you that I wanted you," he said, his eyes still staring straight ahead. "Only you, and only because you're you. How will you twist that into something sinister, I wonder?"

She bit her lips hard. "I never understood it, Stephen." Could he ever know what it meant to be trapped inside this body, imprisoned in this mind that could not forget? "I never did. I never understood why."

He closed his eyes and leaned his head back to let the sun fall on his face. His handsome face, the shape of it that she knew so well, that defined the boundaries of her heart. "Because your real beauty is hidden to all but me," he offered. "Because I thought I knew what honor was until I met you. Because your hair came free and lay against your neck, where I wanted to be."

She stared at the distant target. *Oh, don't listen to pretty words.*

"Do you love her the same way?" she asked, wanting the torture of his answer.

"I loved her," he said. At least he did not try to deny it, and the pain came to her. "A part of me will always love her, because she was the only one who..." He shook his head. "She taught me, before you, taught me to open my heart. I would not know how to do so, otherwise. But she's nothing to you."

"Then why?" she choked out. "Why did you hide so much from me?"

His face lost its soft expression, his eyes opening to stare at the sky. "I could ask the same thing of you."

She was not quick like him: it took her a long time to put meaning to his words, to realize he meant that she had hidden the truth about what had happened to her. He'd only found out because he stumbled into the room as she railed against Henley. She stiffened.

"It's not the same thing." It came out with uncommon force, and his head turned around to her at last. "It's not. Don't look at me like you know, because you don't. It's the one thing you can't ever know, no matter how much you know about everything else in the world." She stood. "Shall I tell you what it was like?"

"No," he said. Immediately, harshly.

"I'll tell you. You never asked for details and I loved you for it. But I'll tell you now," she said, suddenly determined that he should hear. Her anger was surprising – a thing she had hidden from herself. He never had to live with it as she did. Always pressing for the truth. Let him have it, then.

"It's simple. I've told myself how simple it was. He killed them and I saw it. Only by mischance or I would never have known, and I ran back to the house. Maggie was just a chambermaid, but she was steady and so kind that I told her everything. She found Katie, and her family took her in. Then I went the next day early in the morning, back to that place in the little wood."

Her breath came fast but there was not the pressure on her lungs, the force that stole her words.

It had disappeared somewhere along the way. She looked at her husband, refusing to be moved by the look of pain on his face, the denial. It was the only real thing left unsaid between them.

"I loved him. I *still* loved him, even though I saw him kill them. Do you understand? Because I made excuses for his behavior, because I could not bear to believe the worst of him. But I went to see if I could find anything that her family had left behind, and I found it. An apron and some ribbons and a shaving kit. It – saved my life." She let out a laugh, so close to a sob that she thought she might not be able to continue.

This was the hard part. If she could say this part then it would be over. She dimly remembered trying to tell it to Alex, and how tumbled all the words had been, how she had cringed and cowered from it. Better to say it quick and cruel. "And he followed me and told me I had to stay. And he – kissed me." The familiar nausea came, filling her mouth and twisting her face. It would always come, for the rest of her life, she knew. She let him see it, as she had never let anyone see. "And I should have fought but I was s-so stupid and afraid, and he had me on the g-*ground*."

"Stop it," said Stephen urgently, rising from the bench to cross to her. But she stopped him, backing away and raising her hands.

"No, you will hear it!" She drew in a hiccoughing breath as he stopped. She was determined she would not weep. "And I n-never wanted to see blood again, but then he was in me and it – *hurt*. He was *in* me and–" She stopped herself re-imagining it and remembered instead the thing that haunted her even more. The thing lived in her, as it lived in him and everyone, only waiting to come out. The thing that was greedy for blood. "I reached over and the razor was there so I – I put it on his throat and told him to get out of me." She was going mad. She could feel it as she put her hands to her hair and shook her head violently. "I told him to get *out*."

Her voice had risen and now it left a ringing silence. She gave into the weakness in her knees, dropping down hard on the grass and watching her skirt billow up around her. Leaf green silk all around her.

"But he won't get out," she said, feeling the numbness envelop her again, and happy for it. "It's too much a part of me. Not even you can change that. You try to make it better, and it brought him back." She looked at him where he knelt before her now, his knees pressed against her skirt. "You brought him back, and the blood. And now you're part of the nightmares."

She crossed her arms across her belly tightly, wanting to rock back and forth like a child. "He ruined me. You can't know how he's ruined me."

He didn't move to touch her. He knew her that well. She had let him know her so well. But oh, god – what did she *not* know of him? Would it ever be enough?

"Will you let him have you?" Stephen demanded, the harsh edge of his voice cutting into her. "I can't change it. But you let it take you away from me. You make me a part of your nightmares, when all I want to do is hold you when you're afraid."

"I'm afraid all the time." A sob escaped, try as she might to contain it. "Everyone who knows thinks I'm so brave. But I'm terrified, all the time."

He reached his hand up to her face as if he wanted to brush the tears away, but stopped short, letting his hand fall. "He can't hurt you again. Except in this way, and only if you let him."

"I know," she admitted, hearing Maggie's voice telling her the same thing. But that wasn't all there was to fear. *Oh, the thousand terrible things you might be, my love. You could hurt me worse than him.* "You brought him back." How it hurt her, to know Stephen had brought him back. "Why did you bring him back to me?"

"I'm sorry," he said, the words hard and hollow. He looked defeated, there on his knees before her. "I can't tell you how sorry. I didn't know. I never thought he would come." He let out a despairing laugh. "You'll say I should have guessed. And I should have. Always priding myself on knowing the truth and predicting the future," he spat bitterly. "Spending my life on the edges of other people's worlds. They never let me in, except for a moment, to let me run in and steal the secret."

He caught a fold of her dress in his hand, rubbing the silk between his fingers. "Then I met you. And you made me a part of your world. I misjudged you over and over again." His mouth set in its moody curve. "I'm no good at it. I'm not what I thought I was. I'm only good at being in love with you."

She looked at him, the face she knew so well in all his changing moods. And it came to her quietly, unexpected, the thing she had been so afraid to see revealed. Not dark and terrible, but shining with simplicity. Suddenly the thought of all the terrible things he might be were nothing to what she knew he was. Patient and kind and strong. And here, always here by her side in all her worst moments, always giving her the best moments. She saw it like a blinding light all around her, shimmering in the air and reflected in his down-turned eyes.

Caught in the dark woods forever, but he brought her out of it. Her fairy tale knight, her charming prince with the golden key, who shined like a beacon to guide her through the trees to where he waited – always waiting for her.

"You're the one – you taught me not to judge someone only by their worst deed." He was the one who sounded lost, as if she could save him. "Every road leads to you, and I cannot stop traveling it. But at the end you let me in and shut me out. Both, at the same time." He blinked, looking to her in appeal. "Will you never let me stay?"

She was tired of being afraid, tired of being tired. And she only wanted his arms around her. It seemed suddenly so easy.

She leaned forward and rested herself against his broad chest, the only place she felt safe and warm. A sob rose up in her – grief for what she still wanted to run from, and joy because she knew she would not. He gave her the strength to hold on to it, to him.

Her hand reached up and found the nape of his neck, the soft hairs there. "Will you give me an ordinary life?" she asked on a convulsive sob.

And then his arms were around her, holding her fast, anchoring her to him, catching her after the fall. She reveled in it, how he squeezed the breath from her.

"It can't be," he said fiercely against her ear. "It can only be extraordinary. It will be," he promised. "My wife... sweet, strong, beautiful wife. Come home. Laugh in my bed." It was like a prayer, a hymn, his voice pleading and exultant, his heart drumming against hers.

It's frightening, she had told Marie-Anne long ago. To look at love and happiness, to know it was all contained in one place — in his eyes when he looked at her.

That is because it is life, came the answer, and she knew it was true.

"Yes," she answered him. She threw herself into it, into the tears and laughter, into the pain and ecstasy of a life of loving him, a turbulent swirl that took her up and swept her into his arms. He made her brave. She could never be afraid with him. Not of life, not of specters in the dark, not of monsters she imagined breeding in his heart. Never, as long as he was with her.

"Yes?" His hopeful look pierced her. He shook his head in happy disbelief. "Can it be so simple?"

She nodded. "That simple."

A simple story that she would tell him over and over again: how she loved him; how he saved her; how she could never be lost in those woods again.

She smiled through her tears, a laugh of perfect joy that only he could bring. She put her mouth to his in the midst of it, awkward, her teeth bumping against his, as if she'd never kissed anyone before. Her tongue found his and probed deep, pressing against him as he answered her - strong enough to withstand her greedy nature and overcome it, demanding love in return.

He dragged his mouth away, holding her face tight in his hands. "You won't leave me again," he commanded, giving her a little shake.

"Never," she vowed. "We'll be all right? We'll be

happy?"

He wiped her tears and doubts away. "We'll be wonderful." He said it with the certainty only he possessed, and she believed him. He was the Earl of Summerdale, after all, and he knew everything. "You'll always stay with me?"

She laughed again. It bubbled up inside her with a vengeance. "Where would I go?"

"Nowhere without me." His eyes crinkled, his grin warmer than the summer sun above them. "I'll take you to Italy, to Sicily where they modeled the night skies on your eyes. Or to America. To your benighted President Washington."

She laughed as his lips sought hers again. "He's not president anymore," she giggled, drunk with love and life. "Isn't he...dead?" she asked between kisses.

"Ask me if I give a damn," he muttered, returning to her lips, returning again and again to where he belonged.

EPILOGUE

My darling love, my only love—
Where the devil are you? I'm bored to tears without you. Will you disappear from me forever? It's been years already. I'll beg if I have to.

-S

⁂

For Heaven's sake, Stephen, I'm only in the library. And it's only been an hour, is it so boring as that? Get rid of your blustering businessmen and come here. You will delight in Marie-Anne's letter: she has agreed to come to London at the Shipleys' astonishing invitation. It has caused her to write the most eloquent description of this "great pile of cretins" — I think she accepts the invitation only for the comedic possibilities it offers.

I have finished my letter to Katie, taking the liberty to share your wishes for her continued excellent health. (How long will it take to reach her in America?) So you will find me unoccupied.

-H

A month or more to reach her, but her latest communication must assure you that she is so much improved as to be fit to swim the distance herself. Fret instead over the poor Shipley family, who can have no notion what glorious mischief they have invited into their midst.

And fret for me, who perishes of boredom without you.

-S

I am engrossed in the political essays. And waiting for you. So hurry.

-H

I rather like it when you're demanding. I can honestly tell these stuffy old men that I am distracted by important matters, hence Collins coming and going with notes. Thirty minutes, my love. Then come in here and ravish me.

-S

Collins has more to do than carry notes, wasteful man.

Thirty minutes! I am disgruntled in the library. Your invitation to ravish you, though full of charm, is startling from one of your reputation, sir. And they call me the scandalous one.

-H

Disgruntled in the library and waiting to ravish me. I find myself enjoying the scandalous life. I did promise we'd be wonderful, didn't I?

-S

※

You did. Extraordinary, you said - and you were right. You are always right, my love.

THE END

ACKNOWLEDGEMENTS

Here is where I will say what you might not expect from a romance novelist: romantic love is not so important. To get through life intact (to say nothing of being made whole again after devastation) requires rather more than one flavor of love. So in many ways, this book is a hymn in praise of friendship, especially female friendship. I could write fiction for a thousand years and never manage to invent any girlfriends better than the ones that actually exist in my life. These are the women who have cheered me up and cheered me on, who are always on my side, who never fail to tell me the hardest truths with the kindest compassion, who listen to me even when I'm being insane or boring or childish. Their love sustains me.

Snezana Pavlic makes all my writing possible, not only because she is my perfect audience and has a flawless editorial eye, but because she has held my hand all through every stumbling, soaring, monotonous minute of this writer-life. (And there's no room to go into how she vastly enriches the non-writing part of my life.) Also, she is capable of making me laugh so hard that I'm in perpetual danger of wetting myself like a gleeful toddler. Whenever the world and life seem impossibly cruel, I remember that I have such a friend, and know that I am the wealthiest person on earth.

Megan Odett is my fellow texting fiend, my fellow morbid humorist, my Hospital Buddy. She is always there for me, and always has comfort to give - or perspective, or invective, or just really great manicure tips and cocktail suggestions. She is also, as all good girlfriends are, ever-willing to ogle footwear at all appropriate and inappropriate moments.

Rita Milandri has possibly listened to me bitch and moan more than any other person in my life, and has never failed in her duty to tell me to get a grip already. With her willingness to discuss any topic to within an inch of its life, her generosity, curiosity, and hospitality, she could teach master classes in How To Be A Great Friend.

Laura Kinsale is Laura Freakin' Kinsale, first of all, so there's that. But in addition, she is smart and kind and wise and fun and has a heart so expansive it makes Texas look tiny. Plus also, she introduced me to the glories of Taylor's Scottish Breakfast Tea, which is pretty major.

Agnes L, my misiu, kept me sane in The Miserable Office Years and beyond, and is my chief supplier of sunny smiles. **Lyssa M and Beq B**, who are so much more than just my writing buddies. **Heather D**, who is totally allowed to forever forget the members of the G8. **Amanda D**, who sends long and caring emails that always bring a smile to my face. **Randi H,** who pops up at random moments to remind me of how to be joyful. And **Dawn Z**, more like family than friend at this point, who has cheered me on without hesitation or reservation for 36 years. Good GOD, 36 *years*. We are old. It is awesome.

I would be remiss if I did not also acknowledge the contributions of my inanimate, edible friends who made this book possible: my thanks to the humble donut, the fine scotch, the buckets of sugary tea, and carbohydrates in general. May their sacrifice be ne'er forgot.

Made in the USA
San Bernardino, CA
22 April 2017